Joan Haste by H. Rider Haggard

Sir Henry Rider Haggard, KBE was born on June 22nd, 1856 at Bradenham in Norfolk, England.

After his education he was pushed towards an Army career but failed the entrance exam. Next Haggard was positioned to work for the British Foreign Office but he seems not to have sat that exam. Using family connections, he was sent to Southern Africa by his father in search of a further opportunity of a career.

Haggard spent six years there before a return to England and marriage. He had begun to write and publish some non-fiction in Africa but it was only after studying Law in the hope it might prove to be the proper career his father wanted for him that Haggard began to write fiction, using his African experiences as the basis.

His first fiction was published in 1885 and the following year King Solomon's Mines was published. It was a phenomenal success. His career was set.

Haggard wrote well and wrote often. He managed to sympathise with the local populations even though they were exploited and manipulated by Europeans intent on amassing fortunes in money, people and resources. His writing career covered the great sprint to Empire of several European powers and both reflects and criticizes these events through his well-loved characters including Allan Quatermain and Ayesha.

In his later years Haggard pursued much in the way social reform as well as standing for Parliament and writing a great many letters to The Times.

Henry Rider Haggard died on May 14th, 1925 at the age of 68. His ashes were buried at Ditchingham Church.

Index of Contents
CHAPTER I - JOAN HASTE
CHAPTER II - SAMUEL ROCK DECLARES HIMSELF
CHAPTER III - THE BEGINNINGS OF FATE
CHAPTER IV - THE HOME-COMING OF HENRY GRAVES
CHAPTER V - THE LEVINGERS VISIT ROSHAM
CHAPTER VI - MR. LEVINGER PUTS A CASE
CHAPTER VII - A PROPOSAL AND A DIFFERENCE
CHAPTER VIII - TWO CONVERSATIONS
CHAPTER IX - MUTUAL ADMIRATION
CHAPTER X - AZRAEL'S WING
CHAPTER XI - ELLEN GROWS ALARMED
CHAPTER XII - ELLEN FINDS A REMEDY
CHAPTER XIII - A MEETING BY THE MERE
CHAPTER XIV - SOWING THE WIND
CHAPTER XV - THE FIRST FRUITS

CHAPTER XVI - FORTITER IN RE
CHAPTER XVII - BETWEEN DUTY AND DUTY
CHAPTER XVIII - CONGRATULATIONS
CHAPTER XIX - RIGHTEOUS INDIGNATION
CHAPTER XX - "LET IT REMAIN OPEN"
CHAPTER XXI - A LUNCHEON PARTY
CHAPTER XXII - AN INTERLUDE
CHAPTER XXIII - A NEW DEPARTURE
CHAPTER XXIV - MESSRS. BLACK AND PARKER
CHAPTER XXV - "I FORBID YOU."
CHAPTER XXVI - A LOVE LETTER
CHAPTER XXVII - LUCK AT LAST
CHAPTER XXVIII - THE PRICE OF INNOCENT BLOOD
CHAPTER XXIX - THROUGH THE VALLEY OF THE SHADOW
CHAPTER XXX - REAPING THE WHIRLWIND
CHAPTER XXXI - THE GATE OF PARADISE
CHAPTER XXXII - THE CLOSING OF THE GATE
CHAPTER XXXIII - THE GATE OF HELL
CHAPTER XXXIV - THE OPENING OF THE GATE
CHAPTER XXXV - DISENCHANTMENT
CHAPTER XXXVI - THE DESIRE OF DEATH—AND THE FEAR OF HIM
CHAPTER XXXVII - THE TRUTH, THE WHOLE TRUTH
CHAPTER XXXVIII - A GHOST OF THE PAST
CHAPTER XXXIX - HUSBAND AND WIFE
CHAPTER XL - FULL MEASURE, PRESSED DOWN AND RUNNING OVER
H. RIDER HAGGARD – A SHORT BIOGRAPHY
H. RIDER HAGGARD – A CONCISE BIBLIOGRAPHY

CHAPTER I

JOAN HASTE

Alone and desolate, within hearing of the thunder of the waters of the North Sea, but not upon them, stand the ruins of Ramborough Abbey. Once there was a city at their feet, now the city has gone; nothing is left of its greatness save the stone skeleton of the fabric of the Abbey above and the skeletons of the men who built it mouldering in the earth below. To the east, across a waste of uncultivated heath, lies the wide ocean; and, following the trend of the coast northward, the eye falls upon the red roofs of the fishing village of Bradmouth. When Ramborough was a town, this village was a great port; but the sea, advancing remorselessly, has choked its harbour and swallowed up the ancient borough which to-day lies beneath the waters.

With that of Ramborough the glory of Bradmouth is departed, and of its priory and churches there remains but one lovely and dilapidated fane, the largest perhaps in the east of England—that of Yarmouth alone excepted—and, as many think, the most beautiful. At the back of Bradmouth church, which, standing upon a knoll at some distance from the cliff, has escaped the fate of the city that once nestled beneath it, stretch rich marsh meadows, ribbed with raised lines of roadway. But these do not make up all the landscape, for between Bradmouth and the ruins of Ramborough, following the indentations of the sea coast and set back in a fold or depression of the ground, lie a chain of small and melancholy meres, whose brackish waters, devoid of sparkle even on the brightest day, are surrounded by coarse and worthless grass land, the haunt of the shore-shooter, and a favourite feeding-place of curlews, gulls, coots and other wild-fowl. Beyond these meres the ground rises rapidly, and is clothed in gorse and bracken, interspersed with patches of heather, till it culminates in the crest of a bank that marks doubtless the boundary of some primeval fiord or lake, where, standing in a ragged line, are groups of wind-torn Scotch fir trees, surrounding a grey and solitary house known as Moor Farm.

The dwellers in these parts—that is, those of them who are alive to such matters—think that there are few more beautiful spots than this slope of barren land pitted with sullen meres and bordered by the sea. Indeed, it has attractions in every season: even in winter, when the snow lies in drifts upon the dead fern, and the frost-browned gorse shivers in the east wind leaping on it from the ocean. It is always beautiful, and yet there is truth in the old doggerel verse that is written in a quaint Elizabethan hand upon the fly-lead of one of the Bradmouth parish registers—

"Of Rambro', north and west and south,
Man's eyes can never see enough;
Yet winter's gloom or summer's light,
Wide England hath no sadder sight."

And so it is; even in the glory of June, when lizards run across the grey stonework and the gorse shows its blaze of gold, there is a stamp of native sadness on the landscape which lies between Bradmouth and Ramborough, that neither the hanging woodlands to the north, nor the distant glitter of the sea, on which boats move to and fro, can altogether conquer. Nature set that seal upon the district in the beginning, and the lost labours of the generations now sleeping round its rotting churches have but accentuated the primal impress of her hand.

Though on the day in that June when this story opens, the sea shone like a mirror beneath her, and the bees hummed in the flowers growing on the ancient graves, and the larks sang sweetly above her head, Joan felt this sadness strike her heart like the chill of an autumn night. Even in the midst of life everything about her seemed to speak of death and oblivion: the ruined church, the long neglected graves, the barren landscape, all cried to her with one voice, seeming to say, "Our troubles are done with, yours lie before you. Be like us, be like us."

It was no high-born lady to whom these voices spoke in that appropriate spot, nor were the sorrows which opened her ears to them either deep or poetical. To tell the truth, Joan Haste was but a village girl, or, to be more accurate, a girl who had spent most of her life in a village. She was lovely in her own fashion, it is true—but of this presently; and, through circumstances that shall be explained, she chanced to have enjoyed a certain measure of education, enough to awaken longings and to call forth visions that perhaps she would have been happier without. Moreover, although Fate had placed her humbly, Nature gave to her, together with the beauty of her face and form, a mind which, if a little narrow, certainly did not lack for depth, a considerable power of will, and more than her share of that noble dissatisfaction without which no human creature can rise in things spiritual or temporal, and having which, no human creature can be happy.

Her troubles were vulgar enough, poor girl: a scolding and coarse-minded aunt, a suitor toward whom she had no longings, the constant jar of the talk and jest of the ale-house where she lived, and the irk of some vague and half-understood shame that clung to her closely as the ivy clung to the ruined tower above her. Common though such woes be, they were yet sufficiently real to Joan—in truth, their somewhat sordid atmosphere pressed with added weight upon a mind which was not sordid. Those misfortunes that are proper to our station and inherent to our fate we can bear, if not readily, at least with some show of resignation; those that fall upon us from a sphere of which we lack experience, or arise out of a temperament unsuited to its surroundings, are harder to endure. To be different from our fellows, to look upwards where they look down, to live inwardly at a mental level higher than our circumstances warrant, to desire that which is too far above us, are miseries petty in themselves, but gifted with Protean reproductiveness.

Put briefly, this was Joan's position. Her parentage was a mystery, at least so far as her father was concerned. Her mother was her aunt's younger sister; but she had never known this mother, whose short life closed within two years of Joan's birth. Indeed, the only tokens left to link their existences together were a lock of soft brown hair and a faded photograph of a girl not unlike herself, who seemed to have been beautiful. Her aunt, Mrs. Gillingwater, gave her these mementos of the dead some years ago, saying, with the brutal frankness of her class, that they were almost the only property that her mother had left behind her, so she, the daughter, might as well take possession of them.

Of this mother, however, there remained one other memento—a mound in the churchyard of the Abbey, where until quite recently the inhabitants of Ramborough had been wont to be laid to sleep beside their ancestors. This mound Joan knew, for, upon her earnest entreaty, Mr. Gillingwater, her uncle by marriage, pointed it out to her; indeed, she was sitting by it now. It had no headstone, and when Joan asked him why, he replied that those who were neither wife nor maid had best take their names with them six feet underground.

The poor girl shrank back abashed at this rough answer, nor did she ever return to the subject. But from this moment she knew that she had been unlucky in her birth, and though such an accident is by no means unusual in country villages, the sense of it galled her, lowering her in her own esteem. Still she bore no resentment against this dead and erring mother, but rather loved her with a strange and wondering love than which there could be nothing more pathetic. The woman who bore her, but whom she had never seen with remembering eyes, was often in her thoughts; and once, when some slight illness had affected the balance of her mind, Joan believed that she came and kissed her on the brow—a vision whereof the memory was sweet to her, though she knew it to be but a dream. Perhaps it was because she had nothing else to love that she clung thus to the impalpable, making a companion of the outcast dead whose blood ran in her veins. At the least this is sure, that when her worries overcame her, or the sense of incongruity in her life grew too strong, she was accustomed to seek this lowly mound, and, seated by it, heedless of the weather, she would fix her eyes upon the sea and soothe herself with a sadness that seemed deeper than her own.

Her aunt, indeed, was left to her, but from this relation she won no comfort. From many incidents trifling in themselves, but in the mass irresistible, Joan gathered that there had been little sympathy between her mother and Mrs. Gillingwater—if, in truth, their attitude was not one of mutual dislike. It would appear also that in her own case this want of affection was an hereditary quality, seeing that she found it difficult to regard her aunt with any feeling warmer than tolerance, and was in turn held in an open aversion, which to Joan's mind, was scarcely mitigated by the very obvious pride Mrs. Gillingwater took in her beauty. In these circumstances Joan had often wondered why she was not dismissed to seek her fortune. More than once, when after some quarrel she sought leave to go, she found that there was no surer path to reconciliation than to proffer this request; and speeches of apology, which, as she knew well, were not due to any softening of Mrs. Gillingwater's temper, or regret for hasty misbehaviour, were at once showered upon her.

To what, then, were they due? The question was one that Joan took some years to answer satisfactorily. Clearly not to love, and almost as clearly to no desire to retain her services, since, beyond attending to her own room, she did but little work in the way of ministering to the wants and comforts of the few customers of the Crown and Mitre, nor was she ever asked to interest herself in such duties.

Gradually a solution to the riddle forced itself onto Joan's intelligence—namely, that in some mysterious way her aunt and uncle lived on her, not she on them. If this were not so, it certainly became difficult to understand how they did live, in view of the fact that Mr. Gillingwater steadily consumed the profits of the tap-room, if any, and that they had no other visible means of subsistence. Yet money never seemed to be wanting; and did Joan need a new dress, or any other luxury, it was given to her without demur. More, when some years since she had expressed a sudden and spontaneous desire for education; after a few days' interval, which, it seemed to her, might well have been employed in reference to superior powers in the background, she was informed that arrangements had been made for her to be sent to a boarding school in the capital of the county. She went, to find that her fellow-pupils were for the most part the daughters of shopkeepers and large farmers, and that in consequence the establishment was looked down upon by the students of similar, but higher-class institutions in the same town, and by all who belonged to them. Joan being sensitive and ambitious, resented this state of affairs, though she had small enough right to do so, and on her return home informed her aunt that she wished to be taken away from that school and sent to another of a better sort. The request was received without surprise, and again there was a pause as though to allow of reference to others. Then she was told that if she did not like her school she could leave it, but that she was not to be educated above her station in life.

So Joan returned to the middle-class establishment, where she remained till she was over nineteen years of age. On the whole she was very happy there, for she felt that she was acquiring useful knowledge which she could not have obtained at home. Moreover, among her schoolfellows were certain girls, the daughters of poor clergymen and widows, ladies by birth, with whom she consorted instinctively, and who did not repel her advances.

At the age of nineteen she was informed suddenly that she must leave her school, though no hint of this determination had been previously conveyed to her. Indeed, but a day or two before her aunt had spoken of her return thither as if it were a settled thing. Pondering over this decision in much grief, Joan wondered why it had been arrived at, and more especially whether the visit that morning of her uncle's landlord, Mr. Levinger, who came, she understood, to see about some repairs to the house, had anything to do with it. To Mr. Levinger himself she had scarcely spoken half a dozen times in her life, and yet it seemed to her that whenever they met he regarded her with the keenest interest. Also on this particular occasion Joan chanced to pass the bar-parlour where Mr. Levinger was closeted with her aunt, and to overhear his parting words, or rather the tag of them—which was "too much of a lady," a remark that she could not help thinking had to do with herself. Seeing her go by, he stopped her, keeping her in conversation for some minutes, then abruptly turned upon his heel and left the house with the air of a man who is determined not to say too much.

Then it was that Joan's life became insupportable to her. Accustomed as she had become to more refined associations, from which henceforth she was cut off, the Crown and Mitre, and most of those connected with it, grew hateful in her sight. In her disgust she racked her brain to find some means of escape, and could think of none other than the time-honoured expedient of "going as a governess." This she asked leave to do, and the permission was accorded after the usual pause; but here again she was destined to meet with disappointment. Her surroundings and her attainments were too humble to admit of her finding a footing in that overcrowded profession. Moreover, as one lady whom she saw told her frankly, she was far too pretty for this walk of life. At length she did obtain a situation, however, a modest one enough, that of nursery governess to the children of the rector of Bradmouth, Mr. Biggen. This post she held for nine months, till Mr. Biggen, a kind-hearted and scholarly man, noting her beauty and intelligence, began to take more interest in her than pleased his wife—a state of affairs that resulted in Joan's abrupt dismissal on the day previous to the beginning of this history.

To come to the last and greatest of her troubles: it will be obvious that such a woman would not lack for admirers. Joan had several, all of whom she disliked; but chiefly did she detest the most ardent and persistent of them, the favoured of her aunt, Mr. Samuel Rock. Samuel Rock was a Dissenter, and the best-to-do agriculturalist in the neighbourhood, farming some five hundred acres, most of them rich marsh-lands, of which three hundred or more were his own property inherited and acquired. Clearly, therefore, he was an excellent match for a girl in the position of Joan Haste, and when it is added that he had conceived a sincere admiration for her, and that to make her his wife was the principal desire of his life, it becomes evident that in the nature of things the sole object of hers ought to have been to meet his advances half-way. Unfortunately this was not the case. For reasons which to herself were good and valid, however insufficient they may have appeared to others, Joan would have nothing to do with Samuel Rock. It was to escape from him that she had fled this day to Ramborough Abbey, whither she fondly hoped he would not follow her. It was the thought of him that made life seem so hateful to her even in the golden afternoon; it was terror of him that caused her to search out every possible avenue of retreat from the neighbourhood of Bradmouth.

She might have spared herself the trouble, for even as she sighed and sought, a shadow fell upon her, and looking up she saw Samuel Rock standing before her, hat in hand and smiling his most obsequious smile.

CHAPTER II

SAMUEL ROCK DECLARES HIMSELF

Mr. Samuel Rock was young-looking rather than young in years, of which he might have seen some thirty-five, and, on the whole, not uncomely in appearance. His build was slender for his height, his eyes were blue and somewhat shifty, his features sharp and regular except the chin, which was prominent, massive, and developed almost to deformity. Perhaps it was to hide this blemish that he wore a brown beard, very long, but thin and straggling. His greatest peculiarity, however, was his hands, which were shaped like those of a woman, were long, white notwithstanding their exposure to the weather, and adorned with almond-shaped nails that any lady might have envied. These hands were never still; moreover, there was something furtive and unpleasant about them, capable as they were of the strangest contortions. Mr. Rock's garments suggested a compromise between the dress affected by Dissenters who are pillars of their local chapel and anxious to proclaim the fact, and those worn by the ordinary farmer, consisting as they did of a long-tailed black coat rather the worse for wear, a black felt wide-awake, and a pair of cord breeches and stout riding boots.

"How do you do, Miss Haste?" said Samuel Rock, in his soft, melodious voice, but not offering to shake hands, perhaps because his fingers were engaged in nervously crushing the crown of his hat.

"How do you do?" answered Joan, starting violently. "How did you—" ("find me here," she was about to add; then, remembering that such a remark would show a guilty knowledge of being sought after, substituted) "get here?"

"I—I walked, Miss Haste," he replied, looking at his legs and blushing, as though there were something improper about the fact; then added, "You are quite close to my house, Moor Farm, you know, and I was told that—I thought that I should find you here."

"I suppose you mean that you asked my aunt, and she sent you after me?" said Joan bluntly.

Samuel smiled evasively, but made no other reply to this remark.

Then came a pause, while, with a growing irritation, Joan watched the long white fingers squeezing at the black wide-awake.

"You had better put your hat on, or you will catch cold," she suggested, presently.

"Thank you, Miss Haste, it is not what I am liable to—not but what I take it kindly that you should think of my health;" and he carefully replaced the hat upon his head in such a fashion that the long brown hair showed beneath it in a ragged fringe.

"Oh, please don't thank me," said Joan rudely, dreading lest her remark should be taken as a sign of encouragement.

Then came another pause, while Samuel searched the heavens with his wandering blue eyes, as though to find inspiration there.

"You are very fond of graves, Miss Haste," he said at length.

"Yes, Mr. Rock; they are comfortable to sit on—and I don't doubt very good beds to sleep in," she added, with a touch of grim humour.

Samuel gave a slight but perceptible shiver. He was a highly strung man, and, his piety notwithstanding, he did not appreciate the allusion. When you wish to make love to a young woman, to say the least of it, it is disagreeable if she begins to talk of that place whither no earthly love can follow.

"You shouldn't think of such things at your age—you should not indeed, Miss Haste," he replied; "there are many things you have got to think of before you think of them."

"What things?" asked Joan rashly.

Again Samuel blushed.

"Well—husbands, and—cradles and such-like," he answered vaguely.

"Thank you, I prefer graves," Joan replied with tartness.

By this time it had dawned upon Samuel that he was "getting no forwarder." For a moment he thought of retreat; then the native determination that underlay his soft voice and timid manner came to his aid.

"Miss Haste—Joan," he said huskily, "I want to speak to you."

Joan felt that the hour of trial had come, but still sought a feeble refuge in flippancy.

"You have been doing that for the last five minutes, Mr. Rock," she said; "and I should like to go home."

"No, no, not yet—not till you have heard what I have to say." And he made a quick movement as though to cut off her retreat.

"Well, be quick then," she answered, in a voice in which vexation and fear struggled for the mastery.

Twice Samuel strove to speak, and twice words failed him, for his agitation was very real. At last they came.

"I love you," he said, in an intense whisper. "By the God above you, and the dead beneath your feet, I love you, Joan, as you have never been loved before and never will be loved again!"

She threw her head back and looked at him, frightened by his passion. The realities of his declaration were worse than she had anticipated. His thin face was fierce with emotion, his sensitive lips quivered, and the long lithe fingers of his right hand played with his beard as though he were plaiting it. Joan grew seriously alarmed: she had never seen Samuel Rock look like this before.

"I am sorry," she murmured.

"Don't be sorry," he broke in; "why should you be sorry? It is a great thing to be loved as I love you, Joan, a thing that does not often come in the way of a woman, as you will find out before you die. Look here: do you suppose that I have not fought against this? Do you suppose that I wanted to fall into the power of a girl without a sixpence, without even an honest name? I tell you, Joan, I have fought against it and I have prayed against it since you were a chit of sixteen. Chance after chance have I let slip through my fingers for your sake. There was Mrs. Morton yonder, a handsome body as a man need wish for a wife, with six thousand pounds invested and house property into the bargain, who as good as told me that she would marry me, and I gave her the go-by for you. There was the minister's widow, a lady born, and a holy woman, who would have had me fast enough, and I gave her the go-by for you. I love you, Joan—I tell you that I love you more than land or goods, more than my own soul, more than anything that is. I think of you all day, I dream of you all night. I love you, and I want you, and if I don't get you then I may as well die for all the world is worth to me." And he ceased, trembling with passion.

If Joan had been alarmed before, now she was terrified. The man's earnestness impressed her artistic sense—in a certain rude way there was something fine about it—but it awoke no answer within her heart. His passion repelled her; she had always disliked him, now she loathed him. Swiftly she reviewed the position in her mind, searching a way of escape. She knew well enough that he had not meant to affront her by his references to her poverty and the stain upon her birth—that these truths had broken from him together with that great truth which animated his life; nevertheless, with a woman's wit putting the rest aside, it was on these unlucky sayings that she pounced in her emergency.

"How, Mr. Rock," she asked, rising and standing before him, "how can you ask me to marry you, for I suppose that is what you mean, when you throw my poverty—and the rest—in my teeth? I think, Mr. Rock, that you would do well to go back to Mrs. Morton, or the minister's widow who was born a lady, and to leave me in peace."

"Oh, don't be angry with me," he said, with something like a groan; "you know that I did not mean to offend you. Why should I offend you when I love you so, and want to win you? I wish that I had bitten out my tongue before I said that, but it slipped in with the rest. Will you have me, Joan? Look here: you are the first that ever I said a sweet word to, and that ought to go some way with a woman; and I would make you a good husband. There isn't much that you shall want for if you marry me, Joan. If any one had told me when I was a youngster that I should live to go begging and craving after a woman in this fashion, I'd have said he lied; but you have put me off, and pushed me aside, and given me the slip, till at length you have worked me up to this, and I can't live without you—I can't live without you, that's the truth."

"But I am afraid you will have to, Mr. Rock," said Joan more gently, for the tears which trembled in Samuel's light blue eyes touched her somewhat; and after all, although he repelled her, it was flattering that any man should value her so highly: "I do not love you."

His chin dropped upon his breast dejectedly. Presently he looked up and spoke again.

"I did not expect that you would," he said: "it had been too much luck for a miserable sinner. But be honest with me, Joan—if a woman can—and tell me, do you love anybody else?"

"Not a soul," she answered, opening her brown eyes wide. "Who is there that I should love here?"

"Ah! that's it," he answered, with a sigh of relief: "there is nobody good enough for you in these parts. You are a lady, however you were born, and you want to mate with your own sort. It is no use denying it: I have watched you, and I've seen how you look down upon us; and all I've got to say is:—Be careful that it does not bring you into trouble. Still, while you don't love anybody else—and the man you do love had better keep out of my way, curse him!—there is hope for me. Look here, Joan: I don't want to press you—take time to think it over. I'm in no hurry. I could wait five years if I were sure of getting you at last. I dare say I frightened you by my roughness: I was a fool; I should have remembered that it is all new to you, though it is old enough for me. Listen, Joan: tell me that I may wait awhile and come again—though, whether you tell me or not, I shall wait and I shall come, while there is breath in my body and I can find you out."

"What's the use?" said Joan. "I don't love you, and love does not grow with waiting; and if I do not love you, how can I marry you? We had better make an end of the business once and for all. I am very sorry, but it is not been my fault."

"What's the use? Why, all in the world! In time you will come to think differently; in time you will learn that a Christian man's honest love and all that goes with it isn't a thing to be chucked away like dirty water; in time, perhaps, your aunt and uncle will teach you reason about it, though you do despise me since you went away for your fine schooling—"

"Oh, don't tell them!" broke in Joan imploringly.

"Why, I have told them. I spoke to your aunt this very day about it, and she wished me God-speed with all her heart, and I am sure she will be vexed enough when she hears the truth."

As Joan heard these words her face betrayed the perturbation of her mind. Her aunt's fury when she understood that she, Joan, had rejected Samuel Rock would indeed be hard to bear. Samuel, watching, read her thoughts, and, growing cunning in his despair, was not slow to turn them to his advantage.

"Listen, Joan," he said: "say that you will take time to think it over, and I will make matters easy for you with Mrs. Gillingwater. I know how to manage her, and I promise that not a rough word shall be said to you. Joan, Joan, it is not much to ask. Tell me that I may come again for my answer in six months. That can't hurt you, and it will be hope to me."

She hesitated. A warning sense told her that it would be better to have done with this man at once; but then, if she obeyed it, the one thing which she truly feared—her aunt's fury—would fall upon her and crush her. If she gave way, on the other hand, she knew well enough that Samuel would shelter her from this storm for his own sake if not for hers. What could it matter, she argued weakly, if she did postpone her final decision for six months? Perhaps before that time she might be able to escape from Bradmouth and Samuel Rock, and thus avoid the necessity of giving any answer.

"If I do as you wish, will you promise not to trouble me, or interfere with me, or to speak to me about this kind of thing in the meanwhile?" she asked.

"Yes; I swear that I will not."

"Very good: have your own way about it, Mr. Rock; but understand that I do not mean to encourage you by this, and I don't think it likely that my answer six months hence will be any different from what it is to-day."

"I understand, Joan."

"Very well, then: good-bye." And she held out her hand.

He took it, and, overmastered by a sudden impulse, pressed it to his lips and kissed it twice or thrice.

"Leave go," she said, wrenching herself free. "Is that the way you keep your promise?"

"I beg your pardon," he answered humbly. "I could not help it—Heaven knows that I could not help it. I will not break my word again." And he turned and left her, walking through the grass of the graves with a slow and somewhat feline step.

At last he was gone, and Joan sat down once more, with a gasp of relief. Her first feelings were those of exultation at being rid of Mr. Rock; but they did not endure. Would he keep his promise, she wondered, and hide from her aunt the fact that he had proposed and been rejected? If he did not, one thing was clear to her—that she would be forced to fly from Bradmouth, since by many a hint she knew well that it was expected of her that she should marry Samuel Rock, who was considered to have honoured her greatly by his attentions. This, in view of their relative social positions in the small society of Bradmouth, was not wonderful; but Joan's pride revolted at the thought.

"After all this," she said aloud, "how is he so much higher than I am? and why should my aunt always speak of him as though he were a king and I a beggar girl? My blood is as good as his, and better," and she glanced at a row of ancient tombstones, whereof the tops were visible above the herbage of rank grass, yellow crowsfoot, and sheep's-parsley still white with bloom, that marked the resting-places of the Lacons.

These Lacons had been yeoman farmers for many generations, until the last of them, Joan's grandfather, took to evil courses and dissipated his ancestral patrimony, the greater part of which was now in the possession of Samuel Rock.

Yes, that side of her pedigree was well enough, and were it not for the mystery about her father she could have held her head up with the best of them. Oh, it was a bitter thing that, through no fault of her own, Samuel Rock should be able to reproach her with her lack of an "honest name"! So it was, however—she was an outcast, a waif and a stray, and it was useless to cloak this fact. But, outcast or no, she was mistress of herself, and would not be driven into marriage, however advantageous, with Samuel Rock or any other man who was repellent to her.

Having come to this conclusion, Joan's spirits rose. After all, she was young and healthy, and, she believed, beautiful, with the wide world before her. There were even advantages in lacking an "honest name," since it freed her from responsibilities and rendered it impossible for her to disgrace that which she had not got. As it was, she had only herself to please in the world, and within reasonable and decent limits Joan meant to please herself. Most of all did she mean to do so in connection with these matters of the heart. Nobody had ever loved her, and she had never found anybody to love; and yet, as in all true women, love of one sort or another was the great desire and necessity of her life. Therefore on this point she was determined: she would never marry where she could not love.

Thus thought Joan; then, weary of the subject, she dismissed it from her mind for a while, and, lying back upon the grass in idle contentment, watched the little clouds float across the sky till, far out to sea, they melted into the blue of the horizon. It was a perfect afternoon, and she would enjoy what was left of it before she returned to Bradmouth to face Samuel Rock and all her other worries. Grasshoppers chirped in the flowers at her feet, a beautiful butterfly flitted from tombstone to grey tombstone, sunning itself on each, and high over her head flew the jackdaws, taking food to their young in the crumbling tower above.

For a while Joan watched these jackdaws through her half-shut eyes, till suddenly she remembered that her late employer Mr. Biggen's little boy had confided to her his ardent desire for a young bird of that species, and she began to wonder if she could reach the nest and rob it as a farewell gift to him.

Speculation led to desire, and desire to endeavour. The ruined belfry stairway still ran up the interior of the tower for twenty feet or more—to a spot, indeed, in the stonework where a huge fragment of masonry had fallen bodily, leaving a V-shaped opening that reached to the battlements. Ivy grew upon this gap in the flint rubble, and the nest of the two jackdaws that Joan had been watching particularly, did not appear to be more than a dozen feet above the top of the broken stair. This stair she proceeded to climb without further hesitation. It was not at all safe, but she was active, and her head being good, she reached the point where it was broken away without accident, and, taking her stand on the thickness of the wall, supported herself by the ivy and looked up. There, twice her own height above her, was the window slit with the nest in it, but the mortar and stone upon which she must cling to reach it looked so crumbling and insecure that she did not dare to trust herself to them. So, having finished her inspection, Joan decided to leave those young jackdaws in peace and descend to earth again.

CHAPTER III

THE BEGINNINGS OF FATE

It was at this juncture that Captain Henry Archibald Graves, R.N., pursuing his way by the little-frequented sea road that runs along the top of the cliff past the Ramborough ruins to Bradmouth, halted the cob on which he was riding in order that he might admire the scene at leisure. Presently his eyes, following the line of the ruined tower, lit upon the figure of a girl standing twenty feet from the ground in a gap of the broken wall. He was sixty yards away or more, but there was something so striking and graceful about this figure, poised on high and outlined against the glow of the westering sun, that his curiosity became excited to know whose it was and what the girl might be doing. So strongly was it excited, indeed, that, after a fateful moment of hesitation, Captain Graves, reflecting that he had never examined Ramborough Abbey since he was a boy, turned his horse and rode up the slope of broken ground that intervened between him and the churchyard, where he dismounted and made the bridle fast to a stunted thorn. Possibly the lady might be in difficulty or danger, he explained to himself.

When he had tied up the cob to his satisfaction, he climbed the bank whereon the thorn grew, and reached the dilapidated wall of the churchyard, whence he could again see the lower parts of the tower which had been hidden from his view for a while by the nature of the ground. Now the figure of the woman that had stood there was gone, and a genuine fear seized him lest she should have fallen. With some haste he walked to the foot of the tower, to halt suddenly within five paces of it, for before him stood the object of his search. She had emerged from behind a thicket of briars that grew among the fallen masonry; and, holding her straw hat in her hand, was standing with her back towards him, gazing upwards at the unattainable nest.

"She is safe enough, and I had better move on," thought Captain Graves.

At that moment Joan seemed to become aware of his presence; at any rate, she wheeled round quickly, and they were face to face.

She started and blushed—perhaps more violently than the occasion warranted, for Joan was not accustomed to meet strange men of his class thus unexpectedly. Captain Graves scarcely noticed either the start or the blush, for, to tell the truth, he was employed in studying the appearance of the loveliest woman that he had ever beheld. Perhaps it was only to him that she seemed lovely, and others might not have rated her so highly; perhaps his senses deceived him, and Joan was not truly beautiful; but, in his judgment, neither before nor after did he see her equal, and he had looked on many women in different quarters of the world.

She was tall, and her figure was rounded without being coarse, or even giving promise of coarseness. Her arms were somewhat long for her height, and set on to the shoulders with a peculiar grace, her hands were rather thin, and delicately shaped, and her appearance conveyed an impression of vigour and perfect health. These gifts, however, are not uncommon among English girls. What, to his mind, seemed uncommon was Joan's face as it appeared then, in the beginning of her two-and-twentieth year, with its curved lips, its dimpled yet resolute chin, its flawless oval, its arched brows, and the steady, tender eyes of deepest brown that shone beneath them. For the rest, her head was small and covered with ripping chestnut hair gathered into a knot at the back, her loose-bodied white dress, secured about the waist with a leather girdle, was clean and simple, and her bearing had a grace and dignity that Nature alone can give. Lastly, though from various indications he judged that she did not belong to his own station in life, she looked like a person of some refinement.

Such was Joan's outward appearance. It was attractive enough, and yet it was not her beauty only that fascinated Henry Graves. There was something about this girl which was new to him; a mystery more beautiful than beauty shone upon her sweet face—such a mystery as he had noted once or twice in the masterpieces of ancient art, but never till that hour on human lips or eyes. In those days Joan might have posed as a model of Psyche before Cupid kissed her.

Now let us turn for a moment to Henry Archibald Graves, the man destined to be the hero of her life's romance.

Like so many sailors, he was short, scarcely taller than Joan herself indeed, and stout in build. In complexion he was fair, though much bronzed by exposure to foreign climates; his blue eyes were keen and searching, as might be expected in one who had watched at sea by night for nearly twenty years; and he was clean shaved. His features were good though strongly marked, especially as regards the nose and chin; but he could not be called handsome, only a distinguished-looking man of gentlemanly bearing. At first sight the face might strike a stranger as hard, but more careful examination showed it to be rather that of a person who made it a practice to keep guard over his emotions. In repose it was a somewhat proud face, that of one accustomed to command and to be obeyed; but frank and open withal, particularly if its owner smiled, when it became decidedly pleasing.

For a few seconds they stood still in their mutual surprise, looking at each other, and the astonishment and admiration written in the stranger's eyes were so evident, and yet so obviously involuntary, that Joan blushed more deeply than before.

Captain Graves felt the situation to be awkward. His first impulse was to take off his hat and go, his next and stronger one to stay and explain.

"I really beg your pardon," he said, with a shyness which was almost comic; "I saw a lady standing on the tower as I was riding by, and feared that she might be in difficulties."

Joan turned her head away, being terribly conscious of the blush which would not fade. This stranger's appearance pleased her greatly; moreover, she was flattered by his notice, and by the designation of "lady." Hitherto her safety had not been a matter of much moment to any one, except, perhaps, to Samuel Rock.

"It is very kind of you," she answered, with hesitation; "but I was in no danger—I got down quite easily."

Again Captain Graves paused. He was puzzled. The girl's voice was as sweet as her person—low and rich in tone—but she spoke with a slight Eastern-counties accent. Who and what was she?

"Then I must apologise for troubling you, Miss— Miss—?"

"I am only Joan Haste of Bradmouth, sir," she interrupted confusedly, as though she guessed his thoughts.

"Indeed! and I am Captain Graves of Rosham—up there, you know. Bradmouth is—I mean, is the view good from that tower?"

"I think so; but I did not go up to look at it. I went to try to get those young jackdaws. I wanted them for a little boy in Bradmouth, the clergyman's son."

"Ah!" he said, his face lighting up, for he saw an opportunity of prolonging the acquaintance, which interested him not a little; "then perhaps I may be of service after all. I think that I can help you there." And he stepped towards the tower.

"I don't believe that it is quite safe, sir," said Joan, in some alarm; "please do not take the trouble,"—and she stretched out her hand as though to detain him.

"Oh, it is no trouble at all, I assure you: I like climbing. You see, I am well accustomed to it. Once I climbed the second Pyramid, the one with the casing on it, though I won't try that again," he replied, with a pleasant laugh. And before she could interfere further he was mounting the broken stair.

At the top of it Henry halted, surveying the crumbling slope of wall doubtfully. Then he took his coat off, threw it down into the churchyard, and rolled his shirt sleeves up above his elbows, revealing a pair of very powerful and fair-skinned arms.

"Please don't—please!" implored Joan from below.

"I am not going to give in now," he answered; and, grasping a firm and projecting stone with his right hand, he set his foot upon a second fragment and began the ascent of the broken wall. Soon he reached the head of the slope in safety, but only to be encountered by another difficulty. The window slit containing the jackdaws' nest was round the corner, a little above him on the surface of the wall, and it proved impossible to reach it from where he stood. Very cautiously he bent to one side and looked round the angle of the masonry. Close to him a strong stem of ivy grew up the tower, dividing into two branches some five feet below the nest. He knew that it would be dangerous to trust his weight to it, and still more dangerous to attempt the turning of the corner; but at this moment he was more set upon getting the young birds which this village beauty desired, than on his own safety or any other earthly thing. Henry Graves was a man who disliked being beaten.

Very swiftly he shifted his hold, and, stretching out his left hand, he felt about until it gripped the ivy stem. Now he must go on. Exactly how it happened would be difficult to describe on paper, but in two more seconds his foot was in the fork of ivy and his face was opposite to the window slit containing the nest.

"I can see the young ones," he said. "I will throw them out, and you must catch them in your hat, for I can't carry them."

"Oh! pray take care," gasped Joan.

He laughed by way of answer; and next second, with loud squawks and an impotent flapping of untried wings, a callow jackdaw was launched upon its first flight, to be deftly caught in Joan's broad hat before it touched the earth. A second followed, then another, and another. The last bird was the strongest of the four, and flew some yards in its descent. Joan ran to catch it—a process that took a little time, for it lay upon its back behind a broken tombstone, and pecked at her hand in a fashion necessitating its envelopment in her handkerchief. Just as she secured it she heard Captain Graves say: "That's the lot. Now I am coming down."

Next instant there was a sound as of something being torn. Joan looked up, to see him hanging by one arm against the sheer face of the tower. In attempting to repass the corner Henry's foot had slipped, throwing all his weight on to the stem of ivy which he held; but it was not equal to the strain, and a slab of it had come away from the wall. To this ivy he clung desperately, striving to find foothold with his heels, his face towards her, for he had swung round. Uttering a low cry of fear, Joan sped back to the tower like a swallow. She knew that he must fall; but that was not the worst of it, for almost immediately beneath where he hung stood a raised tomb shaped like a stone coffin, having its top set thickly with rusted iron spikes, three inches or more in length, especially designed to prevent the idle youth of all generations from seating themselves upon this home of the dead.

If he struck upon these!

Joan rushed round the spiked tomb, and halted almost, but not quite, beneath Henry's hanging shape. His eyes fell upon her agonised and upturned face.

"Stand clear! I am coming," he said in a low voice.

Watching, she saw the muscles of his arm work convulsively. Then the rough stem of ivy began to slip through his clenched fingers. Another second, and he dropped like a stone from a height of twenty feet or more. Instinctively Joan stretched out her arms as though to catch him; but he struck the ground legs first just in front of her, and, with a sharp exclamation, pitched forward against her.

The shock was tremendous. Joan saw it coming, and prepared to meet it as well as she might by bending her body forward, since, at all hazards, he must be prevented from falling face foremost on the spiked tomb, there to be impaled. His brow cut her lip almost through, his shoulder struck her bosom, knocking the breath out of her, then her strong arms closed around him like a vice, and down they went together.

All this while her mind remained clear. She knew that she must not go down backwards, or the fate from which she strove to protect him would overtake her—the iron spikes would pierce her back and brain. By a desperate effort she altered the direction of their fall, trusting to come to earth alongside the tomb. But she could not quite clear it, as a sudden pang in the right shoulder told her. For a moment they lay on the edge of the tomb, then rolled free. Captain Graves fell undermost, his head striking with some violence on a stone, and he lay still, as did Joan for nearly a minute, since her breath was gone.

Presently the pain of breathlessness passed a little, and she began to recover. Glancing at her arm, she saw that a stream of blood trickled along her sleeve, and blood from her cut lips was falling on the bosom of her dress and upon the forehead of Henry Graves beneath her, staining his white face.

"Oh, he is dead!" mourned Joan aloud; "and it is my fault."

At this moment Henry opened his eyes. Apparently he had overheard her, for he answered: "Don't distress yourself: I am all right."

As he spoke, he tried to move his leg, with the result that a groan of agony broke from him. Glancing at the limb, Joan saw that it was twisted beneath him in a fashion so unnatural that it became evident even to her inexperience that it must be broken. At this discovery her distress overpowered her to so great an extent that she burst into tears.

"Oh! your leg is broken," she sobbed. "What shall I do?"

"I think," he whispered, with a ghastly smile, biting his lips to keep back any further expression of his pain, "that you will find a flask in my coat pocket, if you do not mind getting it."

Joan rose from her knees, and going to the coat, which lay hard by, took from it a little silver flask of whiskey-and-water; then, returning, she placed one arm beneath the injured man's head and with the other contrived to pour some of the liquid down his throat.

"Thank you," he said: "I feel better"; then suddenly fainted away.

In great alarm she poured some more of the spirit down his throat; for now a new terror had taken her that he might be suffering from internal injuries also. To her relief, he came to himself again, and caught sight of the red stain growing upon her white dress.

"You are hurt," he said. "What a selfish fellow I am, thinking only of myself!"

"Oh, don't think of me," Joan answered: "it is nothing—a mere scratch. What is to be done? How can I get you from here? Nobody lives about, and we are a long way from Bradmouth."

"There is my horse," he murmured, "but I fear that I cannot ride him."

"I will go," said Joan; "yet how can I leave you by yourself?"

"I shall get on for a while," Henry answered. "It is very good of you."

Then, since there was no help for it, Joan rose, and running to where the horse was tied, she loosed it. But now a new difficulty confronted her; her wounded arm was already helpless and painful, and without its aid she could not manage to climb into the saddle, for the cob, although a quiet animal enough, was not accustomed to a woman's skirts, and at every effort shifted itself a foot or two away from her. At length, Joan, crying with pain, grief and vexation, determined to abandon the attempt and to set out for Bradmouth on foot, when for the first time fortune favoured her in the person of a red-haired lad whom she knew well, and who was returning homewards from an expedition in search of the eggs of wild-fowl.

"Oh! Willie Hood," she cried, "come and help me. A gentleman has fallen from the tower yonder and broken his leg. Now do you get on this horse and ride as hard as you can to Dr. Child's, and tell him that he must come out here with some men, and a door or something to carry him on. Mind you say his leg is broken, and that he must bring things to tie it up with. Do you understand?"

"Why you're all bloody!" answered the boy, whose face betrayed his bewilderment; "and I never did ride a horse in my life."

"Yes, yes, I am hurt too; but don't think of that. You get on to him, and you'll be safe enough. Why, surely you're not afraid, Willie Hood?"

"Afraid? No, I aren't afraid," answered the boy, colouring, "only I like my legs better than his'n, that's all. Here goes." And with a prodigious and scuffling effort Willie landed himself on the back of the astonished cob.

"Stop," said Joan; "you know what to say?"

"Yes," he answered proudly; "don't you fret—I know right enough. I'll bring the doctor back myself."

"No, Willie: you go on to the Crown and Mitre, and tell my aunt that a gentleman, Captain Graves of Rosham, has hurt himself badly, and that she must get a room ready for him. It had best be mine, for it's the nicest," she added, "and there is nowhere else that he can go."

Willie nodded, and with a loud "gee-up" to the horse, started on his journey, his legs hanging clear of the stirrups, and gripping the pommel of the saddle with his right hand.

Having watched him disappear, Joan returned to where the wounded man lay. His eyes were shut, but apparently he heard her come, for presently he opened them.

"What, back so soon?" he said; "I must have been asleep."

"No, no: I could not leave you. I found a boy and sent him on the horse for the doctor. I only trust that he may get there safely," she added to herself.

"Very well: I am glad you have come back," he said faintly. "I am afraid that I am giving you a great deal of trouble, but do you mind rubbing my hand? It feels so cold."

She sat down on the grass beside him, having first wrapped his coat round him as best she could, and began to chafe his hand. Presently the pain, which had subsided for a while, set in more sharply than ever, and his fingers, that had been like ice, were now burning hot. Another half-hour passed, while the shadows lengthened and the evening waned, and Henry's speech became incoherent. He fancied himself on board a man-of-war, and uttered words of command; he talked of foreign countries, and mentioned many names, among them one that was not strange to Joan's ears—that of Emma Levinger; lastly even he spoke of herself:

"What a lovely girl!" he muttered. "It's worth risking one's neck to please her. Worth risking one's neck to please her!"

A third half-hour passed; the fever lessened, and he grew silent. Then the cold fit took him again—his flesh shivered.

"I am frozen," he murmured through his chattering teeth; "for Heaven's sake help me! Can't you see how cold I am?"

Joan was in despair. Alas and alas! she had nothing to put on him, for even if she took it off, her thin white dress would be no protection. Again and again he prayed for warmth, till at length her tender pity overcame her natural shrinking, and she did the only thing she could. Lying down beside him, she put her arms about him, and held him so, to comfort him if she might.

Apparently it did comfort him, for his moaning ceased, and by slow degrees he sank into stupor. Now twilight was upon them, and still no help came. Where could Willie have gone, Joan wondered: if, he did not come quickly, the man would surely die! Her own strength was failing her—she felt it going with the blood that ebbed continually from the wound in her shoulder. Periods of mist and oblivion alternated in her mind with times of clearest reason. Quick they came and quicker, till at last all was a blank and she knew no more.

And now the twilight had grown into darkness, and these two lay silent, locked in each other's arms among the graves, and the stars shed their light upon them.

CHAPTER IV

THE HOME-COMING OF HENRY GRAVES

Henry Graves, a man of thirty-three years of age, was the second and only surviving son of Sir Reginald Graves, of Rosham Hall, a place situated about four miles from Bradmouth. When a lad he chose the Navy as a profession, and to that profession he clung with such unusual earnestness, that during the last eighteen years or so but little of his time had been passed at home. Some months previous to his meeting with Joan Haste, however, very much against his own will, he was forced to abandon his calling. He was cruising in command of a gunboat off the coast of British Columbia, when one evening a telegram reached him informing him of the death of his elder brother, Reginald, who met his end through an accident whilst riding a steeplechase. There had never been much sympathy or affection between the two brothers, for reasons to be explained presently; still this sudden and terrible intelligence was a heavy shock to Henry, nor did the fact that it left him heir to an entailed property, which he believed to be considerable, greatly mitigate it in his mind.

When there are but two sons, it is almost inevitable that one should be preferred before the other. Certainly that was the case in the Graves family. As children Reginald, the elder, had been wayward, handsome, merry and attractive; whereas Henry was a somewhat plain and silent boy, with a habit of courting his own society, and almost aggressive ideas of honour and duty. Naturally, therefore, the love of father, mother and sister went out to the brilliant Reginald, while Henry was left very much to his own devices. He said nothing, and he was too proud to be jealous, but nobody except the lad himself ever knew what he suffered under this daily, if unintentional, neglect. Though his constitutional reserve prevented him from showing his heart, in truth he was very affectionate, and almost adored the relations who looked on him as a dullard, and even spoke of him at times as "poor Henry," as though he were deficient in intellect.

Thus it came about that very early in his young life, with characteristic determination, Henry arrived at the conclusion that he would be happier away from the home where he was little wanted. Once in the Navy, he applied himself to his profession with industry and intelligence, and as a result did better in the service than most young men who cannot bring to their support any particular interest, or the advantage of considerable private means. In whatever capacity he served, he won the confidence and the respect both of his subordinates and of his superiors. He was a hard-working man, so hard work was thrust upon him; and he never shirked it, though often enough others got the credit of his efforts. At heart, moreover, he was ambitious. Henry could never forget the slights that he had experienced as a child, and he was animated by a great but secret desire to show the relatives who disparaged him in favour of his more showy brother that he was made of better stuff than they were disposed to believe.

To this purpose he subordinated his life. His allowance was small, for their father's means were not in proportion to his nominal estate, and as time went on his brother Reginald grew more and more extravagant. But, such as it was, Henry never exceeded it, though few were aware of the straits to which he was put at times. In the same way, though by nature he was a man of strong passions and genial temperament, he rarely allowed either the one or the other to master him. Geniality meant expense, and he observed that indulgence in passion of any sort, more especially if it led to mixing with the other sex, spelt anxiety and sorrow at the best, or at the worst disgrace and ruin. Therefore he curbed these inclinations till what began in the pride of duty ended in the pride of habit.

Thus time wore on till he received the telegram announcing his brother's shocking death. A fortnight or so afterwards it was followed by a letter from his father, a portion of which may be transcribed. It began:

"My dear Henry,—

"My telegram has informed you of the terrible loss which has overtaken our family. Your brother Reginald is no more; it has pleased Providence to remove him from the world in the fulness of his manhood, and we must accept the fact that we cannot alter with such patience as we may."

Here followed particulars of the accident, and of arrangements for the interment. The letter went on:

"Your mother and sister are prostrated, and for myself I can only say that my heart is broken. Life is a ruin to me henceforward, and I think that when the time comes I shall welcome its close. It does indeed seem cruel that one so brilliant and so beloved as your brother should be snatched from us thus, but God's will be done. Though you have been little together of late years, I know that we shall have your sympathy in our overwhelming sorrow.

"To turn to other matters, of which this event makes it necessary that I should speak: of course your beloved brother's death puts you in the place he held—that is, so far as temporal things are concerned. I may as well tell you at once that the finances of this property are in great confusion. Latterly Reginald had the largest share in its management, and as yet I cannot therefore follow all the details. It seems, however, that, speaking generally, affairs are much worse than I supposed, and already, though he lies unburied, some very heavy claims have come in against his estate, which of course must be met for the honour of the family.

"And now, my dear boy, I—or rather your mother, your sister, and I—must ask you to make a sacrifice, should you look at it in that light: namely, to give up your profession and take the place at home to which the death of your brother has promoted you. This request is not made lightly; but, as you know, my health is now very feeble, and I find myself quite unable to cope with the difficulties of the time and the grave embarrassments by which I am hampered. Indeed, it would be idle to disguise from you that unless matters are speedily taken in hand and some solution is found to our troubles, there is every prospect that before long Rosham will be foreclosed on—a probability of which I can scarcely bear to think, and one that will be equally painful to yourself when you remember that the property has been in our family for full three hundred years, and that we have no resources beyond those of the land."

Then the letter went into details that were black enough, and ended by hinting at some possible mode of escape from the family troubles which would be revealed to him on his return to England.

The receipt of this epistle plunged Henry Graves into a severe mental struggle. As has been said, he was fond of his profession, and he had no wish to leave it. His prospects in the Navy were not especially brilliant, indeed, but his record at the Admiralty was good, and he was popular in the service both with his brother officers and the men, though perhaps more so with the latter than the former. Moreover, he had confidence in himself, and was filled with a sincere ambition to rise to the top of the tree, or near it. Now, after serving many years as a lieutenant, when at last he had earned an independent command, he was asked to abandon his career, and with it the hopes of half a lifetime, in order that he might undertake the management of a bankrupt estate, a task for which he did not conceive himself to be suited.

At first he was minded to refuse altogether; but while he was still hesitating a second letter arrived, from his mother, with whom he was in greater sympathy than with any other member of the family. This epistle, which did not enter into details, was written in evident distress, and implored him to return to England at all hazards if he wished to save them from ruin. In conclusion, like that received from his father, it hinted mysteriously at an unknown something by means of which it would be in his power, and his alone, to restore the broken fortunes of their house.

Duty had always been the first consideration with Henry Graves, and so it remained in this emergency of his life. He had no longer any doubt as to what he ought do do, and, sacrificing his private wishes and what he considered to be his own advantage, he set himself to do it.

An effort to obtain leave on urgent private affairs having failed, he was reduced to the necessity of sending in his papers and begging the Lords of the Admiralty for permission to retire from the service on the ground of his brother's death.

The night that he posted this application was an unhappy one for him: the career he had hoped to make for himself and the future honour which he dreamed of had melted away, and the only prospect left to him was that of one day becoming a baronet without a sixpence to support his title, and the nominal owner of a bankrupt estate. Moreover, however reasonable and enlightened he may be, no sailor is entirely without superstition, and on this matter Henry Graves was superstitious. Something in his heart seemed to tell him that this new start would bring him little luck, whatever advantage might result to his family. Once again he felt the awe of an imaginative boy who for the first time understands that the world is before him, and that he must fight his way through its cruel multitudes, or be trampled to death of them.

In due course my Lords of the Admiralty signified to Commander Graves that his request had been taken into favourable consideration, and that he was granted leave pending the arrangements necessary to his retirement from Her Majesty's Navy. His feelings as for the last time he was rowed away from the ship in the gig which had been his especial property need not be dwelt upon. They were bitter enough, and the evident regret of his messmates at parting from him did not draw their sting: indeed, it would not be too much to say that in this hour of farewell Henry Graves went as near to tears as he had done since he attained to manhood.

But he got through it somehow, and even laughed and waved his hat when the crew of the Hawk—that was the name of the gunboat he had commanded—cheered him as he left her deck for ever.

Eighteen days later he stood in the library of Rosham Hall. Although the season was mid-May the weather held bitterly cold, and such green as had appeared upon the trees did not suffice to persuade the traveller that winter was done with. An indescribable air of gloom hung about the great white house, which, shaped like an early Victorian mausoleum, and treed up to the windows with funereal cedars, was never a cheerful dwelling even in the height of summer. The shadow of death lay upon the place and on the hearts of its inmates, and struck a chill through Henry as he crossed the threshold. His father, a tall and dignified old gentleman with snowy hair, met him in the hall with a show of cordiality that soon flickered away.

"How are you, my dear boy?" he said. "I am very glad to see you home and looking so well. It is most kind of you to have fallen in with our wishes as to your leaving the Navy. I scarcely expected that you would myself. Indeed, was I never more surprised than when I received your letter saying that you had sent in your papers. It is a comfort to have you back again, though I doubt whether you will be able to do any good."

"Then perhaps I might as well have stopped where I was, father," answered Henry.

"No, no, you did well to come. For many reasons which you will understand soon you did well to come. You are looking for your mother and Ellen. They have gone to the church with a wreath for your poor brother's grave. The train is generally late—you were not expected so soon. That was a terrible blow to me, Henry: I am quite broken down, and shall never get over it. Ah! here they are."

As Sir Reginald spoke Lady Graves and her daughter entered the hall and greeted Henry warmly enough. His mother was a person of about sixty, still handsome in appearance, but like himself somewhat silent and reserved in manner. Trouble had got hold of her, and she showed it on her face. For the rest, she was an upright and a religious woman, whose one passion in life, as distinguished from her predilections, had been for her dead son Reginald. He was taken away, her spirit was broken, and there remained to her nothing except an unvarying desire to stave off the ruin that threatened her husband's house and herself.

The daughter, Ellen, now a woman of twenty-five, was of a different type. In appearance she was fair and well-developed, striking and ladylike rather than good-looking; in manner she was quick and vivacious, well-read, moreover, in a certain shallow fashion, and capital company. Ellen was not a person of deep affections, though she also had worshipped Reginald; but on the other hand she was swift to see her own advantage and to shape the course of events toward that end. At this moment her mind was set secretly upon making a rich marriage with the only eligible bachelor in the neighbourhood, Milward by name, a vain man of good extraction but of little strength of character, and one whom she knew that she could rule.

It has been said that his welcome was warm enough to all outward appearance, and yet it left a sense of disappointment in Henry's mind. Instinctively he felt, with the exception, perhaps, of his mother, that they all hoped to use him—that he had been summoned because he might be of service, not because the consolation of his presence was desired in a great family misfortune; and once more he wished himself back on the quarter-deck of the Hawk, dependent upon his own exertions to make his way in the world.

After a somewhat depressing dinner in the great dining-room, of which the cold stone columns and distempered walls, decorated with rather dingy specimens of the old masters, did not tend to expansion of the heart, a family council was held in the study. It lasted far into the night, but its results may be summed up briefly. In good times the Rosham Hall property was worth about a hundred thousand pounds; now, in the depths of the terrible depression which is ruining rural England, it was doubtful if it would find a purchaser at half that amount, notwithstanding its capacities as a sporting estate. When Sir Reginald Graves came into possession the place was burdened with a mortgage of twenty-five thousand pounds, more or less. On the coming of age of his elder son, Reginald, Henry's brother, the entail had been cut and further moneys raised upon resettlement, so that in the upshot the incumbrances upon the property including over-due interests which were added to the capital at different dates, stood at a total of fifty-one thousand, or something more than the present selling value of the estate.

Henry inquired where all the money had gone; and, after some beating about the bush, he discovered that of late years, for the most part, it had been absorbed by his dead brother's racing debts. After this revelation he held his tongue upon the matter.

In addition to these burdens there were unsatisfied claims against Reginald's estate amounting to over a thousand pounds; and, to top up with, three of the principal tenants had given notice to leave at the approaching Michaelmas, and no applicants for their farms were forthcoming. Also the interest on the mortgages was over a year in arrear.

When everything had been explained, Henry spoke with irritation: "The long and the short of it is that we are bankrupt, and badly bankrupt. Why on earth did you force me to leave the Navy? At any rate I could have helped myself to some sort of a living there. Now I must starve with the rest."

Lady Graves sighed and wiped her eyes. The sigh was for their broken fortunes, the tear for the son who had ruined them.

Sir Reginald, who was hardened to money troubles, did not seem to be so deeply affected.

"Oh, it is not so bad as that, my boy," he said, almost cheerfully. "Your poor brother always managed to find a way out of these difficulties when they cropped up, and I have no doubt that you will be able to do the same. For me the matter no longer has much personal interest, since my day is over; but you must do the best for yourself, and for your mother and sister. And now I think that I will go to bed, for business tires me at night."

When his father and mother had gone Henry lit his pipe.

"Who holds these mortgages?" he asked of his sister Ellen, who sat opposite to him, watching him curiously across the fire.

"Mr. Levinger," she answered. "He and his daughter are coming here to-morrow to stay till Monday."

"What, my father's mysterious friend, the good-looking man who used to be agent for the property when I was a boy?"

"Yes, the man who was shooting here when you were on leave eighteen months ago."

"I remember: he had his daughter with him—a pale-faced, quiet girl."

"Yes; but do not disparage his daughter, Henry."

"Why not?"

"Because it is a mistake to find fault with one's future wife. That way salvation lies, my dear brother. She is an heiress, and more than half in love with you, Henry. No, it is not a mistake—I know it for a fact. Now, perhaps, you understand why it was necessary that you should come home. Either you must follow the family tradition and marry an heiress, Miss Levinger or some other, or this place will be foreclosed on and we may all adjourn to the workhouse."

"So that is why I was sent for," said Henry, throwing down his pipe: "to be sold to this lady? Well, Ellen, all I have to say is that it is an infernal shame!"

And, turning, he went to bed without even bidding her good night.

His sister watched him go without irritation or surprise. Rising from her chair, she stood by the fire warming her feet, and glancing from time to time at the dim rows of family portraits that adorned the library walls. There were many of them, dating back to the early part of the seventeenth century or even before it; for the Graveses, or the De Graves as they used to be called, were an ancient race, and though the house had been rebuilt within the last hundred and twenty years, they had occupied this same spot of ground for many generations. During all these years the family could not be said either to have sunk or risen, although one of its members was made a baronet at the beginning of the century in payment for political services. It had produced no great men, and no villains; it had never been remarkable for wealth or penury, or indeed for anything that distinguishes one man, or a race of men, from its fellows.

It may be asked how it came about that these Graveses contrived to survive the natural waste and dwindling of possessions that they never did anything to augment. A glance at the family pedigree supplies an answer. From generation to generation it had been held to be the duty of the eldest son for the time being to marry an heiress; and this rule was acted on with sufficient regularity to keep the fortunes of the race at a dead level, notwithstanding the extravagances of occasional spendthrifts and the claims of younger children.

"They all did so," said Ellen to herself, as she looked upon the portraits of her dead-and-gone forefathers by the light of the flickering flame; "and why shouldn't he? I am not sentimental, but I believe that I'd marry a Russian Jew rather than see the old place go to the dogs, and that sort of thing is worse for a woman than a man. It will be difficult to manage, but he will marry her in the end, even if he hates the very sight of her. A man has no right to let his private inclinations weigh with him in such a matter, for he passes but his family remains. Thank Heaven, Henry always had a strong sense of duty, and when he comes to look at the position coolly he will see it in a proper light; though what made that flaxen-haired little mummy fall in love with him is a mystery to me, for he never spoke a word to her. Blessings on her! It is the only piece of good luck that has come to our family for a generation. And now I must go to bed—those old pictures are beginning to stare at me."

CHAPTER V

THE LEVINGERS VISIT ROSHAM

Seldom did Henry Graves spend a more miserable night than on this occasion of his return to Rosham. He had expected to find his father's affairs in evil case, but the reality was worse than anything that he had imagined. The family was absolutely ruined—thanks to his poor brother's wickedness, for no other word was strong enough to describe his conduct—and now it seemed that the remedy suggested for this stage of things was that he should marry the daughter of their principal creditor. That was why he had been forced to leave the Navy and dragged home from the other side of the world. Henry laughed as he thought of it, for the situation had a comical side. Both in stories and in real life it is common enough for the heroine of the piece to be driven into these dilemmas, in order to save the honour or credit of her family; but it is unusual to hear of such a choice being thrust upon a man, perhaps because, when they chance to meet with them, men keep these adventures to themselves.

Henry tried to recall the appearance of the young lady; and after a while a vision of her came back to him. He remembered a pale-faced, silent girl, with an elegant figure, large grey eyes, dark lashes, and absolutely flaxen hair, who sat in the corner of the room and watched everybody and everything almost without speaking, but who, through her silence, or perhaps on account of it, had given him a curious impression of intensity.

This was the woman whom his family expected him to marry, and, as his sister seemed to suggest, who, directly or indirectly, had intimated a willingness to marry him! Ellen said, indeed, that she was "half in love" with him, which was absurd. How could Miss Levinger be to any degree whatsoever in love with a person whom she knew so slightly? If there were truth in the tale at all, it seemed more probable that she was consumed by a strange desire to become Lady Graves at some future time; or perhaps her father was a victim to the desire and she a tool in his hands. Although personally he had met him little, Henry remembered some odds and ends of information about Mr. Levinger now, and as he lay unable to sleep he set himself to piece them together.

In substance this is what they amounted to: many years ago Mr. Levinger had appeared in the neighbourhood; he was then a man of about thirty, very handsome and courteous in his manners, and, it was rumoured, of good birth. It was said that he had been in the Army and seen much service; but whether this were true or no, obviously he did not lack experience of the world. He settled himself at Bradmouth, lodging in the house of one Johnson, a smack owner; and, being the best of company and an excellent sportsman, gradually, by the help of Sir Reginald Graves, who seemed to take an interest in him and employed him to manage the Rosham estates, he built up a business as a land agent, out of which he supported himself—for, to all appearances, he had no other means of subsistence.

One great gift Mr. Levinger possessed—that of attracting the notice and even the affection of women; and, in one way and another, this proved to be the foundation of his fortunes. At length, to the secret sorrow of sundry ladies of his acquaintance, he put a stop to his social advancement by contracting a glaring masalliance, taking to wife a good-looking but homely girl, Emma Johnson, the only child of his landlord the smack owner. Thereupon local society, in which he had been popular so long as he remained single, shut its doors upon him, nor did the ladies with whom he had been in such favour so much as call upon Mrs. Levinger.

When old Johnson the smack owner died, a few months after the marriage, and it became known that he had left a sum variously reported at from fifty to a hundred thousand pounds behind him, every farthing of which his daughter and her husband inherited, society began to understand, however, that there had been method in Mr. Levinger's madness.

Owing, in all probability, to the carelessness of the lawyer, the terms of Johnson's will were somewhat peculiar. All the said Johnson's property, real and personal, was strictly settled under this will upon his daughter Emma for life, then upon her husband, George Levinger, for life, with remainder "to the issue of the body of the said George Levinger lawfully begotten."

The effect of such a will would be that, should Mrs. Levinger die childless, her husband's children by a second marriage would inherit her father's property, though, should she survive her husband, apparently she would enjoy a right of appointment of the fund, even though she had no children by him. As a matter of fact, however, these issues had not arisen, since Mrs. Levinger predeceased her husband, leaving one child, who was named Emma after her.

As for Mr. Levinger himself, his energy seemed to have evaporated with his, pecuniarily speaking, successful marriage. At any rate, so soon as his father-in-law died, abandoning the land agency business, he retired to a comfortable red brick house situated on the sea shore in a very lonely position some four miles south of Bradmouth, and known as Monk's Lodge, which had come to him as part of his wife's inheritance. Here he lived in complete retirement; for now that the county people had dropped him he seemed to have no friends. Nor did he try to make any, but was content to occupy himself in the management of a large farm, and in the more studious pursuits of reading and archeology.

The morrow was a Saturday. At breakfast Ellen remarked casually that Mr. and Miss Levinger were to arrive at the Hall about six o'clock, and were expected to stay over the Sunday.

"Indeed," replied Henry, in a tone which did not suggest anxiety to enlarge upon the subject.

But Ellen, who had also taken a night for reflection, would not let him escape thus. "I hope that you mean to be civil to these people, Henry?" she said interrogatively.

"I trust that I am civil to everybody, Ellen."

"Yes, no doubt," she replied, in her quiet, persistent voice; "but you see there are ways and ways of being civil. I am not sure that you have quite realised the position."

"Oh, yes, I have—thoroughly. I am expected to marry this lady, that is, if she is foolish enough to take me in payment of what my father owes to hers. But I tell you, Ellen, that I do not see my way to it at present."

"Please don't get angry, dear," said Ellen, more gently; "I dare say that such a notion is unpleasant enough, and in a way—well, degrading to a proud man. Of course no one can force you to marry her if you don't wish to, and the whole business will probably fall through. All I beg is that you will cultivate the Levingers a little, and give the matter fair consideration. For my part I think that it would be much more degrading to allow our father to become bankrupt at his age than for you to marry a good and clever girl like Emma Levinger. However, of course I am only a woman, and have no 'sense of honour,' or at least one that is not strong enough to send my family to the workhouse when by a little self-sacrifice I could keep them out of it."

And with this sarcasm Ellen left the room before Henry could find words to reply to her.

That morning Henry walked with his mother to the church in order to inspect his brother's grave—a melancholy and dispiriting duty—the more so, indeed, because his sense of justice would not allow him to acquit the dead man of conduct that, to his strict integrity, seemed culpable to the verge of dishonour. On their homeward way Lady Graves also began to talk about the Levingers.

"I suppose you have heard, Henry, that Mr. Levinger and his daughter are coming here this afternoon?"

"Yes, mother; Ellen told me."

"Indeed. You will remember Miss Levinger, no doubt. She is a nice girl in every sense; your dear brother used to admire her very much."

"Yes, I remember her a little; but Reginald's tastes and mine were not always similar."

"Well, Henry, I hope that you will like her. It is a delicate matter to speak about, even for a mother to a son, but you know now how terribly indebted we are to the Levingers, and of course if a way could be found out of our difficulties it would be a great relief to me and to your dear father. Believe me, my boy, I do not care so much about myself; but I wish, if possible, to save him from further sorrow. I think that very little would kill him now."

"See here, mother," said Henry bluntly: "Ellen tells me that you wish me to marry Miss Levinger for family reasons. Well, in this matter, as in every other, I will try to oblige you if I can; but I cannot understand what grounds you have for supposing that the young lady wishes to marry me. So far as I can judge, she might take her fortune to a much better market."

"I don't quite know about it, Henry," answered Lady Graves, with some hesitation. "I gathered, however, that, when he came here after you had gone to join your ship about eighteen months ago, Mr. Levinger told your father, with whom you know he has been intimate since they were both young, that you were a fine fellow, and had taken his fancy as well as his daughter's. Also I believe he said that if only he could see her married to such a man as you are he should die happy, or words to that effect."

"Rather a slight foundation to build all these plans on, isn't it, mother? In eighteen months her father may have changed his mind, and Miss Levinger may have seen a dozen men whom she likes better. Here comes Ellen to meet us, so let us drop the subject."

About six o'clock that afternoon Henry, returning from a walk on the estate, saw a strange dogcart being run into the coach-house, from which he inferred that Mr. and Miss Levinger had arrived. Wishing to avoid the appearance of curiosity, he went straight to his room, and did not return downstairs till within a few minutes of the dinner-hour. The large and rather ill-lighted drawing-room seemed to be empty when he entered, and Henry was about to seat himself with an expression of relief, for his temper was none of the best this evening, when a rustling in a distant corner attracted his attention. Glancing in the direction of the noise, he perceived a female figure seated in a big arm-chair reading.

"Why don't you come to the light, Ellen?" he said. "You will ruin your eyes."

Again the figure rustled, and the book was shut up; then it rose and advanced towards him timidly—a delicate figure dressed with admirable taste in pale blue, having flaxen hair, a white face, large and beseeching grey eyes, and tiny hands with tapering fingers. At the edge of the circle of lamp-light the lady halted, overcome apparently by shyness, and stood still, while her pale face grew gradually from white to pink and from pink to red. Henry also stood still, being seized with a sudden and most unaccountable nervousness. He guessed that this must be Miss Levinger—in fact, he remembered her face—but not one single word could he utter; indeed, he seemed unable to do anything except regret that he had not waited upstairs till the dinner-bell rang. There is this to be said in excuse of his conduct, that it is somewhat paralysing to a modest man unexpectedly to find himself confronted by the young woman whom his family desire him to marry.

"How do you do?" he ejaculated at last: "I think that we have met before." And he held out his hand.

"Yes, we have met before," she answered shyly and in a low voice, touching his sun-browned palm with her delicate fingers, "when you were at home last Christmas year."

"It seems much longer ago than that," said Henry—"so long that I wonder you remember me."

"I do not see so many people that I am likely to forget one of them," she answered, with a curious little smile. "I dare say that the time seemed long to you, abroad in new countries; but to me, who have not stirred from Monk's Lodge, it is like yesterday."

"Well, of course that does make a difference;" then, hastening to change the subject, he added, "I am afraid I was very rude; I thought that you were my sister. I can't imagine how you can read in this light, and it always vexes me to see people trying their eyes. If you had ever kept a night watch at sea you would understand why."

"I am accustomed to reading in all sorts of lights," Emma answered.

"Do you read much, then?"

"I have nothing else to do. You see I have no brothers or sisters, no one at all except my father, who keeps very much to himself; and we have few neighbours round Monk's Lodge—at least, few that I care to be with," she added, blushing again.

Henry remembered hearing that the Levingers were considered to be outside the pale of what is called society, and did not pursue this branch of the subject.

"What do you read?" he asked.

"Oh, anything and everything. We have a good library, and sometimes I take up one class of reading, sometimes another; though perhaps I get through more history than anything else, especially in the winter, when it is too wretched to go out much. You see," she added in explanation, "I like to know about human nature and other things, and books teach me in a second-hand kind of way," and she stopped suddenly, for just then Ellen entered the room, looking very handsome in a low-cut black dress that showed off the whiteness of her neck and arms.

"What, are you down already, Miss Levinger!" she said, "and with all your things to unpack too. You do dress quickly,"—and she looked critically at her visitor's costume. "Let me see: do you and Henry know each other, or must I introduce you?"

"No, we have met before," said Emma.

"Oh yes! I remember now. Surely you were here when my brother was on leave last time." At this point Henry smiled grimly and turned away to hide his face. "There's not going to be any dinner-party, you know. Of course we couldn't have one even if we wished at present, and there is no one to ask if we could. Everybody is in London at this time of the year. Mr. Milward is positively the only creature left in these parts, and I believe mother has asked him. Ah! here he is."

As she spoke the butler opened the door and announced—"Mr. Milward."

Mr. Milward was a tall and good-looking young man, with bold prominent eyes and a receding forehead, as elaborately dressed as the plain evening attire of Englishmen will allow. His manner was confident, his self-appreciation great, and his tone towards those whom he considered his inferiors in rank or fortune patronising to the verge of insolence. In short, he was a coarse-fibred person, puffed up with the pride of his possessions, and by the flattery of women who desired to secure him in marriage, either themselves or for some friend or relation.

"What an insufferable man!" was Henry's inward comment, as his eyes fell upon him entering the room; nor did he change his opinion on further acquaintance.

"How do you do, Mr. Milward?" said Ellen, infusing the slightest possible inflection of warmth into her commonplace words of greeting. "I am so glad that you were able to come."

"How do you do, Miss Graves? I had to telegraph to Lady Fisher, with whom I was going to dine to-night in Grosvenor Square, to say that I was ill and could not travel to town. I only hope she won't find me out, that is all."

"Indeed!" answered Ellen, with a touch of irony: "Lady Fisher's loss is our gain, though I think that you would have found Grosvenor Square more amusing than Rosham. Let me introduce you to my brother, Captain Graves, and to Miss Levinger."

Mr. Milward favoured Henry with a nod, and turning to Emma said, "Oh! how do you do, Miss Levinger? So we meet at last. I was dreadfully disappointed to miss you when I was staying at Cringleton Park in December. How is your mother, Lady Levinger? Has she got rid of her neuralgia?"

"I think there has been some mistake," said Emma, visibly shrinking before this bold, assertive man: "I have never been at Cringleton Park in my life, and my mother, Mrs. Levinger, has been dead many years."

"Oh, indeed: I apologise. I thought you were Miss Levinger of Cringleton, the great heiress who was away in Italy when I stayed there. You see, I remember hearing Lady Levinger say that there were no other Levingers."

"I am afraid that I am a living contradiction to Lady Levinger's assertion," answered Emma, flushing and turning aside.

Ellen, who had been biting her lip with vexation, was about to intervene, fearing lest Mr. Milward should make further inquiries, when the door opened and Mr. Levinger entered, followed by her father and mother. Henry took the opportunity of shaking hands with Mr. Levinger to study his appearance somewhat closely—an attention that he noticed was reciprocated.

Mr. Levinger was now a man of about sixty, but he looked much older. Either because of an accident, or through a rheumatic affection, he was so lame upon his right leg that it was necessary for him to use a stick even in walking from one room to another; and, although his hair was scarcely more than streaked with white, frailty of health had withered him and bowed his frame. Looking at him, Henry could well believe what he had heard—that five-and-twenty years ago he was one of the handsomest men in the county. To this hour the dark and sullen brown eyes were full of fire and eloquence—a slumbering fire that seemed to wax and wane within them; the brow was ample, and the outline of the features flawless. He seemed a man upon whom age had settled suddenly and prematurely—a man who had burnt himself out in his youth, and was now but an ash of his former self, though an ash with fire in the heart of it.

Mr. Levinger greeted him in a few courteous, well-chosen words, that offered a striking contrast to the social dialect of Mr. Milward—the contrast between the old style and the new—then, with a bow, he passed on to offer his arm to Lady Graves, for at that moment dinner was announced. As Henry followed him with Miss Levinger, he found himself wondering, with a curiosity that was unusual to him, who and what this man had been in his youth, before he drifted a waif to Bradmouth, there to repair his broken fortunes by a masalliance with the smack owner's daughter.

"Was your father ever in the Army?" he asked of Emma, as they filed slowly down the long corridor. "Forgive my impertinence, but he looks like a military man."

He felt her start at his question.

"I don't know: I think so," she answered, "because I have heard him speak of the Crimea as though he had been present at the battles; but he never talks of his young days."

Then they entered the dining-room, and in the confusion of taking their seats the conversation dropped.

CHAPTER VI

MR. LEVINGER PUTS A CASE

At dinner Henry found himself seated between Mr. Levinger and his daughter. Naturally enough he began to make conversation to the latter, only to find that, either from shyness or for some other reason, she would not talk in public, but contented herself with replies that were as monosyllabic as she could make them.

Somewhat disappointed, for their short tete-a-tete interview had given promise of better things, Henry turned his attention to her father, and soon discovered that he was a most interesting and brilliant companion. Mr. Levinger could talk well on any subject, and whatever the matter he touched, he adorned it by an aptness and facility of illustration truly remarkable in a man who for twenty years and more was reported to have been little better than a hermit. At length they settled down to the discussion of archeological questions, in which, as it chanced, Henry took an intelligent interest, and more particularly of the flint weapons used by the early inhabitants of East Anglia. Of these, as it appeared, Mr. Levinger possessed one of the best collections extant, together with a valuable and unique series of ancient British, Danish and Saxon gold ornaments and arms.

The subject proved so mutually agreeable, indeed, that before dinner was over Mr. Levinger had given, and Henry had accepted, an invitation to stay a night or two at Monk's Lodge and inspect these treasures, and this, be it said, without any arrière-pensée—at any rate, so far as the latter was concerned.

In the silence that followed this pleasant termination to their talk Henry overheard Milward pumping Miss Levinger.

"Miss Graves tells me," he was saying, "er—that you live in that delightful old house beyond—er—Bradmouth—the one that is haunted."

"Yes," she answered, "if you mean Monk's Lodge. It is old, for the friars used it as a retreat in times of plague, and after that it became a headquarters of the smugglers; but I never heard that it was haunted."

"Oh! pray don't rob me of my illusion, Miss Levinger. I drove past there with your neighbours the Marchams; and Lady Marcham, the dowager—the one who wears an eye-glass I mean—assured me that it was haunted by a priest running after a grey nun, or a grey nun running after a priest, which seems more likely; and I am certain she cannot be mistaken: she never was about anything yet, spiritual or earthly, except her own age."

"Lady Marcham may have seen the ghost: I have not," said Emma.

"Oh, I have no doubt that she has seen it: she sees everything. Of course you know her? She is a dear old soul, isn't she?"

"I have met Lady Marcham; I do not know her," answered Emma.

"Not know Lady Marcham!" said Milward, in affected surprise; "why, I should have thought that it would have been as easy to escape knowing the North Sea when one was on it; she is positively surrounding. What do you mean, Miss Levinger?"

"I mean that I have not the honour of Lady Marcham's acquaintance," she replied, in an embarrassed voice.

"If that cad does not stop soon, I shall shut him up!" reflected Henry.

"What! have you quarrelled with her, then?" went on Milward remorselessly. "I wouldn't do that if I were you, for she is a bad enemy; and, besides, it must be so awkward, seeing that you have to meet her at every house about there."

Emma looked round in despair; and just as Henry was wondering how he could intervene without showing the temper that was rapidly getting the mastery of him, with a polite "Excuse me" Mr. Levinger leant across him.

"Perhaps you will allow me to explain, Mr. Milward," he said, in a particularly clear and cutting voice. "I am an invalid and a recluse. What I am my daughter must be also. I have not the honour of the acquaintance of Lady Marcham, or of any other of the ladies and gentlemen to whom you refer. Do I make myself plain?"

"Oh, perfectly, I assure you."

"I am glad, Mr. Milward, since, from what I overheard of your remarks just now, I gathered that you are not very quick of comprehension."

At this point Lady Graves rose with a certain haste and left the room, followed by Miss Levinger and her daughter. Thereupon Sir Reginald fell into talk with Mr. Levinger, leaving Henry and Mr. Milward together.

"Can you tell me who our friend there is?" the latter asked of Henry. "He seems a very touchy as well as a retired person. I should not have thought that there was anything offensive in my suggesting that his daughter knew Lady Marcham."

"Perhaps you insisted upon the point a little too much," said Henry drily. "I am not very well posted about Mr. Levinger myself, although my father has known him all his life; but I understand that he is a rich man, who, from one reason or another, has been more or less of a hermit for many years."

"By George! I have it now," said Milward. "He's the man who was very popular in our mothers' days, then married a wealthy cook or some one of that sort, and was barred by the whole neighbourhood. Of course I have put my foot into it horribly. I am sorry, for really I did not mean to hurt his daughter's feelings."

"I am sure I am glad to hear that you did so inadvertently," answered Henry rather gruffly. "Won't you have a cigarette?"

The rest of the evening passed quietly enough; almost too quietly, indeed, for Emma, dismayed by her former experiences, barricaded herself in a corner behind an enormous photograph album; and Ellen, irritated by a scene which jarred upon her and offended her sense of the social proprieties, grew somewhat tart in speech, especially when addressing her admirer, who quailed visibly beneath her displeasure. Mr. Levinger noticed with some amusement, indeed, that, however largely he might talk, Mr. Milward was not a little afraid of the young lady to whom he was paying his court.

At length the party broke up. Mr. Milward retired to his own place, Upcott Hall, which was situated in the neighbourhood, remarking as he went that he hoped to see them all at church on the morrow in the afternoon; whereon Henry resolved instantly that he would not attend divine service upon that occasion. Then Sir Reginald and Lady Graves withdrew to bed, followed by Ellen and Emma Levinger; but, somewhat to his surprise, Henry having announced his intention of smoking a pipe in the library, Mr. Levinger said that he also smoked, and with his permission would accompany him.

At first the conversation turned upon Mr. Milward, of whom Henry spoke in no complimentary terms.

"You should not judge him so harshly," said Levinger: "I have seen many such men in my day. He is not a bad fellow at bottom; but he is rich and an only child, and has been spoilt by a pack of women—wants taking down a peg or two, in short. He will find his level, never fear. Most of us do in this world. Indeed, unless my observation is at fault," Mr. Levinger added significantly, "there is a lady in this house who will know how to bring him down to it. But perhaps you will think that is no affair of mine."

Henry was somewhat mystified by this allusion, though he guessed that it must have reference to Ellen. Of the state of affairs between Mr. Milward and his sister he was ignorant; indeed, he disliked the young gentleman so much himself that, except upon the clearest evidence, it would not have occurred to him that Ellen was attracted in this direction. Mr. Levinger's remark, however, gave him an opening of which he availed himself with the straightforwardness and promptitude which were natural to him.

"It seems, Mr. Levinger," he said, "from what I have heard since I returned home, that all our affairs are very much your own, or vice versa. I don't know," he added, hesitating a little, "if it is your wish that I should speak to you of these matters now. Indeed, it seems a kind of breach of hospitality to do so; although, if I understand the position, it is we who are receiving your hospitality at this moment, and not you ours."

Mr. Levinger smiled faintly at this forcible way of putting the situation.

"By all means speak, Captain Graves," he said, "and let us get it over. I am exceedingly glad that you have come home, for, between ourselves, your late brother was not a business man, and I do not like to distress Sir Reginald with these conversations—for I presume I am right in supposing that you allude to the mortgages I hold over the Rosham property."

Henry nodded, and Mr. Levinger went on: "I will tell you how matters stand in as few words as possible." And he proceeded to set out the financial details of the encumbrances on the estate, with which we are already sufficiently acquainted for the purposes of this history.

"The state of affairs is even worse than I thought," said Henry, when he had finished. "It is clear that we are absolutely bankrupt; and the only thing I wonder at, Mr. Levinger," he added, with some irritation, "is that you, a business man, should have allowed things to go so far."

"Surely that was my risk, Captain Graves," he answered. "It is I who am liable to lose money, not your family."

"Forgive me, Mr. Levinger, there is another side to the question. It seems to me that we are not only paupers, we are also defaulters, or something like it; for if we were sold up to the last stick to-morrow we should not be able to repay you these sums, to say nothing of other debts that may be owing. To tell you the truth, I cannot quite forgive you for putting my father in this position, even if he was weak enough to allow you to do so."

"There is something in what you say considered from the point of view of a punctiliously honest man, though it is an argument that I have never had advanced to me before," replied Mr. Levinger drily. "However, let me disabuse your mind: the last loan of ten thousand, which, I take it, leaving interest out of the count, would about cover my loss were the security to be realised to-day, was not made at the instance of your father, who I believe did not even know of it at the time. If you want the facts, it was made because of the earnest prayer of your brother Reginald, who declared that this sum was necessary to save the family from immediate bankruptcy. It is a painful thing to have to say, but I have since discovered that it was your brother himself who needed the money, very little of which found its way into Sir Reginald's pocket."

At this point Henry rose and, turning his back, pretended to refill his pipe. He dared not trust himself to speak, lest he might say words that should not be uttered of the dead; nor did he wish to show the shame which was written on his face. Mr. Levinger saw the movement and understood it. Dropping the subject of Reginald's delinquencies, he went on:

"You blame me, Captain Graves, for having acted as no business man should act, and for putting temptation in the path of the weak. Well, in a sense I am still a business man, but I am not an usurer, and it is possible that I may have had motives other than those of my own profit. Let us put a hypothetical case: let us suppose that once upon a time, many years ago, a young fellow of good birth, good looks and fair fortune, but lacking the advantages of careful education and not overburdened with principle, found himself a member of one of the fastest and most expensive regiments of Guards. Let us suppose that he lived—well, as such young men have done before and since—a life of extravagance and debauchery that very soon dissipated the means which he possessed. In due course this young man would not improbably have betaken himself to every kind of gambling in order to supply his pocket with money. Sometimes he would have won, but it is possible that in the end he might have found himself posted as a defaulter because he was unable to pay his racing debts, and owing as many thousands at cards as he possessed five-pound notes in the world.

"Such a young man might not unjustly have hard things said of him; his fellow-officers might call him a scamp and rake up queer stories as to his behaviour in financial transactions, while among outsiders he might be branded openly as no better than a thief. Of course the regimental career of this imaginary person would come to a swift and shameful end, and he would find himself bankrupt and dishonoured, a pariah unfit for the society of gentlemen, with no other opening left to him than that which a pistol bullet through the head can offer. It is probable that such a man, being desperate and devoid of religion, might determine to take this course. He might also be in the act of so doing, when he, who thought himself friendless, found a friend, and that friend one by whom of all others he had dealt ill.

"And now let us suppose for the last time that this friend threw into the fire before his eyes that bankrupt's I.O.U.'s, that he persuaded him to abandon his mad design of suicide, that he assisted him to escape his other creditors, and, finally, when the culprit, living under a false name, was almost forgotten by those who had known him, that he did his best to help him to a fresh start in life. In such a case, Captain Graves, would not this unhappy man owe a debt of gratitude to that friend?"

Mr. Levinger had begun the putting of this "strange case" quietly enough, speaking in his usual low and restrained voice; but as he went on he grew curiously excited—so much so, indeed, that, notwithstanding his lameness, he rose from his chair, and, resting on his ebony stick, limped backwards and forwards across the room—while the increasing clearness and emphasis of his voice revealed the emotion under which he was labouring. As he asked the question with which his story culminated, he halted in his march directly opposite to the chair upon which Henry was sitting, and, leaning on his stick, looked him in the face with his piercing brown eyes.

"Of course he would," answered Henry quietly.

"Of course he would," repeated Mr. Levinger. "Captain Graves, that story was my story, and that friend was your father. I do not say that it is all the story, for there are things which I cannot speak of, but it is some of it—more, indeed, than is known to any living man except Sir Reginald. Forgiving me my sins against him, believing that he saw good in me, your father picked me out of the mire and started me afresh in life. When I came to these parts an unknown wanderer, he found me work; he even gave me the agency of this property, which I held till I had no longer any need of it. I have told you all this partly because you are your father's son, and partly because I have watched you and followed your career from boyhood, and know you to be a man of the strictest honour, who will never use my words against me.

"I repeat that I have not told you everything, for even since those days I have been no saint—a man who has let his passions run riot for years does not grow good in an hour, Captain Graves. But I trust that you will not think worse of me than I deserve, for it still pains me to lose the good opinion of an upright man. One thing at least I have done—though I borrowed from my daughter to do it, and pinched myself till I am thought to be miserly—at length I have paid back all those thousands that I owed, either to my creditors or to their descendants; yes, not a month ago I settled the last and heaviest claim. And now, Captain Graves, you will understand why I have advanced moneys beyond their value upon mortgage of the Rosham estates. Your father, who has long forgotten or rather ignored the past, believes it to have been done in the ordinary way of business; I have told you the true reason."

"Thank you," said Henry. "Of course I shall respect your confidence. It is not for me to judge other men, so I hope that you will excuse my making any remarks about it. You have behaved with extreme generosity to my father, but even now I cannot say that I think your conduct was well advised: indeed, I do not see how it makes the matter any better for us. This money belongs to you, or to your daughter,"—here Henry thought that Mr. Levinger winced a little—"and in one way or another it must be paid or secured. I quite understand that you do not wish to force us into bankruptcy, but it seems that there is a large amount of interest overdue, putting aside the question of the capital, and not a penny to meet it with. What is to be done?"

Mr. Levinger sat down and thought awhile before he answered.

"You have put your finger on the weak spot," he said presently: "this money is Emma's, every farthing of it, for whatever I have saved out of my life interest has gone towards the payment of my own debts, and after all I have no right to be generous with my daughter's fortune. Not long ago I had occasion to appoint a guardian and trustee for her under my will, a respectable solicitor whose name does not matter, and it was owing to the remonstrances that he made when he accepted the office that I was obliged to move in this matter of the mortgages, or at least of the payment of the interest on them. Had it been my own money I would never have consented to trouble your father, since fortunately we have enough to live upon in our quiet way without this interest; but it is not."

"Quite so," said Henry. "And therefore again I ask, what is to be done?"

"Done?" answered Mr. Levinger: "at present, nothing. Let things go awhile, Captain Graves; half a year's interest more or less can make no great difference. If necessary, my daughter must lose it, and after all neither she nor any future husband of hers will be able to blame me for the loss. When those mortgages were made there was plenty of cover: who could foresee that land would fall so much in value? Let matters take their course; this is a strange world, and all sorts of unexpected things happen in it. For aught we know to the contrary, within six months Emma may be dead, or," he added, "in some position in which it would not be necessary that payment should be made to her on account of these mortgages."

For a moment he hesitated, as though wondering whether it would be wise to say something that was on the tip of his tongue; then, deciding that it would not, Mr. Levinger rose, lit a candle, and, having shaken Henry warmly by the hand, he limped off to bed.

When he had gone Henry filled himself another pipe and sat down to think. Mr. Levinger puzzled him; there was something attractive about him, something magnetic even, and yet he could not entirely trust him. Even in his confidences there had been reservations: the man appeared to be unable to make up his mind to tell all the truth. So it was also with his generosity towards Sir Reginald: he had been generous indeed, but it seemed that it was with his daughter's money. Thus too with his somewhat tardy honesty: he had paid his debts even though "he had borrowed from his daughter to do so." To Henry's straightforward sense, upon his own showing Mr. Levinger was a curious mixture, and a man about whom as yet he could form no positive judgment.

From the father his thoughts travelled to the daughter. It was strange that she should have produced so slight an impression upon him when he had met her nearly two years before. Either she was much altered, or his appreciative powers had developed. Certainly she impressed him now. There was something very striking about this frail, flaxen-haired girl, whose appearance reminded him of a Christmas rose. It seemed odd that such a person could have been born of a mother of common blood, as he understood the late Mrs. Levinger to have been, for Emma Levinger looked "aristocratic" if ever woman did. Moreover, it was clear that she lacked neither intellect nor dignity; her conversation, and the way in which she had met the impertinences of the insufferable Milward, proved it.

This was the lady whom Ellen had declared to be "half in love with him." The idea was absurd, and the financial complications which surrounded her repelled him, causing him to dismiss it impatiently. Yet, as Henry followed Mr. Levinger's example and went to bed, a voice in his heart told him that a worse fate might befall a man.

CHAPTER VII

A PROPOSAL AND A DIFFERENCE

The morrow was a Sunday, when, according to immemorial custom, everybody belonging to Rosham Hall was expected to go to church once in the day—a rule, however, from which visitors were excused. Henry made up his mind that Mr. Levinger and his daughter would avail themselves of this liberty of choice and stay at home. There was something so uncommon about both of them that he jumped to the conclusion that they were certainly agnostics, and in all probability atheists. Therefore he was somewhat surprised when at breakfast he heard Mr. Levinger making arrangements to be driven to the church—for, short as was the distance, it was farther than he could walk—and Emma announced her intention of accompanying him.

Henry walked down to church by himself, for Sir Reginald had driven with his guests and his mother and sister were not going until the afternoon. Finding the three seated in the front pew of the nave, he placed himself in that immediately behind, where he thought that he would be more comfortable, and the service began. It was an ordinary country service in an ordinary country church celebrated by an ordinary rather long-winded parson: conditions that are apt to cause the thoughts to wander, even in the best regulated mind. Although he did his utmost to keep his attention fixed, for it was characteristic of him that even in such a matter as the listening to ill-sung psalms his notions of duty influenced him, Henry soon found himself lost in reflections. We need not follow them all, since, wherever they began, they ended in the consideration of the father and daughter before him, and of all the circumstances connected with them. Even now, while the choir wheezed and the clergyman droned, the respective attitudes of these two struck him as exceedingly interesting. The father followed every verse and every prayer with an almost passionate devotion, that afforded a strange insight into an unsuspected side of his character. Clearly, whatever might have been the sins of his youth, he was now a religious devotee, or something very like it, for Henry felt certain that his manner was not assumed.

With Emma it was different. Her demeanour was one of earnest and respectful piety—a piety which with her was obviously a daily habit, since he noticed that she knew all the canticles and most of the psalms by heart. As it chanced, the one redeeming point in the service was the reading of the lessons. These were read by Sir Reginald Graves, whose fine voice and impressive manner were in striking contrast to the halting utterance of the clergyman. The second lesson was taken from perhaps the most beautiful of the passages in the Bible, the fifteenth chapter of the first Epistle to the Corinthians, wherein the Apostle sets out his inspired vision of the resurrection of the dead and of the glorious state of them who shall be found alive in it. Henry, watching Emma's face, saw it change and glow as she followed those immortal words, till at the fifty-third verse and thence to the end of the chapter it became alight as though with the effulgence of a living faith within her. Indeed, at the words "for this corruptible must put on incorruption and this mortal must put on immortality," it chanced that a vivid sunbeam breaking from the grey sky fell full upon the girl's pale countenance and spiritual eyes, adding a physical glory to them, and for one brief moment making her appear, at least in his gaze, as though some such ineffable change had already overtaken her, and the last victory of the spirit was proclaimed in her person.

Henry looked at her astonished; and since in his own way he lacked neither sympathy nor perception, in that instant he came to understand that this woman was something apart from all the women whom he had known—a being purer and sweeter, partaking very little of the nature of the earth. And yet his sister had said that she was half in love with him! Weighing his own unworthiness, he smiled to himself even then, but with the smile came a thought that he was by no means certain whether he was not "half in love" with her himself.

The sunbeam passed, and soon the lesson was finished, and with it the desire for those things which are not yet, faded from Emma's eyes, leaving in the mind of the man who watched her a picture that could never fade.

At lunch Ellen, who had been sitting silent, suddenly awoke from her reverie and asked Emma what she would like to do that afternoon. Emma replied that she wished to take a walk if it were convenient to everybody else.

"That will do very well," said Ellen with decision. "My brother can escort you down to the Cliff: there is a good view of the sea there; and after church I will come to meet you. We cannot miss each other, as there is only one road."

Henry was about to rebel, for when Ellen issued her orders in this fashion she invariably excited an opposition in his breast which was sometimes unreasonable; but glancing at Miss Levinger's face he noticed that she seemed pleased at the prospect of a walk, or of his company, he could not tell which, and held his peace.

"That will be very pleasant," said Emma, "if it does not bore Captain Graves."

"Not at all; the sea never bores me," replied Henry. "I will be ready at three o'clock if that suits you."

"I must say that you are polite, Henry," put in his sister in a sarcastic voice. "If I were Miss Levinger I would walk by myself and leave you to contemplate the ocean in solitude."

"I am sure I did not mean to be otherwise, Ellen," he replied. "There is nothing wrong in saying that one likes the sea."

At this moment Lady Graves intervened with some tact, and the subject dropped.

About three o'clock Henry found Emma waiting for him in the hall, and they started on their walk.

Passing through the park they came to the high road, and for some way went on side by side in silence. The afternoon was cloudy, but not cold; there had been rain during the previous night, and all about them were the evidences of spring, or rather of the coming of summer. Birds sang upon every bush, most of the trees were clothed in their first green, the ashes, late this year, were bursting their black buds, the bracken was pushing up its curled fronds in the sandy banks of the roadway, already the fallen blackthorn bloom lay in patches like light snow beneath the hedgerows, while here and there pink-tipped hawthorns were breaking into bloom. As she walked the promise and happy spirit of the spring seemed to enter into Emma's blood, for her pale cheeks took a tinge of colour like that which blushed upon the May-buds, and her eyes grew joyful.

"Is it not beautiful?" she said suddenly to her companion.

"Well, it would be if there were some sunshine," he replied, in a somewhat matter-of-fact way.

"Oh, the sunshine will come. You must not expect everything in this climate, you know. I am quite content with the spring."

"Yes," he answered; "it is very pleasant after the long winter."

She hesitated a little, and then said, "To me it is more than pleasant. I cannot quite tell you what it is, and if I did you would not understand me."

"Won't you try?" he replied, growing interested.

"Well, to me it is a prophecy and a promise; and I think that, although perhaps they do not understand it, that is why almost all old people love the spring. It speaks to them of life, life arising more beautiful out of death; and, perhaps unconsciously, they see in it the type of their own spiritual fortune and learn from it resignation to their fate."

"Yes, we heard that in the lesson this morning," said Henry. "'Thou fool! that which thou sowest is not quickened except it die.'"

"Oh, I know that the thought is an old one," she answered, with some confusion, "and I put what I mean very badly, but somehow these ancient truths always seem new to us when we find them out for ourselves. We hit upon an idea that has been the common property of men for thousands of years, and think that we have made a great discovery. I suppose the fact of it is that there are no new ideas, and you see each of us must work out his own salvation. I do not mean in a spiritual sense only. Nobody else's thoughts or feelings can help us; they may be as old as the world, but when we feel them or think them, for us they are fresh as the spring. A mother does not love her child less because millions of mothers have loved theirs before."

Henry did not attempt to continue the argument. This young lady's ideas, if not new, were pretty; but he was not fond of committing himself to discussion and opinions on such metaphysical subjects, though, like other intelligent men, he had given them a share of his attention.

"You are very religious, Miss Levinger, are you not?" he said.

"Religious? What made you think so? No; I wish I were. I have certain beliefs, and I try to be—that is all."

"It was watching your face in church that gave me the idea, or rather assured me of the fact," he answered.

She coloured, and then said: "Why do you ask? You believe in our religion, do you not?"

"Yes, I believe in it. I think that you will find few men of my profession who do not—perhaps because their continual contact with the forces and dangers of nature brings about dependence upon an unseen protecting Power. Also my experience is that religion in one form or another is necessary to all human beings. I never knew a man to be quite happy who was devoid of it in some shape."

"Religion does not always bring happiness, or even peace," said Emma. "My experience is very small—indeed, I have none outside books and the village—but I have seen it in the case of my own father. I do not suppose it possible that a man could be more religious than he has been ever since I can remember much about him; but certainly he is not happy, nor can he reconcile himself to the idea of death, which to me, except for its physical side, does not seem such a terrible matter."

"I should say that your father is a very nervous man," Henry answered; "and the conditions of your life and of his may have been quite different. Everybody feels these things according to his temperament."

"Yes, he is nervous," she said; then added suddenly, as though she wished to change the subject, "Look! there is the sea. How beautiful it is! Were you not sorry to leave it, Captain Graves?"

By now they had turned off the main road, and, following a lane which was used to cart sand and shingle from the beach, had reached a chalky slope known as the Cliff. Below them was a stretch of sand, across which raced the in-coming tide, and beyond lay the great ocean, blue in the far distance, but marked towards the shore with parallel lines of white-crested billows.

Hitherto the afternoon had been dull, but as Emma spoke the sunlight broke through the clouds, cutting a path of glory athwart the sea.

"Sorry to leave it!" he said, staring at the familiar face of the waters, and speaking almost passionately: "it has pretty well broken my heart—that is all. I loved my profession, it was everything to me: there I was somebody, and had a prospect before me; now I am nobody, and have none, except—" And he stopped.

"And why did you leave?" she asked.

"For the same reason that we all do disagreeable things: because it was my duty. My brother died, and my family desired my presence, so I was obliged to retire from the Service, and there is an end of it."

"I guessed as much," said Emma softly, "and I am very sorry for you. Well, we cannot go any farther, so we had better turn."

Henry nodded an assent, and they walked homewards silently, either because their conversation was exhausted, or because they were lost in their own thoughts.

It may be remembered that Mr. Milward had announced his intention of attending Rosham church that afternoon. As Ellen knew that he was not in the habit of honouring any place of worship with his presence, this determination of her admirer gave her cause for thought.

For a year or more Mr. Milward's attentions towards herself had been marked, but as yet he had said nothing of a decisive nature. Could it be that upon this occasion he intended to cross the line which divides attention from courtship? She believed that he did so intend, for, otherwise, why did he take the trouble to come several miles to church, and why had he suggested to her that they might go out walking together afterwards, as he had done privately on the previous evening? At any rate, if such were his mind, Ellen determined that he should have every opportunity of declaring it; and it was chiefly for this reason that she had arranged Emma's expedition with her brother, since it would then be easy for her to propose that Mr. Milward should escort herself in search of them.

Ellen did not deceive herself. She knew Mr. Milward's faults, his vulgarity and assumption made her wince, and on the whole perhaps she disliked him. But on the other hand his admiration flattered her vanity, for many were the women who had tried to excite it and failed; his wealth appealed to her love of luxury and place, and she was well aware that, once in the position of his wife, she could guide his weaker will in whatever direction she desired. Moreover his faults were all on the surface, he had no secret vices, and she trusted to her own tact if not to counterbalance, at least to divert attention from his errors of manner.

In due course Ellen and Lady Graves went to church, but to the private mortification of the former Mr. Milward did not appear. At length, much to her relief, towards the middle of the second lesson a disturbance in the nave behind her assured her of his presence. She would not look round, indeed, but her knowledge of him told her that nobody else arriving so painfully late would have ventured to interrupt the congregation in this unnecessary fashion. Meanwhile Mr. Milward had entered the pew behind her, occupying the same place that Henry had sat in that morning, whence by many means, such as the dropping of books and the shifting of hassocks, he endeavoured to attract her attention; but in vain, for Ellen remained inflexible and would not so much as turn her head. His efforts, however, did not altogether fail of their effect, inasmuch as she could see that they drove her mother almost to distraction, for Lady Graves liked to perform her devotions in quiet.

"My dear," she whispered to her daughter at the termination of the service, "I really wish that when he comes to church Mr. Milward could be persuaded not to disturb other people by his movements, and generally to adopt a less patronising attitude towards the Almighty,"—a sarcasm that in after days Ellen was careful to repeat to him.

At the doorway they met, and Ellen greeted him with affected surprise:

"I thought that you had given up the idea of coming, Mr. Milward."

"Oh no; I was a little late, that was all. Did you not hear me come in?"

"No," said Ellen sweetly.

"If Ellen did not hear you I am sure that everybody else did, Mr. Milward," remarked Lady Graves with some severity, and then with a sigh she glided away to visit her son's grave. By this time they were at the church gate, and Ellen turned up the path that ran across the park to the Hall.

"How about our walk?" said Milward.

"Our walk? Oh! I had forgotten. Do you wish to walk?"

"Yes; that is what I came for."

"Indeed! I thought you had come to church. Well, my brother and Miss Levinger have gone to the Cliff, and if you like we can meet them—that is, unless you think that it is going to rain."

"Oh no, it won't rain," he answered.

In a few minutes they had left the park and were following the same road that Henry and Emma had taken. But Ellen did not talk of the allegorical mystery of the spring, nor did Edward Milward set out his views as to the necessity of religion. On the contrary, he was so silent that Ellen began to be afraid they would meet the others before he found the courage to do that which, from the nervousness of his manner, she was now assured he meant to do.

At length it came, and with a rush.

"Ellen," said Edward in a husky voice.

"I beg your pardon," replied that young lady with dignity.

"Miss Graves, I mean. I wish to speak to you."

"Yes, Mr. Milward."

"I want—to ask—you to marry me."

Ellen heard the fateful words, and a glow of satisfaction warmed her breast. She had won the game, and even then she found time to reflect with complacency upon the insight into character which had taught her from the beginning to treat her admirer with affected coldness and assumed superiority.

"This is very sudden and unexpected," she said, gazing over his head with her steady blue eyes.

Her tone frightened Edward, and he stammered—

"Do you really think so? You are so clever that I should have thought that you must have seen it coming for a long while. I know I have only just been able to prevent myself from proposing on two or three occasions—no, that's a mistake, I don't mean that. Oh! there! Ellen, will you have me? I know that you are a great deal too good for me in a way—ever so much cleverer, and all that sort of thing; but I am truly fond of you, I am really. I am well off, and I know that you would be a credit to me and help me on in the world, for I want to go into Parliament some time, and—there, I think that is all I have got to say."

Ellen considered this speech rapidly. Its manner was somewhat to seek, but its substance was most satisfactory and left nothing to be desired. Accordingly she concluded that the time had come when she might with safety unbend a little.

"Really, Mr. Milward," she said in a softer voice, and looking for a second into his eyes, "this is very flattering to me, and I am much touched. I can assure you I had no idea that my friend had become a"—and Ellen hesitated and even blushed as she murmured the word—"lover. I think that perhaps it would be best if I considered your offer for a while, in order that I may make perfectly sure of the state of my own feelings before I allow myself to say words which would be absolutely irrevocable, since, were I once to pledge myself—" and she ceased, overcome.

"Oh! pray don't take time to consider," said Edward. "I know what that means: you will think better of it, and tell me to-morrow that you can only be a sister to me, or something of the sort."

Ellen looked at him a while, then said, "Do you really understand what you ask of me, and mean all you say?"

"Why, of course I do, Ellen: I am not an idiot. What do you suppose I should mean, if it is not that I want you to marry me?"

"Then, Edward," she whispered, "I will say yes, now and for always. I will be your wife."

"Well, that's all right," answered Edward, wiping his brow with his pocket-handkerchief. "Why couldn't you tell me so at first, dear? It would have spared me a great deal of agitation."

Then it occurred to him that further demonstrations were usual on these occasions, and, dropping the handkerchief, he made a somewhat clumsy effort to embrace her. But Ellen was not yet prepared to be kissed by Mr. Milward. She felt that these amatory proceedings would require a good deal of leading up to, so far as she was concerned.

"No, no," she murmured—"not now and here: I am upset." And, withdrawing her cheek, she gave him her hand to kiss.

It struck Edward that this was a somewhat poor substitute, more especially as she was wearing dogskin gloves, whereon he must press his ardent lips. However, he made the best of it, and even repeated the salute, when a sound caused him to look up.

Now, the scene of this passionate encounter was in a lane that ran from the main road to the coast; moreover, it was badly chosen, for within three paces of it the lane turned sharply to the right. Down this path, still wrapped in silence, came Henry and Emma, and as Edward was in the act of kissing Ellen's hand they turned the corner. Emma was the first to perceive them.

"Oh!" she exclaimed, with a start.

Then Henry saw. "What the deuce—!" he said.

Ellen took in the situation at a glance. It was discomposing, even to a person of her considerable nerve; but she felt that on the whole nothing could have happened more opportunely. Recovering themselves, Henry and Emma were beginning to advance again, as though they had seen nothing, when Ellen whispered hurriedly to her fiance:

"You must explain to my brother at once."

"All right," said Edward. "I say, Graves, I dare say you were surprised when you saw me kissing Ellen's hand, weren't you?"

"Yes, Mr. Milward, I was surprised."

"Well, you won't be any more when I tell you that we are engaged to be married."

"Forgive me," said Henry, somewhat icily: "I am still surprised." And in his heart he added, "How could Ellen do it!—how could she do it!"

Guessing what was passing in his mind, his sister looked at him warningly, and at that moment Emma began to murmur some confused congratulations. Then they set out homewards. Presently Ellen, who was a person of decision, and thought that she had better make the position clear without delay, managed to attach herself to her brother, leaving the other two to walk ahead out of hearing, much to their mutual disgust.

"You have not congratulated me, Henry," she said, in a steady voice.

"Congratulated you, Ellen! Good Lord! how can I congratulate you?"

"And why not, pray? There is nothing against Mr. Milward that I have ever heard of. His character is irreproachable, and his past has never been tarnished by any excesses, which is more than can be said of many men. He is well born, and he has considerable means."

"Very considerable, I understand," interrupted Henry.

"And, lastly, he has a most sincere regard for me, as I have for him, and it was dear Reginald's greatest wish that this should come about. Now may I ask you why I am not to be congratulated?"

"Well, if you want to know, because I think him insufferable. I cannot make out how a lady like yourself can marry such a man just for—" and he stopped in time.

By this time Ellen was seriously angry, and it must be admitted not altogether without cause.

"Really, my dear Henry," she said, in her most bitter tones, "I am by no means sure that the epithet which you are so good as to apply to Mr. Milward would not be more suitable to yourself. You always were impossible, Henry—you see I imitate your frankness—and certainly your manners and temper have not improved at sea. Please let us come to an understanding once and for all: I mean to marry Mr. Milward, and if by chance any action or words of yours should cause that marriage to fall through, I will never forgive you. On reflection you must admit that this is purely my own affair. Moreover, you are aware of the circumstances of our family, which by this prudent and proper alliance I at any rate propose to do my best to improve."

Henry looked at his stately and handsome sister and the cold anger that was written on her face, and thought to himself, "On the whole I am sorry for Milward, who, whatever his failings may be, is probably an honest man in his way." But to Ellen he said:

"I apologise. In nautical language, I come up all I have said. You are quite right: I am a bear—I have often thought so myself—and my temper, which was never of the best, has been made much worse by all that I have seen and learned since I returned home, and because I am forced by duty to leave my profession. You must make allowances for me, and put up with it, and I for my part will do my best to cultivate a better frame of mind. And now, Ellen, I offer you my warm congratulations on your engagement. You are of an age to judge for yourself, and doubtless, as you say, you know your own business. I hope that you may be happy, and of course I need hardly add, even if my prejudice makes him uncongenial to me, that I shall do my best to be friendly with Mr. Milward, and to say nothing that can cause him to think he is not welcome in our family."

Ellen heard and smiled: once more she had triumphed. Yet, while the smile was on her face, a sadness crept into her heart, which, if it was hard and worldly, was not really bad; feeling, as she did, that this bitterly polite speech of her brother's had shut an iron door between them which could never be reopened. The door was shut, and behind her were the affectionate memories of childhood and many a loving delusion of her youth. Before her lay wealth and pride of place, and every luxury, but not a grain of love—unless indeed she should be so happy as to find the affection whereof death and the other circumstances of her life and character had deprived her, in the hearts of children yet to be. From her intended husband, be it noted, when custom had outward his passion and admiration for her, she did not expect love even in this hour of her engagement, and if it were forthcoming she knew that from him it would not satisfy her. Well, she knew also if she had done with "love" and other illusions, that she had chosen the better part according to her philosophy.

CHAPTER VIII

TWO CONVERSATIONS

On arriving at the Hall, Ellen went at once to her mother's room, while Edward retired to the library, where he was informed that Sir Reginald was to be found. Lady Graves received the news of her daughter's engagement kindly, but without emotion, for since her son's death nothing seemed to move her. Sir Reginald was more expansive. When Edward told him that he was engaged to Ellen, he took his hand and shook it warmly—not, indeed, that he had any especial affection for that young man, whose tone and manners did not chime in with his old-fashioned ideas of gentlemanly demeanour, but because he knew his wealth to be large, and rejoiced at the prospect of an alliance that would strengthen the tottering fortunes of his family.

Edward had always been a little afraid of Sir Reginald, whose stately and distant courtesy oppressed him, and this fear or respect stood the older man in good stead on the present occasion. It enabled him even to explain that Ellen would inherit little with as much dignity as though he were announcing that she had ten thousand a year in her own right, and, striking while the iron was hot, to extract a statement as to settlements.

Edward mentioned a sum that was liberal enough, but by a happy inspiration Sir Reginald hummed and hawed before making any answer—whereupon, fearing opposition to his suit, his would-be son-in-law corrected himself, adding to the amount he proposed to put into settlement a very handsome rentcharge on his real property in the event of his predeceasing Ellen.

"Yes, yes," said Sir Reginald. "I think your amended proposal proper and even generous. But I am no business man—if I had been, things would be very different with me now—and my head for figures is so shockingly bad that perhaps you will not mind jotting down what you suggest on a piece of paper, so that I can think it over at my leisure and submit it to my lawyers. And then, will it be too much trouble to ask you to find Ellen, as I should like to congratulate her?"

"Shall I go at once? I can do the writing afterwards," suggested Edward, with an instinctive shrinking from the cold record of pen and ink.

"No, no," answered the old gentleman testily; "these money matters always worry me"—which was true enough—"and I want to be done with them."

So Edward wrote first and went afterwards, albeit not without qualms.

The sight of his lawyer's face when he explained to him the terms of settlement on his intended marriage, that he himself had propounded in black and white, amply justified his doubts.

"Well, I never!" said the man of law; "they must know their way about at Rosham Hall. However, as you have put it in writing, you cannot get out of it now. But perhaps, Mr. Milward, next time you wish to make proposals of settlement on an almost penniless lady, you will consult me first."

That night there was more outward show of conviviality in the cold Hall dining-room than there had been for many a day. Everybody drank champagne, and all the gentlemen made speeches with the exception of Henry, who contented himself with wishing health and happiness to Edward and his sister.

"You see," Mr. Levinger whispered to him in the drawing-room, "I did well to caution you to be patient with the foibles of your future brother-in-law, and I was not far out in a surmise that at the time you may have thought impertinent."

Henry shrugged his shoulders and made no answer.

After dinner Lady Graves, who always retired early, vanished to her room, Sir Reginald and Mr. Levinger went to the library, and Henry, after wandering disconsolately for a while about the great drawing-room, in a distant corner of which the engaged couple were carrying on a tete-a-tete, betook himself to the conservatory. Here he chanced upon Emma.

To-night she was dressed in white, wearing pearls upon her slender neck; and seated alone upon a bench in the moonlight, for the conservatory was not otherwise illuminated, she looked more like a spirit than a woman. Indeed, to Henry, who came upon her unobserved, this appearance was much heightened by a curious and accidental contrast. Immediately behind Emma was a life-sized marble replica of one of the most beautiful of the statues known to ancient art. There above this pale and spiritual maiden, with outstretched arms and alluring lips stood the image of Aphrodite, triumphing in her perfect nakedness.

Henry looked from one to the other, speculating as to which was the more lovely of these types of the spirit and the flesh. "Supposing," he thought to himself, "that a man were obliged to take his choice between them, I wonder which he would choose, and which would bring him the greater happiness. For the matter of that, I wonder which I should choose myself. To make a perfect woman the two should be merged."

Then he came forward, smiling at his speculation, and little knowing that before all was done this very choice would be forced upon him.

"I hope that I am not disturbing you, Miss Levinger," he said; "but to tell you the truth I fled here for refuge, the drawing-room being engaged."

Emma started, and seeing who it was, said, "Yes, I thought so too; that is why I came away. I suppose that you are very much pleased, Captain Graves?"

"What pleases others pleases me," he answered grimly. "I am not going to marry Mr. Milward."

"Why don't you like him?" she asked.

"I never said I did not like him. I have no doubt that he is very well, but he is not quite the sort of man with whom I have been accustomed to associate—that is all."

"Well, I suppose that I ought not to say it, but I do not admire him either; not because he was rude to me last night, but because he seems so coarse. I dislike what is coarse."

"Do you? Life itself is coarse, and I fancy that a certain amount of that quality is necessary to happiness in the world. After all, the flesh rules here, and not the spirit,"—and again he looked first at the marble Aphrodite, then at the girl beneath it. "We are born of the flesh, we are flesh, and all our affections and instincts partake of it."

"I do not agree with you at all," Emma answered, with some warmth. "We are born of the spirit: that is the reality; the flesh is only an accident, if a necessary accident. When we allow it to master us, then our troubles begin."

"Perhaps; but it is rather a pervading accident for many of us. In short, it makes up our world, and we cannot escape it. While we are of it the most refined among us must follow its routine—more or less. A day may come when that routine will be different, and our desires, aims, and objects will vary with it, but it is not here or now. Everything has its season, Miss Levinger, and it is useless to try to escape from the facts of life, for at last in one shape or another they overtake us, who, strive as we may, can very rarely defy our natures."

Emma made no answer, though she did not look convinced, and for a while they remained silent.

"My father tells me that you are coming to see us," she said at last.

"Yes; he kindly asked me. Do you wish me to come?"

"Of course I do," she answered, colouring faintly. "It will be a great change to see a stranger staying at Monk's Lodge. But I am afraid that you will find it very dull; we are quite alone, at this time of year there is nothing on earth to do, unless you like birdnesting. There are plenty of wild fowl about, and I have rather a good collection of eggs."

"Oh, I have no doubt that I shall amuse myself," he answered. "Don't you think that we had better be going back? They must have had enough of each other by this time."

Making no answer, Emma rose and walked across the conservatory, Henry following her. At the door, acting on a sudden impulse, she stopped suddenly and said, "You do really mean to come to Monk's Lodge, do you not, Captain Graves?" And she looked up into his face.

"If you wish it," he answered in a low voice.

"I have said that I do wish it," she replied, and turning led the way into the drawing-room.

Meanwhile another conversation had taken place in the library, where Sir Reginald and Mr. Levinger were seated.

"I think that you are to be very much congratulated on this engagement, Graves," said his companion. "Of course the young man is not perfect: he has faults, and obvious ones; but your daughter knows what she is about, and understands him, and altogether in the present state of affairs it is a great thing for you."

"Not for me—not for me," answered Sir Reginald sadly; "I seem to have neither interests nor energies left, and so far as I am concerned literally I care for nothing. I have lived my life, Levinger, and I am fading away. That last blow of poor Reginald's death has killed me, although I do not die at once. The only earthly desire which remains to me is to provide, if possible, for the welfare of my family. In furtherance of that end this afternoon I condescended even to get the best possible terms of settlement out of young Milward. Twenty years ago I should have been ashamed to do such a thing, but age and poverty have hardened me. Besides, I know my man. He blows hot to-day, a month hence he may blow cold; and as it is quite on the cards that he and Ellen will not pull together very well in married life, and I have nothing to leave her, I am anxious that she should be properly provided for. By the way, have you spoken to Henry about these mortgages?"

"Yes, I explained the position to him on Saturday night. It seemed to upset him a good deal."

"I don't wonder at it, I am sure. You have behaved very kindly in this matter, Levinger. Had it been in anybody else's hands I suppose that we should all have been in the workhouse by now. But, frankly, I don't see the end of it. The money is not yours—it is your daughter's fortune, or the greater part of it—and you can't go on being generous with other people's fortunes. As it is, she stands to lose heavily on the investment, and the property is sinking in value very day. It is very well to talk of our old friendship and of your gratitude to me. Perhaps you should be grateful, and no doubt I have pulled you out of some nasty scrapes in bygone days, when you were the Honourable—"

"Don't mention the name, Graves!" said Levinger, striking his stick fiercely on the floor: "that man is dead; never mention his name again to me or to anybody else."

"As you like," answered Sir Reginald, smiling. "I was only going to repeat that you cannot continue to be grateful on your daughter's money, and if you take your remedy Rosham must go to the hammer after all these generations. I shall be dead first, but it breaks my heart to think of it." And the old man covered his face with his thin hand and groaned aloud.

"Don't distress yourself, Graves," said Levinger gently; "I have hinted to you before that there is a possible way of escape."

"You mean if Henry were to take a fancy to your daughter, and she were to reciprocate it?"

"Yes, that is what I mean; and why shouldn't they? So far as Emma is concerned the matter is already done. I am convinced of it. She was much struck with your son when she was here nearly two years ago, and has often spoken of him since. Emma has no secrets from me, and her mind is clear as a glass. It is easy to read what is passing there. I do not say that she has thought of marrying Henry, but she is attached to him, and admires him and his character—which shows her sense, for he is a fine fellow, a far finer fellow than any of you give him credit for. And on his side, why shouldn't he take to her? It is true that her mother's origin was humble, though she was a much more refined woman than people guessed, and that I, her father, am a man under a cloud, and deservedly. But what of that? The mother is dead, and alas! my life is not a good one, so that very soon her forbears will be forgotten. For the rest, she is a considerable, if not a large, heiress; there should be a matter of at least fifteen thousand pounds to come to her besides the mortgages on this place and real property as well. In her own way—to my mind at any rate—she is beautiful, and there never lived a sweeter, purer, or more holy-minded woman. If your son were married to her, within a year he would worship the ground she trod on. Why shouldn't it come about, then?"

"I don't know, except that things which are very suitable and very much arranged have a way of falling through. Your daughter Emma is all you say, though perhaps a little too unearthly. She strikes me as rather ghost-like—that is, compared with the girls of my young days, though I understand this sort of thing has become the fashion. The chief obstacle I fear, however, is Henry himself. He is a very queer-grained man, and as likely as not the knowledge that this marriage is necessary to our salvation will cause him to refuse to have anything to do with it."

"For his own sake I hope that it may not be so," answered Levinger, with some approach to passion, "for if it is I tell you fairly that I shall let matters take their course. Emma will either come into possession of this property as the future Lady Graves or as Miss Levinger, and it is for your son to choose which he prefers."

"Yes, yes, I understand all that. What I do not understand, Levinger, is why you should be so desperately anxious for this particular marriage. There are plenty of better matches for Emma than my son Henry. We are such old friends, I do not mind telling you I have not the slightest doubt but that you have some secret reason. It seems to me—I know you won't mind my saying it—that you carry the curious doublesidedness of your nature into every detail of life. You cannot be anything wholly—there is always a reservation about you: thus, when you seemed to be thoroughly bad, there was a reservation of good in you; and now, when you appear to be the most righteous man in the county, I sometimes think that there is still a considerable leaven of the other thing."

Mr. Levinger smiled and shrugged his shoulders, but he did not take offence at these remarks. That he refrained from doing so showed the peculiar terms on which the two men were—terms born of intimate knowledge and long association.

"Most people have more reasons for desiring a thing than they choose to publish on the housetops, Graves; but I don't see why you should seek for secret motives here when there are so many that are obvious. You happen to be the only friend I have in the world; it is therefore natural that I should wish to see my daughter married to your son, and for this same reason I desire that your family, which has been part and parcel of the country-side for hundreds of years, should be saved from ruin. Further, I have taken a greater liking to Henry than to any man I have met for many a long day, and I know that Emma would love him and be happy with him, whereas did she marry elsewhere, with her unusual temperament, she might be very unhappy.

"Also, the match would be a good one for her, which weighs with me a great deal. Your son may never be rich, but he has done well in his profession, he is the inheritor of an ancient name, and he will be a baronet. As you know, my career has been a failure, and more than a failure. Very probably my child will never even know who I really am, but that she is the granddaughter of a Bradmouth smack owner is patent to everybody. I am anxious that all this should be forgotten and covered up by an honourable marriage; I am anxious, after being slighted and neglected, that she should start afresh in a position in which she can hold her head as high as any lady in the county, and I do not think that in my case this is an unnatural or an exorbitant ambition. Finally, it is my desire, the most earnest desire of my life, and I mean to live to see it accomplished. Now have I given you reasons enough?"

"Plenty, and very good ones too. But I still think that you have another and better in the background. Well, for my part I shall only be too thankful if this can be brought about. It would be a fair marriage also, for such disadvantages as there are seem to be very equally divided; and I like your daughter, Levinger—she is a sweet girl and interesting, even if she is old Will Johnson's grandchild. Now I must be off and say something civil to my future son-in-law before he goes,"—and, rising with something of an effort, Sir Reginald left the room.

"Graves is breaking up, but he is still shrewd," said Mr. Levinger to himself, gazing after him with his piercing eyes. "As usual he put his finger on the weak spot. Now, if he knew my last and best reason for wishing to see Emma married to his son, I wonder what he would do? Shrug his shoulders and say nothing, I expect. Beggars cannot be choosers, and bankrupts are not likely to be very particular. Poor old friend! I am sorry for him. Well, he shall spend his last days in peace if I can manage it—that is, unless Henry proves himself an obstinate fool, as it is possible he may."

Next morning Mr. Levinger and his daughter returned to Monk's Lodge; but before they went it was settled that Henry was to visit them some three weeks later, on the tenth of June, that date being convenient to all concerned.

On the following day Henry went to London for a week to arrange about a little pension to which he was entitled, and other matters. This visit did not improve his spirits, for in the course of his final attendances at the Admiralty he discovered for the first time how well he was thought of there, and that he had been looked on as a man destined to rise in the Service.

"Pity that you made up your mind to go, Captain Graves—great pity!" said one of the head officials to him. "I always thought that I should see you an admiral one day, if I lived long enough. We had several good marks against your name here, I can tell you. However, it is too late to talk of all this now, and I dare say that you will be better off as a baronet with a big estate than banging about the world in an ironclad, with the chance of being shot or drowned. You are too good a man to be lost, if you will allow me to say so, and now that you are off the active list you must go into Parliament and try to help us there."

"By Heavens, sir," answered Henry with warmth, "I'd rather be captain of an ironclad in the Channel Fleet than a baronet with twenty thousand a year, though now I have no chance of either. But we can't always please ourselves in this world. Good-bye." And, turning abruptly, he left the room.

"I wonder why that fellow went," mused the official as the door closed. "For a young man he was as good a sailor as there is in the Service, and he really might have got on. Private affairs, I suppose. Well, it can't be helped, and there are plenty ready to step into his shoes."

Henry returned to Rosham very much depressed, nor did he find the atmosphere of that establishment conducive to lightness of the heart. Putting aside his personal regrets at leaving the Navy, there was much to sadden him. First and foremost came financial trouble, which by now had reached an acute stage, for it was difficult to find ready money wherewith to carry on the ordinary expenses of the house. Then his mother's woeful face oppressed him as she went about mourning for the dead, mourning also for their fallen fortunes, and his father's failing health gave great reason for anxiety.

Furthermore, though here he knew that he had no just cause of complaint, the constant presence of Edward Milward irritated him to a degree that he could not conceal. In vain did he try to like this young man, or even to make it appear that he liked him; his efforts were a failure, and he felt that Ellen, with whom otherwise he remained on good, though not on cordial terms, resented this fact, as he on his part resented the continual false pretences, or rather the subterfuges and suppressions of the truth, in which she indulged in order to keep from her fiance a knowledge of the real state of the Rosham affairs. These arts exasperated Henry's pride to an extent almost unbearable, and Ellen knew that it was so, but not on this account would she desist from them. For she knew also the vulgar nature of her lover, and feared, perhaps not without reason, lest he should learn how great were their distresses, and how complete was the ruin which overshadowed them, and break off an engagement that was to connect him with a bankrupt and discredited family.

In the midst of these and other worries the time passed heavily enough, till at length that day arrived on which Henry was engaged to visit Monk's Lodge. Already he had received a note from Emma Levinger, writing on behalf of her father, to remind him of his promise. It was a prettily expressed note, written in a delicate and beautiful hand; and he answered it saying that he proposed to send his portmanteau by train and to ride over to Monk's Lodge, arriving there in time for dinner.

Henry had not thought much of Emma during the last week or two; or, if he had thought of her, it was in an impersonal way, as part of a sordid problem with which he found himself called upon to cope. At no time was he much given to allow his mind to run upon the fascinations of any woman; and, charming and original as this lady might be, he was not in a mood just now to contemplate her from the standpoint of romance. None the less, however, was he glad of the opportunity which this visit gave him to escape for a while from Rosham, even if he could not leave his anxieties behind him.

He had no further conversation with Ellen upon the subject of Emma. The terms upon which they stood implied a mutual truce from interference in each other's affairs. His father, however, did say a word to him when he went to bid him good-bye. He found the old man in bed, for now he did not rise till lunch-time.

"Good-bye, my boy," he said. "So you are going to Monk's Lodge? Well, it will be a pleasant change for you. Old Levinger is a queer fish, and in some ways not altogether to be trusted, as I have known for many a year, but he has lots of good in him; and to my mind his daughter is charming. Ah, Henry! I wish, without doing violence to your own feelings, that you could manage to take a fancy to this girl. There, I will say no more; you know what I mean."

"I know, father," answered Henry, "and I will do my best to fall in with your views. But, all the same, however charming she may be, it is a little hard on me that I should be brought down to this necessity."

Then he rode away, and in due course reached the ruins of Ramborough Abbey.

CHAPTER IX

MUTUAL ADMIRATION

That Henry and Joan were left lying for so many hours among the graves of Ramborough Abbey is not greatly to be wondered at, since, before he had ridden half a mile, Master Willie Hood's peculiar method of horsemanship resulted in frightening the cob so much that, for the first time in its peaceful career, it took the bit between its teeth and bolted. For a mile or more it galloped on at right angles to the path, while Willie clung to its mane, screaming "Wo!" at the top of his voice, and the sea-birds' eggs with which his pockets were filled, now smashed into a filthy mass, trickled in yellow streams down the steed's panting sides.

At length the end came. Arriving at a fence, the cob stopped suddenly, and Willie pitched over its head into a bramble bush. By the time that he had extricated himself—unharmed, but very much frightened, and bleeding from a dozen scratches—the horse was standing five hundred yards away, snorting and staring round in an excited manner. Willie, who was a determined youth, set to work to catch it.

Into the details of the pursuit we need not enter: suffice it to say that the sun had set before he succeeded in his enterprise. Mount it again he could not, for the saddle had twisted and one stirrup was lost; nor would he have done so if he could. Therefore he determined to walk into Bradmouth, whither, after many halts and adventures, he arrived about ten o'clock, leading the unwilling animal by the reins.

Now Willie, although exceedingly weary, and somewhat shaken, was a boy of his word; so, still leading the horse, he proceeded straight to the residence of Dr. Childs, and rang the bell.

"I want the doctor, please, miss," he said to the servant girl who answered it.

"My gracious! you look as if you did," remarked that young lady, surveying his bleeding countenance.

"Tain't for myself, Silly!" he replied. "You ask the doctor to step out, for I don't trust this here horse to you or anybody: he's run away once, and I don't want no more of that there game."

The girl complied, laughing; and presently Dr. Childs, a middle-aged man with a quiet manner, appeared, and asked what was the matter.

"Please, sir, there's a gentleman fallen off Ramborough Tower and broken his leg; and Joan Haste she's with him, and she's all bloody too—though I don't know what she's broken. I was to ask you to go and fetch him with a shutter, and to take things along to tie him up with."

"When did he fall, and what is his name, my boy?" asked the doctor.

"I don't know when he fell, sir; but I saw Joan Haste about six o'clock time. Since then I've been getting here with this here horse; and I wish that I'd stuck to my legs, for all the help he's been to me—the great idle brute! I'd rather wheel a barrow of bricks nor pull him along behind me. Oh! the name? She said it was Captain Graves of Rosham: that was what I was to tell her aunt."

"Captain Graves of Rosham!" said Dr. Childs to himself. "Why, I heard Mr. Levinger say that he was coming to stay with him to-day!"

Then he went into the house, and ten minutes later he was on his way to Ramborough in a dogcart, followed by some men with a stretcher. On reaching the ruined abbey, the doctor stood up and looked round; but, although the moon was bright, he could see no one. He called aloud, and presently heard a faint voice answering him. Leaving the cart in charge of his groom, he followed the direction of the sound till he came to the foot of the tower. Here, beneath the shadow of the spiked tomb, clasping the senseless body of a man in her arms, he found a woman—Joan Haste—whose white dress was smirched with blood, and who, to all appearance, had but just awakened from a faint. Very feebly—for she was quite exhausted—she explained what had happened; and, without more words, the doctor set to work.

"It's a baddish fracture," he said presently. "Lucky that the poor fellow is insensible."

In a quarter of an hour he had done all that could be done there and in that light, and by this time the men who were following with the stretcher, were seen arriving in another cart. Very gently they lifted Henry, who was still unconscious, on to the stretcher, and set out upon the long trudge back to Bradmouth, Dr. Childs walking by their side. Meanwhile Joan was placed in the dogcart and driven forward by the coachman, to see that every possible preparation was made at the Crown and Mitre, whither it was rapidly decided that the injured man must be taken, for it was the only inn at Bradmouth, and the doctor had no place for him in his own house.

At length they arrived, and Henry, who by now was recovering consciousness, was carried into Joan's room, an ancient oak-panelled apartment on the ground floor. Once this room served as the justice-chamber of the monks; for what was now the Crown and Mitre had been their lock-up and place of assize, when, under royal charter, they exercised legal rights over the inhabitants of Bradmouth. There the doctor and his assistant, who had returned from visiting some case in the country, began the work of setting Henry's broken leg, aided by Mrs. Gillingwater, Joan's aunt, a hard-featured, stout and capable-looking woman of middle age. At length the task was completed, and Henry was sent to sleep under the influence of a powerful narcotic.

"And now, sir," said Mrs. Gillingwater, as Dr. Childs surveyed his patient with a certain grave satisfaction, for he felt that he had done well by a very difficult bit of surgery, "if you have a minute or two to spare, I think that you might give Joan a look: she's got a nasty hole in her shoulder, and seems shaken and queer."

Then she led the way across the passage to a little room that in the monastic days had served as a cell, but now was dedicated to the use of Mr. Gillingwater whenever his wife considered him too tipsy to be allowed to share the marital chamber.

Here Joan was lying on a truckle bed, in a half-fainting condition, while near her, waving a lighted candle to and fro over her prostrate form, stood Mr. Gillingwater, a long, thin-faced man, with a weak mouth, who evidently had taken advantage of the general confusion to help himself to the gin bottle.

"Poor dear! poor dear! ain't it sad to see her dead?" he said, in maudlin tones, dropping the hot grease from the candle upon the face of the defenceless Joan; "and she, what she looks, a real lady. Oh! ain't it sad to see her dead?" And he wept aloud.

"Get out, you drunken sot, will you!" exclaimed his wife, with savage energy. "Do you want to set the place on fire?" And, snatching the candle from Mr. Gillingwater's hand, she pushed him through the open door so vigorously that he fell in a heap in the passage. Then she turned to Dr. Childs, and said, "I beg your pardon, sir; but there's only one way to deal with him when he's on the drink."

The doctor smiled, and began to examine Joan's shoulder.

"It is nothing serious," he said, when he had washed the wound, "unless the rust from the spike should give some trouble in the healing. Had it been lower down, it would have been another matter, for the lung might have been pierced. As it is, with a little antiseptic ointment and a sleeping draught, I think that your niece will be in a fair way to recovery by to-morrow morning, if she has not caught cold in that damp grass."

"However did she come by this, sir?" asked Mrs. Gillingwater.

"I understand that Captain Graves climbed the tower to get some young jackdaws. He fell, and she tried to catch him in her arms, but of course was knocked backwards."

"She always was a good plucked one, was Joan," said Mrs. Gillingwater, with a certain reluctant pride. "Well, if no harm comes of it, she has brought us a bit of custom this time anyhow, and when we want it bad enough. The Captain is likely to be laid up here some weeks, ain't he, sir?"

"For a good many weeks, I fear, Mrs. Gillingwater, even if things go well with him."

"Is he in any danger, then?"

"There is always some danger to a middle-aged man in such a case: it is possible that he may lose his leg, and that is a serious matter."

"Lord! and all to get her young jackdaws. You have something to answer for, miss, you have," soliloquised Mrs. Gillingwater aloud; adding, by way of explanation, as they reached the passage, "She's an unlucky girl, Joan is, for all her good looks—always making trouble, like her mother before her: I suppose it is in the blood."

Leaving his assistant in charge, Dr. Childs returned home, for he had another case to visit that night. Next morning he wrote two notes—one to Sir Reginald Graves and one to Mr. Levinger, both of whom were patients of his, acquainting them with what had occurred in language as little alarming as possible. Having despatched these letters by special messengers, he walked to the Crown and Mitre. As he had anticipated, except for the pain of the wound in her shoulder, Joan was almost herself again: she had not caught cold, the puncture looked healthy, and already her vigorous young system was shaking off the effects of her shock and distress of mind. Henry also seemed to be progressing as favourably as could be expected; but it was deemed advisable to keep him under the influence of opiates for the present.

"I suppose that we had better send for a trained nurse," said the doctor. "If I telegraph to London, we could have one down by the evening."

"If you do, sir, I am sure I don't know where she's to sleep," answered Mrs. Gillingwater; "there isn't a hole or corner here unless Joan turns out of the little back room, and then there is nowhere for her to go. Can't I manage for the present, sir, with Joan to help? I've had a lot to do with sick folk of all sorts in my day, worse luck, and some knack of dealing with them too, they tell me. Many and many's the eyes that I have shut for the last time. Then it isn't as though you was far off neither: you or Mr. Salter can always be in and out if you are wanted."

"Well," said the doctor, after reflecting, "we will let the question stand over for the present, and see how the case goes on."

He knew Mrs. Gillingwater to be a capable and resourceful woman, and one who did not easily tire, for he had had to do with her in numerous maternity cases, where she acted the part of sage-femme with an address that had won her a local reputation.

About twelve o'clock a message came to him to say that Lady Graves and Mr. Levinger were at the inn, and would be glad to speak to him. He found them in the little bar-parlour, and Emma Levinger with them, looking even paler than her wont.

"Oh! doctor, how is my poor son?" said Lady Graves, in a shaken voice. "Mrs. Gillingwater says that I may not see him until I have asked you. I was in bed this morning and not very well when your note came, but Ellen had gone over to Upcott, and of course Sir Reginald could not drive so far, so I got up and came at once." And she paused, glancing at him anxiously.

"I think that you would have done better to stop where you were, Lady Graves, for you are not looking very grand," answered Dr. Childs. "I thought, of course, that your daughter would come. Well, it is a bad double fracture, and, unluckily, Captain Graves was left exposed for some hours after the accident; but at present he seems to be going on as well as possible. That is all I can say."

"How did it happen?" asked Mr. Levinger.

"Joan Haste can tell you better than I can," the doctor answered. "She is up, for I saw her standing in the passage. I will call her."

At the mention of Joan's name Mr. Levinger's face underwent a singular contraction, that, quick as it was, did not escape the doctor's observant eye. Indeed, he made a deprecatory movement with his hand, as though he were about to negative the idea of her being brought before them; then hearing Lady Graves's murmured "by all means," he seemed to change his mind suddenly and said nothing. Dr. Childs opened the door and called Joan, and presently she stood before them.

Her face was very pale, her under lip was a little cut, and her right hand rested in a sling on the bosom of her simple brown dress; but her very pallor and the anxiety in her dark eyes made her beauty the more remarkable, by touching it with an added refinement. Joan bowed to Mr. Levinger, who acknowledged her salute with a nod, and curtseyed to Lady Graves; then she opened her lips to speak, when her eyes met those of Emma Levinger, and she remained silent.

The two women had seen each other before; in childhood they had even spoken together, though rarely; but since they were grown up they had never come thus face to face, and now it seemed that each of them found a curious fascination in the other. It was of Emma Levinger, Joan remembered, that Captain Graves had spoken on the previous night, when his mind began to wander after the accident; and though she scarcely knew why, this gave her a fresh interest in Joan's eyes. Why had his thoughts flown to her so soon as his mental balance was destroyed? she wondered. Was he in love with her, or engaged to be married to her? It was possible, for she had heard that he was on his way to stay at Monk's Lodge, where they never saw any company.

Joan has almost made up her mind, with considerable perspicuity, that there was something of the sort in the air, when she remembered, with a sudden flush of pleasure, that Captain Graves had spoken of herself also yonder in the churchyard, and in singularly flattering terms, which seemed to negative the idea that the fact of a person speaking of another person, when under the influence of delirium, necessarily implied the existence of affection, or even of intimacy, between them. Still, thought Joan, it would not be wonderful if he did love Miss Levinger. Surely that sweet and spiritual face and those solemn grey eyes were such as any man might love.

But if Joan was impressed with Emma, Emma was equally impressed with Joan, for in that instant of the meeting of their gaze, the thought came to her that she had never before seen so physically perfect a specimen of womanhood. Although Emma could theorise against the material, and describe beauty as an accident, and therefore a thing to be despised, she was too honest not to confess to herself her admiration for such an example of it as Joan afforded. This was the girl whose bravery, so she was told, had saved Captain Graves from almost certain death; and, looking at her, Emma felt a pang of envy as she compared her health and shape with her own delicacy and slight proportions. Indeed, there was something more than envy in her mind—something that, if it was not jealousy, at least partook of it. Of late Emma's thoughts had centred themselves a great deal round Captain Graves, and she was envious of this lovely village girl with whom, in some unknown way, he had become acquainted, and whose good fortune it had been to be able to protect him from the worst effects of his dreadful accident.

At that moment a warning voice seemed to speak in Emma's heart, telling her that this woman would not readily let go the man whom fate had brought to her, that she would cling to him indeed as closely as though he were her life. It had nothing to do with her, at any rate as yet; still Emma grew terribly afraid as the thought went home, afraid with a strange, impalpable fear she knew not of what. At least she trembled, and her eyes swam, and she wished in her heart that she had never seen Joan Haste, that they might live henceforth at different ends of the world, that she might never see her again.

All this flashed through the minds of the two girls in one short second; the next Emma's terror, for it may fitly be so called, had come and gone, and Lady Graves was speaking.

"Good day, Joan Haste," she said kindly: "I understand that you were with my son at the time of this shocking accident. Will you tell us how it came about?"

"Oh, my Lady," answered Joan with agitation, "it was all my fault—at least, in a way it was, though I am sure I never meant that he should be so foolish as to try and climb the tower." And in a simple straightforward fashion she went on to relate what had occurred, saying as little as possible, however, about her own share in the adventure.

"Thank you," said Lady Graves when Joan had finished. "You seem to have behaved very bravely, and I fear that you are a good deal hurt. I hope you will soon be well again. And now, Dr. Childs, do you think that I might see Henry for a little?"

"Well, perhaps for a minute or two, if you will keep as quiet as possible," he answered, and led the way to the sick room.

By this time the effects of the sleeping draughts had passed off, and when his mother entered Henry was wide awake and talking to Mrs. Gillingwater. He knew her step at once, and addressed her in a cheery voice, trying to conceal the pain which racked him.

"How do you do, mother?" he said. "You find me in a queer way, but better off than ever I expected to be again when I was hanging against the face of that tower. It is very good of you to come to see me, and I hope that the news of my mishap has not upset my father."

"My poor boy," said Lady Graves, bending over him and kissing him, "I am afraid that you must suffer a great deal of pain."

"Nothing to speak of," he answered, "but I am pretty well smashed up, and expect that I shall be on my back here for some weeks. Queer old place, isn't it? This good lady tells me that it is her niece's room. It's a very jolly one, anyhow. Just look at the oak panelling and that old mantelpiece. By the way, I hope that Miss Joan—I think that she said her name was Joan—is not much hurt. She is a brave girl, I can tell you, mother. Had it not been that she caught me when I fell, I must have gone face first on to that spiked tomb, and then—"

"Had it not been for her you would never have climbed the tower," answered Lady Graves with a shudder. "I can't think what induced you to be so foolish, at your age, my dear boy."

"I think it was because she is so pretty, and I wanted to oblige her," he answered, with the candour of a mind excited by suffering. "I say, I hope that somebody has written to the Levingers, or they will be wondering what on earth has become of me."

"Yes, yes, dear; they are here, and everything has been explained to them."

"Oh, indeed. Make them my excuses, will you? When I am a bit better I should like to see them, but I don't feel quite up to it just now."

Henry made this last remark in a weaker voice; and, taking the hint, Dr. Childs touched Lady Graves on the shoulder and nodded towards the door.

"Well, dear, I must be going," said his mother; "but Ellen or I will come over to-morrow to see how you are getting on. By the way, should you like us to send for a trained nurse to look after you?"

"Most certainly not," Henry answered, with vigour; "I hate the sight of hospital nurses—they always remind me of Haslar, where I was laid up with jaundice. There are two doctors, and this good lady taking care of me here, and if that isn't enough for me, nothing will be."

"Well, dear, we will see how you get on," said his mother doubtfully. Then she kissed him and went; but the doctor stopped behind, and having taken his patient's temperature, ordered him another sleeping draught.

So soon as Lady Graves had left the parlour, Joan followed her example, murmuring with truth that she felt a little faint.

"What a beautiful girl, father!" said Emma to Mr. Levinger. "Who is she? Somebody said the other day that there was a mystery about her."

"How on earth should I know?" he answered. "She is Mrs. Gillingwater's niece and I believe that her parents are dead; that is the only mystery I ever heard."

"I think that there must be something odd, all the same," said Emma. "If you notice, her manners are quite different from those of most village girls, and she speaks almost like a lady."

"Been educated above her station in life, I fancy," her father answered snappishly. "That is the way girls of this kind are ruined, and taught to believe that nothing in their own surroundings is good enough for them. Anyhow, she has led poor Graves into this mess, for which I shall not forgive her in a hurry."

"At least she did her best to save him, and at great risk to herself," said Emma gently. "I don't see what more she could have done."

"That's woman's logic all over," replied the father. "First get a man who is worth two of you into some terrible scrape, physical or otherwise, and then do your 'best to save him,' and pose as a heroine. It would be kinder to leave him alone altogether in nine cases out of ten, only then it is impossible to play the guardian angel, as every woman loves to do. Just to gratify her whim—for that is the plain English of it—this girl sends poor Graves up that tower; and because, when he falls off it, she tries to throw her arms round him, everybody talks of her wonderful courage. Bother her and her courage! The net result is that he will never be the same man again."

Her father spoke with so much suppressed energy that Emma looked at him in astonishment, for of late years, at any rate, he had been accustomed to act calmly and to speak temperately.

"Is Captain Graves's case so serious?"

"From what young Salter tells me I gather that it is about as bad as it can be of its kind. He has fractured his leg in a very awkward place, there is some haemorrhage, and he lay exposed for nearly five hours, and had to be carried several miles."

"What will happen to him, then?" asked Emma in alarm. "I thought that the worst of it was over."

"I can't tell you. It depends on Providence and his constitution; but what seems likely is that they will be forced to amputate his leg and make him a hopeless cripple for life."

"Oh!" said Emma, catching her breath like one in pain; "I had no idea that it was so bad. This is terrible." And for a moment she leant on the back of a chair to support herself.

"Yes, it is black enough; but we cannot help by stopping here, so we may as well drive home. I will send to inquire for him this evening."

So they went, and never had Emma a more unhappy drive. She was looking forward so much to Captain Graves's visit, and now he lay wounded—dangerously ill. The thought wrung her heart, and she could almost find it in her gentle breast to detest the girl who, however innocently, had been the cause of all the trouble.

CHAPTER X

AZRAEL'S WING

For the next two days, notwithstanding the serious condition of his broken leg, Henry seemed to go on well, till even his mother and Emma Levinger, both of whom were kept accurately informed of his state, ceased to feel any particular alarm about him. On the second day Mrs. Gillingwater, being called away to attend to some other matter, sent for Joan—who, although her arm was still in a sling, had now almost recovered—to watch in the sick room during her absence. She came and took her seat by the bed, for at the time Henry was asleep. Shortly afterwards he awoke and saw her.

"Is that you, Miss Haste?" he said. "I did not know that you cared for nursing."

"Yes, sir," answered Joan. "My aunt was obliged to go out for a little while, and, as you are doing so nicely, she said that she thought I might be trusted to look after you till she came back."

"It is very kind of you, I am sure," said Henry. "Sick rooms are not pleasant places. Perhaps you wouldn't mind giving me some of that horrid stuff—barley-water I think it is. I am thirsty."

Joan handed him the glass and supported his head while he drank. When he had satisfied his thirst he said:

"I have never thanked you yet for your bravery. I do thank you sincerely, Miss Haste, for if I had fallen on to those spikes there would have been an end of me. I saw them as I was hanging, and thought that my hour had come."

"And yet he told me to 'stand clear'!" reflected Joan; but aloud she said:

"Oh! pray, pray don't thank me, sir. It is all my fault that you have met with this dreadful accident, and it breaks my heart to think of it." And as she spoke a great tear ran down her beautiful face.

"Come, please don't cry: it upsets me; if the smash was anybody's fault, it was my own. I ought to have known better."

"I will try not, sir," answered Joan, in a choking voice; "but aunt said that you weren't to talk, and you are talking a great deal."

"All right," he replied: "you stop crying and I'll stop talking."

As may be guessed after this beginning, from that hour till the end of his long and dangerous illness, Joan was Henry's most constant attendant. Her aunt did the rougher work of the sick room, indeed, but for everything else he depended upon her; clinging to her with a strange obstinacy that baffled all attempts to replace her by a more highly trained nurse. On one occasion, when an effort of the sort was made, the results upon the patient were so unfavourable that, to her secret satisfaction, Joan was at once reinstalled.

After some days Henry took a decided turn for the worse. His temperature rose alarmingly, and he became delirious, with short coherent intervals. Blood poisoning, which the doctors feared, declared itself, and in the upshot he fell a victim to a dreadful fever that nearly cost him his life. At one time the doctors were of opinion that his only chance lay in amputation of the fractured limb; but in the end they gave up this idea, being convinced that, in his present state, he would certainly die of the shock were they to attempt the operation.

Then followed three terrible days, while Henry lay between life and death. For the greater part of those days Lady Graves and Ellen sat in the bar-parlour, the former lost in stony silence, the latter pale and anxious enough, but still calm and collected. Even now Ellen did not lose her head, and this was well, for the others were almost distracted by anxiety and grief. Distrusting the capacities of Joan, a young person whom she regarded with disfavour as being the cause of her brother's accident, it was Ellen who insisted upon the introduction of the trained nurses, with consequences that have been described. When the doctors hesitated as to the possibility of an operation, it was Ellen also who gave her voice against it, and persuaded her mother to do the same.

"I know nothing of surgery," she said, with conviction, "and it seems probable that poor Henry will die; but I feel sure that if you try to cut off his leg he will certainly die."

"I think that you are right, Miss Graves," said the eminent surgeon who had been brought down in consultation, and with whom the final word lay. "My opinion is that the only course to follow with your brother is to leave him alone, in the hope that his constitution will pull him through."

So it came about that Henry escaped the knife.

Emma Levinger and her father also haunted the inn, and it was during those dark days that the state of the former's affections became clear both to herself and to every one about her. Before this she had never confessed even to her own heart that she was attached to Henry Graves; but now, in the agony of her suspense, this love of hers arose in strength, and she knew that, whether he stayed or was called away, it must always be the nearest and most constant companion of her life. Why she loved him Emma could not tell, nor even when she began to do so; and indeed these things are difficult to define. But the fact remained, hard, palpable, staring: a fact which she had no longer any care to conceal or ignore, seeing that the conditions of the case caused her to set aside those considerations of womanly reserve that doubtless would otherwise have induced her to veil the secret of her heart for ever, or until circumstances gave opportunity for its legitimate expression.

At length on a certain afternoon there came a crisis to which there was but one probable issue. The doctors and nurses were in Henry's room doing their best to ward off the fate that seemed to be approaching, while Lady Graves, Mr. Levinger, Ellen and Emma sat in the parlour awaiting tidings, and striving to hope against hope. An hour passed, and Emma could bear the uncertainty no longer. Slipping out unobserved, she stole towards the sick room and listened at a little distance from it. Within she could hear the voice of a man raving in delirium, and the cautious tread of those who tended him. Presently the door opened and Joan appeared, walking towards her with ashen face and shaking limbs.

"How is he?" asked Emma in an intense whisper, catching at her dress as she passed.

Joan looked at her and shook her head: speak she could not. Emma watched her go with vacant eyes, and a jealousy smote her, which made itself felt even through the pain that tore her heart in two. Why should this woman be free to come and go about the bedside of the man who was everything to her—to hold his dying hand and to lift his dying head—while she was shut outside his door? Emma wondered bitterly. Surely that should be her place, not the village girl's who had been the cause of all this sorrow. Then she turned, and, creeping back to the parlour, she flung herself into a chair and covered her face with her hands.

"Have you heard anything?" asked Lady Graves.

Emma made no reply but her despair broke from her in a low moaning that was very sad to hear.

"Do not grieve so, dear," said Ellen kindly.

"Let me grieve," she answered, lifting her white face; "let me grieve now and always. I know that Faith should give me comfort, but it fails me. I have a right to grieve," she went on passionately, "for I love him. I do not care who knows it now: though I am nothing to him, I love him, and if he dies it will break my heart."

So great was the tension of suspense that Emma's announcement, startling as it was, excited no surprise. Perhaps they all knew how things were with her; at any rate Lady Graves answered only, "We all love him, dear," and for a time no more was said.

Meanwhile, could she have seen into the little room behind her, Emma might have witnessed the throes of a grief as deep as her own, and even more abandoned; for there, face downwards on her bed, lay Joan Haste, the girl whom she had envied. Sharp sobs shook her frame, notwithstanding that she had thrust her handkerchief between her teeth to check them, and she clutched nervously at the bedclothes with her outstretched hands. Hitherto she had been calm and silent; now, at length, when she was of no more service, she broke down, and Nature took its way with her.

"O my God!" she muttered between her strangling sobs, "spare him and kill me, for it was my fault, and I am his murderess. O my God! my God! What have I done that I should suffer so? What makes me suffer so? Oh! spare him, spare him!"

Another half-hour passed, and the twilight began to gather in the parlour.

"It is very long," murmured Lady Graves.

"While they do not come to call us there is hope," answered Ellen, striving to keep up a show of courage.

Once more there was silence, and the time went on and the darkness gathered.

At length a step was heard approaching, and they knew it for that of Dr. Childs. Instinctively they all rose, expecting the last dread summons. He was among them now, but they could not see his face because of the shadows.

"Is Lady Graves there?" he asked.

"Yes," whispered the poor woman.

"Lady Graves, I have come to tell you that by the mercy of Heaven your son's constitution has triumphed, and, so far as my skill and knowledge go, I believe that he will live."

For a second the silence continued; then, with a short sharp cry, Emma Levinger went down upon the floor as suddenly as though she had been shot through the heart.

Joan also had heard Dr. Child's footsteps, and, rising swiftly from her bed, she followed him to the door of the parlour, where she stood listening to his fateful words—for her anxiety was so intense that the idea of intrusion did not even cross her mind.

Joan heard the words, and she believed that they were an answer to her prayer; for her suffering had been too fierce and personal to admit of her dissociating herself from the issue, at any rate at present. She forgot that she was not concerned alone in this matter of the life or death of Henry Graves—she who, although as yet she did not know it, was already wrapped with the wings and lost in the shadow of a great and tragic passion. She had prayed, and she had been answered. His life had been given back to her.

Thus she thought for a moment; the next she heard Emma's cry, and saw her fall, and was undeceived. Now she was assured of what before she had suspected, that this sweet and beautiful lady loved the man who lay yonder; and, in the assurance of that love, she learned her own. It became clear to her in an instant, as at night the sudden lightning makes clear the landscape to some lost wanderer among mountains. As in the darkness such a wanderer may believe that his feet are set upon a trodden road, and in that baleful glare discover himself to be surrounded by dangers, amid desolate wastes; so at this sight Joan understood whither her heart had strayed, and was affrighted, for truly the place seemed perilous and from it there was no retreat. Before her lay many a chasm and precipice, around her was darkness, and a blind mist blew upon her face, a mist wet as though with tears.

Somebody in the parlour called for a light, and the voice brought her back from her vision, her hopeless vision of what was, had been, and might be. What had chanced or could chance to her mattered little, she thought to herself, as she turned to seek the lamp. He would live, and that was what she had desired, what she had prayed for while as yet she did not know why she prayed it, offering her own life in payment. She understood now that her prayer had been answered more fully than she deemed; for she had given her life, her true life, for him and to him, though he might never learn the price that had been exacted of her. Well, he would live—to be happy with Miss Levinger—and though her heart must die because of him, Joan could be glad of it even in those miserable moments of revelation.

She returned with the lamp, and assisted in loosening the collar of Emma's dress and in sprinkling her white face with water. Nobody took any notice of her. Why should they, who were overcome by the first joy of hope renewed, and moved with pity at the sight of the fainting girl? They even spoke openly before her, ignoring her presence.

"Do not be afraid," said Dr. Childs: "I have never known happiness to kill people. But she must have suffered a great deal from suspense."

"I did not know that it had gone so far with her," said her father in a low voice to Lady Graves. "I believe that if the verdict had been the other way it would have killed her also."

"She must be very fond of him," answered Lady Graves; "and I am thankful for it, for now I have seen how sweet she is. Well, if it pleases God that Henry should recover, I hope that it will all come right in the end. Indeed, he will be a strange man if it does not."

Just then Ellen, who was watching and listening, seemed to become aware of Joan's presence.

"Thank you," she said to her; "you can go now."

So Joan went, humbly enough, suffering a sharper misery than she had dreamed that her heart could hold, and yet vaguely happy through her wretchedness. "At least," she thought to herself, with a flash of defiant feeling, "I am his nurse, and they can't send me away from him yet, because he won't let them. It made him worse when they tried before. When he is well again Miss Levinger will take him, but till then he is mine—mine. Oh! I wish I had known that she was engaged to him from the beginning: no, it would have made no difference. It may be wicked, but I should have loved him anyhow. It is my doom that I should love him, and I would rather love him and be wretched, than not love him and be happy. I suppose that it began when I first saw him, though I did not understand it then—I only wondered why he seemed so different to any other man that I had seen. Well, it is done now, and there is no use crying over it, so I may as well laugh, if one can laugh with a heart like a lump of ice."

Once out of danger, Henry's progress towards recovery was sure, if slow. Three weeks passed before he learned how near he had been to death. It was Joan who told him, for as yet he had been allowed only the briefest of interviews with his mother and Ellen, and on these occasions, by the doctor's orders, their past anxieties were not even alluded to. Now, however, all danger was done with, and that afternoon Joan had been informed by Dr. Childs that she might read to her patient if he wished it, or talk to him upon any subject in which he seemed to take interest.

It was a lovely July day, and Joan was seated sewing in Henry's, or rather in her own room, by the open window, through which floated the scent of flowers and a murmuring sound of the sea. Henry had been dozing, and she laid her work upon her knee and watched him while he slept. Presently she saw that his eyes were open and that he was looking at her.

"Do you want anything, sir?" she said, hastily resuming her sewing. "Are you comfortable?"

"Quite, thank you; and I want nothing except to go on looking at you. You make a very pretty picture in that old window place, I assure you."

She coloured faintly and did not answer. Presently he spoke again.

"Joan," he said—he always called her Joan now—"was I very bad at any time?"

"Yes, sir; they almost gave you up three weeks ago—indeed, they said the chances were ten to one against your living."

"It is strange: I remember nothing about it. Do you know, it gives me rather a turn. I have been too busy a man and too occupied with life to think much of death, and I don't quite like the sensation of having been so near to it; though perhaps it is not as bad as one thinks, and Heaven knows it would have saved me plenty of worry here below," and Henry sighed.

"I am very grateful to you all," he went on after a moment's pause, "for taking so much trouble about me—especially to you, Joan, for somehow or other I realised your presence even when I was off my head. I don't know how you occupy yourself generally, but I am sure you are fond of fresh air. It is uncommonly good of you to mew yourself up here just to look after me."

"Don't talk like that, sir. It is my business."

"Your business! Why is it your business? You are not a professional nurse, are you?"

"No, sir, though they offered to pay me to-day," and she flushed with indignation as she said it.

"Well, don't be angry if they did. Why shouldn't you have a week's wage for a week's work? I suppose you like to earn something, like the rest of us."

"Because I don't choose to," answered Joan, tapping the floor with her foot: "I'd rather starve. It is my fault that you got into this trouble, and it is an insult to offer me money because I am helping to nurse you out of it."

"Well, there is no need to excite yourself about it. I have no doubt they thought that you would take a different view, and really I cannot see why you should not. Tell me what happened on the night that they gave me up: it interests me."

Then in a few graphic words Joan sketched the scene so vividly, that Henry seemed to see himself lying unconscious on the bed, and sinking fast into death while the doctors watched and whispered round him.

"Were you there all the time?" he asked curiously.

"Most of it, till I was of no further use and could bear no more."

"What did you do then?"

"I went to my room."

"And what did you do there? Go to sleep?"

"Go to sleep! I—I—cried my heart out. I mean—that I said my prayers."

"It is very kind of you to take so much interest in me," he answered, in a half bantering voice; then, seeming to understand that she was very much in earnest, he changed the subject, asking, "And what did the others do?"

"They were all in the bar-parlour; they waited there till it grew dark, and then they waited on in the dark, for they thought that presently they would be called in to see you die. At last the change came, and Dr. Childs left you to tell them when he was sure. I heard his step, and followed him. I had no business to do it, but I could not help myself. He went into the room and stood still, trying to make out who was in it, and you might have heard a pin drop. Then he spoke to your mother, and said that through the mercy of Heaven he believed that you would live."

"Yes," said Henry; "and what did they say then?"

"Nobody said anything, so far as I could hear; only Miss Levinger screamed and dropped on the floor in a faint."

"Why did she do that?" asked Henry. "I suppose that they had been keeping her there without any dinner, and her nerves were upset."

"Perhaps they were, sir," said Joan sarcastically: "most women's nerves would be upset when they learned that the man they were engaged to was coming back to them from the door of the dead."

"Possibly; but I don't exactly see how the case applies."

Joan rose slowly, and the work upon which she had been employed fell from her hand to the floor.

"I do not quite understand you, sir," she said. "Do you mean to say that you are not engaged to Miss Levinger?"

"Engaged to Miss Levinger! Certainly not. Whatever may happen to me if I get out of this, at the present moment I am under no obligations of that sort to any human creature."

"Then I am sorry that I said so much," answered Joan. "Please forget my silly talk: I have made a mistake. I—think that I hear my aunt coming, and—if you will excuse me, I will go out and get a little air."

"All this is Greek to me," thought Henry, looking after her. "Surely Ellen cannot have been right! Oh, it is stuff and nonsense, and I will think no more about it."

CHAPTER XI

ELLEN GROWS ALARMED

On the morrow Henry had his first long interview with his mother and Ellen, who again detailed to him those particulars of his illness of which he had no memory, speaking more especially of the events of the afternoon and evening when he was supposed to be dying. To these Ellen added her version of the incident of Emma's fainting fit, which, although it was more ample, did not differ materially from that given him by Joan.

"I have heard about this," said Henry, when she paused; "and I am sorry that my illness should have pained Miss Levinger so much."

"You have heard about it? Who told you—Dr. Childs?"

"No; Joan Haste, who is nursing me."

"Then I can only say that she had no business to do so. It is bad enough that this young woman, to whom we certainly owe no gratitude, should have thrust herself upon us at such a terrible moment; but it is worse that, after acting the spy on poor Emma's grief, she should have the hardihood to come and tell you that she had done so, and to describe what passed."

"You must really excuse me, Ellen," her brother answered; "but I for one owe a great deal of gratitude to Joan Haste—indeed, had it not been for her care, I doubt if I should be here to be grateful to-day. Also it does not seem to have struck you that probably she took some interest in my case, and that her motive was not to spy upon you, but to hear what the doctor had to say."

"A great deal of interest—too much, indeed, I think," said Ellen drily; and then checked herself, for, with a warning glance at her daughter, Lady Graves suddenly changed the conversation.

A few minutes later his mother went out of the room to speak to Mrs. Gillingwater, leaving Ellen and Henry alone.

"I am sorry, dear, if I spoke sharply just now," said Ellen presently. "I am afraid that I am an argumentative creature, and it is not good for you to argue at present. But, to tell the truth, I was a little put out because you took the story of dear Emma's distress so coolly, and also because I had wished to be the first to tell it to you."

"I did not mean to take it coolly, Ellen, and I can only repeat that I am sorry. I think it a pity that a girl of Miss Levinger's emotional temperament, who probably has had no previous experience of illness threatening the life of a friend, should have been exposed to such a strain upon her nerves."

"A friend—a friend?" ejaculated Ellen, arching her eyebrows.

"Yes, a friend—at least I suppose that I may call myself so. Really, Ellen, you mystify me," he added petulantly.

"Really, Henry, you astonish me," his sister answered. "Either you are the most simple of men, or you are pretending ignorance out of sheer contrariness."

"Perhaps if you would not mind explaining, it might simplify matters, Ellen. I never was good at guessing riddles, and a fall off a church tower has not improved my wits."

"Oh, how can you talk in that way! Don't you remember what I told you when you came home?"

"You told me a good many things, Ellen, most of which were more or less disagreeable."

"I told you that Emma Levinger was half in love with you, Henry."

"Yes, I know you did; and I didn't believe you."

"Well, perhaps you will believe me now, when I say that she is wholly in love with you—as much in love as ever woman was with man."

"No," said Henry, shaking his head; "I don't wish to contradict, but I must decline to believe that."

"Was there ever so obstinate a person! Listen now, and if you are not satisfied of the truth of what I say, ask mother, ask Mr. Levinger, ask the girl herself." And word for word she repeated the passionate confession that had been wrung from poor Emma's agony. "Now will you believe me?"

"It seems that I must," he answered, after a pause; "though I think it quite possible that Miss Levinger's words sprang from her excitement, and did not mean what they appeared to convey. I think also, Ellen, that you ought to be ashamed of yourself for repeating to me what slipped from her in a moment of mental strain, and thus putting her in a false position. Supposing that the doctor, or Joan Haste, were to tell you every foolish thing which I may have uttered during my delirium, what would you think of them, I wonder? Still, I dare say that I led you on and you meant it kindly; but after this I am sure I do not know how I shall dare to look that poor girl in the face. And now I think I am a little tired. Would you call Mrs. Gillingwater or some one?"

Ellen left her brother's room in a state of irritation which was not the less intense because it was suppressed. She felt that her coup had not come off—that she had even made matters worse instead of better. She had calculated, if Henry's affections were not touched, that at least his vanity would be flattered, by the tale of Emma's dramatic exhibition of feeling: indeed, for aught she knew, either or both of these conjectures might be correct; but she was obliged to confess that he had given no sign by which she could interpret his mind in any such sense. The signs were all the other way, indeed, for he had taken the opportunity to lecture her on her breach of confidence, and it angered her to know that the reproof was deserved. In truth, she was so desperately anxious to bring about this marriage as soon as possible, that she had allowed herself to be carried away, with the result, as she now saw, of hindering her own object.

Ellen had a very imperfect appreciation of her brother's character. She believed him to be cold and pharisaical, and under this latter head she set down his notions concerning the contraction of marriages that chanced to be satisfactory from a money point of view. It did not enter into her estimate of him to presume that he might possess a delicacy of feeling which was lacking in her own nature; that the idea of being thrust into marriage with any woman in order to relieve the pecuniary necessities of his family, might revolt him to the extent of causing a person, whom perhaps he would otherwise have loved, to become almost distasteful to him. She did not understand even that the premature and unsought declaration of affection for himself on the part of the lady who was designed by others to be his wife, might produce a somewhat similar effect. And yet a very slight consideration of the principles of human nature would have taught her that this was likely to be the case.

These were solutions of Henry's conduct that did not suggest themselves to Ellen, or, if they did, she dismissed them contemptuously in her search for a more plausible explanation. Soon she found one which seemed to explain everything: Joan was the explanation. Nothing escaped Ellen's quick eyes, and she had noticed that Joan also was distressed at Henry's danger. She had marked, moreover, how he clung to this girl, refusing to be parted from her even in his delirium, and with what tenderness she nursed him; and she knew how often men fall in love with women who tend them in sickness.

Now, although she did not like Joan Haste, and resented as an impertinence, or worse, her conduct in following Dr. Childs to the parlour and reporting what took place there to Henry, Ellen could not deny that she was handsome, indeed beautiful, or that her manners were refined beyond what was to be expected of one in her station, and her bearing both gracious and dignified. Was it not possible, Ellen reflected, that these charms had produced an effect even upon her puritan brother, who already expressed his gratitude with such unnecessary warmth?

The thought filled her with alarm, for if once Henry became entangled with this village beauty, she knew enough of him to be sure that there would be an end of any prospect of his engagement to Emma—at least for the present. Meanwhile the girl was about him all day and every day, and never had a woman a better opportunity of carrying her nefarious schemes to a successful issue; for that Joan had schemes she soon ceased to doubt.

In this dilemma Ellen took counsel with her fiancé, whom she knew to possess a certain shrewdness; for she preferred to say nothing to her mother, and Sir Reginald was so unwell that he could not be troubled with such matters. By this time Edward Milward was aware that the Graves family desired greatly to bring about a match between Henry and Emma, though he was not aware how pressing were the money difficulties which led them to be anxious for this alliance. He listened with interest to Ellen's tale, then chuckled and said—

"Depend upon it you have knocked the right nail on the head as usual, Ellen. Those sanctimonious fellows like your brother are always the deepest, and of course he is playing his little game."

"I don't know what you mean by 'his little game,' Edward, and I wish that you would not use such vulgar expressions to me; nor can I see how Henry can be playing anything, considering that he never saw this person till the day of his accident, and that he has been laid up in bed ever since."

"Oh, well, he is getting ready to play it, which is much the same thing, and of course it puts him off the other girl. I am sure I don't blame him either, for I think that Joan—what's her name—is about the loveliest woman I ever saw, and one can't wonder that he prefers her to that thin ghost of a Miss Levinger with her die-away airs and graces. After all flesh and blood is the thing, and you may depend upon it Henry thinks so."

In this speech, had he but known it, Edward contrived to offend his betrothed in at least three separate ways, but she thought it prudent to suppress her resentment, at any rate for the moment.

"Do you think, dear," Ellen said blandly, "that you could manage to remember that you are not in a club smoking-room? I did not ask for these reflections; I asked you to give me your advice as to the best way to deal with a difficulty."

"All right, love: please don't look so superior; and save up your sarcasm for the wicked Henry. As for my advice, here it is in a nutshell: get the girl out of his way, and then perhaps he will begin to think of the other one, to whom you are so anxious to tie him up, though I can't say that I consider the connection desirable myself."

Having delivered himself thus, Edward put his hands into his pockets and strolled off in a huff. Although he was not thin-skinned, to tell the truth Ellen's slings and arrows sometimes irritated this young man.

"I wonder if she will always go on like this after we are married?" he thought to himself. "Perhaps she'll get worse. What's that about a green and a dry tree? She's dry enough anyway when she likes, and sometimes I think that I am pretty green. By George! if I believed that she always meant to keep up this game of snubs and sharp answers, fond as I am of her, I think I would cut the show before it is too late. There are a good many things that I don't like about it; I sometimes suspect that the whole set of them are pretty well broke, and I don't want to marry into a bankrupt family. Then that fellow Henry is an infernal prig—not but what I would be careful to see precious little of him. I wonder why Ellen is so anxious that he should take up with the Levinger girl? From all I can find out the father is a disreputable old customer, who made a low marriage, and whom everybody declines to know. It is shady, deuced shady," and, filled with these gloomy musings, Edward made his way into the dining-room to lunch.

Here Ellen, who in the interval had bethought herself that she was showing a little too much of the iron hand, received him graciously enough: indeed, she was so affectionate and pleasant in her manner, that before the afternoon was over Edward's doubts were dispelled, and he forgot that he had that morning contemplated a step so serious as the breaking off of his engagement.

However coarsely he might express himself, Ellen had wit enough to see that Edward's advice was of the soundest. Certainly it was desirable that Joan Haste should be got rid of, but how was this to be brought about? She could not tell her to go, nor could she desire Mrs. Gillingwater to order her out of the house. Ellen pondered the question deeply, and after sleeping a night over it she came to the conclusion that she would take Mr. Levinger into her counsel. She knew him to be a shrewd and resourceful man; she knew, moreover—for her father had repeated the gist of the conversation between them—that he was bent upon the marriage of Henry with his daughter; and lastly she knew that he was the landlord of the Crown and Mitre, in which the Gillingwaters lived. Surely, therefore, if any one could get rid of Joan, Mr. Levinger would be able to do so.

As it chanced upon this particular morning, Ellen was to drive over in the dogcart to lunch at Monk's Lodge, calling at the Crown and Mitre on her way through Bradmouth in order to hear the latest news of Henry. This programme she carried out, only stopping long enough at the inn, however, to run to her brother's room for a minute while the cart waited at the door. Here she discovered him propped up with pillows, while by his side was seated Joan, engaged in reading to him, and, worse still, in reading poetry. Now, for poetry in the abstract Ellen did not greatly care, but she had heard the tale of Paolo and Francesca, and knew well that when a young man and woman are found reading verses together, it may be taken as a sign that they are very much in sympathy.

"Good morning, Henry," said Ellen. "Good gracious, my dear! what are you doing?"

"Good morning, Ellen," he answered. "I am enjoying myself listening to Joan here, who is reading me some poetry, which she does very nicely indeed."

Ellen would not even turn her head to look at Joan, who had risen and stood book in hand.

"I had no idea that you wasted your time upon such nonsense, especially so early in the morning," she said, glancing round, "when I see that your room has not yet been dusted. But never mind about the poetry. I only came in to ask how you were, and to say that I am going to lunch with the Levingers. Have you any message for them?"

"Nothing particular," he said precisely, and with a slight hardening of the face, "except my best thanks to Miss Levinger for her note and the fruit and flowers she has so kindly sent me."

"Very well, then; I will go on, as I don't want to keep the mare standing. Good-bye, dear; I shall look in again in the afternoon." And she went without waiting for an answer.

"I wished to ask her how my father was," said Henry, "but she never gave me a chance. Well, now that the excitement is over, go on, Joan."

"No, sir; if you will excuse me, I don't think that I will read any more poetry."

"Why not? I am deeply interested. I think it must be nearly twenty years since I have seen a line of 'Lancelot and Elaine.'" And he looked at her, waiting for an answer.

"Because," blurted out Joan, blushing furiously, "because Miss Graves doesn't wish me to read poetry to you, and I dare say she is right, and—it is not my place to do so. But all the same it is not true to say that the room wasn't dusted, for you know that you saw me dust it yourself after aunt left."

"My dear girl, don't distress yourself," Henry answered, with more tenderness in his voice than perhaps he meant to betray. "I really am not accustomed to be dictated to by my sister, or anybody else, as to who should or should not read me poems. However, as you seem to be upset, quite unnecessarily I assure you, let us give it up for this morning and compromise on the Times."

Meanwhile Ellen was pursuing her course along the beach road towards Monk's Lodge, where she arrived within half an hour.

Monk's Lodge, a quaint red-brick house of the Tudor period, was surrounded on three sides by plantations of Scotch firs. To the east, however, stretching to the top of the sea cliff, was a strip of turf, not more than a hundred yards wide, so that all the front windows of the house commanded an uninterrupted view of the ocean. Behind the building lay the gardens, which were old-fashioned and beautiful, and sheltered by the encircling belts of firs; but in front were neither trees nor flowers, for the fierce easterly gales, and the salt spray which drifted thither in times of storm, would not allow of their growth.

Descending from the dogcart, Ellen was shown through the house into the garden, where she found Emma seated reading, or pretending to read, under the shade of a cedar; for the day was hot and still.

"How good of you to come, Ellen!" she said, springing up—"and so early too."

"I can't take credit for any particular virtue in that respect, my dear," Ellen answered, kissing her affectionately; "it is pleasant to escape to this delightful place and be quiet for a few hours, and I have been looking forward to it for a week. What between sickness and other things, my life at home is one long worry just now."

"It ought not to be, when you are engaged to be married," said Emma interrogatively.

"Even engagements have their drawbacks, as no doubt you will discover one day," she answered, with a little shrug of her shoulders. "Edward is the best and dearest of men, but he can be a wee bit trying at times: he is too affectionate and careful of me, if that is possible, for you know I am an independent person and do not like to have some one always running after me like a nurse with a child."

"Perhaps he will give up that when you are married," said Emma doubtfully. Somehow she could not picture her handsome and formidable friend—for at times the gentle Emma admitted to herself that she was rather formidable—as the constant object and recipient of petits soins and sweet murmured nothings.

"Possibly he will," answered Ellen decisively. "By the way, I just called in to see Henry, whom I found in a state of great delight with the note and roses which you sent him. He asked me to give you his kindest regards, and to say that he was much troubled by your thought of him."

"They were lilies, not roses," answered Emma, looking down.

"I meant lilies—did I say roses?" said Ellen innocently. "And, talking of lilies, you look a little pale, dear."

"I am always pale, Ellen; and, like you, I have been a good deal worried lately."

"Worried! Who can worry you in this Garden of Eden?"

"Nobody. It is—my own thoughts. I dare say that even Eve felt worried in her garden after she had eaten that apple, you know."

Ellen shook her head. "I am not clever, like you," she said, smiling, "and I don't understand parables. If you want my advice you must come down to my level and speak plainly."

Emma turned, and walked slowly from the shadow of the cedar tree into the golden flood of sunlight. Very slowly she passed down the gravel path, that was bordered by blooming roses, pausing now and again as though to admire some particular flower.

"She looks more like a white butterfly than a woman, in that dress of hers," thought Ellen, who was watching her curiously; "and really it would not seem wonderful if she floated away and vanished. It is hot out there, and I think that I had better not follow her. She has something to say, and will come back presently."

She was right. After a somewhat prolonged halt at the end of the path, Emma turned and walked, or rather flitted, straight back to the cedar tree.

"I will speak plainly," she said, "though I could not make up my mind to do so at first. I am ashamed of myself, Ellen—so bitterly ashamed that sometimes I feel as though I should like to run away and never be seen again."

"And why, my dear?" asked Ellen, lifting her eyes. "What dreadful crime have you committed, that you should suffer such remorse?"

"No crime, but a folly, which they say is worse—an unpardonable folly. You know what I mean—those words that I said when your brother was supposed to be dying. You must have heard them."

"Yes, I heard them; and now that he is not dying, they please me more than any words that I ever listened to from your lips. It is my dearest wish that things should come about between Henry and you as I am sure that they will come about, now that I know your mind towards him."

"If they please you, the memory of them tortures me," Emma answered, passionately clenching her slim white hands. "Oh! how could I be so shameless as to declare my—my love for a man who has never spoken a single affectionate word to me, who probably looks on me with utter indifference, or, for aught I know, with dislike! And the worst of it is I cannot excuse myself: I cannot say that they were nonsense uttered in a moment of fear and excitement, for it was the truth, the dreadful truth, that broke from me, and which I had no power to withhold. I do love him; I have loved him from the day when I first saw him, nearly two years ago, as I shall always love him; and that is why I am disgraced."

"Really, Emma, I cannot see what there is shocking in a girl becoming fond of a man. You are not the first person to whom such a thing has happened."

"No, there is nothing shocking in the love itself. So long as I kept it secret it was good and holy, a light by which I could guide my life; but now that I have blurted it, it is dishonoured, and I am dishonoured with it. That I was myself half dead with the agony of suspense is no excuse; I say that I am dishonoured."

To the listening Emma all these sentiments, natural as they might be to a girl of Emma's exalted temperament and spotless purity of mind, were as speeches made in the Hebrew tongue—indeed, within herself she did not hesitate to characterise her friend as "a high-flown little idiot." But, as she could not quite see what would be the best line to take in answering her, she satisfied herself with shaking her head as though in dissent, and looking sympathetic.

"What torments me most," went on Emma, who by now was thoroughly worked up—"I can say it to you, for you are a woman and will understand—is the thought that those shameless words might possibly come to your brother's ears. Three people heard them—Lady Graves, yourself and my father. Of course I know that neither you nor your mother would betray me, for, as I say, you are women and will feel for me; but, oh! I cannot be sure of my father. I know what he desires; and if he thought that he could advance his object, I am not certain that I could trust him—no, although he has promised to be silent; though, indeed, to tell your brother would be the surest way to defeat himself; for, did he learn the truth, such a man would despise me for ever."

"My dear girl," said Ellen boldly, for she felt that the situation required courage, "do calm yourself. Of course no one would dream of betraying to Henry what you insist upon calling an indiscretion, but what I thought a very beautiful avowal made under touching circumstances." Then she paused, and added reflectively, "I only see one danger."

"What danger?" asked Emma.

"Well, it has to do with that girl—Joan somebody—who brought about all this trouble, and who is nursing Henry, very much against my wish. I happen to have found out that she was listening at the door when Dr. Childs came into the room that night, just before you fainted, and it is impossible to say how long she had been there, and equally impossible to answer for her discretion."

"Joan Haste—that lovely woman! Of course she heard, and of course she will tell him. I was afraid of her the moment that I saw her, and now I begin to see why, though I believe that this is only the beginning of the evils which she will bring upon me. I am sure of it: I feel it in my heart."

"I think that you are alarming yourself quite unnecessarily, Emma. It is possible that this girl may repeat anything that she chances to overhear, and it is probable that she will do her best to strike up a flirtation with Henry, if he is foolish enough to allow it; for persons of this kind always avail themselves of such an opportunity—generally with a view to future compensation. But Henry is a cautious individual, who has never been known to commit himself in that fashion, and I don't see why he should begin now; though I do think it would be a good thing if that young lady could be sent about her business. At the worst, however, there would only be some temporary entanglement, such as happens every day, and means nothing serious."

"Nothing serious? I am sure it would be serious enough if that girl had to do with it: she is not a flirt—she looks too strong and earnest for that kind of thing; and if once she made him fond of her, she would never let him go."

"Perhaps," answered Ellen; "but first of all she has to make him fond of her, and I have reasons for knowing, even if she wishes to do this, that she will find it a little difficult."

"What reasons?" asked Emma.

"Only that a man like Henry does not generally fall in love with two women at the same time," Ellen answered drily.

"Is he—is he already in love, then?"

"Yes, dear; unless I am very much mistaken, he is already in love—with you."

"I doubt it," Emma answered, shaking her head. "But even if it should be so, there will be an end of it if he hears of my behaviour on that night. And he is sure to hear: I know that he will hear."

And, as though overcome by the bitterness of her position, Emma put her hands before her eyes, then turned suddenly and walked into the house.

CHAPTER XII

ELLEN FINDS A REMEDY

When Emma had gone Ellen settled herself comfortably in a garden chair, sighed, and began to fan her face with a newspaper which lay at hand. Her mind was agitated, for it had become obvious to her that the position was full of complications, which at present her well-meant efforts had increased rather than diminished.

"I only hope that I may be forgiven for all the white lies I have been forced to tell this morning," she reflected. Ellen did not consider her various embellishments of the truth as deserving of any harsher name, since it seemed to her not too sensitive conscience, that if Jove laughs at lovers' perjuries, he must dismiss with a casual smile the prevarications of those who wish to help other people to become lovers.

Still Ellen felt aggrieved, foreseeing the possibility of being found out and placed in awkward positions. Oh, what fools they were, and how angry she was with both of them—with Emma for her schoolgirlish sentiment, and with Henry for his idiotic pride and his headstrong obstinacy! Surely the man must be mad to wish to fling away such a girl as Emma and her fortune, to say nothing of the romantic devotion that she cherished for him, little as he deserved it—a devotion which Ellen imagined would have been flattering to the self-conceit of any male. It was hard on her that she should be obliged to struggle against such rank and wrong-headed stupidity, and even driven to condescend to plots and falsehoods. After all, it was not for her own benefit that she did this, or only remotely so, since she was well provided for; though it was true that, should she become involved in an immediate financial scandal, her matrimonial prospects might be affected.

No, it was for the benefit of her family, the interests of which, to do her justice, Ellen had more at heart than any other earthly thing, her own welfare of course expected. Should this marriage fall through, ruin must overtake their house, and their name would be lost, in all probability never to be heard again. It seemed impossible to her that her brother should wish to reject the salvation which was so freely proffered to him; and yet, maddening as the thought might be, she could not deny that she saw signs of such a desire. Well, she would not give up the game; tired as she was of it, she would fight to the last ditch. Were she to draw back now, she felt that she should fail in her most sacred duty.

As Ellen came to this determination she saw Mr. Levinger walking towards her. He was leaning on his stick, as usual, and looked particularly refined in his summer suit and grey wide-awake hat.

"How do you do, Miss Graves?" he said, in his gentle voice: "I heard that you were here, but did not come out because I thought you might wish to have a chat with Emma. Where has she gone?"

"I don't know," Ellen answered, as they shook hands.

"Well, I dare say that she will be back presently. How hot it is here! Would you like to come and sit in my study till luncheon is ready?" And he led the way to a French window that opened on to the lawn.

Mr. Levinger's study was a very comfortable room, and its walls were lined with books almost to the ceiling. Books also lay about on the desk. Evidently he had risen from reading one of them, and Ellen noticed with surprise that it was Jeremy Taylor's "Holy Living."

"How is your brother to-day?" he asked, when they were seated.

Ellen reflected a moment, and determined to take advantage of the opportunity to unbosom herself.

"He is doing as well as possible, thank you. Still I am anxious about him."

"Why? I thought that he was clear of all complications except the chance of a limp like mine."

"I did not mean that I was anxious about his health, Mr. Levinger. I am sure that you will forgive me if I am frank with you, so I will speak out."

He bowed expectantly, and Ellen went on:

"My father has told me, and indeed I know it from what you have said to me at different times, that for various reasons you would be glad if Henry and Emma—made a match of it."

Again Mr. Levinger bowed.

"I need not say that our family would be equally glad; and that Emma herself would be glad we learned from what she said the other day. There remains therefore only one person who could object—Henry himself. As you know, he is a curiously sensitive man, especially where money matters are concerned, and I believe firmly that the fact of this marriage being so greatly to his advantage, and to that of his family, is the one thing which makes him hesitate, for I am sure, from the way in which he has spoken of her, that he is much attracted by Emma. Had he come here to stay, however, I fancy that all this would have passed off, and by now they might have been happily engaged, or on the verge of it; but you see, this accident happened, and he is laid up—unfortunately, not here."

"He will not be laid up for ever, Miss Graves. As you say, I am anxious for this marriage, and I hope that it will come about in due course."

"No, he will not be laid up for ever; but what I fear is, that it may be too long for Emma's and his own welfare."

"You must pardon me, but I do not quite understand."

"Then you must pardon me if I speak to you without reserve. You may have noticed that there is a singularly handsome girl at the Bradmouth inn. I mean Joan Haste."

At the mention of this name Mr. Levinger rose suddenly from his chair and walked to the end of the room, where he appeared to lose himself in the contemplation of the morocco backs of an encyclopedia. Presently he turned, and it struck Ellen that his face was strangely agitated, though at this distance she could not be sure.

"Yes, I know the girl," he said in his usual voice—"the one who brought about the accident. What of her?"

"Only this: I fear that, unless something is done to prevent it, she may bring about another and a greater accident. Listen, Mr. Levinger. I have no facts to go on, or at least very few, but I have my eyes and my instinct. If I am not mistaken, Joan Haste is in love with Henry, and doing her best to make him in love with her—an effort in which, considering her opportunities, her great personal advantages, and the fact that men generally do become fond of their nurses, she is likely enough to succeed, for he is just the kind of person to make a fool of himself in this way."

"What makes you think so?" asked Mr. Levinger, with evident anxiety.

"A hundred things: when he was not himself he would scarcely allow her out of his sight, and now it is much the same. But I go more by what I saw upon her face during all that day of the crisis, and the way in which she looks at him when she fancies that no one is observing her. Of course I may be wrong, and a passing flirtation with a village beauty is not such a very serious matter, or would not be in the case of most men; but, on the other hand, perhaps I am right, and where an obstinate person like my brother Henry is concerned, the consequences might prove fatal to all our hopes."

Mr. Levinger seemed to see the force of this contention, and indeed Ellen had put the case very sensibly and clearly. At any rate he did not try to combat it.

"What do you suggest?" he asked. "You are a woman of experience and common sense, and I am sure that you have thought of a remedy before speaking to me."

"My suggestion is, that Joan should be got out of the way as quickly as possible; and I have consulted you, Mr. Levinger, because your interest in the matter is as strong as my own, and you are the only person who can get rid of her."

"Why do you say that?" he asked, rising for the second time. "The girl is of age, and I cannot control her movements."

"Is she? I was not aware of her precise age," answered Ellen; "but I have noticed, Mr. Levinger, that you seem to have a great deal of authority in all sorts of unsuspected places, and perhaps if you think it over a little you may find that you have some here. For instance, I believe that you own the Crown and Mitre, and I should fancy, from what I have seen of her, that Mrs. Gillingwater, the aunt, is a kind of person who might be approached with some success. There goes the bell for luncheon, and as I think I have said everything that occurs to me, I will run up to Emma's room and wash my hands."

"The bell for luncheon," mused Mr. Levinger, looking after her. "Well, I have not often been more glad to hear it. That woman has an alarming way of putting things; and I wonder how much she knows, or if she was merely stabbing in the dark? Gone to wash her hands, has she? Yes, I see, and left me to wash mine, if I can. Anyway, she is sharp as a needle, and she is right. The man will have no chance with that girl if she chooses to lay siege to him. Her mother before her was fascinating enough, and she was nothing compared to Joan, either in looks or mind. She must be got rid of: but how?" and he looked round as though searching for a clue, till his eye fell upon the book that lay open before him.

"Holy Living," he said, shutting it impatiently: "no more of that for me to-day, or for some time to come. I have other things to think of now, things that I hoped I had done with. Well, there goes the bell for luncheon, and I must go too, but without washing my hands," and he stared at his delicate fingers. "After all, they do not look so very dirty; even Ellen Graves will scarcely notice them"; and laughing bitterly at his own jest he left the room.

That afternoon Mr. Levinger had a long conversation with Mrs. Gillingwater, whom he sent for to see him after Ellen had gone.

With the particulars of this interview we need not concern ourselves, but the name of Samuel Rock was mentioned in it.

On the following morning it chanced that Mr. Samuel Rock received a letter from Mr. Levinger referring to the erection of a cattle-shed upon some fifty acres of grass land which he held as that gentleman's tenant. This cattle-shed Samuel had long desired; indeed, it is not too much to say that he had clamoured for it, for he did not belong to that class of tenant which considers the landlord's pocket, or makes shift without improvements when they can be had by importunity. Consequently, as was suggested in the letter, he hastened to present himself at Monk's Lodge on that very afternoon, adorned in his shiniest black coat and his broadest-brimmed wide-awake.

"The man looks more like a Methodist parson than ever," thought Mr. Levinger, as he watched his advent. "I wonder if she will have anything to say to him? Well, I must try."

In due course Samuel Rock was shown in, and took the chair that was offered to him, upon the very edge of which he seated himself in a gingerly fashion, his broad hat resting on his knee. Mr. Rock's manner towards his landlord was neither defiant nor obsequious, but rather an unhappy combination of these two styles. He did not touch his forehead according to the custom of the old-times tenant, nor did he offer to shake hands. His greeting consisted of a jerky bow, lacking alike dignity and politeness, a half-hearted salute which seemed to aim at compromise between a certain respect for tradition and a proper sense of the equality of all men in the sight of Heaven.

"How do you do, Mr. Rock?" said Mr. Levinger cheerfully. "I thought that I would ask you to have a chat with me on the matter of that cowshed, about which you spoke at the audit last January—rather strongly, if I remember."

"Yes, Mr. Levinger, sir," answered Samuel, in a hesitating but mellifluous voice. "I shall be very glad to speak about it. A shed is needed on those marshes, sir, where we look to let the cattle lie out till late in autumn, untempered to all the winds of heaven, which blow keen down there, and also in the spring; and I hope you see your way to build one, Mr. Levinger, else I fear that I shall have to give you notice and find others more accommodating."

"Really! do you think so? Well, if you wish to do that, I am ready to meet you half way and accept short service, so that you can clear out next Michaelmas; for I don't mind telling you that I know another party who will be glad to take the land."

"Indeed, sir, I was not aware," answered Samuel, running his fingers through his straight hair uncomfortably—for the last thing that he desired was to part with these particular marshes. "Not that I should wish to stand between a landlord and a better offer in these times. Still, Mr. Levinger, I don't hold it right, as between man and man, to slip like that behind a tenant's back as has always paid his rent."

The conversation, which was a long one, need not be pursued further. Samuel was of the opinion that Mr. Levinger should bear the entire cost of the shed, which the latter declined to do. At length, however, an arrangement was effected that proved mutually satisfactory; the "said landlord" agreeing to find all material necessary, and to pay the skilled labour, and the "said tenant" undertaking to dig the holes for the posts and to cut the reed for the thatch.

"Ah, Mr. Rock," said Levinger, as he signed a note of their contract, "it is very well for you to pretend that you are hard up; but I know well enough, notwithstanding the shocking times, that you are the warmest man in these parts. You see you began well, with plenty of capital; and though you rent some, you have been wise enough to keep your own land in hand, and not trust it to the tender mercies of a tenant. That, combined with good farming, careful living and hard work, is what has made you rich, when many others are on the verge of ruin. You ought to be getting a wife, Mr. Rock, and starting a family of your own, for if anything happened to you there is nowhere for the property to go."

"We are in the Lord's hands, sir, and man is but grass," answered Samuel sententiously, though it was clear from his face that he did not altogether appreciate this allusion to his latter end. "Still, under the mercy of Heaven, having my health, and always being careful to avoid chills, I hope to see a good many younger men out yet. And as for getting married, Mr. Levinger, I think it is the whole duty of man, or leastways half of it, when he has earned enough to support a wife and additions which she may bring with her. But the thing is to find the woman, sir, for it isn't every girl that a careful Christian would wish to wed."

"Quite so, Mr. Rock. Have a glass of port, won't you?"—and Mr. Levinger poured out some wine from a decanter which stood on the table and pushed it towards him. Then, taking a little himself by way of company, he added, "I should have thought that you could find a suitable person about here."

"Your health, sir," said Samuel, drinking off the port and setting down the glass, which Mr. Levinger refilled. "I am not saying, sir," he added, "that such a girl cannot be found—I am not even saying that I have not found such a girl: that's one thing, marrying is another."

"Ah! indeed," said Mr. Levinger.

Again Samuel lifted his glass and drank half its contents. The wine was of the nature that is known as "full-bodied," and, not having eaten for some hours, it began to take effect on him. Samuel grew expansive.

"I wonder, sir," he said, "if I might take a liberty? I wonder if I might ask your advice? I should be grateful if you would give it to me, for I know that you have the cleverest head of any gentleman in these parts. Also, sir, you are no talker."

"I shall be delighted if I can be of any service to an old friend and tenant like yourself," answered Mr. Levinger airily. "What is the difficulty?"

Samuel finished the second glass of wine, and felt it go ever so little to his head; for which he was not sorry, as it made him eloquent.

"The difficulty is this, sir. Thank you—just a taste more. I don't drink wine myself, as a rule—it is too costly; but this is real good stuff, and maketh glad the heart of man, as in the Bible. Well, sir, here it is in a nutshell: I want to marry a girl; I am dead set on it; but she won't have me, or at least she puts me off."

"Why not try another, then?"

"Because I won't want no other, Mr. Levinger, sir," he answered, suddenly taking fire. The wine had done its work with him, and moreover this was the one subject that had the power to break through the cold cunning which was a characteristic of his nature. "I want this girl or none, and I mean to have her if I wait half a lifetime for her."

"You are in earnest, at any rate, which is a good augury for your success. And who may the lady be?"

"Who may she be? Why, I thought you knew! There's only one about here that she could be. Joan Haste, of course."

"Joan Haste! Ah! Yes, she is a handsome and attractive girl."

"Handsome and attractive? Eh! she is all that. To me she is what the sun is to the corn and the water to the fish. I can't live without her. Look here: I have watched her for years, ever since she was a child. I have summered her and wintered her, as the saying is, thinking that I wouldn't make no mistake about her, whatever I might feel, nor give myself away in a hurry, seeing that I wanted to keep what I earn for myself, and not to spend it on others just because a pretty face chanced to take my fancy."

"Perhaps you have been a little too careful under the circumstances, Mr. Rock."

"Maybe I have: anyway, it has come home to me now. A month or so back I spoke out, because I couldn't keep myself in no longer."

"To Joan Haste?"

"Yes, to Joan Haste. Her aunt knew about it before, but she didn't seem able to help me much."

"And what did Joan say?"

"She said that she did not love me, and that she never would love me nor marry me; but she said also that she had no thought for any other man."

"Excuse me, Mr. Rock, but did this interview happen before Captain Graves and Joan Haste met with their accident in Ramborough Abbey? I want to fix the date, that's all."

"It happened on that same afternoon, sir. The Captain must have come along just after I left."

And Samuel paused, passing his white hands over each other uneasily, as though he were washing them, for Mr. Levinger's question seemed to suggest some new and unpleasant idea in his mind.

"Well?"

"Well, there isn't much more to say, sir, except that I think I was a bit unlucky in the way I put it to her; for it slipped out of my mouth about her father never having had a name, and that seemed to anger her."

"Perhaps it was not the best possible way to ingratiate yourself with the young woman," replied Mr. Levinger sweetly. "So you came to no understanding with her?"

"Well, I did and I didn't. I found out that she is afraid for her life of her aunt, who favours me; so I made a bargain with her that, if she would let the matter stand open for six months, I'd promise to say nothing to Mrs. Gillingwater."

"I see: you played upon the girl's fears. Doubtful policy again, I think."

"It was the best I could do, sir; for starving dogs must eat offal, as the saying is. And now, Mr. Levinger, if you can help me, I shall be a grateful man all my days. They do say down in Bradmouth that you know something about Joan's beginnings, and have charge of her in a way, and that is why I made bold to speak to you; for I only promised to be mum to her aunt."

"Do they indeed, Mr. Rock? Truly in Bradmouth their tongues are long and their ears are open. And yet, as you are seeking to marry her, I do not mind telling you that there is enough truth in this report to give it colour. As it chances, I did know something of Joan's father, though I am not at liberty to mention his name. He was a gentleman, and has been dead many years; but he left me, not by deed but in an informal manner, in a position of some responsibility towards her, and entrusted me with a sum of money—small, but sufficient—to be employed for her benefit, at my entire discretion, which was only hampered by one condition—namely, that she should not be educated as a lady. Now, Mr. Rock, I have told you so much in order to make matters clear; but I will add this to it: if you repeat a single word, either to Joan herself or to anybody else, you need hope for no help from me in your suit. You see I am perfectly frank with you. I ask no promises, but I appeal to your interests."

"I understand, sir; but the mischief of it is, whether you wished it or not, you have made a lady of her, and that is why she looks down on me; or perhaps, being in her blood, it will out."

"It would be possible to suggest other reasons for her unwillingness to accept your offer," replied Mr. Levinger drily; "but this is neither here nor there. On the whole I approve of your suit, provided that you are ready to make proper settlements upon Joan, for I know you are a thriving man, and I see that you are attached to her."

"I'll do anything that I can, sir, for I have no mind to stint money in this matter. But though you are so kind as to wish me well, I don't see how that sets me any forrarder with Joan."

"Perhaps you will in a few days' time, though. And now I've got a bit of advice to give you: don't you bother about that six months' promise. You go at her again—in a week, let us say. You know how she is employed now, do you not?"

"I have heard that she is helping to nurse the Captain."

"Quite so: she is helping to nurse the Captain. Now, please understand that I make no imputations, but I don't know if you consider this a suitable occupation for a beautiful young woman whom you happen to wish to marry. Captain Graves is a very fine fellow, and people sometimes grow intimate under such circumstances. Joan told you that she cared for no man on the tenth of June. Perhaps if you wait till the tenth of December she may not be able to say so much."

By this time the poison of Mr. Levinger's hints had sunk deep into his hearer's mind; though had he known Samuel's character more thoroughly, he might have thought the danger of distilling it greater than any advantage that was to be gained thereby. Indeed, a minute later, he regretted having said so much, for, glancing at him, he saw that Rock was deeply affected. His sallow face had become red, his quivering lips were livid, and he was snatching at his thin beard.

"Damn him!" he said, springing to his feet; "if he leads her that way, fine fellow or not, I'll do for him. I tell you that if he wants to keep a whole skin, he had better leave my ewe-lamb alone."

In an instant Mr. Levinger saw, that he had set fire to a jealousy fierce enough to work endless mischief, and too late he tried to stamp out the flame.

"Sit down, sir," he said quietly, but in the tone of one who at some time in his career had been accustomed to the command of men; "sit down, and never dare to speak before me like that again. Now," he added, as Samuel obeyed him, "you will apologise to me for those words, and you will dismiss all such thoughts from your mind. Otherwise I tell you that I take back everything I have said, and that you shall never even speak to Joan Haste again."

Samuel's fit of passion had passed by now, or perhaps it had been frightened away, for his face grew pale, paler than usual, and the constant involuntary movement of his furtive hands was the only sign left of the storm that shook him.

"I beg your pardon, sir," he said in a whining voice: "the Lord knows I beg your pardon; and what's more, I didn't mean nothing of what I said. It was jealousy that made me speak so, jealousy bitter as the grave; and when I heard you talk of her getting fond of that Captain—my Joan fond of another man, a gentleman too, who would be bound to treat her as her mother was treated by some villain—it seemed as though all the wickedness in the world bubbled up in my heart and spoke through my mouth."

"There, that will do," answered Mr. Levinger testily. "See that you do not let such wickedness bubble again in your heart, or anywhere else, that's all; for at the first sign of it—and remember I shall have my eye on you—there will be an end of your courtship. And now you had better go. Take my advice and ask her again in a week or so; you can come and tell me how you get on. Good-day."

Samuel picked up his broad hat, bowed, and departed, walking delicately, like Agag, as though he expected at every moment to put his foot upon an egg.

"Upon my word," thought Mr. Levinger, "I'm half afraid of that fellow! I wonder if it is safe to let the girl marry him. On the whole I should think so; he has a great deal to recommend him, and this kind of thing will pass off. She isn't the woman to stand much of it. Anyway, it seems necessary for everybody's welfare, though somehow I doubt if good will come of all this scheming."

CHAPTER XIII

A MEETING BY THE MERE

Mr. Levinger's confidential interview with Mrs. Gillingwater was not long in bearing fruit. Joan soon became aware that her aunt was watching her closely, and most closely of all whenever she chanced to be in attendance on Henry, with whom she now was left alone as little as possible. The effect of this knowledge was to produce an intense irritation in her mind. Her conscience was guilty, but Joan was not a woman to take a warning from a guilty conscience. Indeed, its sting only drove her faster along the downward road, much as a high-mettled horse often rebels furiously under the punishment of the whip. There was a vein of self-willed obstinacy and of "devil-may-caredness" in Joan's nature that, dormant hitherto, at this crisis in her life began to assert itself with alarming power. Come what might, she was determined to have her way and not to be thwarted. There is this to be said in excuse for her, that now her whole being was dominated by her passion for Henry. In the ordinary sense of the word it was not love that possessed her, nor was it strictly what is understood by passion, but rather, if it can be defined at all, some strange new force, some absorbing influence that included both love and passion, and yet had mysterious qualities of its own. Fortunately, with English women such infatuations are not common, though they are to found frequently enough among people of the Latin race, where sometimes they result in blind tragedies that seem almost inexplicable to our sober sense. But, whatever the cause, Joan had fallen a victim to this fate, and now it mastered her, body and mind and soul. She had never cared for any one before, and on Henry she let loose the pent-up affections of a lifetime. No breath of passion had ever moved her, and now a look from his eyes or a touch of his hand stirred all the fibres of her nature as the wind stirs every leaf upon a tree. He was her darling, her desire. Till she had learnt to love him she had not know the powers and the possibilities of life, and if she could win his love she would even have been willing to pay for it at the price of her own death.

The approach of such an infatuation would have terrified most girls: they would have crushed it, or put themselves beyond its reach before it took hold of them. But then the majority of young English women, even of those who belong to the humbler walks of life, do not stand by their own strength alone. Either they have an inherited sense of the proprieties that amounts almost to an instinct, or they possess strong religious principles, or there are those about them who guide and restrain any dangerous tendency in their natures. At the very least they are afraid of losing the respect and affection of their friends and relatives, and of becoming a mark for the sneers and scandal of the world in which they move.

In Joan's case these influences were for the most part lacking. From childhood she had lived beneath the shadow of a shame that, in some degree, had withered her moral sense; no father or mother gave her their tender guidance, and of religion she had been taught so little that, though she conformed to its outward ceremonies, it could not be said to have any real part in her life. Relatives she had none except her harsh and coarse-minded aunt; her few friends made at a middle-class school were now lost to her, for with the girls of her own rank in the village she would not associate, and those of better standing either did, or affected to look down upon her. In short, her character was compounded of potentialities for good and evil; she was sweet and strong-natured and faithful, but she had not learned that these qualities are of little avail to bring about the happiness or moral well-being of her who owns them, unless they are dominated by a sense of duty. Having such a sense, the best of us are liable to error in this direction or in that; wanting it, we must indeed be favoured if we escape disaster among the many temptations of life. It was Joan's misfortune rather than her fault, for she was the victim of her circumstances and not of any innate depravity, that she lacked this controlling power, and in this defenceless state found herself suddenly exposed to the fiercest temptation that can assail a woman of her character and gifts, the temptation to give way to a love which, if it did not end in empty misery, could only bring shame upon herself and ceaseless trouble and remorse to its object.

Thus it came about that during these weeks Joan lived in a wild and fevered dream, lived for the hour only, thinking little and caring less of what the future might bring forth. Her purpose, so far as she can be said to have had one, was to make Henry love her, and to the consummation of this end she brought to bear all her beauty and every power of her mind. That success must mean sorrow to her and to him did not affect her, though in her wildest moments she never dreamed of Henry as her husband. She loved him to-day, and to-day he was there for her to love: let the morrow look to itself, and the griefs that it might bring.

If such was Joan's attitude towards Henry, it may be asked what was Henry's towards Joan. The girl attracted him strangely, after a fashion in which he had never been attracted by a woman before. Her fresh and ever-varying loveliness was a continual source of delight to him, as it must have been to any man; but by degrees he became conscious that it was not her beauty alone which moved him. Perhaps it was her tenderness—a tenderness apparent in every word and gesture; or more probably it may have been the atmosphere of love that surrounded her, of love directed towards himself, which gradually conquered him mind and body, and broke down the barrier of his self-control. Hitherto Henry had never cared for any woman, and if women had cared for him he had not understood it. Now he was weak and he was worried, and in his way he also was rebellious, and fighting against a marriage that men and circumstances combined to thrust upon him. Under such conditions it was not perhaps unnatural that he should shrink back from the strict path of interest, and follow that of a spontaneous affection. Joan had taken his fancy from the first moment that he saw her, she had won his gratitude by her bravery and her gentle devotion, and she was a young and beautiful woman. Making some slight allowances for the frailties of human nature, perhaps we need not seek for any further explanation of his future conduct.

For a week or more nothing of importance occurred between them. Indeed, they were very seldom alone together, for whenever Joan's duty took her to the sick room Mrs. Gillingwater, whom Henry detested, made a point of being present, or did she chance to be called away, his sister Ellen would be certain to appear to take her place, accompanied at times by Edward Milward.

At length, on a certain afternoon, Mrs. Gillingwater ordered Joan to go out walking. Joan did not wish to go out, for the weather threatened rain, also for her own reasons she preferred to remain where she was. But her aunt was peremptory, and Joan started, setting her face towards Ramborough Abbey. Very soon it came on to rain and she had no umbrella, but this accident did not deter her. She had been sent out to walk, and walk she would. To tell the truth, she was thinking little of the weather, for her mind was filled with resentment against her aunt. It was unbearable that she should be interfered with and ordered about like a child. There were a hundred things that she wished to do in the house. Who would give Captain Graves his tea? And she was sure that he would never remember about the medicine unless she was there to remind him.

As Joan proceeded on her walk along the edge of the cliff, she noticed the figure of a man, standing about a quarter of a mile to her right on the crest or hog's back of land, beyond which lay the chain of melancholy meres, and wondered vaguely what he could be doing there in such weather. At length it occurred to her that it was time to return, for now she was near to Ramborough Abbey. She was weary of the sight of the sea, that moaned sullenly beneath her, half hidden by the curtain of the rain; so she struck across the ridge of land, heedless of the wet saline grasses that swept against her skirt, purposing to walk home by the little sheep-track which follows the edge of the meres in the valley. As she was crossing the highest point of the ridge she saw the man's figure again. Suddenly it disappeared, and the thought struck her that he might have been following her, keeping parallel to her path. For a moment Joan hesitated, for the country here was very lonely, especially in such weather; but the next she dismissed her fears, being courageous by nature, and passed on towards the first mere. Doubtless this person was a shepherd looking for a lost sheep, or perhaps a gamekeeper.

The aspect of the lakes was so dreary, and the path so sopping wet, that soon Joan began to wish that she had remained upon the cliff. However, she trudged on bravely, the rain beating in her face till her thin dress was soaked and clung to her shape in a manner that was picturesque but uncomfortable. At the head of the second mere the sheep-walk ran past some clumps of high reeds; and as she approached them Joan, whose eye for natural objects was quick, observed that something had disturbed the wild fowl which haunted the place, for a heron and a mallard rose and circled high in the air, and a brace of curlew zigzagged away against the wind, uttering plaintive cries that reached her for long after they vanished into the mist. Now she had come to the first clump of reeds, when she heard a stir behind them, and a man stepped forward and stood in the middle of the path within three paces of her.

The man was Samuel Rock, clad in a long cloak; and, recognising him, Joan understood that she had been waylaid. She halted and said angrily—for her first feeling was one of indignation:

"What are you doing here, Mr. Rock?"

"Walking, Miss Haste," he answered nervously; "the same as you."

"That is not true, Mr. Rock: you were hiding behind those reeds."

"I took shelter there against the rain."

"I see; you took shelter from the rain, and on the weather side of the reeds," she said contemptuously. "Well, do not let me keep you standing in this wet." And she attempted to pass him.

"It is no use telling you lies," he muttered sullenly: "I came here to speak to you, where there ain't none to disturb us." And as he spoke Samuel Rock placed himself in such a position that it was impossible for her to escape him without actually breaking into a run.

"Why do you follow me," she said in an indignant voice—"after what you promised, too? Stand aside and let me go home."

Samuel made no move, but a curious light came into his blue eyes, a light that was not pleasant to see.

"I am thinking I've stood aside enough, Joan," he answered, "and I ain't a-going to stand aside till all the mischief is done and I am ruined. As for promises, they may go hang: I can't keep no more of them. So please, you'll just stand for once, and listen to what I have to say to you. If you are wet you can take my cloak. I don't mind the rain, and I seem to want some cooling."

"I'd rather drown than touch anything that belongs to you," she replied, for her hatred of the man mastered her courtesy and reason. "Say what you've got to say and let me go on."

The remark was an unfortunate one, for it awoke in Samuel's breast the fury that accompanied and underlay his passion, that fury which had astonished Mr. Levinger.

"Would you, now!" he broke out, his lips turning white with rage. "Well, if half I hear is true, there's others whose things you don't mind touching."

"What do you mean, Mr. Rock?"

"I mean that Captain whom you're not ashamed to be hanging after all day long. Oh, I know about you. I heard how you were found holding him in your arms, the first day that you met him by the tower yonder, after you'd been flirting with him like any street girl, till you brought him to break his leg. Yes, holding him in those arms of yours—nothing less."

"Oh! how dare you! How dare you!" she murmured, for no other words would come to her.

"Dare? I dare anything. You've worked me up to that, my beauty. Now I dare ask you when you'll let me make an honest woman of you, if it isn't too late."

By this time Joan was positively speechless, so great were the rage and loathing with which this man and his words filled her.

"Oh! Joan," he went on, with a sudden change of tone, "do you forgive me if I have said sharp things, for it's you that drives me to them with your cruelty; and I'm ready to forgive you all yours—ay! I'd bear to hear them again, for you look so beautiful when you are like that."

"Forgive you!" gasped Joan.

But he did not seem to hear. "Let's have done with this cat-and-dog quarrelling," he went on; "let's make it up and get married, the sooner the better—to-morrow if you like. You will never regret it; you'll be happier then than with that Captain who loves Miss Levinger, not you; and I, I shall be happy too—happy, happy!" And he flung his arms wide, in a kind of ecstasy.

Of all this speech only one sentence seemed to reach Joan's understanding at any rate at the time: "who loves Miss Levinger, not you." Oh! was it true? Did Captain Graves really love Miss Levinger as she knew that Emma loved him? The man spoke certainly, as though he had knowledge. Even in the midst of her unspeakable anger, the thought pierced her like a spear and caused her face to soften and her eyes to grow troubled.

Samuel saw these signs, and misinterpreted them, thinking that her resentment was yielding beneath his entreaties. For a moment he stood searching his mind for more words, but unable to find them; then suddenly he sought to clinch the matter in another fashion, for, following the promptings of an instinct that was natural enough under the circumstances, however ill-advised it might be, suddenly he caught Joan in his long arms, and drawing her to him, kissed her twice passionately upon the face. At first Joan scarcely seemed to understand what had happened—indeed, it was not until Samuel, encouraged by his success, was about to renew his embraces that she awoke to the situation. Then her action was prompt enough. She was a strong woman, and the emergency doubled her strength. With a quick twisting movement of her form and a push of her hands, she shook off Samuel so effectively, that in staggering back his foot slipped in the greasy soil and he fell upon his side, clutching in his hand a broad fragment from the bosom of Joan's dress, at which he had caught to save himself.

"Now," she said, as Samuel rose slowly from the mire, "listen to me. You have had your say, and I will have mine. First understand this: if ever you try to kiss me again it will be the worse for you; for your own sake I advise you not, for I think that I should kill you if I could. I hate you, Samuel Rock, for you have lied to me, and you have insulted me in a way that no woman can forgive. I will never marry you—I had rather beg my bread; so if you are wise, you will forget all about me, or at the least keep out of my way."

Samuel faced the beautiful woman, who, notwithstanding her torn and draggled dress, looked royal in her scorn and anger. He was very white, but his passion seemed to have left him, and he spoke in a quiet voice.

"Don't be afraid," he said; "I'm not going to try and kiss you again. I have kissed you twice; that is enough for me at present. And what's more, though you may rub your face, you can't rub it out of your mind. But you are wrong when you say that you won't marry me, because you will. I know it. And the first time I kiss you after we are married, I will remind you of this, Joan Haste. I am not going to ask you to have me again. I shall wait till you ask me to take you, and then I shall be revenged upon you. That day will come, the day of your shame and need, the day of my reward, when, as I have lain in the dirt before you, you will lie in the dirt before me. That is all I have to say. Good-bye." And he walked past her, vanishing behind the reeds.

Now it was for the first time that Joan felt afraid. The insult and danger had gone by, yet she was frightened, horribly frightened; for though the thing seemed impossible, it was borne in upon her mind that Samuel Rock's presentiment was true, and that an hour might come when, in some sense, she would lie in the mire before him and seek a refuge as his wife. She could not conceive any circumstances in which a thing so horrible might happen, for however sore her necessity, though she shrank from death, it seemed to her that it would be better to die rather than to suffer such a fate. Yet so deeply did this terror shake her, that she turned and looked upon the black waters of the mere, wondering if it would not be better to give it the lie once and for all. Then she thought of Henry, and her mood changed, for her mind and body were too healthy to allow her to submit herself indefinitely to such forebodings. Like many women, Joan was an opportunist, and lived very much in the day and for it. These things might be true, but at least they were not yet; if she was destined to be the wife of Samuel Rock in the future, she was her own mistress in the present, and the shadow of sorrow and bonds to come, so she argued, suggested the strongest possible reasons for rejoicing in the light and liberty of the fleeting hour. If she was doomed to an earthly hell, if her hands must be torn by thorns and her eyes grow blind with tears, at least she was minded to be able to remember that once she had walked in Paradise, gathering flowers there, and beholding her heart's desire.

Thus she reasoned in her folly, as she tramped homewards through the rain, heedless of the fact that no logic could be more fatal, and none more pleasing to that tempter who as of old lurks in paradises such as her fancy painted.

When she reached home Joan found her aunt awaiting her in the bar parlour.

"Who has been keeping you all this time in the wet, Joan?" she asked in a half expectant voice.

Joan lit a candle before she answered, for the place was gloomy.

"Do you wish to know?" she said: "then I will tell you. Your friend, Mr. Samuel Rock, whom you set after me."

"My friend? And what if he is my friend? I'd be glad if I had a few more such." By this time the light had burnt up, and Mrs. Gillingwater saw the condition of her niece's attire. "Good gracious! girl, what have you been doing?" she asked. "Ain't you ashamed to walk about half stripped like that?"

"People must do what they can't help, aunt. That's the work of the friend you are so proud of. I may as well tell you at once, for if I don't, he will. He came making love to me again, as he has before, and finished up by kissing me, the coward, and when I threw him off he tore my dress."

"And why couldn't you have let him kiss you quietly, you silly girl?" asked her aunt with indignation. "Now I dare say that you have offended him so that he won't come forward again, to say nothing of spoiling your new dress. It ain't a crime for a man to kiss the girl he wants to marry, is it?"

"Why? Because I would rather kiss a rat—that's all. I hate the very sight of him; and as for coming forward again, I only hope that he won't, for my sake and for his too."

Now Mrs. Gillingwater arose in her wrath; her coarse face became red and her voice grew shrill.

"You good-for-nothing baggage!" she said; "so that is your game, is it? To go turning up your nose and chucking your impudence in the face of a man like Mr. Rock, who is worth twenty of you, and does you honour by wishing to make a wife of you, you that haven't a decent name to your back, and he rich enough to marry a lady if he liked, or half a dozen of them for the matter of that. Well, I tell you that you shall have him, or I will know the reason why—ay, and so will others too."

"I can't be violent, like you, aunt," answered Joan, who began to feel as though this second scene would be too much for her; "it isn't in my nature, and I hate it. But whether I have a name or not—and it is no fault of mine if I have none, though folk don't seem inclined to let me forget it—I say that I will not marry Samuel Rock. I am a woman full grown and of age; and I know this, that there is no law in the land which can force me to take a husband whom I don't want. And so perhaps, as we have got to live together, you'll stop talking about him."

"Stop talking about him? Never for one hour, till I see you signing your name in the book with him, miss. And as for living together, it won't be long that we shall do that, unless you drop these tantrums and become sensible. Else you may just tramp it for your living, or go and slave as a housemaid if any one will take you, which I doubt they won't without a character, for nobody here will say a good word for you, you wilful, stuck-up thing, for all your fine looks that you are so proud of, and that'll be the ruin of you yet if you're not careful, as they were of your mother before you."

Joan sank into a chair and made no answer. The woman's violence beat her down and was hateful to her. Almost rather would she have faced Samuel Rock, for with him her sex gave her certain advantages.

"I know what you are after," went on Mrs. Gillingwater, with gathering vehemence. "Do you suppose that I have not seen through you all these weeks, though you are so cunning? You are making up to him, you are; not that I have a word to say against him, for he is a nice gentleman enough, only, like the rest of them, so soft that he'll let a pretty face fool him for all his seafaring in foreign parts. Well, look here, Joan: I'll speak to you plain and plump. We never were mother and daughter, so it is no use pretending what we don't feel, and I won't put up with that from you which I might perhaps from my own child, if I had one. You've given me lots of 'truck,' with your contrary ways, ever since you were a little one, and I'm not minded to stand much more of it, for the profit don't run to the worry. What I want you to understand is, that I am set on your pulling it off with Samuel Rock like a broody hen on a nest egg, and I mean to see that chick hatch out; never you mind for why—that's my affair. If you can't see your way to that, then off you go, and pretty sharp too. There, I have said my say, and you can think it over. Now you had best change your clothes and go and look after the Captain, for I have got business abroad to-night. If you don't mend your manners, it will be for the last time, I can tell you."

Joan rose and obeyed without a word.

Mrs. Gillingwater watched her pass, and fell into a reflective mood.

"She is a beauty and no mistake," she thought to herself; "I never saw such another in all my born days. Her mother was well enough, but she wasn't in it with Joan; and what's more, I like her pride. Why should she take that canting chap if she don't want to? I'm paid to back him, and a day's work for a day's wage, that's my motto. But I'd rather see her marry the Captain, and sit in the church a lady, with a fur round her neck and a carriage waiting outside, than snuffle in a chapel praising the Lord with a pack of oily-faced children. If she had the go of a heifer calf, she would marry him though; he is bound to be a baronet, and it would make a ladyship of her, which with a little teaching is just what she is fit to be; for if he ain't almost as sweet on her—and small wonder after all that nursing—as she is on him, I was born in the Flegg Hundred, that's all. But go is just what Joan ain't got, not when she can make anything for herself out of it anyway; she'd do what you like for love, but she wouldn't turn her finger round a teacup to crown herself a queen. Well, there is no helping them as won't help themselves, so I am all for Samuel Rock and a hundred pounds in my pocket, especially as I dare say that I can screw another hundred out of him if I can square Joan, to say nothing of a trifle from the Captain over and above the board for holding my tongue. I suppose he will marry old Levinger's girl, the Captain will; a pale, puling-faced thing she is, and full of soft words as a boiled potato with flour, but she's got plenty of that as will make her look rosy to any landlord in these times. Still, hang me, if I was a man, if I wouldn't rather take Joan and those brown eyes of hers, and snap my fingers at the world, the flesh, and the devil."

Who or what Mrs. Gillingwater meant by "the world, the flesh, and the devil" is not quite evident, but certainly they symbolised persons or conveyed some image to her mind in this connection, for, suiting the action to the word, she snapped her fingers thrice at the empty air, and then sought her bonnet prior to some private expedition in pursuance of pleasure, or more probably of profit.

CHAPTER XIV

SOWING THE WIND

Joan went to her room and took off her wet things, for she was soaked to the skin, clothing herself anew in her Sunday dress—a soft grey garment, with little frills about the neck and wrists. Then she brushed her waving brown hair, twisting it into a loose knot at the back of her head; and, though she did not think of it, no style could have been more becoming to her. Her toilet completed, a few minutes after her aunt left the house, she went to the parlour to get herself some tea, of which she drank two or three cups, for she felt unusually thirsty, but she could scarcely swallow a mouthful. The food seemed to choke her, and when she attempted to eat the effort brought on a feeling of dizziness and a tingling sensation in her limbs.

"I wonder what is the matter with me?" she said to herself. "I feel as though my veins were on fire. I suppose that these scenes have upset me; or perhaps that tea was too strong. Well, I must go and look after Captain Graves. Aunt won't be back till twelve o'clock or so, and it's my last night, so I had better make the most of it. I dare say that they will turn me out of the house to-morrow." And, with a bitter little laugh, she took up the candle preparatory to going to Henry's room.

Near the door Joan paused, and, whether by chance or by design, turned to look at herself in an oak-framed mirror that hung upon the wall, whither doubtless it had been brought from some old house in the neighbourhood, for it was costly and massive in make. Her first glance was cursory, then she held up the candle and began to examine herself more attentively, since, perhaps for the first time in her life, her appearance fascinated her, and she became fully aware of her own loveliness. Indeed, in that moment she was lovely—as lovely as we may imagine the ancient Helen to have been, or any of those women who have set the world aflame. Her brown eyes were filled with a strange light beneath their curving lashes and the clear-cut heavy lids; her sweet mouth dropped a little, like that of a sleeping child, showing the ivory of her teeth between the parted lips; her cheeks glowed like the bloom on a peach; and above, the masses of her gold-brown hair shone faintly in the candlelight. Perhaps it was that the grey dress set it off more perfectly than usual—at least it seemed to Joan, considering herself critically, that her form was worthy of the face above it; and, in truth, it would have been hard to find a woman cast in a more perfect mould. Tall, and somewhat slender for her height, her every movement was full of grace, and revealed some delicacy of limb or neck or carriage.

Seeing herself thus, a new light broke upon Joan's mind, and she understood how it came about that Samuel Rock worshipped her so madly. Well, if mere beauty could move one man thus, why should not beauty and tenderness and love—ah! love that could not be measured—suffice to move another? She smiled at the thought—a slow, sweet smile; and with the smile a sense of her own power entered into her, a power that she had never learned until this moment.

Except for the occasional visits of Mrs. Gillingwater, bringing him his tea or dinner, Henry had been alone that day since one o'clock. Nearly nine weeks had passed from the date of his accident, and although he did not dare as yet to set his injured limb to the ground, in all other respects he was perfectly well, but thinner in the face, which was blanched by confinement and adorned with a short chestnut-coloured beard. So well was he, indeed, that he had been allowed to leave his bed and to take exercise on crutches in the room, though the doctor considered that it would not be wise for him to risk the shaking of a journey home, or even to venture out at present. In this view Henry had acquiesced, although his sister Ellen pooh-poohed it, saying that she was certain that he could be brought safely. The truth was that at the time he had no yearning for the society of his family, or indeed for any other society than that in which he found himself. He was glad to be away from Rosham and the carking care that brooded on the place; he was glad to escape from Ellen and the obnoxious Edward.

Nor did he wish to visit Mr. Levinger at present, for he knew that then he would be expected to propose to his daughter, which for many reasons he did not desire to do. Although she had exaggerated its effects—for, in fact, the matter had almost slipped from his memory—Emma, poor girl, had been right to some extent in her forebodings as to the results of her passionate outburst upon Henry's mind, should he ever hear the story of it. Not that he thought the worse of her: no man thinks the worse of a woman because she either is, or pretends to be, in love with him; but the incident irritated him in that it gave a new twist to a tangled skein. How could he remain on terms of ordinary friendship with a girl who had made such an avowal? It seemed to him difficult, if not impossible. Surely he must either place himself in regard to her upon the footing which she appeared to desire, or he must adopt the easier alternative and keep away from her altogether.

No, he wanted none of their company, and he was glad that it was still unsafe for him to travel, though he longed for the fresh air. But that he did wish for some company became evident to him this afternoon, although he had received with a certain amount of resignation a note in which Ellen informed him that their father seemed so fidgety and unwell that she could not drive over to Bradmouth that day. He could no longer disguise the truth from himself—it was the society of Joan that he desired; and of Joan he had seen less and less during the last fortnight. Neither she nor anybody else had said anything to that effect, but he was convinced that she was being kept out of his way. Why should she be kept out of his way? A guilty conscience gave him the answer readily enough: because it was not desirable that they should remain upon terms of such intimacy. Alas! it was so. He had fought against the fact, ridiculing and denying it up to this very hour, but now that fact had become too strong for him, and as he sat a prey to loneliness and uncomfortable thoughts, he was fain to acknowledge before the tribunal of his own heart that, if he was not in love with Joan, he did not know what was the matter with him. At the least it had come to this: her presence seemed necessary to him, and the prospective pain of parting from her absolutely intolerable.

It is not too much to say that this revelation of his sad plight dismayed Henry. For a moment, indeed, his faculties and judgment were paralysed. To begin with, for him it was a new experience, and therefore the more dangerous and crushing. If this were not a mere momentary madness, and if the girl cared for him as it would appear that he cared for her, what could be the issue? He had no great regard for the prejudice and conventions of caste, but, circumstanced as he was, it seemed absolutely impossible that he should marry her. Had he been independent, provided always that she did care for him, he would have done it gladly enough. But he was not independent, and such an act would mean the utter ruin of his family. More, indeed: if he could bring himself to sacrifice them, he had now no profession and no income. And how would a man hampered and dragged down by a glaring masalliance be able to find fresh employment by means of which he could support a wife?

No, there was an end of it. The thing could not possibly be done. What, then, was the alternative? Clearly one only. To go, and at once. Some men so placed might have found a third solution, but Henry did not belong to this class. His character and sense of right rebelled against any such notion, and the habits of self-restraint in which he had trained himself for years afforded what he believed to be an impregnable rampart, however frail might be the citadel within.

So thought Henry, who as yet had never matched himself in earnest in such a war. There he sat, strong in his rectitude and consciousness of virtue, however much his heart might ache, making mental preparations for his departure on the morrow, till at last he grew tired of them, and found himself wishing that Joan would come to help him to get ready.

He was lying with his back to the door on a sofa placed between the bed and the wide hearth, upon which a small fire had been lighted, for the night was damp and chilly; and just as this last vagrant wish flitted through his mind, a sound attracted his attention, and he turned to discover that it had been realized as swiftly as though he were the owner of Aladdin's lamp. For there, the candle still in her hand, stood Joan, looking at him from the farther side of the hearth.

It has been said that she was struck by her own appearance as she passed towards his room; and that the change she saw in herself cannot have been altogether fancy is evident from the exclamation which burst from Henry as his eyes fell upon her, an exclamation so involuntary that he scarcely knew what he was saying until the words had passed his lips:

"Great Heaven! Joan, how lovely you are to-night! What have you been doing to yourself?"

Next second he could have bitten out his tongue: he had hardly ever paid her a compliment before, and this was the moment that he had chosen to begin! His only excuse was that he could not help himself; the sudden effect of her beauty, which was so strangely transfigured, had drawn the words from him as the sun draws mist.

"Am I?" she asked dreamily; "I am glad if it pleases you."

Here was a strange beginning to his pending announcement of departure, thought Henry. Clearly, he must recover the situation before he made it.

"Where have you been all this afternoon?" he asked in an indifferent voice.

"I have been out walking."

"What, alone, and in the rain?"

"I did not say that I was alone."

"Whom were you with, then? It can't have been your aunt."

"I was with Mr. Samuel Rock: I mean that he met me."

"What, that farmer who Mrs. Gillingwater told me admires you so much?"

"Yes. And what else did she tell you?"

"Well, I think she said she hoped that he would propose to you; but I didn't pay much attention, it seemed too odd."

"Well, however odd it may be, that is just what he has been doing," answered Joan deliberately.

Now Henry understood it all: Joan had accepted this man, and it was love for him that made her breast heave and her eyes shine like stars. He ought to have been delighted—the difficulty was done with, and no trouble could possibly ensue—and behold, instead he was furious. He ought to have congratulated her, to have said the right thing in the right way; but instead of congratulation the only words that passed his lips were such as might have been uttered by a madly jealous and would-be sarcastic boy.

"He proposed to you, did he, and in the rain? How charming! I suppose he kissed you too?"

"Yes," replied Joan—"twice." And slowly she raised her eyes and fixed them upon his face.

What Henry said immediately after that announcement he was never quite able to remember, but it was something strong and almost incoherent. Set on fire by his smouldering jealousy, suddenly his passion flamed up in the magnetised atmosphere of her presence, for on that night her every word and look seemed to be magnetic and to pierce him through and through. For a minute or more he denounced her, and all the while Joan stood silent, watching him with her wide eyes, the light shining on her face. At last he ceased and she spoke.

"I do not understand you," she said. "Why are you angry with me? What do you mean?"

"I don't know," he gasped. "I have no right to be angry, I think I must be mad, for I can't even recollect what I have been saying. I suppose that I was astonished to hear that you were engaged to Mr. Rock, that's all. Please forgive me and forget my words. And, if you don't mind, perhaps you had better go away."

"I don't wish to forget them, although I dare say that they mean nothing; and I am not engaged to Mr. Rock—I hate him," answered Joan in the same slow voice; adding, "If you have patience, will you listen to a story? I should like to tell it you before we part, for I think that we have been good friends, and friends should know each other, so that they may remember one another truly when their affection has become nothing but a memory."

Henry nodded; and still very deliberately, as though she wished to avoid all appearance of haste or of excitement, Joan sat herself down upon a footstool in front of the dying fire and began to speak, always keeping her sad eyes fixed upon his face.

"It is not such a very long story," she said, "and the only part of it that has any interest began on that day when we met. I suppose they have told you that I am nobody, and worse than nobody. I do not know who my father was, though I think"—and she smiled as though some coincidence had struck her—"that he was a gentleman whom my mother fell in love with. Mr. Levinger has to do with me in some way; I believe that he paid for my education when I went to school, but I am not sure even about this, and why he should have done so I can't tell. Mr. Samuel Rock is a dissenter and a farmer; they say that he is the richest man in Bradmouth. I don't know why—it was no fault of mine, for I always disliked him every much—but he took a fancy to me years ago, although he said nothing about it at the time. After I came back from school my aunt urged me continually to accept his attentions, but I kept out of his way until that afternoon when I met you. Then he found me sitting under the tower at Ramborough Abbey, where I had gone to be alone because I was cross and worried; and he proposed to me, and was so strange and violent in his manner that he frightened me. What I was most afraid of, however, was that he would tell my aunt that I had refused him—for I did refuse him—and that she would make my life more of a misery than it is already, for you see I have no friends here, where everybody looks down upon me, and nothing to do. So in the end I struck a bargain with him, that he should leave me alone for six months, and that then I would give him a final answer, provided that he promised to say nothing of what had happened to my aunt. He has not kept his promise, for to-day he waylaid me and was very insolent and brutal, so much so that at last he caught hold of me and kissed me against my will, tearing my dress half off me, and I pushed him away and told him what I thought of him. The end of it was that he swore that he would marry me yet, and left me. Then I came back home, and an hour ago I told my aunt what had happened, and there was a scene. She said that either I should marry Samuel Rock or be turned out of the house in a day or two, so I suppose that I must go. And that is all my story."

"The brute!" muttered Henry. "I wish I had him on board a man-of-war: I'd teach him manners. And what are you going to do, Joan?"

"I don't know. Work if I can, and starve if I can't. It doesn't matter; nobody will miss me, or care what happens to me."

"Don't say that, Joan," he answered huskily; "I—I care, for one."

"It is very good of you to say so, but you see you have others to care for besides me. There is Miss Levinger, for instance."

"I have told you once already that I am not engaged to Miss Levinger."

"Yes, but a time will come when you will tell me, or others, that you are; and I think that you will be right—she is a sweet girl. And now, sir," she added, with a total change of manner, "I think that I had better tidy up and bid you good night, and good-bye, for I dare say that I shall come back here no more. I can't wait to be driven out like a strange dog." And she began to perform her various sickroom duties with a mechanical precision.

Henry watched her for a while, until at length all was done and she made ready to go. Then the heart which he had striven to repress burst its bonds, and he sat up and said to her, in a voice that was almost a cry—

"Oh! Joan, I don't know what has come to me, but I can't bear to part with you, though it is best that you should go, for I cannot offer to marry you. I wish to Heaven that I could."

She came and stood beside him.

"I will remember those words as long as I live," she said, "because I know that they are true. I know also why you could not marry me; for we hear all the gossip, and putting that aside it would be your ruin, though for me it might be heaven."

"Do you really care about me, then, Joan?" he asked anxiously, "and so much as that? You must forgive me, but I am ignorant in these things. I didn't quite understand. I feel that I have become a bit foolish, but I didn't know that you had caught the disease."

"Care about you! Anyway, I care enough not to let you marry me even if you would. I think that to bring ruin and disgrace upon a man and all his family would be a poor way to show one's love for him. You see, you have everything to lose. You are not like me who have nothing, not even a name. Care about you!" she went on, with a strange, almost unnatural energy—and her low, caressing voice seemed to thrill every fibre of his heart and leave them trembling, as harp-strings thrill and tremble beneath the hand of the player—"I wonder if there are any words in the world that could make you understand how much I care. Listen. When first I saw you yonder by the Abbey, a change crept over me; and when you lay there senseless in my arms, I became a new woman, as though I were born again—a woman whose mind I could not read, for it was different from my own. Afterwards I read it; it was when they thought you were dying, and suddenly I learned that you would live. When I heard Miss Levinger cry out and saw her fall, then I read it, and knew that I also loved you. I should have gone; but I didn't go, for I could not tear myself away from you. Oh! pity me, and do not think too hardly of me; for remember who and what I am—a woman who has never had any one to love, father or mother or sister or friend, and yet who desires love above everything. And now it had come to me at last; and that one love of mine made up for all that I had missed, and was greater and stronger in itself than the hundred different loves of happier girls can be. I loved you, and I loved you, and I love you. Yes, I wish you to know it before we part, and I hope that you will never quite forget it, for none will ever love you so much again as I have, and do, and shall do till I die. And now it is all done with, and of it there will remain nothing except some pain for you, and for me my memories and a broken heart. What is that you say again about marrying me? Have I not told you that you shall not do it?—though I shall never forget that you have even thought of such a thing."

"I say that I will marry you, Joan," broke in Henry, in a hoarse voice. "Why should I spoil your life and mine for the sake of others?"

"No, no, you will not. Why should you spoil Emma Levinger's life, and your sister's, and your mother's, and bring yourself to disgrace and ruin for the sake of a girl like me? No, you will not. You will bid me farewell, now and for ever." And she held out her hand to him, while two great tears ran slowly down her face.

He saw the tears, and his heart melted, for they moved him more than all her words.

"My darling!" he whispered, drawing her towards him.

"Yes," she answered: "kiss away my tears this once, that, remembering it, whatever befalls me, I may weep no more for ever."

CHAPTER XV

THE FIRST FRUITS

Some days had passed since this night of avowal when, very early one morning, Henry was awakened from sleep by the sound of wheels and of knocking at the inn door. A strange apprehension took hold of him, and he rose from his bed and limped to the window. Then he saw that the carriage which had arrived was the old Rosham shooting brake, a long plain vehicle with deal seats running down its length on either side, constructed to carry eight or nine sportsmen to and from the more distant beats. Knocking at the door was none other than Edward Milward, and Henry guessed at once that he must have come to fetch him.

"Well, perhaps it is as well," he thought to himself grimly; then again his heart was filled with fear. What had happened? Why did Milward come thus, and at such an hour?

In another minute Edward had entered the room, followed by Mrs. Gillingwater.

"Your father is dying, Graves," he blurted out. "I don't know what it is; he collapsed suddenly in the middle of the night. If you want to see him alive—and you had better, if you can, while he has got his senses—you must make shift to come along with me at once. I have brought the brake, so that you can lie in it at full length. That was Ellen's idea: I should never have thought of it."

"Great Heaven!" said Henry. Then, assisted by Mrs. Gillingwater, he began to get into his clothes.

In ten minutes they were off, Henry lying flat upon a mattress at the bottom of the brake. Once he lifted his head and looked through the open rails of the vehicle towards the door of the house. Mrs. Gillingwater, who was a shrewd woman, interpreted the glance.

"If you are looking for Joan, sir, to say good-bye to her, it is no use, for she's in her room there sleeping like the dead, and I couldn't wake her. I don't think she is quite herself, somehow; but she'll be sorry to miss you, and so shall I, for the matter of that; but I'll tell her."

"Thank you, thank you—for everything," he answered hastily, and they started.

The drive was long and the road rough, having been much washed by recent rains; but after a fashion Henry enjoyed it, so far as his pressing troubles of mind would allow him to enjoy anything, for it was a lovely morning, and the breath of the open air, the first that he had tasted for many weeks, was like wine to him. On the way he learned from his companion all that there was to be told about his father. It appeared, as Henry had heard already, that he had been unwell for the last two months—not in a way to give alarm, though sufficiently to prevent him from leaving the house except on the finest days, or at times his room. On the previous day, however, he seemed much better, and dined downstairs. About ten o'clock he went to bed, and slept soundly till a little past midnight, when the household was aroused by the violent ringing of Lady Graves's bell, and they rushed upstairs to find that Sir Reginald had been seized with a fit. Dr. Childs was sent for at once, and gave an opinion that death might occur at any moment. His treatment restored the patient's consciousness; and Sir Reginald's first words expressed the belief that he was dying, and an earnest wish to see his son, whereupon Edward, who chanced to be spending the night at Rosham, was despatched with the brake to Bradmouth.

At length they reached the Hall, and Henry was helped from the vehicle; but in ascending the stone steps, which he insisted upon doing by himself, one of his crutches slipped, causing the foot of his injured limb to come down with some force upon the edge of the step. The accident gave him considerable pain, but he saved himself from falling, and thought little more of it at the time.

In the dining-room he found Ellen, who looked pale, and seemed relieved to see him.

"How is my father?" he asked.

"Insensible again, just now. But I am so glad that you have come, Henry, for he has been asking for you continually. All this business about the property seems to weigh more upon his mind now than it has done for years, and he wants to speak to you on the subject."

Then his mother came down, and her eyes were red with weeping.

"You have returned to a sad home, Henry," she said kissing him. "We are an unlucky family: death and misfortune are always at our doors. You look very white, my dear boy, and no wonder. You had better try to eat something, since it useless for you to attempt to see your poor father at present."

So Henry ate, or made a pretence of doing so, and afterwards was helped upstairs to a room opposite to that in which his father lay dying, where he settled himself in an invalid chair which Sir Reginald had used on the few occasions when he had been outside the house during the past weeks, and waited. All that day and all the next night he waited, and still his father did not recover consciousness—indeed, Dr. Childs now appeared to be of opinion that he would pass from coma to death. Much as he wished to bid a last farewell to his father, Henry could not repress a certain sense of relief when he heard that this was likely to be the case, for an instinct, coupled with some words which Ellen had let fall, warned him that Sir Reginald wished to speak to him upon the subject of Miss Levinger.

But the doctor was mistaken; for about six o'clock in the morning, nearly twenty-four hours after he had reached the house, Henry was awakened by Ellen, who came to tell him that their father was fully conscious and wished to see him at once. Seating himself in the invalid chair, he was wheeled across the passage to the red bedroom, in which he had himself been born. The top halves of some of the window-shutters were partly open, and by the light that streamed though them into the dim death-chamber, he saw his father's gaunt but still stately form propped up with pillows in the great four-post bed, of which the red curtains had been drawn back to admit the air.

"Here comes Henry," whispered Lady Graves.

The old man turned his head, and shaking back his snowy hair, he peered round the room.

"Is that you, my son?" he said in a low voice, stretching out a trembling hand, which Henry took and kissed. "You find me in a bad way: on the verge of death, where you have so lately been."

"Yes, it is I, father."

"God bless you, my boy! and God be thanked that you have been able to come to listen to my last words and that I have recovered my senses so that I can speak to you! Do not go away, my dear, or you, Ellen, for I want you all to hear what I have to say. You know, Henry, the state of the property. Mismanagement and bad times have ruined it. I have been to blame, and your dear brother, whom I hope soon to see, was to blame also. It has come to this, that I am leaving you beggars, and worse than beggars, since for the first time in the history of our family we cannot pay our debts."

Here he stopped and groaned, and Lady Graves whispered to him to rest awhile.

"No, no," he answered. "Give me some brandy; I will go on; it does not matter if I use myself up, and my brain may fail me at any moment. Henry, I am dying here, on this spot of earth where so many of our forefathers have lived and died before me; and more than the thought of leaving you all, more than the memory of my sins, or than the fear of the judgment of the Almighty, Whose mercy is my refuge, the thought crushes me that I have failed in my trust, that my children must be beggared, my name dishonoured, and my home—yes, and my very grave—sold to strangers. Henry, I have but one hope now, and it is in you. I think that I have sometimes been unjust to you in the past; but I know you for an upright and self-denying man, who, unlike some of us, has always set his duty before his pleasure. It is to you, then, that I appeal with my last breath, feeling sure that it will not be in vain, since, even should you have other wishes, you will sacrifice them to my prayer, to your mother's welfare, and to the honour of our name. You know that there is only one way of escape from all our liabilities—for I believe you have been spoken to on the subject; indeed, I myself alluded to it—by a marriage between yourself and Emma Levinger, who holds the mortgages on this property, and has other means. Her father desires this, and I have been told that the girl herself, who is a good and a sweet woman, has declared her affection for you; therefore it all rests with you. Do you understand me?"

"Say yes, and that you will marry her on the first opportunity," whispered Ellen into Henry's ear. "He will kill himself with talking so much." Then she saw her brother's face, and drew back her head in horror. Heavens! could it be that he was going to refuse?

"I will try to make myself plain," went on Sir Reginald after a pause, and swallowing another sip of brandy. "I want you to promise, Henry, before us all, that nothing, except the death of one of you, shall prevent you from marrying Emma Levinger so soon as may be possible after my funeral. When I have heard you say that, I shall be able to die in peace. Promise, then, my son, quickly; for I wish to turn my mind to other matters."

Now all eyes were bent upon Henry's face, and it was rigid and ashen. Twice he tried to speak and failed; the third time the words came, and they sounded like a groan.

"Father, I cannot."

Ellen gasped, and Lady Graves murmured, "O! cruel, cruel!" As for the dying man, his head sank back upon the pillow, and he lay there bewildered. Presently he lifted it and spoke again.

"I do not think—my hearing—I must have misunderstood. Did you say you could not promise, Henry? Why not? With everything at stake, and my dying prayer—mine, your father's. Oh! why not? Are you married, then?"

The sweat broke from Henry's brow and rolled down his face in large drops, as he answered, always in the voice that sounded like a groan—

"I am not married, father; and, before God, sooner than be forced to refuse you I would lie as you lie now. Have pity, I beseech you, on my cruel strait, between my honour and the denial of your wish. I cannot promise that I will marry Emma Levinger, because I am bound to another woman by ties that may not be broken, and I cannot be so base as to desert her."

"Another woman? I am too late, then?" murmured his father more and more feebly. "But stay: there is still hope. Who is she? At least you will not refuse to tell me her name."

"Her name is Joan Haste."

"Joan Haste? What! the girl at the inn? The bastard! My son, my only remaining son, denies his dying father, and brings his mother and his name to disgrace and ruin, because he is bound in honour to a village bastard!" he screamed. "Oh, my God! that I should have lived to hear this! Oh, my God! my God!"

And suddenly the old man flung his arms wide and fell back. Lady Graves and Ellen ran to him. Presently the former came away from the bed.

"Your father is dead, Henry," she said. "Perhaps, after what has passed, you will feel that this is no fit place for you. I will ring for some one to take you to your room."

But the last bitterness of these words, so awful from a mother's lips, was spared to Henry, for he had swooned. As he sank into unconsciousness a solemn voice seemed to speak within his tortured brain, and it said, "Behold the firstfruits of iniquity."

Henry did not attend his father's funeral, for the good reason that he was ill in bed. In the first place, though he made light of it at the time, that slip of his on the stone steps had so severely affected his broken limb as to necessitate his lying by for at least another month; and in the second he had received a shock to his nerves, healthy as they were, from which he could not hope to recover for many a month. He was kept informed of all that went on by Thomson, the old butler, for neither his mother nor Ellen came near him during those dark days. He heard the footsteps of the carpenter who measured his father's body, he heard the coffin being brought upstairs; and the day afterwards he heard the shuffling tramp of the tenants, who, according to ancient custom, bore down the corpse of the dead owner of Rosham to lie in state in the great hall. He heard the workmen nailing the hatchment of the departed baronet beneath his window; and then at last a day came when he heard a noise of the rolling wheels of carriages, and the sound of a church bell tolling, as his father was laid to rest among the bones of his ancestors.

So bitter was the resentment against him, that none had asked Henry to look his last upon his father's face. For a while he thought it better that he should not do so, but on the second night after the death nature grew too strong for him, and he determined to do that alone which, under happier circumstances, it should have been his duty to do with his widowed mother and his sister at his side.

Painfully he dragged himself from the bed, and, placing a candle and a box of matches in the pocket of his dressing-gown, he limped upon his crutches across the silent corridor and into the death-chamber, where the atmosphere was so heavy with the scent of flowers that for a moment it brought back his faintness. Recovering himself, he closed the door and made shift to light his candle. Then by its solitary light he approached the bed on which his father's corpse was lying, half hidden by wreaths and covered with a sheet. With a trembling hand he drew down the wrapping and exposed the dead man's face. It was calm enough now: there was no trace there of the tormenting grief that had been upon it in the moment of dissolution; it bore the seal of perfect peace, and, notwithstanding the snowy hair, a more youthful aspect than Henry could remember it to have worn, even in the days of his childhood.

In sad and solemn silence Henry gazed upon the clay that had given him life, and great bitterness and sorrow took hold of him. He covered his eyes with his hand, and prayed that God might forgive him for the pain which he had caused his father in his last hour, and that his father might forgive him too in the land where all things are understood, for there he would learn that he could not have spoken otherwise. Well, he was reaping as he had sown, and there remained nothing to him except to make amendment as best he could. Then with a great effort he dragged himself up upon the bed, and kissed his father's forehead.

Having replaced the sheet, he extinguished the candle and turned to leave the room. As he opened the door he saw a figure draped in black, who stood in the passage listening. It was his mother. She advanced towards him with a cold, sad mien, and opened her lips as though to speak. Then the light fell upon his face, and she saw that it was torn by grief and stained with tears, and her look softened, for now she understood something of what her son's sufferings must be. Still she did not speak, and in silence, except for the tapping of his crutches on the polished floor, Henry passed her with bowed head, and reached his room again.

In due course the family returned from the funeral, and, outwardly at any rate, a break occurred in the conspiracy of silence and neglect of which Henry was the object, for it was necessary that he should be present at the reading of the will. This ceremony took place in the bedroom of the new baronet, and gathered there were a representative from the London firm of lawyers that had managed, or mismanaged, the Graves's affairs for several generations, the widow, Ellen, and Edward Milward. Bowing gravely to Sir Henry, the lawyer broke the seals of the document and began the farce—for a farce it was, seeing that the will had been signed nearly five-and-twenty years before, when the position of the family was very different. After reciting the provisions of the entail—that, by the way, had long been cut—under which his deceased brother Reginald should have entered into the enjoyment of all the land and hereditaments and the real property generally, with remainder to his children, or, in the event of his death without issue, to Henry, the testator went on to deal with the jointure of the widow, which was fixed at eight hundred a year in addition to the income arising from her own fortune, that, alas! had long since been lost or muddled away. Then it made provision for the younger children—ten thousand to Henry and eight thousand to Ellen—to be paid out of the personalty, or, should this prove insufficient, to be raised by way of rentcharge on the estate, as provided for under the marriage settlement of Sir Reginald and his wife; and, after various legacies and directions as to the disposal of heirlooms, ended by constituting Reginald, or, in the event of his death without issue, Henry, residuary legatee.

When he had finished reading this lengthy document, which he well knew not to be worth the paper on which it was written, the lawyer solemnly exhibited the signatures of the testator and of the attesting witnesses, and laid it down with a sigh. Three of the listeners were aware that the will might as well have affected to dispose of the crown of England as to devise to them these various moneys, lands and chattels; but the fourth, Edward Milward, who had never been admitted to full confidence as to the family position, was vastly pleased to learn that his future wife inherited so considerable a sum, to say nothing of her chance of succeeding to the entire estate should Henry die without issue. That there had been embarrassments and mortgage charges he knew, but these, he concluded, were provided for by life insurances, and had rolled off the back of the property on the death of the late owner. Indeed, he showed his pleasure so plainly in his face that the lawyer, guessing he was labouring under some such delusion, hesitated and looked at him pointedly before he proceeded to make remarks upon the document. Ellen, always on the watch, took the hint, and, laying her hand affectionately on Milward's shoulder, said in a low voice:

"Perhaps you will not mind leaving us for a few moments, Edward: I fancy there are one or two matters that my mother would not like to be discussed outside her own family at present."

"Certainly," answered Edward, who, having learned all he wished to know, rejoiced at the chance of escape, seeing that funerals and will-reading exercised a depressing effect upon his spirits.

Lady Graves was at the other end of the room and looking out of an open window, so that she did not overhear these remarks. Henry, however, did hear them, and spoke for the first time.

"I think that you had better stay, Milward," he said: "there is nothing to conceal," and he smiled grimly at his own double-entendre.

"No, thanks," answered Edward airily: "I have heard all I want to know, so I will go into the garden and smoke a cigarette." And before Henry could speak again he was gone.

"You are probably aware, Sir Henry," began the lawyer, "that all the main provisions of this document"—and he tapped the will with his knuckle—"fall to the ground, for the reason that the capital sums with which they dealt were exhausted some years since; though I am bound to tell you that, in my opinion, the legality of the methods by which some of those sums were brought into possession might even now be contested."

"Yes," answered Henry, "and good money thrown after bad."

"Of course," went on the lawyer, "you succeed to the estates, which have been little, if at all, diminished in acreage; but they are, I believe, mortgaged to more than their present value in favour of a Mr. Levinger, who holds the securities in trust for his daughter, and to whom there is a large sum due by way of back interest."

"Yes, I am aware of it."

"Hem," said the lawyer. "Then I am afraid that there is not much more to say, is there? I trust that you may be able—to find means to meet—these various liabilities, in which case we shall be most happy to act for you in the matter. By the way, we still have a small sum in our hands that was sent to us by our late esteemed client to pay a debt of your late brother's, which on enquiry was found not to be owing. This we propose to remit to you, after deducting the amount of our account current."

"By all means deduct the account current," said Henry; "for, you see, you may not get another chance of paying yourselves. Well, the carriage is waiting for you. Good afternoon."

The lawyer gathered up his papers, shook hands all round, bowed and went.

"Well," he thought to himself as he drove towards the station, "I am glad to be clear of this business: somehow it was more depressing than most funerals. I suppose that there's an end of a connection that has lasted a hundred years, though there will be some pickings when the estate is foreclosed on. I am glad it didn't happen in Sir Reginald's time, for I had a liking for the old man and his grand last-century manners. The new baronet seems a roughish fellow, with a sharp edge to his tongue; but I dare say he has a deal to worry him, and he looks very ill. What fools they were to cut the entail! They can't blame us about it, anyway, for we remonstrated with them strongly enough. Sir Reginald was under the thumb of that dead son of his—that's the fact, and he was a scamp, or something like it. Now they are beggared, absolutely beggared: they won't even be able to pay their debts. It's not one man's funeral that I have been assisting at—it is that of a whole ancient family, without benefit of clergy or hope of resurrection. The girl is going to marry a rich man: she knows which side her bread is buttered, and has a good head on her shoulders—that's one comfort. Well, they are bankrupt and done with, and it is no good distressing myself over what can't be helped. Here's the station. I wonder if I need tip the coachman. I remember he drove me when I came down to the elder boy's christening; we were both young then. Not necessary, I think: I sha'n't be likely to see him again."

CHAPTER XVI

FORTITER IN RE

When the lawyer had gone, for a while there was silence in Henry's room. Everybody seemed to wish to speak, and yet no one could find any words to say. Of course Henry was aware that the subject which had been discussed at the last dreadful scene of his father's life would be renewed on the first opportunity, but he was nervously anxious that it should not be now, when he did not feel able to cope with the bitter arguments which he was sure Ellen was preparing for him, and still less with the pleadings of his mother, should she condescend to plead. After all it was he who spoke the first.

"Perhaps, Ellen," he said, "you will tell me who were present at our father's funeral."

"Everybody," she answered; adding, with meaning, "You see, the truth about us has not yet come out. We are still supposed to be people of honour and position."

Her mother turned and made a gesture with her hand, as though to express disapproval of the tone in which she spoke; and, taking the hint, Ellen went on in a dry, clear voice, like that of one who reads an inventory, to give the names of the neighbours who attended the burial, and of more distant friends who had sent wreaths, saying in conclusion:

"Mr. Levinger of course was there, but Emma did not come. She sent a lovely wreath of eucharist lilies and stephanotis."

At this moment the old butler came in, his face stained with grief—for he had dearly loved Sir Reginald, who was his foster-brother—and announced that Dr. Childs was waiting to see Sir Henry.

"Show him up," said Henry, devoutly thankful for the interruption.

"How do you do, Captain—I mean Sir Henry Graves?" said the doctor, in his quiet voice, when Lady Graves and Ellen had left the room. "I attended your poor father's funeral, and then went on to see a patient, thinking that I would give you a look on my way back. However, don't let us talk of these things, but show me your leg if you will. Yes, I thought so; you have given it a nasty jar; you should never have tried to walk up those steps without help. Well, you will have to stop quiet for a month or so, that is all; and I think that it will be a good thing for you in more ways than one, for you seem very much shaken, my dear fellow, and no wonder, with all this trouble after a dangerous illness."

Henry thanked him; and then followed a little general conversation, in which Dr. Childs was careful not to let him know that he was aware of the scene that had occurred at his father's death, though as a matter of fact the wildest rumours were floating up and down the country side, based upon hints that had fallen from Lady Graves in her first grief, and on what had been overheard by listeners at the door. Presently he rose to go, saying that he would call again on the morrow.

"By the way," he added, "I have got to see another patient to-night—your late nurse, Joan Haste."

"What is the matter with her?" asked Henry, flushing suddenly red, a symptom of interest or distress that did not escape the doctor's practised eye.

"So the talk is true," he thought to himself. "Well, I guessed as much; indeed, I expected it all along: the girl has been in love with him for weeks. A pity, a sad pity!"

"Oh! nothing at all serious," he answered; "a chill and a touch of fever. It has been smouldering in her system for some time, I think. It seems she got soaked about ten days ago, and stood in her wet things. She is shaking it off now, however."

"Indeed; I am glad to hear that," Henry answered, in a tone of relief which he could not quite conceal. "Will you remember me to Miss Haste when you see her, and tell her that—"

"Yes?" said the doctor, his hand on the door.

"That I am glad she has recovered, and—that—I was sorry not to be able to say good-bye to her," he added hurriedly.

"Certainly," answered Dr. Childs, and went.

Henry saw no more of his mother or his sister that evening, which was a sorrowful one for him. He grieved alone in his room, comforted only by the butler Thomson, who came to visit him, and told him tales of his father's boyhood and youth; and they grieved elsewhere, each according to her own nature. On the morrow the doctor called early and reported favourably of Henry's condition. He told him that Joan was doing even better than he had expected, that she sent him her duty and thanked him kindly for his message, and with this Henry was fain to be content. Indeed, what other message could she have sent him, unless she had written? and something told him that she would not write. Any words that could be put on paper would express both too much and too little.

Henry was not the only person at Rosham whose rest was troubled this night, seeing that Ellen also did not sleep well. She had loved her father in her own way and sorrowed for him, but she loved her family better than any individual member of it, and mourned still more bitterly for its sad fate. Also she had her own particular troubles to overcome, for she was well aware that Edward imagined her to possess the portion of eight thousand pounds which had been allotted to her under the will, and it was necessary that he should be undeceived and enlightened on various other points in connection with the Rosham affairs, which could no longer be concealed from him. On the morrow he rode over from Upcott, and very soon gave Ellen a chance of explanation, by congratulating her upon the prospective receipt of the eight thousand. Like a bold woman she took her opportunity at once, though she did not care about this task and had some fears for the issue.

"Don't congratulate me, Edward," she said, "for I must tell you I have discovered that this eight thousand pounds is very much in the clouds."

Edward whistled. "Meaning—?" he asked.

"Meaning, my dear, that after you left the lawyer explained our financial position. To put it shortly, the entail has been cut, the estate has been mortgaged for more than its value, and there is not a farthing for anybody."

"Indeed!" answered Edward: "that's jolly good news. Might I ask what is going to happen then?"

"It all depends upon Henry. If he is not a fool, and marries Miss Levinger, everything will come right, except my eight thousand pounds of course, for she holds the mortgages, or her father does for her. If he is a fool—which I have reason to believe is the case—and declines to marry Miss Levinger, then I suppose that the estate will be made bankrupt and that my mother will be left to starve."

At this announcement Edward uttered an indignant grunt.

"Look here, Ellen," he said; "it is all very fine, but you have been playing it pretty low down upon me. I never heard a word of this mess, although, of course, I knew that you were embarrassed, like most people nowadays. What I did not know—to say nothing of your not having a penny—was that I am to have the honour of marrying into a family of bankrupts; and, to tell you the truth, I am half inclined to reconsider my position, for I don't wish to be mixed up with this sort of thing."

"About that you must do as you like, Edward," she answered, with dignity; "but let me tell you that this state of affairs is not my fault. In the first place, it is the fault of those who are dead and gone, and still more is it the fault of my brother Henry, whose wickedness and folly threaten to plunge us all into ruin."

"What do you mean by his 'wickedness and folly'?"

"I mean that matter of which I spoke to you before—the matter of this wretched girl, Joan Haste. It seems that he has become involved in some miserable intrigue with her, after the disgusting fashion of you men, and on this account he refuses to marry Emma Levinger. Yes, although my father prayed him to do so with his dying breath, he still refuses, when he knows that it would be his own salvation and that of his family also."

"He must be mad," said Edward—"stark, staring mad: it's no such great wonder about the girl, but that he should decline to marry Miss Levinger is sheer insanity; for, although I don't think much of her, and the connection is a bad one, it is clear that she has got the dollars. What does he mean to do, then? Marry the other one?"

"Very possibly, for all I know to the contrary. It would be quite in keeping with his conduct."

"Oh, hang it, Ellen!—that I could not stand. It is not to be expected of any man that he should come into a family of which the head will be a bankrupt, who insists upon marrying a barmaid."

"Again I say that you must please yourself, Edward; but if you feel so strongly about Henry's conduct—and I admit that it is quite natural that you should do so—perhaps you had better speak to him yourself."

"All right: I will," he answered. "Although I don't like meddling with other people's love affairs, for I have quite enough to do to manage my own, I will give him my mind pretty straight. He's a nasty customer to tackle; but if he doesn't know before he's an hour older that there are other people to be considered in the world besides himself, it sha'n't be my fault, that's all."

"I am sure it is very brave of you, dear," said Ellen, with veiled sarcasm. "But, if I may venture to advise, I would suggest what my poor father used to call the suaviter in modo in preference to the fortiter in re."

"Oh, bother your Latin!" said Edward. "Please speak English."

"I mean that were I you I should go fair and softly; for, as you remarked just now in your own classic tongue, Henry is a 'nasty customer to tackle.' Well, I happen to know that he is up and alone just now, so you cannot have a better opportunity." Then she rang the bell, which was almost immediately answered by the butler, and added, "Will you be so good, Thomson, as to show Mr. Milward to Sir Henry's room?"

Edward hesitated, for, like another hero, he felt his courage oozing out of his finger-tips. Looking up, he saw Ellen watching him with a little smile, and remembered that to draw back now would mean that for many a long day to come he must be the target of the bitter arrows of her irony. So he set his teeth and went as to a forlorn hope.

In another minute he was in the presence of the man whom he came to annihilate. Henry was seated in a chair, against which his crutches were resting, looking out of the window, with an open book upon his knee, and it cannot be said that he appeared pleased on hearing the name of his visitor. Indeed, he was about to tell Thomson that he was engaged, when Edward blundered in behind him, leaving him no option but to shake hands and ask his visitor to sit down. Then ensued this conversation.

"How do you do, Graves? I have come to see you on business."

"As well as I can expect, thank you."

A pause.

"Beautiful weather, isn't it?"

"It seems fine; but as you have been out, you will know more about it than I do."

Another pause.

"The pheasants ought to do well this year; they have had a wonderful fine time for hatching."

"Indeed. I think you said that you wished to speak to me about some business."

"You are not rearing any this season, are you?"

"No: I am sorry to say that I have other chicks to hatch at present. But about the business?"

"All right, Graves; I am coming to that. The pheasants lead up to it. Fortiter in modo, as Ellen says."

"Does she? Well, it is not a bad motto for her, though it's wrong. Well, if we have done with the pheasants—"

There was yet another pause, and then Edward said suddenly, and with effort:

"You are not rearing any pheasants, Graves, because you can't afford to; in fact, I have just found out that you are bankrupt, and the whole thing is a swindle, and that Ellen won't have a farthing of her eight thousand pounds. She has sent me up here to talk to you about it."

"Has she? That is fortiter in modo and no mistake. Well, talk on, Mr. Milward. But, before you begin, let me remind you that I asked you to stop and hear what passed after the reading of the will yesterday, and you would not."

"Oh, bother the will! It is a fraud, like everything else in this place. I tell you, Graves—"

"One moment. Pray lower your voice, keep your temper, and remember that you are speaking to a gentleman."

"Speaking to a gentleman? A nice sort of gentleman! You mean an uncertified bankrupt, who won't do the right thing by his family and marry the girl who could set them on their legs again; a pious humbug who preaches to everybody else, but isn't above carrying on a low intrigue with a barmaid, and then having the impudence to say that he means to disgrace us by marrying her."

"I have asked you to lower your voice, Mr. Milward."

"Lower my voice? I think it is high time to raise it when I find myself let in for an engagement with the sister of a man who does such things. You needn't look at me, Sir Henry Graves—Sir Henry indeed! I repeat, 'let in.' However, you must mend your manners, or Ellen will suffer for it, that is all; for I shall throw her over and wash my hands of the whole show. The bankruptcy is bad enough, but I'm hanged if I will stand the barmaid. Edward Milward of Upcott with a barmaid for a sister-in-law! Not if he knows it."

Then Henry answered, in a quiet and ominous voice:

"You have been so good, Mr. Milward, doubtless more in kindness than in anger, as to point out to me with great directness the errors, or assumed errors, of my ways. Allow me, before I say anything further, to point out to you an error in yours, about which there is no possibility of doubt. You say that you propose 'to throw over' my sister, not on account of anything that she has done, but because of acts which I am supposed to have done. In my judgment it will indeed be fortunate for her should you take this course. But not the less do I feel bound to tell you, that the man who behaves thus towards a woman, having no cause of offence against her, is not what is usually understood by the term gentleman. So much for my sister: now for myself. It seems to me that there is only one answer possible to conduct and language such as you have thought fit to make use of; and were I well, much as I dislike violence, I should not hesitate to apply it. I should, Mr. Milward, kick you out of this room and down yonder stairs, and, should my strength not fail me, across that garden. Being crippled at present, I am unable to advance this argument. I must, therefore, do the best I can." And, taking up the crutch that stood by his chair, Henry hurled it straight at him. "Now go!" he thundered; and Mr. Milward went.

"I hope that Ellen will feel pleased with the effect of her embassy," thought Henry; then suddenly he turned white, and, choking with wrath, said aloud, "Great Heaven! to think that I should have come so low as to be forced to suffer such insults from a cur like that! What will be the end of it? One thing is clear: I can't stand much more. I'm done for in the Service; but I dare say that I could get a billet as mate on a liner, or even a command of some vessel in the Canadian or Australian waters where I am known. Unless there is a change soon, that is what I'll do, and take Joan with me. Nobody will sneer at her there, anyway—at least, nobody who sees her."

Meanwhile Ellen was standing in the hall making pretence to arrange some flowers, but in reality waiting, not without a certain sense of anxiety, to learn the result of the interview which she had been instrumental in bringing about. She hoped that Henry would snub her fiance in payment of sundry remarks that Edward had made to her, and which she had by no means forgotten, although she was not at present in a position to resent them. She hoped also, with some lack of perspicuity, that Henry would be impressed by Edward's remonstrances, and that, when he came to understand that her future was imperilled, he would hasten to sacrifice his own. But here she made her great mistake, not foreseeing that a man of Milward's moral fibre could not by any possibility neglect to push a fancied vantage home, any more than he could refrain from being insolent and brutal towards one whom he thought at his mercy; for, even in the upper walks of life, individuals do exist who take pleasure in grinding the heads of the fallen deeper into the mire.

Presently Ellen was alarmed to hear Henry's words "Now go" echo through the house, followed by the sound of a banging door. Next instant Edward appeared upon the stairs, and the expression of his features betrayed a wondrous mixture of astonishment, fear and indignation.

"What have you been doing, Edward?" she said, as he approached. "You do not mean to tell me that you have been brawling, and in this house?"

"Brawling? Oh, yes, say that I have been brawling," gasped Edward, when at last he managed to speak. "That infernal brother of yours has thrown a crutch at me; but by all means say that I have been brawling."

"Thrown a crutch? And what had you been doing to make him throw a crutch?"

"Doing? Why, nothing, except tell him that he was a fraud and a bankrupt. He took it all quite quietly till the end, then suddenly he said that if he wasn't a cripple he would kick me downstairs, and threw a crutch at my head; and, by George! I believe from the look of him that if he could he would have done it too!"

"It is very possible," said Ellen, "if you were foolish enough to use such language towards him. You have had an escape. Henry has a fearful temper when roused."

"Then why on earth didn't you say so before you sent me up there? Do you suppose that I enjoy being pelted with crutches by a mad sailor? Possible! Yes, it seems that anything is possible in this house; but I will tell you one thing that isn't, and it is that I should stay here any longer. I scratch, now, on the spot. Do you understand, Ellen? The game is up, and you can marry whom you like."

At this point Ellen touched him on the shoulder, and said, in a cold voice:

"Perhaps you are not aware that there are at least two servants listening to you? Will you be so kind as to follow me into the drawing-room?"

Edward obeyed. When Ellen put on her coldest and most imperious manner he always did obey, and it is probable that he will always continue to do so. He was infuriated, and he was humbled, still he could not resist that invitation into the drawing-room. It was a large apartment, and by some oversight the shutters that were closed for the funeral had never been reopened, therefore its aspect could not be called cheerful, though there was sufficient light to see by.

"Now, Mr. Milward," said Ellen, stationing herself in the centre of a wide expanse of floor, for there were no little tables and knickknacks at Rosham, "I will ask you to be so good as to repeat what you were saying."

Thus adjured, Edward looked around him, and his spirits sank. He could be vociferous enough in the sunlit hall, but here in this darkened chamber, that reminded him unpleasantly of corpses and funerals, with Ellen, of whom he was secretly afraid, standing cool and collected before him, a sudden humility fell upon him.

"Why do you call me Mr. Milward?" he asked: "it doesn't sound right; and as for what I was saying, I was saying that I could not stand this sort of thing any more, and I think that we had better shut up the shop."

"If you mean by 'shutting up the shop' that our engagement is at an end, Mr. Milward, so be it. But unfortunately, as you must understand, questions will be asked, and I shall be glad to know what explanation you propose to furnish."

"Oh! you can settle that."

"Very well; I presume you admit that I am not to blame, therefore we must fall back upon the cause which you have given: that you insulted my brother, who—notwithstanding his crippled condition—inflicted a physical punishment upon you. Indeed, unless I can succeed in stopping it, thanks to your own indiscretion, the story will be all over the place before to-morrow, and I must leave you to judge what will be thought of it in the county, or let us say at the militia mess, which I believe you join next Wednesday."

Edward heard and quailed. He was excessively sensitive to public opinion, and more especially to the chaff of his brother officers in the militia, among whom he was something of a butt. If it became known there that Sir Henry Graves, a man with a broken leg, had driven him out of the room by throwing crutches at his head, he felt that his life would speedily become a burden to him.

"You wouldn't be so mean as that, Ellen," he said.

"So mean as what? To some people it might seem that the meanness is on the other side. There are difficulties here, and you have quarrelled with my brother; therefore, as I understand, you wish to desert me after being publicly engaged to me for some months, and to leave me in an utterly false position. Do so if you will, but you must not be surprised if you find your conduct called by strong names. For my part I am indifferent, but for your own sake I think that you would do well to pause. Do not suppose that I shall sit still under such an affront. You know that I can be a good friend; you have yet to learn that I can be a good enemy. Possibly, though I do not like to think it of you, you believe that we are ruined and of no account. You will find your mistake. There are troubles here, but they can be overcome, and very soon you will live to regret that you dared to put such a deadly affront upon me and my family. You foolish man!" she went on, with gathering vehemence, "have you not yet realized the difference between us? Have you not learned that with all your wealth you are nobody and I am somebody—that though I can stand without you, without me you will fall? Now I am tired of talking: choose, Edward Milward, choose whether you will jilt me and incur an enmity that shall follow you to your death, or whether you will bide by me and be placed where of late it has been the object of my life to set you."

If Edward had quailed before, now he positively trembled, for he knew that Ellen spoke truth. Hers was the master mind, and to a great extent he had become dependent on her. Moreover he had ambitions, for the most part of a social and personal nature—which included, however, his entry into Parliament, where he hoped that his power of the purse would ultimately earn him some sort of title—and these ambitions he felt sure would never be gratified without the help of Ellen. Lastly, he was in his own way sincerely attached to her, and quite appreciated the force of her threats to make of him an object of ridicule among his neighbours and brother-officers. Smarting though he was under a sense of moral and physical injury, the sum of these considerations turned the balance in favour of the continuance of his engagement. Perhaps Ellen was right, and her family would ride out this trouble; but whether they did so or not, he was convinced that without Ellen he should sink below his present level, and what was more, that she would help him on his downward career. So Edward gave in; indeed, it would not be too much to say that he collapsed.

"You shouldn't speak so harshly, dear," he said, "for you know that I did not really mean what I told you about breaking off our engagement. The fact is that, what between one thing and another, I scarcely knew what I was saying."

"Indeed!" answered Ellen. "Well, I hope that you know what you are saying now. If our engagement is to be continued, there must be no further talk of breaking it off on the next occasion that you happen to have a quarrel with my brother, or to be angry about the mortgages on this property."

"The only thing that I bargain about your brother is, that I shall not be asked to see him, or have anything to do with him. He can go to the deuce in his own way so far as I am concerned, and we can cut him when we are married—that is, if he becomes bankrupt and the rest of it. I am sorry if I have behaved badly, Ellen; but really and truly I do mean what I say about our engagement, and I tell you what, I will go home and put it on paper if you like, and bring you the letter this afternoon."

"That is as you like, Edward," she answered, with a perceptible softening of her manner. "But after what has happened, you may think yourself fortunate that I ever consent to see you again."

Edward attempted no reply, at least in words, for he was crushed; but, bending down, he imprinted a chaste salute upon Ellen's smooth forehead, which she acknowledged by touching him frostily on the cheek with her lips.

This, then, is the history of the great quarrel between these lovers, and of their reconciliation.

"Upon my word," said Ellen to herself, as she watched him depart, "I am by no means certain that Henry's obstinacy and violence have not done be a good turn for once. They have brought things to a crisis, there has been a struggle, and I have won the day. Whatever happens, I do not think it likely that Edward will try to match himself against me again, and I am quite certain that he will never talk any more of breaking off our engagement."

CHAPTER XVII

BETWEEN DUTY AND DUTY

For a while Ellen stood silent, enjoying the luxury of a well-earned victory; then she turned and went upstairs to Henry's room. The first thing that she saw was the crutch which her brother had used as a missile of war with such effect, still lying where it had fallen on the carpet. She picked it up and placed it by his chair.

"How do you do, Henry?" she said blandly. "I hear that you have surpassed yourself this morning."

"Now, look here, Ellen," he answered, in a voice that was almost savage in its energy, "if you have come to bait me, I advise you to give it up, for I am in no mood to stand much more. You sent Mr. Milward up here to insult me, and I treated him as he deserved; though now I regret that under intolerable provocation I forgot myself so far as to condescend to violence. I am very sorry if I have interfered with your matrimonial projects, though there is a certain justice about it, seeing how constantly you attempt to interfere with mine; but I could not help it. No man of honour could have borne the things that fellow thought fit to say, and it is your own fault for encouraging him to say them."

"Oh, pray, my dear Henry, let us leave this cant about 'men of honour' out of the question. It really seems to me that after all that has happened and is happening, the less said of honour the better. It is quite useless for you to look angry, since I presume that you will not try to silence me by throwing things in my face. And now let me tell you that, although you have done your best, you have not succeeded in 'interfering with my matrimonial projects,' which, in fact, were never so firmly established as they are at this moment."

"Do you mean to say," asked Henry in astonishment, "that the man has put up with—well, with what I was obliged to inflict upon him, and that you still contemplate marrying him after the way in which he has threatened to jilt you?"

"Certainly I mean to say it. We have set the one thing against the other and cried quits, though of course he has bargained that he shall have nothing more to do with you, and also that, should you persist in your present conduct, he shall not be forced to receive you at his house after our marriage."

"Really he need not have troubled to make that stipulation."

"We are not all fools, Henry," Ellen went on; "and I did not feel called upon to break an engagement that in many ways suits me very well because you have chosen to quarrel with Edward and to use violence towards him. Do not be afraid, Henry: I have not come here to lecture you; I come to say that I wash my hands of you. In the interests of the family, of which you are the head, I still venture to hope that you will repent of the past and that better counsels may prevail as to the future. I hope, for instance, that you will come to see that your own prosperity and good name should not be sacrificed in order to gratify a low passion. But this is merely a pious wish and by the way. You are a middle-aged man, and must take your own course in life; only I decline to be involved in your ruin. If in the future I should however be able to do anything to mitigate its consequences so far as this property is concerned, I will do it; for I at least think more of my family than of myself, and most of all of the dying wishes of our father. And now, Henry, as a sister to a brother I say good-bye to you for so long as you persist in your present courses. Henceforth when we meet it will be as acquaintances and no more. Good-bye, Henry." And she left the room.

"That is a pleasant speech to have to listen to," reflected Henry as the door closed behind her. "Of the two I really think that I prefer Mr. Milward's mode of address, for he can be answered, or at any rate dealt with; but it is difficult to answer Ellen, seeing that to a great extent she has the right on her side. What a position for a man! If I had tried, I could not have invented a worse one. I shall never laugh again at the agonies of a heroine placed between love and duty, for it is my own case. Or rather let us leave the love out of it, and say that I stand between duty and duty, the delicate problem to deceive being: Which is the higher of these duties and who shall be sacrificed?"

As he thought thus, sadly enough, there was a knock upon his door, and Lady Graves entered the room, looking very sorrowful and dignified in her widow's robe.

"So I haven't seen the worst of it," Henry muttered. "Well, I may as well get it over." Then he added aloud, "Will you sit down, mother? I am sorry that I cannot rise to receive you."

"My boy," she said in a low voice, "I have been thinking a great deal of the sad scene which took place in connection with your dear father's death, and of my subsequent conduct towards you, and I have come to apologise to you. I do not know the exact circumstances that led you to act as you have done—I may even say that I scarcely wish to know them; but on reflection I feel that nothing but the strongest reasons of considerations of honour would have induced you to refuse your father's last request, and that I have therefore no right to judge you harshly. This came home to me when I saw you leaving the room yonder a few nights since, and your face showed me what you were suffering. But at that time my heart was too frozen with grief, and, I fear, also too much filled with resentment against you to allow me to speak. If you can tell me anything that will give me a better understanding of the causes of all this dreadful trouble, I shall be grateful to you; for then we may perhaps consult together and find some way out of it. But I repeat that I do not come to force your confidence. I come, Henry, to express my regret, and to mourn with you over a husband and a father whom we both loved dearly,"—and, moved by a sudden impulse of affection, she bent down and kissed her son upon the forehead.

He returned the embrace, and said, "Mother, those are the first kind words that I have heard for a long while from any member of my family; and I can assure you that I am grateful for them, and shall not forget them, for I thought that you had come here to revile me like everybody else. You say that you do not ask my confidence, but fortunately a man can speak out to his mother without shame, even when he has cause to be ashamed of what he must tell her. Now listen, mother: as you know, I never was a favourite in this house; I dare say through my own fault, but so it is. From boyhood everybody more or less looked down upon me, and, with the exception of yourself, I doubt if anybody cared for me much. Well, I determined to make my own way in the world and to show you all that there was something in me, and to a certain extent I succeeded. I worked hard to succeed too; I denied myself in many ways, and above all I kept myself clear from the vices that most young men fall into in one shape or another. Then came this dreadful business of my brother's death, and just as I was beginning really to get on I was asked to leave the profession which was everything to me. From the letters that reached me I gathered that in some mysterious way it lay in my power, and in mine alone, to pull the family affairs out of the mire if I returned home. So I retired from the Service and I came, because I thought that it was my duty, for hitherto I have tried to do my duty when I could see any way to it. On the first night of my arrival here I learned the true state of affairs from Ellen, and I learned also what it was expected that I should do to remedy it—namely, that I should marry a young lady with whom I had but a slight acquaintance, but who, as it chances, is the owner of the mortgages on this estate."

"It was most indiscreet of Ellen to put the matter like that," said Lady Graves.

"Ellen is frequently indiscreet, mother; but doubtless it never occurred to her that I should object to doing what she is ready to do for herself—marry for money. I am glad you see, however, that her method was not exactly calculated to prepossess any man in favour of a marriage, of which he did not happen to have thought for himself. Still the young lady came, and I liked her exceedingly; I liked her more than any woman that I had met before, the one inexplicable thing about her to my mind being—why on earth she should wish to marry me, as I understand is, or was, the case."

"You foolish boy!" said Lady Graves, smiling a little; "do you not understand that she had become fond of you during that week when you were here together the year before last?"

"I can't say that I understand it, mother, for I had not much to do with her. But even if it is so, it does not satisfactorily explain why her father should be equally anxious for this match. Of course I know that he has given lots of reasons, but I cannot help thinking that there is something behind them all. However, that is neither here nor there."

"I fancy, Henry, that the only thing behind Mr. Levinger's reasons is an earnest desire for the happiness of a daughter to whom he is much attached."

"Well, mother, as I was saying, I took a great fancy to the girl, and though I did not like at all the idea of making advances to a lady to whom we are under such obligations, I determined to put my pride in my pocket, and, if I still continued to admire her after further acquaintance, to ask her if she would allow me to share her fortune, for I think that is an accurate way of putting it. So I went off to stay at Monk's

Lodge, and the chapter of troubles began. The girl who indirectly was the cause of my accident became my nurse, and it seems that—she grew attached to me, and—I grew attached to her. It was not wonderful: you know her; she is very beautiful, she has a good heart, and in most ways she is a lady. In short, she is a woman who in any less prejudiced country would certainly be received into society if she had the means to enter it. Well, so things went on without anything remarkable happening, until recently." And he repeated to her fairly and fully all that had passed between himself and Joan.

"Now, mother," he said, "I have made my confession to you, and perhaps you will understand how it came about that, fresh from such scenes, and taken as I was utterly by surprise, I was unable to promise what my father asked. I do not know what your judgment of my conduct may be; probably you cannot think of it more harshly than I do myself, and in excuse of it I can only say that the circumstances were strange, and, as I have discovered, I love the woman. What, therefore, is my duty towards her?"

"Did you ever promise to marry her, Henry?"

"Promise? Yes, I said that I would; for, as you know, I am a bit of a puritan, although I have little right to that title now, and it seemed to me that marriage was the only way out of the trouble."

"Does she expect you to marry her, then?"

"Certainly not. She declares that she would not allow it on any consideration. But this goes for nothing, for how can I take advantage of her inexperience and self-sacrificing folly? You have the whole facts: what do you think that I should do?"

"Henry, I am older than you are; I have seen a great deal of life, and perhaps you, who are curiously unworldly, may think me the reverse. I accept your story as it stands, well knowing that you have told me the exact truth, without hiding anything which would weigh against yourself; and on the face of that story, I cannot say that I consider it to be your duty to marry this poor girl, with whom, through your own weakness and folly, you have placed yourself in such false relations—though undoubtedly it is your duty to do everything in your power to provide for her. If you had deliberately set yourself to lead her astray, the case might be different; only, were you capable of such conduct—which I know that you are not—you would not now be tormented by doubts as to your duty towards her. You talk of Joan Haste's 'inexperience.' Are you sure that this is so? The whole history of her conduct seems to show experience, and even art, or at any rate a knowledge, very unusual in a girl of her age and position, of how best to work upon a man's tenderness and to move his feelings. That art may have been unconscious, an art which Nature gave her; and that knowledge may have been intuitive, for of course all things are possible, and I can only judge of what is probable. At least it is clear that she never expected that you would marry her, because she knew that such an act would bring you to ruin, and I respect her for her honesty in this particular."

"Should a man shrink from his duty because duty means disaster, mother?"

"Not if it is his duty, perhaps, Henry; but in the present case that, to say the least of it, is not proved. I will answer your question by another: Should a man neglect many undoubted duties, among them that of obeying the dying petition of his father, in order to indulge his conscience with the sense that he has fulfilled one which is open to doubt? Henry, I do not wish to push you about this matter, for I see that, even if you do not love Joan Haste so much as you think, at the least you are strongly attracted to her; also I see that your self-questionings are honest, and that you are anxious to do what is right, independently of the possible consequences to yourself. But I do pray of you not to be led away, and, if you can avoid it, not to see this girl again at present. Take time to consider: one month, two, three, as you like; and in the meanwhile do not commit yourself beyond redemption. Remember all that is at stake; remember that a man in your position is not entirely his own master. Of myself I will not speak. Why should I? I am old, and my day is done; such years as remain to me I can drag out in obscurity without repining, for my memories are enough for me, and I have little care left for any earthly advantage. But of your family I do venture to speak. It has been here so long, and your father loved this place so well, that it breaks my heart to think of its going to the hammer—after three centuries,"—and the old lady turned her head and wiped her eyes furtively, then added: "And it will go to the hammer—it must. I know Mr. Levinger well; he is a curious man, and whatever his real reasons may be, his mind is set upon this marriage. If he is disappointed about it, he will certainly take his remedy; indeed, he is bound to do so, for the money at stake is not his, but his daughter's."

"You tell me to take three months to consider, mother; but, looking at the matter from the family point of view, how am I to do this? It seems that we have scarcely a sixpence in the world, and a heavy accumulation of debt. Where is the money to come from to enable us to carry on for another three months?"

"Beyond the overdue interest there are not many floating liabilities, Henry, for I have always made it a practice to pay cash. Of course, when the farms come on hand at Michaelmas the case will be different, for then, unless they can be let in the meantime, a large sum of money must be found to pay the covenants and take them over, or they must go out of cultivation. Till then, however, you need have no anxiety, for, as it chances, at the moment I have ample funds at command."

"Ample funds! Where do they come from?"

"Of all my fortune, Henry, there remained to me my jewels, the diamonds and sapphires that my grandmother left me, which she inherited from her grandmother. They should have gone to Ellen, but when our need was pressing, rather than trouble your poor father any more, I sold them secretly. They realized between two and three thousand pounds—about half their value, I believe—of which I have a clear two thousand left. Do not tell Ellen of this, I pray you, for she would be very angry, and I do not feel fit to bear any scenes at present. And now, my dear, it is luncheon time, so I think that I will leave you, hoping that you will consider the advice which I have ventured to give you." And again she kissed him affectionately and left the room.

"Sold her jewels!" thought Henry, "the jewels that she valued above any possession in the world! My poor mother! And if I marry this girl, or do not marry the other, what will her end be? The workhouse, I suppose, unless Milward gives her a home out of charity, or I can earn sufficient to keep her, of which I see no prospect. Indeed, I begin to think that she is right, and that my first duty is owing to my family. And yet how can I abandon Joan? Or if I do, how can I marry Emma Levinger with this affair upon my hands, begun since I became acquainted with her? Oh! what an unhappy man am I! Well, there is one thing to be said—my evil doing is being repaid to me full measure, pressed down and running over. It is not often that punishment follows so hard upon the heels of error."

CHAPTER XVIII

CONGRATULATIONS

Joan was not really ill: she had contracted a chill, accompanied by a certain amount of fever, but this was all. Indeed, the fever had already taken her on the night of her love scene with Henry, and to its influence upon her nerves may be attributed a good deal of the conduct which to Lady Graves had seemed to give evidence of art and experienced design. Nothing further was said by her aunt as to her leaving the house, and things went on as usual till the morning when she woke up and learned that her lover had gone under such sad circumstances. It was a shock to her, but she grieved more for him than for herself. Indeed, she thought it best that he should be gone; it even seemed to her that she had anticipated it, that she had always known he must go and that she would see him no more. The curtain was down for ever; her short tragedy had culminated and was played out, so Joan believed, unaware that its most moving acts were yet to come. It was terrible, and henceforth her life must be a desolation; but it cannot be said that as yet her conscience caused her to grieve for what had been: sorrow and repentance were to overtake her when she learned all the trouble and ruin which her conduct had caused.

No, at present she was glad to have met him and to have loved him, winning some share of his love in return; and she thought then that she would rather go broken-hearted through the remainder of her days than sponge out those memories and be placid and prosperous without them. Whatever might be her natural longings, she had no intention of carrying the matter any further, least of all had she any intention of persuading or even of allowing Henry to marry her, for she had been quite earnest and truthful in her declarations to him upon this point. She did not even desire that his life should be burdened with her in any way, or that she should occupy his mind to the detriment of other persons and affairs; though of course she hoped that he would always think of her with affection, or perhaps with love, and she would have been no true woman had she not done so. Curiously enough, Joan seemed to expect that Henry would adopt the same passive attitude towards herself which she contemplated adopting towards him. She knew that men are for the most part desirous of burying their dead loves out of sight—sometimes, in their minds, marking the graves with a secret monument visible to themselves alone, be it a headstone with initials and a date, or only a withered wreath of flowers; but more often suffering the naked earth of oblivion to be trodden hard upon them, as though fearful lest their poor ghosts should rise again, and, taking flesh and form, come back to haunt a future in which they have no place.

She did not understand that Henry was not of this class, that in many respects his past life had been different to the lives of the majority of men, or that she was absolutely the first woman who had ever touched his heart. Therefore she came to the conclusion, sadly enough, and with an aching jealousy which she could not smother, but with resignation, that the next important piece of news she was likely to hear about her lover would be that of his engagement to Miss Levinger.

As it chanced, tidings of a totally different nature reached her on the following day, though whether they were true or false she could not tell. It was her aunt who brought them, when she came in with her supper, for Joan was still confined to her room.

"There are nice doings up there at Rosham," said Mrs. Gillingwater, eyeing her niece curiously.

Joan's heart gave a leap.

"What's the matter?" she asked, trying not to look too interested.

"Well, the old baronet is gone for one thing, as was expected that he must; and they say that he slipped off while he was cursing and swearing at his son, the Captain, which don't seem a right kind of way to die, to my mind."

"Died cursing and swearing at Captain Graves? Why?" murmured Joan faintly.

"I can't tell you rightly. All I know about it came to me from Lucilla Smith, who is own sister to Mary Roberts, the cook up there, who, it seems, was listening at the door, or, as she puts it, waiting to be called in to say good-bye to her master, and she had it from the gardener's boy."

"She? Who had it, aunt?"

"Why, Lucilla Smith had, of course. Can't you understand plain English? I tell you that old Sir Reginald sat up in bed and cursed and swore at the Captain till he was black in the face. Then he screeched out loud and died."

"How dreadful!" said Joan. "But what was he cursing about?"

"About? Why, because the Captain wouldn't promise to marry Miss Levinger, who's got bonds on all the property, down to the plate in the pantry, in her pocket. That old fox of a father of hers stole them when he was agent there, I expect—" Here Mrs. Gillingwater checked herself, and added hastily, "But that's neither here nor there; at any rate she's got them, and can sell the Graves's up to-morrow if she likes, which being so, it ain't wonderful that old Sir Reginald cursed when he heard his son turn round coolly and say that he wouldn't marry her at any price."

"Did he tell why he wouldn't marry her?" asked Joan, with a desperate effort to look unconcerned beneath her aunt's searching gaze.

"I don't know that he did. If so, Lucilla doesn't know, so I suppose that Mary Roberts couldn't hear. She did hear one thing, however: she heard your name, miss, twice, so there wasn't no mistake about it."

"My name? Oh! my name!" gasped Joan.

"Yes, yours, unless there is another Joan Haste in these parts, which I haven't heard on. And now, perhaps, you will tell me what it was doing there?"

"How can I tell you when I don't know, aunt?"

"How can you tell me when you won't say, miss? That's what you mean. Look here, Joan: do you take me for a fool? Do you suppose that I haven't seen through your little game? Why, I have watched it all along, and I'm bound to say that you don't play half so bad for a young hand. Well, it seems that you pulled it off this time, and I'm not saying but what I am proud of you, though I still hold that you would have done better to have married Samuel; for I believe, when all is said and finished, he will be the richer man of the two. It's very nice to be a baronet's lady, no doubt; but if you have nothing to live in—and I don't fancy that there are many pickings left up there at Rosham—I can't see that it helps you much forrarder."

"What do you mean, aunt?"

"Mean? Now, Joan, don't you begin trying your humbug on me: keep that for the men. You're not going to pretend that you haven't been making love to the Captain—I beg his pardon, Sir Henry he is now—as hard as you know how. Well, it seems that you have bamboozled him finely, and have made him so sweet on your pretty face that he's going to throw over marrying the Levinger girl in order to marry you, for that's what it comes to, and you may very well be proud of it. But don't you be carried away; you wouldn't take my advice about Samuel Rock, and I spoke to you rough that night on purpose, for I wanted you to make sure of one or the other. Well, take my advice about Sir Henry. Remember there is many a slip between the cup and the lip, and that out of sight is apt to be out of mind. Don't you keep out of sight too long. You strike while the iron is hot, and marry him; on the quiet if you like, but marry him. Of course there will be a row, but all the rows under heaven can't unmake a wife and a ladyship. Now listen to me. I have gone out of my way to talk to you like this, because you are a fine girl and I'm fond of you, which is more than you are of me, and I should like to see you get on in the world; and perhaps when you're up you will not forget your old aunt who is down. I tell you I have gone out of my way to give you this tip, for there's some as won't be pleased to see you turned into Lady Graves. Yes, there's some who'd give a good deal to stop it: Samuel Rock, for instance; he don't like parting, but he'd lay down something handsome, and I doubt if I'll ever see the coin out of you that I might out of him and others, for after all you won't be a rich woman at best. However, we must sacrifice ourselves at times, and that's what I am doing on your account, Joan. And now, if you want to get a note up to Rosham, I will manage it for you. But perhaps you had better wait and go yourself."

Joan listened to this long address in amazement mingled with scorn. It would be hard to say which of its qualities disgusted her the most—its coarseness, its cunning, or its avarice. Above all these, however, it revolted her to learn that her aunt thought her capable of conceiving and carrying out so disgraceful a plot. What must the woman's mind be like, that she could imagine such evil in others? And what had she, Joan, ever done, that she should be so misunderstood?

"I don't understand you, aunt; I don't wish to marry Captain Graves," she said simply.

"Do you mean to tell me that you ain't blind gone on him, and that's he's not gone on you, Joan?"

"I said that I did not wish to marry him," she answered, evading the question. "To marry a girl like me would be the ruin of him."

Mrs. Gillingwater stared at her niece as she lay on the bed before her; then she burst into a loud laugh.

"Oho! you're a simple one, you are," she said, pointing her finger at her. "You're downright innocent, if ever a girl was, with your hands folded and your hair hanging about your face, like a half-blown angel, more fit for a marble monument than for this wicked world. You couldn't give anybody a kiss on the quiet, could you? Your lips would blush themselves off first, wouldn't they? And as for marrying him if his ma didn't like it, that you'd never, never do. I'll tell you what it is, Joan: I'm getting a better opinion of you every day; you ain't half the fool I thought you, after all. You remember what I said to you about Samuel, and you think that I've got his money in my pocket and other people's too perhaps, and that I'm just setting a trap for you and going to give you away. Well, as a matter of fact I wasn't this time, so you might just as well have been open with me. But there you are, girl: go about your own business in your own fashion. I see that you can be trusted to look after yourself, and I won't spoil sport. I've been blind and deaf and dumb before now—yes, blinder than you think, perhaps, for all your psalm-singing air—and I can be again. And now I'm off; only I tell you fair I won't work for nothing, so don't you begin to whine about poor relations when once you're married, else I may find a way to make it hot for you yet, seeing that there's things you mightn't like spoke of when you're 'my lady' and respectable." And with this jocular threat on her lips Mrs. Gillingwater vanished.

When her aunt had gone, Joan drew the sheet over her face as though she sought to hide herself, and wept in the bitterness of her shame. She was what she was; but did she deserve to be spoken to like this? She would rather a hundred times have borne her aunt's worst violence than be made the object of her loathly compliments. How much did this woman know? Surely everything, or she would not dare to address her as she had done. She had no longer any respect for her, and that must be the reason of her odious assumption that there was nothing to choose between them, that they were equal in evil. She would not believe her when she said that she had no wish to marry Henry—she thought that the speech was dictated by a low cunning like her own. Well, perhaps it was fortunate that she did not believe her; for, if she had, what would have happened?

Very soon it became clear to Joan that on this point it would be best not to undeceive her aunt, since to do so might provoke some terrible catastrophe of which she could not foresee the consequences. After further reflection, another thing became clear to her: that she must vanish from Bradmouth. What was truth and what was falsehood in Mrs. Gillingwater's story, she could not say, but obviously it contained an alloy of fact. There had been some quarrel between Henry and his dying father, and in that quarrel her name had been mentioned. Strange as it seemed, it might even be that he had declared an intention of marrying her. Now that she thought of it, she remembered that he had spoken of such a thing several times. The idea opened new possibilities to her—possibilities of a happiness of which she had not dared to dream; but, to her honour be it said, she never allowed them to take root in her mind—no, not for a single hour. She knew well what such a marriage would mean for Henry, and that was enough. She must disappear; but whither? She had no means and no occupation. Where, then, could she go?

For two or three days she stayed in her room, keeping her aunt as much at a distance as possible, and pondering on these matters, but without attaining to any feasible solution of them.

On the day of Sir Reginald's funeral, which Mrs. Gillingwater attended, and of which she gave a full account, she received Henry's message brought to her by the doctor, and returned a general answer to it. Next morning her uncle Gillingwater, who chanced to be sober, brought her word that Mr. Levinger had called, and asked that she would favour him with a visit at Monk's Lodge so soon as she was about again. Joan wondered for what possible reason Mr. Levinger could wish to see her, and her conscience answered that it had to do with Henry. Well, if he was not her guardian, he took an undefined interest in her, and it occurred to her that he might be able to help her to escape from Bradmouth, so for this reason, if for no other, she determined to comply with his wish.

Two days later, accordingly, Joan started for Monk's Lodge, having arranged with the local grocer to give her a lift to the house, whither his van was bound to deliver some parcels; for, after being laid up, she did not feel equal to walking both ways. About two o'clock, arrayed in her best grey dress, she went to the grocer's shop and waited outside. Presently she heard a shrill voice calling to her from the stable-yard, that joined the shop, and a red-haired boy poked his head through the open door.

"Sorry to keep you waiting, Joan Haste," said the boy, who was none other than Willie Hood; "but I've been cleaning up the old horse's bit in honour of having such a swell as you to drive. Stand clear now;

here we come." And he led out the van, to which a broken-kneed animal was harnessed, that evidently had seen better days.

"Why, you're never going to drive me, Willie, are you?" asked Joan in alarm, for she remembered the tale of that youth's equestrian efforts.

"Yes, I am, though. Don't you be skeered. I know what you're thinking of; but I've been grocer's boy for a month now, and have learned all about hosses and how to ride and drive them. Come, up you get, unless you'd rather walk behind."

Thus adjured, Joan did get up, and they started. Soon she perceived that her fears as to Willie Hood's powers of driving were not ill-founded; but, fortunately, the animal that drew them was so reduced in spirit that it did not greatly matter whether any one was guiding him or no.

"Is he all right again?" said Willie presently, as, leaving the village, they began to travel along the dusty road that lay like a ribbon upon the green crest of the cliff.

"Do you mean Captain Graves?"

"Yes: who else? I saw him as they carried him into the Crown and Mitre that night. My word! he did look bad, and his trouser was all bloody too. I never seed any one so bloody before; though, now I come to think of it, you were bloody also, just like people in a story-book. That was a bad beginning for you both, they say."

"He is better; but he is not all right," answered Joan, with a sigh. Why would every one talk to her about Henry? "Captain Graves is not here now, you know."

"No; he's up at the Hall. And the old Squire is dead and buried. I went to see his funeral, I did. It was a grand sight—such lots of carriages, and such a beautiful polished coffin, with a brass cross and a plate with red letters on it. I'd like to be buried like that myself some day."

Joan smiled, but made no answer; and there was silence for a little time, while Willie thrashed the horse till his face was the colour of his hair.

"I say, Joan," he said, when at last that long-suffering animal broke into a shuffling trot, which caused the dust to rise in clouds, "is it true that you are going to marry him?"

"Marry Sir Henry Graves! Of course not. What put that idea into your head, you silly boy?"

"I don't know; it's what folks say, that's all. At least, they say that if you don't you ought to—though I don't rightly understand what they mean by that, unless it is that you are pretty enough to marry anybody, which I can see for myself."

Joan blushed crimson, and then turned pale as the dust.

"No need to pink up because I pay you a compliment, Joan," said Willie complacently.

"Folks say?" she gasped. "Who are the folks that say such things?"

"Everybody mostly—mother for one. But she says that you're like to find yourself left on the sand with the tide going out, like a dogfish that's been too greedy after sprats, for all that you think yourself so clever, and are so stuck-up about your looks. But then mother never did like a pretty girl, and I don't pay no attention to her—not a mite; and if I was you, Joan, I'd just marry him to spite them."

"Look here, Willie," answered Joan, who by now was almost beside herself: "if you say another word about me and Sir Henry Graves, I'll get out and walk."

"Well, I dare say the old horse would thank you if you did. But I don't see why you should take on so just because I've been answering your questions. I expect it's all true, and that you do want to marry him, or else you're left on the beach like the dogfish. But if you are, it's no reason why you should be cross with me."

"I'm not cross, Willie, I am not indeed; but you don't understand that I can't bear this kind of gossip."

"Then you'd better get out of Bradmouth as fast as you can, Joan, for you'll have lots of it to bear there, I can tell you. Why, I'm downright sick of it myself," answered the merciless Willie. Then he lapsed into a dignified silence, that for the rest of the journey was only broken by his exhortations to the sweating horse, and the sound of the whacks which he rained upon its back.

At length they reached Monk's Lodge, and drove round to the side-entrance, where Joan got down hurriedly and walked to the servants' door.

CHAPTER XIX

RIGHTEOUS INDIGNATION

On the day before Sir Reginald's funeral Mr. Samuel Rock presented himself at Monk's Lodge, and was shown into the study. As he entered Mr. Levinger noticed that his mien was morose, and that dejection beamed from his pale blue eyes, if indeed dejection can be said to beam.

"I fancy that my friend's love affairs have gone wrong," he thought to himself; "he would scarcely look so sulky about a cow shed." Yet it was of this useful building that he began to speak.

"Well, Mr. Rock," he said cheerfully, "have they dug out the foundations of that shed yet?"

"Shed, sir?" answered Samuel (he pronounced it shodd): "I haven't come to speak to you about no sheds. I have come to speak to you about the advice you gave me as to Joan Haste."

"Oh! yes, I remember: you wanted to marry her, didn't you? Well, did you take it?"

"I took it, sir, to my sorrow, for she wouldn't have nothing to do with me. I went so far as to try and kiss her."

"Yes. And then?"

"And then, sir, she pushed me off, that's all, and stood there saying things that I would rather forget. But here's the story, sir." And with a certain amount of glozing and omission, he told the tale of his repulse.

"Your case does not seem very promising," said Mr. Levinger lightly, for he did not wish to show his vexation; "but perhaps the lady will change her mind. As you know, it is often darkest before the dawn."

"Oh yes, sir," answered Samuel, with a kind of sullen confidence, "sooner or later she will change her mind, never fear, and I shall marry her, I am sure of it; but she won't change her heart, that's the point, for she's given that to another."

"Well, perhaps, if you get the rest of her, Mr. Rock, you may leave the heart to the other, for that organ is not of very much practical use by itself, is it? Might I ask who the other is?"

Samuel shook his head gloomily, and answered:

"It's all very well for you to joke about hearts, sir, as haven't got one—I mean, as don't take no interest in them; but they're everything to me—least Joan's is. And as for who it is, sir, if half I hear is true, it's that Captain, I mean Sir Henry Graves. You warned me against him, you remember, and you spoke strong because I grew angry. Well, sir, I did right to be angry, for it's him she loves, Mr. Levinger, and that's why she hates me. They're talking about them all over Bradmouth."

"Indeed. Well, Bradmouth always was a great place for scandal, and I should not pay much attention to their tongues, were I you, Mr. Rock. Girls will have their fancies, you know, and I do not think it is necessary to hunt round for explanations because this one happens to flout you. I dare say it will all come right in time, if you have a little patience. Anyway there will be no more gossip about Joan Haste and Sir Henry Graves, for he has gone home, where he will find plenty of other things to occupy him, poor fellow. And now I have a plan of the shed here: perhaps you can explain it to me."

Samuel expounded his plan and went away, this time without the offer of any port wine, for it seemed to his host that he was already quite sufficiently excited.

When he had gone, Mr. Levinger rose from his chair and began to limp up and down the room, as was his custom when thinking deeply. To Samuel he had made light of the talk about Sir Henry Graves and Joan Haste, but he knew well that this was no light matter. He had been kept informed of the progress of their intimacy by his paid spy, Mrs. Gillingwater, but at the time he could find no pretext that would enable him to interfere without exposing himself to the risk of questions, which he preferred should be left unasked. On the previous day only, Mrs. Gillingwater had come to see him, and given him her version of the rumours which were flying about as to the scene that occurred at the death-bed of Sir Reginald. Discount these rumours as he would, he could not doubt but that they had a basis in fact. That Henry had declined to bind himself to marry his daughter Emma was clear; and it seemed probable that this refusal, made in so solemn an hour, had something to do with the girl Joan. And now, on top of it, came Samuel Rock with the story of his angry and ignominious rejection by this same Joan, a rejection that he unhesitatingly attributed to her intimacy or intrigue with Henry Graves.

The upshot of these reflections was the message received by Joan summoning her to Monk's Lodge.

Having escaped from Willie Hood, Joan paused for a minute to recover her equanimity, then she rang the back-door bell and asked for Mr. Levinger. Apparently she was expected, for the servant showed her straight to the study, where she found Mr. Levinger, who rose, shook hands with her courteously, and invited her to be seated.

"You sent for me, sir," she began nervously.

"Yes: thank you for coming. I wanted to speak to you about a little matter." And he went to the window and stood with his face to the light, so that she could only see the back of his head.

"Yes, sir."

"I trust that you will not be pained, my dear girl, if I begin by alluding to the circumstances of your birth; for, believe me, I do not wish to pain you."

"I so often hear them alluded to, in one way or another, sir," answered Joan, with some warmth, "that it really cannot matter who speaks to me about them. I know what I am, though I don't know any particulars; and such people should have no feelings."

Mr. Levinger's shoulders moved uneasily, and he answered, still addressing the window-pane, "I fear I can give you no particulars now, Joan; but pray do not distress yourself, for you least of all people are responsible for your—unfortunate—position."

"The sins of the fathers shall be visited on the children," answered Joan aptly enough. "Not that I have a right to judge anybody," and she sighed.

"As I have said," went on Mr. Levinger, taking no notice of her interruption, "I am not in a position to give you any details about those circumstances, or even the name of your father, since to do so would be to violate a sacred confidence and a solemn promise."

"What confidence and what promise, sir?"

Mr. Levinger hesitated a little, then answered, "Your dead father's confidence, and my promise to him."

"So, sir, the father who brought me into the world to be the mock of every one made you promise that you would never tell me his name, even after he was dead? I am sorry to hear it, sir, for it makes me think worse of him than ever I did before. Father or no father, he must have been a coward—yes, such a coward that I can hardly believe it."

"The case was a very peculiar one, Joan; but if you require any such assurance, that I am telling you nothing but the truth is evident from the fact that it would be very easy to tell you a lie. It would not have been difficult to invent a false name for your father."

"No, sir; but it would have been awkward, seeing that sooner or later I should have found out that it was false."

"Without entering into argument on the question of the morality of his decision, which is a matter for which he alone was responsible," said Mr. Levinger, in an irritated voice, "as I have told you, your father decided that it would be best that you should never know his name, or anything about him, except that he was of gentle birth. I believe that it was not cowardice, as you suggest, which made him take this course, but a regard for the rights and feelings of others whom he left behind him."

"And have I no rights and feelings, sir, and did he not leave me behind him?" Joan answered bitterly. "Is it wonderful that I, who have no mother, should wish to know who my father was? and could he not have foreseen that I should wish it? Was it not enough that he should desert me to be brought up in a public-house by a man who drinks, and a rough woman who hates me and would like to see me as bad as herself, with no one even to teach me my prayers when I was little, or to keep me from going to the bad when I grew older? Why should he also refuse to let me know his name, or the kin from which I come? Perhaps I am no judge of such matters, sir; but it seems to me that if ever a man behaved wickedly to a poor girl, my father has done so to me, and, dead or living, I believe that he will have to answer for it one day, since there is justice for us all somewhere."

Suddenly Mr. Levinger wheeled round, and Joan saw that his face was white, as though with fear or anger, and that his quick eyes gleamed.

"You wicked girl!" he said in a low voice, "are you not ashamed to call down curses upon your own father, your dead father? Do you not know that your words may be heard—yes, even outside this earth, and perhaps bring endless sorrow on him? If he has wronged you, you should still honour him, for he gave you life."

"Honour him, sir? Honour the man who deserted me and left me in the mud without a name? It isn't such fathers as this that the Prayer-book tells us to honour. He is dead, you say, and beyond me; and how can my words touch the dead? But even if they can, could they do him more harm, wherever he is, than he has done to me here? Oh! you do not understand. I could forgive him everything, but I can't forgive that he should make me go through my life without even knowing his name, or who he was. Had he only left me a kind word, or a letter, I dare say that I could even have loved him, though I never saw him. As it is, I think I hate him, and I hope that one day he will know it."

As she said these words, Mr. Levinger slowly turned his back upon her and began to look out of the window again, as though he felt himself unable to face the righteous indignation that shone in her splendid eyes.

"Joan Haste," he said, speaking quietly but with effort, "if you are going to talk in this way I think that we had better bring our interview to an end, as the conversation is painful to me. Once and for all I tell you, that if you are trying to get further information out of me you will fail."

"I have said my say, sir, and I shall ask you no more questions, except one; but none the less I believe that the truth will come out some time, for others must have known what you know, and perhaps after all my father had a conscience. I'm told that people often see things differently when they come to die, and he may have done so. The question that I want to ask, sir, if you will be so kind as to answer it, is: You knew my father, so I suppose that you knew my mother also, though she's been dead these twenty years. How did she come by her death, sir? I have heard say that she was drowned, but nobody seems able to tell me any more about it."

"I believe that your mother was found dead beneath the cliff opposite the meres. How she came there is not known, but it is supposed that she missed her footing in the dark and fell over. The story of her drowning arose from her being found at high tide in the shallow water; but the medical evidence at the inquest showed that death had resulted from a fall, and not from suffocation."

"My poor mother!" said Joan, with a sigh. "She was unlucky all her life, it seems, so I dare say that she was well rid of it, and her death must have been good news to some. There's only one thing I'm sorry for—that I wasn't in her arms when she went over the edge of that cliff. And now, sir, about the business."

"Yes, about the business," replied Mr. Levinger, with a hard little laugh; "after so much sentiment it is quite refreshing to come to business, although unfortunately this has its sentimental side also. You must understand, Joan, that the parent whom you are so hard on, and whose agent I chanced to be in bygone years, left me more or less in a fiduciary position as regards yourself—that is to say, he entrusted me with a certain sum of money to be devoted to your education, and generally to your advancement in life, making the proviso that you were not to be brought up as a lady, since, rightly or wrongly, he did not think that this would conduce to your happiness. Well, I have strained the letter of my instructions, and you have had a kind of half-and-half education. Now I think that I should have done better to have held closer to them; for so far as I can judge, the result has been to make you dissatisfied with your position and surroundings. However, that is neither here nor there. You are now of age; the funds at my disposal are practically exhausted; and I desire to wind up my trust by settling you happily in life, if I can do so. You will wonder what I am driving at. I will tell you. I understand that a very worthy farmer, a tenant of mine, who is also a large freeholder—I mean Mr. Samuel Rock—wishes to make you his wife. Is this so?"

"Yes, sir."

"Very well. Don't think me rude; but I should be glad to know if you are inclined to fall in with his views."

"On the whole, sir," answered Joan composedly, "I think that I would rather follow my mother's example and walk over the cliff at high tide."

"That statement seems pretty comprehensive," said Mr. Levinger, after a pause; "and, to be frank, I don't see any way round it. I am to understand, then, that Mr. Rock is so distasteful to you that you decline to have anything to do with him?"

"Absolutely, sir: I detest Mr. Rock, and I can scarcely conceive any circumstances under which I would consent to marry him."

"Well, Joan, I am sorry, because I think that the marriage would have been to your advantage; but this is a free country. Still, it is a pity—a great pity—especially, to be candid, as I have heard your name pretty roughly handled of late; in a way, indeed, that is likely to bring disgrace upon it."

"You are forgetting, sir, that I have no name to disgrace. What I do, or leave undone, can matter to nobody. I have only myself to think of."

"Really this is a most unfortunate tone for any young woman to adopt; still, I did hope that, if you considered nobody else, you would at least consider your own reputation. Perhaps you know to what I allude?"

"Yes, sir; I know."

"Might I ask you if there is any truth in it?"

Then for the first time Joan lied. So far as she was aware, she had never before told a deliberate falsehood; but now she had entered on a path in which falsehood of necessity becomes a weapon of self-defence, to be used at all times and places. She did not pause to think; she knew that she must protect herself and her lover from this keen-eyed, plausible man, who was searching out their secret for some purpose of his own.

"No, sir," she said boldly, looking him in the face, "there is no truth. I nursed Sir Henry Graves, and I tried to do my duty by him, and of course people talked about us. For years past I never could speak to a man but what they talked about me in Bradmouth."

Mr. Levinger shrugged his shoulders.

"I have asked my question, and I have got my answer. Of course I believe you; but even if the story were ever so true, I should not have expected any other reply. Well, I am glad to hear that it is not true, for it would have been much to the detriment of both yourself and Sir Henry Graves—especially of Sir Henry Graves."

"Why especially of Sir Henry, sir? I have always understood that it is the girl who suffers if there is any talk, because she is the weaker. Not that talk matters to one like me who has nothing to lose."

"Because it might interfere with his matrimonial prospects, that is all. As you may have heard, the affairs of this family are in such a condition that, if Sir Henry does not marry advantageously, he will be utterly ruined. He may as well commit suicide as attempt to take a wife without money, however fond he might be of her, or however charming she was," Mr. Levinger said meaningly, watching Joan's face.

She understood him perfectly, and did not hesitate as to her answer, though it must have cost her much to speak it.

"I have heard, sir. I have a great regard and respect for Sir Henry Graves, and I hope that he will settle himself well in life. I happen to know, also, that there is a young lady who has fortune and is fond of him. I trust that he will marry her, as she will make him a good wife."

Mr. Levinger nodded.

"I trust so too, Joan, for everybody's sake. Thank you for your good wishes. I was afraid, to speak frankly, that there was some truth in these tales; that you might selfishly, though naturally enough, adopt a course towards Sir Henry Graves which would be prejudicial to his true interests; and that he would possibly be so foolish as to suffer himself to be led away—as, indeed, any man might be without much blame—by the affection of such a woman as you are, Joan."

"I have given you my answer about it, sir. If you think for a minute you will understand that, had there been any truth in these tales, the more reason would there be that I should speak as I have done, seeing that no true woman could wish to injure the man whom she—dearly loves, no, not even if it broke her heart to part with him."

And Joan turned her head, in a somewhat ineffectual attempt to hide the tears that welled into her eyes.

Mr. Levinger looked at her with admiration. He did not believe a word of her statement with reference to herself and Henry. Indeed, he knew it to be false, and that her denial amounted merely to a formal plea of "not guilty"

"Of course, of course," he said; "but all the same you are a brave girl, Joan, and I am sure that it will be made up to you in some way or other. And now—what do you intend to do with yourself?"

"It was of this that I wished to speak to you, sir. I want to go away from Bradmouth. I am not fit to be a governess: I don't know enough, and there are very few people who would care to take me. But I could do as a shop-girl in London. I have a decent figure, and I dare say that they will employ me to hang cloaks on for the ladies to look at, only you see I have no money to start with."

Mr. Levinger hesitated. Her plan had great advantages from his point of view, and yet—

"I suppose that you really mean to seek honest employment, Joan? Forgive me, but you know—you have been talking a little wildly once or twice this afternoon as to your being without responsibilities to anybody."

"You need not be afraid, sir," she said, with a sad smile; "I want to earn my bread away from here, that is all. If there has been talk about me in Bradmouth, there shall be none in London, or anywhere else I may go."

"I am glad to hear it, Joan. Without some such assurance, an assurance in which I put the most implicit faith, I could never have helped you in your plan. As it is, you shall not lack for money. I will give you five-and-twenty pounds to put in your pocket, and make you an allowance of five pounds a month for so long as you require it. If you wish to go to London, I know a respectable woman who takes in girls to lodge, mostly ladies in reduced circumstances who are earning their living in one way or another. Here is the address: Mrs. Thomas, 13, Kent Street, Paddington. By the way, you will do well to get a certificate of character from the clergyman at Bradmouth; my name would carry no weight, you see. But of course, if you fall into any difficulties, you will communicate with me at once; and as I have said I propose to allow you sixty pounds a year, which will be a sufficient sum to keep you in comfort whether or no you succeed in obtaining employment. Now for the money," and he drew his cheque-book from a drawer, but replaced it, saying, "No, perhaps gold would be more convenient."

Then he went to a small safe, and, unlocking it, extracted twenty-four pounds in sovereigns, which, with the exception of some bank-notes, was all that it contained.

"Twenty-four," he said, counting them. "I dare say that I can make up the other sovereign;" and he searched his pockets, producing a ten-shilling bit and some loose silver.

"Why don't you give me one of the notes, sir, instead of so much money?" asked Joan innocently.

"No, no. I always like to make payments in gold, which is the legal tender, you know; though I am afraid I must give you some silver in this case. There you are, all but threepence. I shall have to owe you the threepence. What, you haven't got a purse? Then tie up the money in the corner of your pocket-handkerchief, and put it in the bosom of your dress, where it can't fall out. I have found that the safest way for a woman to carry valuables."

Joan obeyed, saying, "I don't know if I have to thank you for this money, sir."

"Not at all, not at all. It is a portion of your trust fund."

"I thought you said that the amount was almost exhausted, sir; and if so, how can you give me this and promise to pay me sixty pounds a year?"

"No, no, you are mistaken; I did not say that—I said it was getting rather low. But really I don't quite know how the account stands. I must look into it. And now, is there anything more?"

"Yes, one thing, sir. I do not want anybody in Bradmouth, or anybody anywhere, and more especially my aunt, to know whither I have gone, or what my address is. I have done with the old life, and I wish to begin a new one."

"Certainly; I understand. Your secret will be safe with me, Joan. And now good-bye."

"Good-bye, sir; and many thanks for all that you have done for me in the past, and for your kindness to-day. You must not think too much of any bitter words I may have said: at times I remember how lonely I am in the world, and I think and speak like that, not because I mean it, but because my heart is sore."

"It is perfectly natural, and I do not blame you," answered Mr. Levinger, as he showed her out of the room. "Only remember what I say: for aught you know, even the dead may have ears to hear and hearts to feel, and when you judge them, they, whose mouths are closed, cannot return to explain what you believe to be their wickedness. Where are you going? To the kitchen? No, no—the front door, if you please. Good-bye again: good luck to you!"

"Thank Heaven that she has gone!" Mr. Levinger thought to himself, as he sat down in his chair. "It has been a trying interview, very trying, for both of us. She is a plucky woman, and a good one according to her lights. She lied about Henry Graves, but then it was not to be expected that she would do anything else; and whatever terms they are on, she is riding straight now, which shows that she must be very fond of him, poor girl."

CHAPTER XX

"LET IT REMAIN OPEN"

Outside the door of Monk's Lodge, Joan met Emma returning from a walk. As usual she was dressed in white, and, to Joan's fancy, looked pure as a wild anemone in the April sun, and almost as frail. She would have passed her with a little salutation that was half bow, half curtsey, but Emma held out her hand.

"How do you do, Miss Haste?" she said, with a slight nervous tremor in her voice. "I did not know that you were up here," and she stopped; but her look seemed to add, "And I wonder why you have come."

"I am going to leave Bradmouth, and I came to say good-bye to Mr. Levinger, who has always been very kind to me," Joan replied, with characteristic openness, answering the look and not the words. She felt that, in the circumstances, it was best that she should be open with Miss Levinger.

Emma looked surprised. "I was not aware that you were going," she said; but again Joan felt that what astonished her was not the news of her approaching departure, but the discovery that she was on intimate terms with her father. She was right. Emma remembered that he had spoken disparagingly of this girl, and as though he knew nothing about her. It seemed curious, then, that he should have been "very kind" to her, and that she should come to bid him good-bye. Here was another of those mysteries with which her father's life seemed to be surrounded, and which so frequently made her feel uncomfortable and afraid of she knew not what. "Won't you come in and have some tea?" Emma asked kindly.

"No, thank you, miss; I have to walk home, and I must not stay any longer."

"It is a long way, and you look tired. Let me order the dogcart for you."

"Indeed no, thank you. I haven't been very well—that is why I am paler than usual. But I am quite strong again now," and Joan made a movement as though to start on her walk.

"If you will allow me, I will come a little way with you," said Emma timidly.

"I shall be very pleased, miss."

The two girls turned, and, for a while, walked side by side in silence, each of them wondering about the other and the man who was dear to both.

"Are you going to be a nurse?" asked Emma at length.

"Oh no! What made you think that?"

"Because you nursed Captain—I mean Sir Henry—Graves so wonderfully," Emma answered, colouring. "Dr. Childs told me he believed that you saved his life."

"Then I have done something in the world," said Joan, with a little laugh; "but it is the first that I have heard of it."

"Really! Haven't they thanked you?"

"Somebody offered to pay me, if you mean that, miss."

"No, no; I didn't mean it. I meant that we are all grateful to you, so very grateful—at least, his family are. Then what do you intend to do when you go away?" she asked, changing the subject suddenly.

"I don't know, miss. Earn my living as best I can—as a shop girl, probably."

"It seems rather terrible starting by oneself out into the unknown, like this. Does it not frighten you?"

"Perhaps it does," answered Joan; "but beggars cannot be choosers. I can't stop here, where I have nothing to do; and, you see, I am alone in the world."

Emma understood the allusion, and said hastily:

"I am very sorry for you—I am indeed, if you won't be angry with me for saying so. It is cruel that you should have to suffer like this for no fault of your own. It would kill me if I found myself in the same position—yes, I am sure that it would."

"Luckily, or unluckily, it doesn't kill me, miss, though sometimes it is hard enough to bear. You see that the burden is laid upon the broadest back, and I can carry what would crush you. Still, I thank you for your sympathy and the kind thought which made you speak it. I have very few memories of that sort, and I shall never forget this one."

For another five minutes or so they went on without speaking, since their fount of conversation seemed to have dried up. At length, beginning to feel the silence irksome, Emma stopped and held out her hand, saying that she would now return.

"Would you listen to a word or two from me before you go, miss? And would you promise not to repeat it—no, not to Mr. Levinger even?" said Joan suddenly.

"Certainly, if you wish it. What is it about?"

"About you and myself and another person. Miss Levinger, I am going away from here—I believe for good—and I think it likely that we shall not meet again. When I am gone you will hear all sorts of tales about me and Sir Henry."

"Really—really!" said Emma, in some distress.

"Listen to me, miss: there is nothing very dreadful, and I speak for your own good. While all this sickness was on I learned something—I learned that you are fond of Sir Henry, never mind how—"

"I know how," murmured Emma. "Oh! did you tell him?"

"I told him nothing; indeed, I had nothing to tell. I saw you faint, and guessed the rest. What I want to ask you is this: that you will believe no stories which may be told against Sir Henry, for he is quite blameless. Now I have only one thing more to say, and it is, that I have watched him and known him well; and, if you do not cling to him through good and through evil, you will be foolish indeed, for there is no better man, and you will never find such another for a husband. I wish that it may all come about, and that you may be happy with him through a long life, Miss Levinger."

Emma heard, and, though vaguely as yet, understood all the nobility and self-sacrifice of her rival. She also loved this man, and she renounced him for the sake of his own welfare. Otherwise she would never have spoken thus.

"I do not know what to answer you," she said. "I do not deny it is true that I am attached to Sir Henry, though I have no right to be. What am I to answer you?"

"Nothing, except this: that under any circumstances you will not believe a word against him."

"I can promise that, if it pleases you."

"It does please me; for, wherever I am, I should like to think of you and him as married and happy, for I know that he will make you a good husband, as you will make him a good wife. And now again, good-bye."

Emma looked at Joan and tried to speak, but could find no words; then suddenly she put out her arms and attempted to kiss her.

"No," said Joan, holding her back; "do not kiss me, but remember what I have said, and think kindly of me if you can."

Then she walked away swiftly, without looking back, leaving Emma standing bewildered upon the road.

"I have done it now," thought Joan to herself—"for good or evil I have done it, though I don't quite know what made me speak like that. She will understand now: some women might not take it well, but I think that she will, because she wants to. Oh! if I had known all that was at stake, I'd have acted very differently. I thought that I could only harm myself, but it seems I may ruin him, and that I'll never do; I'd rather make away with myself. I suppose that we cannot sin against ourselves alone; the innocent must suffer with the guilty, that's the truth of it, as I suffer to-day because my father and mother were guilty more than twenty years ago. Still, it is hard—very hard—to have to go away and give him up to her; to have to humble myself before her, and to tell lies to her father, when I know that if it wasn't for my being nobody's child, and not fit to marry an honest man, and for this wretched money, I could be the best wife to him that ever he could have. Yes, and make him love me too, though I am almost sure that he does not really love me now. Well, she has the name and the fortune, and will do as well, I dare say; and some must dig thistles while others pluck flowers. Still, it is cruel hard, and, though I am afraid to die, I wish that I were dead, I do—I do!"

Then the poor girl began to sob as she walked, and, thus sobbing and furtively wiping away the tears that would run from her eyes, she crept back to the inn in the twilight, thoroughly weary and broken in spirit.

When Emma reached Monk's Lodge she found her father leaning over the front gate, as though he were waiting for her.

"Where have you been, love?" he said, in that tone of tenderness which he always adopted when speaking to his daughter. "I thought that I saw you on the road with somebody, and began to wonder why you were so late."

"I have been walking with Joan Haste," she answered absently.

"Why have you been walking with her?" he asked, in a quick and suspicious voice. "She is very well in her way, but not altogether the sort of person for you to make a companion of."

"I don't know about that, father. I should say that she was quite my equal, if not my superior, except that I have been a little better educated."

"Well, well, perhaps so, Emma; but I should prefer that you did not become too intimate with her."

"There is no need to fear that, father, as she is going away from Bradmouth."

"Oh! she told you that she was leaving here, did she? And what else did she tell you?"

"A good deal about herself. Of course I knew something of her story before; but I did not know that she felt her position so bitterly. Poor girl! she has been cruelly treated."

"I really fail to see it, Emma. Considering the unfortunate circumstances connected with her, it seems to me that she has been very well treated."

"I don't think so, father, and you only believe it because you are not a woman and do not understand. Suppose, now, that I, your daughter whom you are fond of, were in her place to-day, without a friend or home, feeling myself a lady and yet obliged to mix with rough people and to be the mark of their sneers, jealousy and evil-speaking, should you say that I was well treated? Suppose that I was going to-morrow to be thrown, without help or experience, on to the world to earn my bread there, should you—"

"I absolutely decline to suppose anything of the sort, Emma," he answered passionately. "Bother the girl! Why does she put such ideas into your head?"

"Really, father," she said, opening her eyes wide, "there is no need for you to get angry with Joan Haste, especially as she told me that you had always been kind to her."

"I am not angry, Emma, but one way and another that girl gives me more trouble than enough. She might make a very good marriage, and settle herself in life out of reach of all these disagreeables, about which she seems to have been whining to you, but she is so pig-headed that she won't."

"But surely, father, you wouldn't expect her to marry a man she doesn't like, would you? Why, I have heard you say that you thought it better that a woman should never be born than that she should be forced into a distasteful marriage."

"Circumstances alter cases, and certainly it would have been better if she had never been born," answered Mr. Levinger, who seemed quite beside himself with irritation. "However, there it is: she won't marry, she won't do anything except bring trouble upon others with her confounded beauty, and make herself the object of scandal."

"I think that it is time for me to go and dress," said Emma coldly.

"I forgot, my dear; I should not have spoken of that before you, but really I feel quite unhinged to-night. I suppose that you have no idea of what I am alluding to, but if not you soon will have, for some kind friend is sure to tell you."

"I—have an idea, father."

"Very well. Then I may as well tell you that it is all nonsense."

"I am not sure that it is all nonsense," she answered, in the same restrained voice; "but whether it is nonsense or no, it has nothing to do with me."

"Nothing to do with you, Emma! Do you mean that? Listen, my love: these are delicate matters, but if any one may speak to a woman about them, her father may. Do you remember that nearly two years ago, when you were more intimate and open with me than you are now, Emma, you told me that Henry Graves had—well, taken your fancy?"

"I remember. I told you because I did not think it likely that I should meet him again, and because you said something to me about marrying, and I wished to put a stop to the idea."

"Yes, I quite understand; but I gathered from what took place the other day, when poor Graves was so ill, that you still entertain an affection for him."

"Oh! pray do not speak of that," she murmured; "I cannot bear it even from you; it covers me with shame. I was mad, and you should have paid no attention to it."

"I am sorry to give you pain or to press you, Emma, but I should be deeply grateful if you would make matters a little clearer. Never mind about Henry Graves and his attitude towards you: I want to understand yours towards him. As you know, or if you do not know I beg you to believe it, your happiness is the chief object of my life, and to secure that happiness to you I have planned and striven for years. What I wish to learn now is: do you desire to have done with Henry Graves? If so, tell me at once. It will be a great blow to me, for he is the man of all others to whom, for many reasons, I should like to see you married, and doubtless if matters are left alone he will marry you. But in this affair your wish is my law, and if you would prefer it I will wind up the mortgage business, cut the connection to-morrow, and then we can travel for a year in Egypt, or wherever you like. Sometimes I think that this would be the best course. But it is for you to choose, not for me. You are a woman full grown, and must know your own mind. Now, Emma."

"What do you mean by winding up the mortgage business, father?"

"Oh! the Graves's owe us some fifty or sixty thousand pounds, and it is not a paying investment, that is all. But don't you bother about that, Emma: confine yourself to the personal aspect of the question, please."

"It is very hard to have to decide so quickly. Can I not give you an answer in a few days, father?"

"No, Emma, you can't. I will not be kept halting between two opinions any longer. I want to know what line to take at once."

"Well, then, on the whole I think that perhaps you had better not 'wind up the business.' I very much doubt if anything will come of this. I am by no means certain that I wish anything to come of it, but we will let it remain open."

"In making that answer, Emma, I suppose that you are bearing in mind that, though I believe it to be all nonsense, the fact is not to be concealed that there is some talk about Graves and Joan Haste."

"I am bearing it in mind, father. The talk has nothing to do with me. I do not wish to know even whether it is false or true, at any rate at present. True or false, there will be an end of it now, as the girl is going away. I hope that I have made myself clear. I understand that, for reasons of your own, you are very anxious that I should marry Sir Henry Graves, should it come in my way to do so; and I know that his family desire this also, because it would be a road out of their money difficulties. What Sir Henry wishes himself I do not know, nor can I say what I wish. But I think that if I stood alone, and had only myself to consider, I should never see him again. Still I say, let it remain open, although I decline to bind myself to anything definite. And now I must really go and dress."

"I do not know that I am much 'for'arder,' after all, as Samuel Rock says," thought Mr. Levinger, looking after her. "Oh, Joan Haste! you have a deal to answer for." Then he also went to dress.

The two interviews in which Emma had taken part this afternoon—that with Joan and that with her father—had, as it were, unsealed her eyes and opened her ears. Now she saw the significance of many a hint of Ellen's and her father's which hitherto had conveyed no meaning to her, and now she understood what it was that occasioned the forced manner which had struck her as curious in Henry's bearing towards herself, even when he had seemed most at his ease and pleased with her. Doubtless the knowledge that he was expected to marry a particular girl, in order that by so doing he might release debts to the amount of fifty thousand pounds, was calculated to cause the manner of any man towards that girl to become harsh and suspicious, and even to lead him to regard her with dislike. This was why he had been forced to leave the Service, for this reason "his family had desired his presence," and the opening in life, the only one that remained to him, to which he had alluded so bitterly, but significantly enough avoided specifying, was to marry a girl with fortune, to marry her—Emma Levinger.

It was a humiliating revelation, and though perhaps Emma had less pride than most women, she felt it sorely. She was deeply attached to this man; her heart had gone out to him when she first saw him, after the unaccountable fashion that hearts sometimes affect. Still, having learned the truth, she was quite in earnest when she told her father that, were she alone concerned, she would meet him no more. But she was not alone in the matter, and it was this knowledge that made her pause. To begin with, there was Henry himself to be considered, for it seemed that if he did not marry her he would be ruined or something very like it; and, regarding him as she did, it became a question whether she ought not to outrage her pride in order to save him if he would be saved. Also she knew that her father wished for this marriage above all things—that it was, indeed, one of the chief objects of his life; though it was true that in an inexplicable fit of irritation with everything and everybody, he had but now offered to bring the affair to nothing. Why he should be so set upon it she could not understand, any more than she could understand why he should have been so vexed when she illustrated her sense of the hardship of Joan's position by supposing herself to be similarly placed. These were some of the mysteries by which their life was surrounded, mysteries that seemed to thicken daily. After what she had seen and heard this afternoon she began to believe that Joan Haste herself was another of them. Joan had told her that her father had always been kind to her. Taken by itself there was nothing strange about this, for Emma knew him to be charitable to many people, but it was strange that he should have practically denied all knowledge of the girl some few weeks before. Perhaps he knew more about her than he chose to say—even who she was and where she came from.

Now it appeared that her presentiment was coming true, and that Joan herself was playing some obscure and undefined part in the romance or intrigue in which she, Emma, was the principal though innocent actor. In effect, Joan had given her to understand that she was in love with Henry, and yet she had implored her to marry Henry. Why, if Joan was in love with him, should she desire another woman to marry him? It was positively bewildering, also it was painful, and, like everything else connected with this business, humbling to her pride. She felt herself being involved in a network of passions, motives, and interests of which she could only guess the causes, and the issues whereof were dark; and she longed, ah, how she longed to escape from it back into the freedom of clear purpose and honest love! But would she ever escape? Could she ever hope to be the cherished wife of the man whom too soon she had learned to love? Alas! she doubted it. And yet, whatever was the reason, she could not make up her mind to have done with him, either for his sake or her own.

CHAPTER XXI

A LUNCHEON PARTY

Two days after her visit to Mr. Levinger Joan began her simple preparations for departure, for it was her intention to leave Bradmouth by the ten o'clock train on the following morning. First, however, after much thought she wrote this note to Henry:—

"Dear Sir Henry Graves,—

"Thank you for the kind message you sent asking after me. There was never much the matter, and I am quite well again now. I was very sorry to hear of the death of Sir Reginald. I fear that it must have been a great shock to you. Perhaps you would like to know that I am leaving Bradmouth for good and all, as I have no friends here and do not get on well; besides, it is time that I should be working for my own living. I am leaving without telling my aunt, so that nobody will know my address or be able to trouble me to come back. I do not fear, however, but that I shall manage to hold my own in the world, as I am strong and active, and have plenty of money to start with. I think you said that I might have the books which you left behind here, so I am taking them with me as a keepsake. If I live, they will remind me of the days when I used to nurse you, and to read to you out of them, long years after you have forgotten me. Good-bye, dear Sir Henry. I hope that soon you will be quite well again and happy all your life. I do not think that we shall meet any more, so again good-bye.

"Obediently yours,
"Joan Haste."

When Joan had finished her letter she read it once, kissed it several times, then placed it in an envelope which she directed to Sir Henry Graves. "There," she thought, as she dropped it into the post-box, "I must go now, or he will be coming to look after me."

On her way back to the inn she met Willie Hood standing outside the grocer's shop, with his coat off and his thumbs hooked in the armholes of his waistcoat.

"Will you do something for me, Willie?" she asked.

"Anything to oblige a customer, I am sure, Joan Haste," answered that forward youth.

"Very well: then will you come round to-morrow morning with a hand-barrow at six o'clock time—not later, mind—and take a box for me to the station? If so, I will give you a shilling."

"I'll be there," said Willie, "and don't you bother about the shilling. Six o'clock, did you say? Very well, I'll book it. Anything else to-day, miss?"

Joan shook her head, smiling, and returned home, where she busied herself with packing the more valued of her few possessions into the deal box that had been given her when she first went to school. Her wardrobe was not large, but then neither was the box, so the task required care and selection. First there were her few books, with which she could not make up her mind to part—least of all with those that Henry had given her; then there was the desk which she had won at school as a prize for handwriting, a somewhat bulky and inconvenient article, although it contained the faded photograph of her mother and many other small treasures. Next came the doll that some kind lady had given her many years before, the companion of her childhood, from which she could not be separated; and an ink-stand presented to her by the Rectory children, with "from your loving Tommy" scrawled upon the bottom of it. These, with the few clothes that she thought good enough to take with her, filled the box to the brim. Having shut it down, Joan thrust it under the bed, so that it might escape notice should her aunt chance to enter the room upon one of her spying expeditions, for it was Mrs. Gillingwater's unpleasant habit to search everything belonging to her niece periodically, in the hope of discovering information of interest. Her preparations finished, Joan wrote another letter. It ran thus:—

"Dear Aunt,—

"When you get this I shall be gone away, for I write to say good-bye to you and uncle. I am tired of Bradmouth, and am going to try my fortune in London, with the consent of Mr. Levinger. I have not told you about it before, because I don't wish my movements to come to the ears of other people until I am gone and can't be found, and least of all to those of Mr. Rock. It is chiefly on his account that I am leaving Bradmouth, for I am afraid of him and want to see him no more. Also I don't care to stay in a place where they make so much talk about me. I dare say that you have meant to deal kindly with me, and I thank you for it, though sometimes you have not seemed kind. I hope that the loss of the money, whatever it is, that Mr. Levinger pays on my account, will not make any great difference to you. I know that my going away will not put you out otherwise, as I do no work here, and often and often you have told me what a trouble I am; indeed, you will remember that the other day you threatened to turn me out of the house. Good-bye: please do not bother about me, or let any one do so, as I shall get on quite well.

"Your affectionate niece
"Joan."

Mrs. Gillingwater received this letter on the following afternoon, for Joan posted it at the station just before the train left. When slowly and painfully she had made herself mistress of its contents, her surprise and indignation broke forth in a torrent.

"The little deceitful cat!" she exclaimed, addressing her husband, whose beer-soaked intelligence could scarcely take in the position, even when the letter had been twice read to him—"to think of her sneaking away like an eel into a rat hole! Hopes the money won't make much difference to us, does she!

Well, it is pretty well everything we have to live on, that's all; though there's one thing, Joan or no Joan, that old Levinger shall go on paying, or I'll know the reason why. It seems that he helped her off. Well, I think that I can see his game there, but hang me if I can see hers, unless Sir Henry is going to look after her wheresoever she's gone, which ain't likely, for he can't afford it. I call to mind that's just how her mother went off two or three and twenty years ago. And you know how she came back and what was the end of her. Joan will go the same way and come to the same end, or something like it. It's in the blood, and you mark my words, Gillingwater. Oh! that girl's a master fool if ever there was one. She might have been the lawful wife of either of them, and now she'll let both slip through her fingers to earn six shillings a week by sewing, or some such nonsense. Well, she did right not to let me know what she was after, or I'd have given her what for by way of good-bye. And now what shall I say to Samuel? I suppose that he will want his money back. No play, no pay—that'll be his tune. Well, want must be his master, that's all. He was a fool not to make a better use of his chances when he had them. But I shall never get another stiver out of him unless I can bring her back again. The sly little hypocrite!" And Mrs. Gillingwater paused exhausted, and shook her fist in her husband's face, more from habit than for any other reason.

"Do you mean to say that Joan is gone?" said that worthy, twirling his hat vacantly on the table. "Then I'm sorry."

"Sorry, you lout?—why didn't you stop her, then?"

"I didn't stop her because I didn't know that she was going; and if I had, I shouldn't have interfered. But I'm real sorry, because she was a lady, she was, who always spoke soft and civil—nor a red-faced, screeching varmint of a woman such as some I knows on. Well, she's gone, and a good job too for her sake; I wish that I could go after her,"—and, dodging the blow which his enraged wife aimed at his head, Mr. Gillingwater sauntered off to drown his regrets at Joan's departure in some of the worst beer in Bradmouth.

Henry received Joan's letter in due course of post, and it would be difficult to analyse the feelings with which he perused it. He could guess well enough what were the real causes that had led to her departure from Bradmouth. She desired to escape from Samuel Rock and the voice of scandal; for by now he knew that there was scandal about her and himself, though he did not know how loud and persistent it had become. The hidden tenderness of the letter, and more especially of those sentences in which she told him that she was taking his books to remind her, in after years, of the days when she had nursed him, touched him deeply, and he knew well that no lapse of time would enable him to attain to that forgetfulness which she prophesied for him. It was dreadful to him to think that this woman, who had grown so dear to him, should be cast thus alone into the roaring tide of London life, to sink or to swim as it might chance. In one sense he had few fears for her indeed: he felt sure that she would not drift into the society of disreputable people, or herself become disreputable. He gathered also that she had sufficient funds to keep her from want, should she fail in obtaining work, and he hazarded a guess as to who it was that supplied those funds. Still, even under the most favourable conditions, in such a position a girl like Joan must of necessity be exposed to many difficulties, dangers, annoyances and temptations. From these he desired to shield her, as she had a right—the best of rights—to be shielded by him; but now, of her own act, she removed herself beyond his reach and knowledge. More, he was secretly afraid that, in addition to those which first occurred to him, Joan had another reason for her flight: he feared lest she should have gone, or rather vanished, in order that his path might be made easier for him and his doubts dissolved.

What was he to do? To ascertain her whereabouts seemed practically impossible. Doubtless she had gone to London, but even so how was he to find her, unless, indeed, he employed detectives to search her out, which he had not the slightest authority to do? He might, it was true, make inquiries in Bradmouth, where it was possible that somebody knew her address although she declared that she was leaving none; but, for obvious reasons, he was very loath to take this course. Indeed, at present he was scarcely in a position to prosecute such researches, seeing that he was still laid up and likely to remain so for some weeks. Very soon he came to the conclusion that he must remain passive and await the development of events. Probably Joan would write to him, but if nothing was heard of her for the next few weeks or months, then it would be time to search for her.

Meanwhile Henry found plenty of other things to occupy him. For the first time he went thoroughly into the affairs of the estate, and was shocked to discover, firstly, the way at once extravagant and neglectful in which it had been administered, and secondly, the total amount of its indebtedness. It was in connection with this painful subject that, about a week after Joan's departure, Henry sought an interview with Mr. Levinger. It chanced that another half-year's interest on the mortgage was due, also that some money had been paid in to the credit of the estate on account of the year's rents. About the same time there arrived the usual formal letter from Mr. Levinger, addressed to the executor of Sir Reginald Graves deceased, politely demanding payment of the interest owing for the current half-year, and calling attention to the sums overdue, amounting in all to several thousand pounds.

Henry stared at the total and sighed. How was he to meet these overwhelming liabilities? It seemed impossible that things should be allowed to go on like this; and yet what was to be done? In the issue he wrote a note to Mr. Levinger, asking him to call whenever it might be convenient, as unfortunately he was not able to wait on him.

On the morrow Mr. Levinger arrived, about eleven o'clock in the morning; indeed, he had expected some such summons, and was holding himself in readiness to obey it. Nor did he come alone, for, Ellen having learned the contents of Henry's letter, had supplemented it by a note to Emma, inviting her to lunch on the same day, giving, as an excuse, that she wished particularly to consult her upon some matters connected with dress. This invitation Emma was very unwilling to accept, for reasons known to herself and the reader, but in the end her father overruled her, and she consented to accompany him.

Henry was carried downstairs for the first time on the day of their visit, and, seating himself in the invalid chair, was wheeled into the library. A few minutes later Mr. Levinger arrived, and greeted him with the refined and gentle courtesy which was one of his characteristics, congratulating him on the progress that he had made towards recovery.

"Thank you," said Henry, "I am perfectly well except for this wretched leg of mine, which, I fear, will keep me cooped up for some weeks to come, though I hope to get out a little in the chair. I can't say that you look very well, however, Mr. Levinger. You seem thinner and paler than when we last met."

"My health has not been grand for years, Graves, and I am sorry to say that it gets steadily worse. Heart trouble, you know; and that is not a pleasant thing for a man to have, especially," he added significantly, "if his worldly affairs are in an unsettled condition. I have been a good deal worried of late, and it has told upon me. The truth is that my life is most precarious, and the sooner I can reconcile myself to the fact the better."

"I did not know that things were so serious," Henry answered, and then hastened to change the subject. "I received your notice, Mr. Levinger, and thought that I had better talk the matter over with you. To be plain, as executor to my father's estate I find myself able to pay the sum of five hundred pounds on account of the interest of these mortgages, and no more."

"Well, that is something," said Mr. Levinger, with a little smile. "For the last two years I have been accustomed to receive nothing."

"I know, I know," said Henry: "really, I am almost ashamed to look you in the face. As you are aware, the position was not of my making, but I inherit it, and am therefore, indirectly, to some extent responsible for it. I really think, Levinger, that the best thing you can do will be to sell us up, or to take over the property and manage it yourself. In either case you must, I fear, suffer a loss, but as things are at present that loss grows daily greater. You see, the worst of it is that there are several farms coming on hand at Michaelmas, and I can neither find money to work them nor tenants to take them. Should they be suffered to go out of cultivation, your security will be still further depreciated."

"I should be most sorry to take such a course, Graves, for many reasons, of which friendship to your family is not the least; and I have no desire to find the management of a large estate thrust upon me in my condition of health. Of course, should no other solution be found, some steps must be taken sooner or later, for, after all, I am only a trustee, and dare not allow my daughter's property to be dissipated; but I still hope that a solution may be found—though, I admit, not so confidently as I did a few months back."

"It is no good playing with facts," answered Henry doggedly: "for my part I have no such hope."

Mr. Levinger rose and, laying his hand upon Henry's shoulder spoke earnestly.

"Graves," he said, "think again before you say that. I beg of you not to force me to measures that would be most distasteful to me, as I shall be forced if you persist in this declaration—not from any motives of pique or revenge, mind you, but because I am bound to protect the financial interests of another person. Will you forgive me if I speak more clearly, as one friend to another?"

"I'd rather you didn't; but as you like," answered Henry.

"I do like, my dear fellow; because I wish, if possible, to save you from yourself, and also because my own interests are involved. Graves, what is there against her? Why don't you marry her, and have done with all this miserable business? If you could find a sweeter or a better girl, I might understand it. But you cannot. Moreover, though her pride may be a little hurt just now, at heart she is devoted to you."

"Every word that you say is true, Mr. Levinger, except perhaps your last statement, which I am modest enough to doubt. But surely you understand, supposing your daughter to be willing, that it is most humiliating, even for a bankrupt, to take a wife upon such terms."

"I understand your pride, Graves, and I like you for it. Remember, it is not you who are bankrupt, but your father's estate, of which you are executor, and that there are occasions in life when pride should give way. After all, pride is a strictly personal possession; when you die your pride will die with you, but if you have allowed it to ruin your family, that can never be repaired. Are you therefore justified in indulging in this peculiar form of selfishness? And, my dear fellow, are you giving me your true, or rather your only reason?"

"What makes you ask that question, Mr. Levinger?"

"I have heard some gossip, that is all, Graves, as to a scene that is supposed to have occurred at your father's death-bed, in which the name of a certain young woman was mentioned."

"Who told you of this? my sister?"

"Certainly not. If walls have ears to hear, do you suppose that nurses and servants generally are without them? The point is, I have heard it, and, as you make no contradiction, I presume that it contains a proportion of truth."

"If this is so, Mr. Levinger, one might think that it would induce you to request me to abandon the idea of making any advances to your daughter; but it seems to have had an opposite effect."

"Did the story that has reached me prove you to be a confirmed evil liver, or an unprincipled libertine, this might be the case; but it proves nothing of the sort. We are liable to fall into folly, all of us, but some of us can fall out again."

"You are charitable," said Henry; "but it seems to me, as there are two people concerned in this sort of folly, that they owe a duty to each other."

"Perhaps, in some cases; but it is one which has not been recognised by the other person in this instance, seeing that she has gone off and left no address."

"Perhaps she felt obliged to go, or perhaps she was sent, Mr. Levinger."

"If you mean that I sent her, Graves, you are very much mistaken. I have had some queer fiduciary relations with this girl for years, and the other day she came and told me that she was going to London to earn her living. I raised objections, but she overruled them. She is of age, and I have no control over her actions; indeed, on reflection, I thought it best that she should go, for I will not conceal from you that there is a certain amount of loose talk about yourself in Bradmouth. When a young woman gets mixed up in this sort of thing, my experience is, that she had better either marry or try a change of air. In this case she declined to marry, although she had an excellent opportunity of so doing, therefore I fell in with the change of air proposal, and I learn that within a day or two she went away nobody knows whither. I have no doubt, however, that sooner or later I shall hear of her whereabouts, for she is entitled to an allowance of sixty pounds a year, which she will certainly not forget to draw. Till then—unless, indeed, you know her address already—you will scarcely find her; and if you are not going to marry her, which I gather she has never desired, I'll do you the justice to suppose that you cannot wish to follow her, and disturb her in her employment, whatever it may be, since such a course would probably lead to her losing it."

"You are right there: I never wish to see her again, unless it is in order to ask her to become my wife."

"Then do not see her, Graves. For her sake, for your own, for your mother's, and mine, or rather for my daughter's, I beg you not to see her, or to allow these quixotic notions of yours to drag you down to ruin. Let the thing alone, and all will be well; follow it up, and you are a lost man. Do you think that you would find happiness in such a marriage?—I am putting aside all questions of duty, position and means—I tell you, 'no.' I am not speaking without my book," he added fiercely, "and I warn you that when you have grown accustomed to her beauty, and she had ceased to wonder at your generosity, your life would become a hell. What sympathy can there be between individuals so different in standing, in taste, and in education? How could you bear the jealousies, the passions, and the aggressive ignorance of such a woman? How could you continue to love her when you remembered in what fashion your affection had begun; when for her sake you found yourself a social outcast, and when, every time that you beheld her face, you were constrained to recollect that it was the wrecker's light which lured you, and through you all whom you hold dear, to utter and irretrievable disaster? I tell you that I have seen such cases, and I have seen their miserable ends; and I implore you, Henry Graves, to pause before you give another and a signal example of them."

"You speak very feelingly," said Henry, "and no doubt there is a great deal of truth in what you say. I had two messmates who made masalliances, and certainly it didn't answer with them, for they have both gone to the dogs—indeed, one poor fellow committed suicide. However, it is very difficult to argue on such matters, and still more difficult to take warning from the fate of others, since the circumstances are never similar. But I promise you this, Levinger, that I will do nothing in a hurry—for two or three months, indeed—and that I will take no step in the matter without informing you fully of my intentions, for I think that this is due to you. Meanwhile, if you are good enough to allow me to remain upon friendly terms with your daughter and yourself, I shall be glad, though I am sure I do not know how she will receive me. Within a few months I shall finally have decided upon my course of action, and if I then come to the conclusion that I am not bound in honour elsewhere, perhaps I may ask you to allow me to try my fortune with Miss Levinger, unworthy of her as I am and always shall be."

"I can find no fault with that arrangement, Graves. You have set out your mind like an honest man, and I respect you for it. It will make me the more anxious to learn, when the three months are up, that you have decided to forget all this folly and to begin afresh. Now I have something to ask you: it is that, so soon as you can get about again, you will pay us the visit which was so unfortunately postponed. Please understand I do not mean that I wish you to make advances to my daughter, but I should like you to grow to know each other better in an ordinary and friendly fashion. Will you come?"

Henry reflected, and answered, "Thank you, yes, I will."

At this moment the door was opened, and the butler, Thomson, announced that lunch was ready, adding, "Shall I wheel you in, Sir Henry? Her ladyship bids me say she hopes that you will come."

"Yes, I suppose so," he answered. "Here, give me a hand into the chair."

In another minute they were advancing in solemn procession across the hall, Mr. Levinger walking first, leaning on his stick, and Henry following after in the invalid chair propelled by Thomson. So agitated was he at the thought of meeting Emma, and by a secret fear, born of a guilty conscience that she should know what he and her father had been employing the last hour in discussing her, that he forgot to guide the chair properly, and despite Thomson's warning, "To the right, Sir Henry," he contrived to strike the jamb of the door so sharply that he must have overturned had not Emma, who was standing close by, sprung forward and seized the wheel.

In one way this accident was fortunate, for it lessened the awkwardness of their meeting. Henry apologised and she laughed; and presently they were seated side by side at table, discussing the eccentricities of invalid chairs with somewhat unnecessary persistence and fervour.

After this the lunch went off well enough. It was not an altogether cheerful meal, indeed; but then nothing at Rosham was ever quite cheerful, and probably nothing had been for generations. The atmosphere of the place, like its architecture, was oppressive, even lugubrious, and the circumstances in which the present company were assembled did not tend towards unrestrained gaiety. Ellen talked energetically of matters connected with dress, in which Emma did not seem to take any vivid interest; Lady Graves threw in an occasional remark about the drought and the prevalence of blight upon the roses; while Henry for the most part preserved a discreet, or rather an embarrassed, silence; and Mr. Levinger discoursed sweetly upon the remote and impersonal subject of British coins, of a whole potful of which it appeared that he had recently become the proud possessor.

"Sir Henry has promised to come and see them, my dear," he said to Emma pointedly, after he had at length succeeded in stirring his audience into a flabby and intermittent interest in the crown that Caractacus wore, or was supposed to wear, upon a certain piece of money.

"Indeed," she answered quickly, bending her head as though to examine the pattern of her plate.

"Your father has been so kind as to ask me for the second time, Miss Levinger," Henry remarked uneasily, "and I propose to avail myself of his invitation so soon as I am well enough not to be a nuisance—that is, if it is convenient."

"Of course it will always be convenient to see you, Sir Henry Graves," Emma replied coldly, "or indeed anybody whom my father likes to ask."

"That's one for Henry," reflected Ellen. "Serves him right too." Then she added aloud: "A few days at Monk's Lodge will be a very nice change for you, dear, and I hope that you may arrive safely this time. Would you like to take a walk round the garden, Emma, while your father smokes a cigarette?"

Emma rose gladly, for she felt the moral atmosphere of the dining-room to be in a somewhat volcanic state, and was terribly afraid lest a few more sparks of Ellen's sarcastic wit should produce an explosion. For half an hour or so they sauntered through the old-fashioned shrubberies and pleasure grounds, the charms of which their overrun and neglected condition seemed to enhance, at least at this season of the year. Then it was that Ellen confided to her companion that she expected to be married about the middle of November, and that she hoped that Emma would come to town with her some time in October to assist in completing her trousseau. Emma hesitated for a moment, for she could not disguise from herself the fact that her friendship for Ellen, at no time a very deep one, had cooled; indeed, she was not sure whether she quite trusted her. In the end, however, she assented, subject to her father's consent, for she had very rarely been in London, and she felt that a change of scene and ideas would do her good. Then they turned back to the house, to find that the dog-cart was standing at the door.

"One word, my dear," said Ellen, halting: "I am so glad that Henry is going to stop at Monk's Lodge. He is a most curious creature, and I hope that you will be patient with him, and forgive him all his oddities."

"Really, Ellen," answered Emma, with suppressed irritation, "I have nothing to forgive Sir Henry, and of course I shall be glad to see him whenever he chooses to come."

"I am by no means sure," reflected Ellen, as she watched the Levingers drive away, "but that this young lady has got more spirit than I gave her credit for. Henry had better look out, or he will lose his chance, for I fancy that she will become as difficult to deal with in the future as he has been in the past."

CHAPTER XXII

AN INTERLUDE

A month or five weeks went by at Rosham almost without incident. For the moment money troubles were in abeyance, seeing that the payment of the interest due on the mortgages was not pressed, and the sale of Lady Graves's jewels had provided sufficient funds to meet the most immediate claims, to pay household expenses, and even to provide for Ellen's trousseau upon a moderate scale. By degrees Henry regained the use of his injured limb, though it was now evident that he would carry the traces of his accident to the grave in the shape of a pronounced limp. In all other respects he was bodily as well as ever he had been, though he remained much troubled in mind. Of Joan he had heard nothing; and it appeared that nobody knew where she had gone, or what she was doing, except possibly Mr. Levinger, whom he scarcely cared to ask for tidings. That her aunt did not know was evident from the fact that one morning she arrived at the Hall and, adopting a tone in which obsequiousness and violence were curiously mixed, taxed him roundly with having spirited her niece away. In vain did Henry assure her that he knew no more of Joan's whereabouts than she did herself; since she either did not or would not believe him, and at length departed, breathing threats that if the girl was not forthcoming shortly, she would "make it hot for him, baronet or no baronet." For his part Henry was somewhat at a loss to understand Mrs. Gillingwater's conduct, since he knew well that she had no sort of affection for her niece, and it was obvious from her words that she was rather proud than otherwise of the gossip connecting Joan's name with his own.

"I know all about your goings on," she had said, "though I haven't come here to preach to you, for that's your affair and hers; but I do say that if you call yourself a gentleman you should do what is handsome by the girl, seeing that you've stood in the way of her making a good marriage; and, to put it plump, Sir Henry, I think that you are in duty bound to do something for me too, bearing in mind all the 'truck' that I've had about the two of you, and that one has been taken away from me as was dearer than a daughter."

The real explanation of this estimable person's behaviour was twofold. In the first place, Joan being gone, she had lost the monthly sum that was paid for her board, and in the second she had been bribed by Samuel Rock to win the secret of her hiding-place from Henry. In due course Mrs. Gillingwater reported the failure of her mission to Samuel, who, needless to say, did not believe a word of Henry's denial. Indeed, he accused Mrs. Gillingwater first of being a fool, and next of taking money from the enemy as well as from himself, with the result that a very pretty quarrel ensued between the pair of them.

After a few days' reflection Samuel determined to take the matter into his own hands. Already he had attempted to extract information about Joan from Mr. Levinger, who, however, professed ignorance, and would give him none. Having ascertained that the man was hateful to Joan, Mr. Levinger had the good feeling to wish to protect her from his advances; for he saw well that if once Rock learned her address he would follow her like a shadow, and if necessary hunt her from place to place, importuning her to marry him. The girl was out of the way, which was much, though of course it would be better were she safely married. But, greatly as he might desire such a thing, he would be no party to her persecution. Joan, he felt, was doing her best to further his plans; in return he would do everything in his power—at least, everything that circumstances permitted—to promote her comfort and welfare. She should not lack for money, nor should she be tormented by Samuel Rock.

Having drawn the Monk's Lodge covers blank, Mr. Rock turned his attention to those of Rosham. As a first step he sent Mrs. Gillingwater to whine and threaten, with results that we have already learned. Then he determined to go himself. He did not, however, drive up to the Hall and ask boldly to see Sir Henry, as Mrs. Gillingwater had done, for such an act would not have been in keeping with his character. Samuel's nature was a furtive one. Did he desire to see a person, he would lurk about for hours in order to meet him on some path which he knew that he must follow, rather than accost him in a public place. Even in business transactions, of which he had many, this custom clung to him. He was rarely seen on market days, and so well were his habits known, that customers desiring to buy his fat stock or his sheep or his hay would wait about the land till he "happened" on them in the course of his daily round.

Thus he made three separate visits to Rosham before he succeeded in meeting Henry. On the first occasion he discovered that it was his practice—for by now Henry could get about—to walk round the home-farm after breakfast. Accordingly Rock returned on the following day; but the weather chanced to be bad, and Henry did not come out. Next morning he was more fortunate. Having put up his cart at the village inn, he took his stand upon an eminence, as though he were a wandering poet contemplating the beauties of Nature, and waited. Presently he saw Henry appear out of a cow-shed and cross some fields in his direction, whereon Samuel retreated behind a hay-stack. Five minutes passed, and Henry hobbled by within three yards of him. He followed at his heels, unable to make up his mind how to begin the interview, walking so softly on the grass that it was not until Henry observed another shadow keeping pace with his own that he became aware of his presence. Then, not unnaturally, he wheeled round suddenly, for the apparition of this second shadow in the open field, where he had imagined himself to be alone, was almost uncanny. So quickly did he turn, indeed, that Samuel ran into him before he could stop himself.

"Who the devil are you?" said Henry, lifting his stick, for his first thought was that he was about to be attacked by a tramp. "Oh! I beg your pardon," he added: "I suppose that you are the person who is coming to see me about the Five Elms farm?"

"I've been waiting to see you, sir," said Samuel obsequiously, and lifting his hat—"in fact, I've been waiting these three mornings."

"Then why on earth didn't you come and speak to me, my good man, instead of crawling about after me like a Red Indian? It's easy enough to find me, I suppose?"

"It isn't about a farm that I wish to see you, sir," went on Samuel, ignoring the question. "No, sir, this ain't no matter between a proud landlord and a poor tenant coming to beg a few pounds off his rent for his children's bread, as it were. This is a matter between man and man, or perhaps between man and woman."

"Look here," said Henry, "are you crazed, or are you asking me riddles? Because if so, you may as well give it up, for I hate them. What is your name?"

"My name, sir, is Samuel Rock"—here his manner suddenly became insolent—"and I have come to ask you a riddle; and what's more, I mean to get an answer to it. What have you done with Joan Haste?"

"Oh! I see," said Henry. "I wonder I didn't recognise you. Now, Mr. Samuel Rock, by way of a beginning let me recommend you to keep a civil tongue in your head. I'm not the kind of person to be bullied, do you understand?"

Samuel looked at Henry's blue eyes, that shone somewhat ominously, and at his determined chin and mouth, and understood.

"I'm sure I meant no offence, sir," he replied, again becoming obsequious.

"Very well: then be careful to give none. It is quite easy to be polite when once you get used to it. Now I will answer your question. I have done nothing with Joan Haste—about whom, by the way, you have not the slightest right to question me. I don't know where she is, and I have neither seen nor heard of her for several weeks. Good morning!"

"That, sir, is a—"

"Now, pray be careful." And Henry turned to go.

"We don't part like that, sir," said Rock, following him and speaking to him over his shoulder. "I've got some more to say to you."

"Then say it to my face; don't keep sneaking behind me like an assassin. What is it?"

"This, sir: you have robbed me, sir; you have taken my ewe-lamb as David did to Nathan, and your reward shall be the reward of David."

"Oh, confound you and your ewe-lamb!" said Henry, who was fast getting beyond argument. "What do you want?"

"I want her back, sir. I don't care what's happened; I don't care if you have stolen her; I tell you I want her back."

"Very well, then, go and find her; but don't bother me."

"Oh yes, I'll find her in time; I'll marry her, never you fear; but I thought that you might be able to help me on with it, for she's nothing to you; but you see it's this way—I can't live without her."

"I have told you, Mr. Rock, that I don't know where Joan Haste is; and if I did, I may add that I would not help you to find her, as I believe she is hiding herself to keep out of your way. Now will you be so good as to go?"

Then Samuel burst into a flood of incoherent menaces and abuse, born of his raging hate and jealousy. Henry did not follow the torrent—he did not even attempt to do so, seeing that his whole energies were occupied in a supreme effort to prevent himself from knocking this creature down.

"She's mine, and not yours," he ended. "I'm an honest man, I am, and I mean to marry her like an honest man; and when I've married her, just you keep clear, Sir Henry Graves, or, by the God that made me, I'll cut your throat!"

"Really," ejaculated Henry, "this is too much! Here, Jeffries, and you, Bates," he called to two men in his employ who chanced to be walking by: "this person seems to be the worse for drink. Would you be so good as to take him off the premises? And look here—be careful that he never comes back again."

Messrs. Jeffries and Bates grinned and obeyed; for, as it happened, they both knew Samuel, and one of them had a grudge against him.

"You hear what Sir Henry says. Now come you on, master," said Jeffries. "Surely it is a scandal to see a man the worse for beer at this time of day. Come on, master."

By now Samuel's passion had spent itself, and he went quietly enough, followed by the two labourers. Henry watched him disappear towards the road, and then said aloud:—

"Upon my word, Joan Haste, fond as I am of you, had I known half the trouble and insult that I must suffer on your account, I would have chosen to go blind before ever I set eyes upon your face."

Within a week of this agreeable interview with Samuel Rock, Henry set out to pay his long-promised visit to Monk's Lodge. This time he drove thither, and no further accident befell him. But as he passed by Ramborough Abbey he reflected sadly enough on the strange imbroglio in which he had become involved since the day when he attempted to climb its ruined tower. At present things seemed to be straightening themselves out somewhat, it was true; but a warning sense told him that there were worse troubles to come than any which had gone before.

The woman who was at the root of these evils had vanished, indeed; but he knew well that all which is hidden is not necessarily lost, and absence did not avail to cure him of his longing for the sight of her dear face. He might wish that he had been stricken blind before his eyes beheld it; but he had looked upon it, alas! too long, nor could he blot out its memory. He tried to persuade himself that he did not care; he tried to believe that his sensations were merely the outcome of flattered vanity; he tried, even, to forbid his mind to think of her—only to experience the futility of one and all of these endeavours.

Whether or no he was "in love" with Joan, he did not know, since, never having fallen into that condition, he had no standard by which to measure his feelings. What he had good cause to know, however, was that she had taken possession of his waking thoughts in a way that annoyed and bewildered him—yes, and even of his dreams. The vision of her was all about him; most things recalled her to him, directly or indirectly, and he could scarcely listen to a casual conversation, or mix in the society of other women, without being reminded—by inference, contrast, or example—of something that she had said or done. His case was by no means helpless; for even now he knew that time would cure the trouble, or at least draw its sting. He was not a lad, to be carried away by the wild passion which is one of the insane privileges of youth; and he had many interests, ambitions, hopes and fears with which this woman was not connected, though, as it chanced at present, her subtle influence seemed to pervade them all.

Meanwhile his position towards her was most painful. She had gone, leaving him absolutely in the dark as to her wishes, motives, or whereabouts; leaving him also to suffer many things on her account, not the least of them being the haunting knowledge of what, in her silence and solitude, she must be suffering upon his.

Well, he had debated the matter till his mind grew weary, chiefly with the object of discovering which among so many conflicting duties were specious and which were sacred, and now he was inclined to give up the problem as insoluble, and to allow things to take their chance.

"By George!" he thought to himself, glancing at the old tower, "this is the kind of thing that they call romance: well, I call it hell. No more romance for me if I can avoid it. And now I am going to stay with old Levinger, and, as I suppose that I shall not be expected to make love to his daughter—at any rate, at present—I'll try to enjoy myself, and forget for a few days that there is such a thing as a woman in the world."

Henry reached Monk's Lodge in time to dress for dinner, and was at once shown by Mr. Levinger, who greeted him with cordiality and evident pleasure, to his room—a low and many-cornered apartment commanding a delightful view of the sea. Having changed, he found his way to the drawing-room, where Emma was waiting to receive him, which she did very courteously, and with more self-possession than might have been expected of her. It struck Henry, as he stood by the window and chatted to her on indifferent subjects in the pearly light of the September evening, that he had never seen her look so charming. Perhaps it was that her secret troubles had added dignity to her delicate face and form, or that the dress she wore became her, or that the old-fashioned surroundings of the place among which she had grown up, and that doubtless had exercised their influence upon her character, seemed to combine with and to set off her quaint and somewhat formal grace of mien and movement. At least it seemed to him that she was almost beautiful that night, not with the rich and human loveliness of a woman like Joan, but in a certain spiritual fashion which was peculiar to her.

Presently they went in to dinner. It was a pleasant meal enough, and Henry enjoyed the change from the cold-looking Rosham dining-room, with its pillars and its dingy old masters, even more than he had hoped to do. Here there were no old masters and no marble, but walls wainscoted with a dado of black oak, and hung with quaint Flemish pictures painted on panels or on copper, such as are still to be picked up by the discerning at sales in the Eastern counties. Here also were no melancholy cedars shutting off the light, but open windows wreathed about with ivy, through which floated the murmur of the sea. The dinner was excellent, moreover, as was Mr. Levinger's champagne; and by the time that they reached the dessert Henry found himself in a better mood than he had known for many a long week.

Abandoning his reserve, he fell into some harmless snare that was set by his host, and began to speak of himself and his experiences—a thing that he very rarely did. Though for the most part he was a somewhat silent man, and at his best could not be called a brilliant conversationalist, Henry could talk well when he chose, in a certain plain and forcible manner that attracted by its complete absence of exaggeration or of straining after effect. He told them tales of wars in Ashantee and Egypt; he described to them a great hurricane off the coast of Madagascar, when the captain and first lieutenant of the ship in which he was serving were swept overboard by a single sea, leaving him in command of her; and several other adventures, such as befall Englishmen who for twenty years or more have served their country in every quarter of the globe. By now the coffee and cigarettes had been brought in; but Emma did not leave the room—indeed, it was not her custom to do so, and the presence of a guest at Monk's Lodge was so rare an event that it never occurred to her to vary it. She sat, her face hidden in the shadow, listening with wide-opened eyes to Henry's "moving accidents by flood and field"; and yet she grew sad as she listened, feeling that his talk was inspired by a vain regret which was almost pitiful. He was speaking as old men speak of their past, of events that are gone by, of things in which they have no longer any share.

Evidently Mr. Levinger felt this also, for he said, "It is unfortunate, Graves, that prospects like yours should have been snapped short. What do you mean to do with yourself now?"

"Yes," answered Henry, "it is very unfortunate; but these things will happen. As for the future it must look after itself. Ninety-nine naval officers out of a hundred have no future. They live—or rather starve—upon their half-pay in some remote village, and become churchwardens—that is, if they do not quarrel with the parson."

"I hope that you will do something more than this," said Mr. Levinger. "I look forward to seeing you member for our division if I live long enough. You might do more good for the Navy in the house than ever you could have done at sea."

"That's just what a man told me at the Admiralty, and I think I answered him that I preferred a command at sea. Not but that I should like the other thing very well, if it came in my way. However, as both careers are as much beyond my reach as the moon, it is no use talking of them, is it?"

"I don't agree with you—I don't agree at all. You will be a great authority yet. And now let us go into the other room."

So they went into the drawing-room, where Emma sang a little, sweetly enough; and after she had bidden them good-night they adjourned to the study to smoke and drink weak whiskies-and-sodas. Here Mr. Levinger was the talker and Henry the listener, and it seemed to the latter that he had rarely met a man with so much knowledge and power of observation, or one who could bring these to bear in a more interesting manner upon whatever subject he chanced to be discussing. His intellect was keen, his knowledge of life and men large and varied, and he seemed to know every book worth reading, and, what is more, to remember its contents.

Thus Henry's first evening at Monk's Lodge passed very pleasantly, and as his visit began so it went on and ended. In the daytime he would take his gun, and accompanied by Mr. Levinger on a pony and by an old man, half bailiff and half gamekeeper, would limp through the bracken in search of partridges and rabbits, an occupation in which he took great delight, although he was still too lame to follow it for long at a time.

Failing the shooting, his host organised some expedition to visit a distant church or earthwork, and accompanied by Emma they drove for hours through the mellow September afternoon. Or sometimes they sat upon the beach beneath the cliff, chatting idly on everything under heaven; or, if it chanced to rain, they would take refuge in the study and examine Mr. Levinger's collection of coins, ancient weapons and other antiquities.

Then at last arrived the dinner-hour, and another delightful evening would be added to the number of those that had gone. Before he had been in the house a week, Henry felt a different man; indeed, had any one told him, when he came to Monk's Lodge, that he was about to enjoy himself so much, he would not have believed it. He could see also that both Mr. Levinger and his daughter were glad that he should be there. At first Emma was a little stiff in her manner towards him, but by degrees this wore off, and he found himself day by day growing more friendly with her.

The better they became acquainted, the greater grew their mutual liking, and the more complete their understanding of each other. There was now no question of love-making or even of flirtation between them; their footing was one of friendship, and both of them were glad that it should be so. Soon the sharpest sting of Emma's shame passed away, since she could not believe that the man who greeted her with such open fellowship had learned the confession which broke from her on that night of her despair, for if it were so, surely he would look down upon her and show it in his manner. Taking this for granted, in some dim and illogical fashion she was grateful to him for not having heard; or if by any chance he had heard, as she was bound to admit was possible, still more was she grateful in that he dissembled his knowledge so completely as to enable her to salve her pride with the thought that he was ignorant. Indeed, in this event, so deeply did she feel upon the point, she was prepared in her own mind to forgive any sins of omission or commission with which he stood charged, setting against them the generosity of his conduct in this particular. Of the future Emma did not think; she was content to live in the present, and to feel that she had never been so happy before. Neither did she think of the past, with its disquieting tales of Joan Haste, and its horrible suggestions that Henry was bring driven into marriage with herself for pecuniary reasons. If a day should ever come when he proposed to her, then it would be time enough to take all these matters into consideration, and to decide whether she should please her pride and do violence to her heart, or sacrifice her pride and satisfy her heart. There was no need to come to a decision now, for she could see well that, whatever might be his thoughts with reference to her, Henry had no immediate intention of asking her to be his wife.

Although of course he could not follow all the secret workings of Emma's mind, Henry grasped the outlines of the situation accurately enough. He knew that this was a time of truce, and that by a tacit agreement all burning questions were postponed to a more convenient season. Mr. Levinger said no word to him of his daughter, of Joan Haste, or even of the financial affairs connected with the Rosham mortgages, for all these subjects were tabooed under the conditions of their armistice. Tormented as he had been, and as he must shortly be again, he also was deeply grateful for this indulgence, and more than content to forget the past and let the future take care of itself. One thing grew clear to him, however; indeed, before he left Monk's Lodge he admitted it to himself in so many words: it was, that had there been no Joan Haste and no mortgages in the question, he would certainly ask Emma Levinger to be his wife.

The more he saw of this lady, the more attached he grew to her. She attracted him in a hundred ways—by her gentleness, her delicacy of thought, her ever-present sympathy with distress and with all that was good and noble, and by the quaintness and culture of her mind. For these and many other reasons he could imagine no woman whom he should prefer to marry were he fortunate enough to win her. But always when he thought of it two spectres seemed to rise and stand before him—one of Joan, passionate, lovely and loving, and the other shaped like a roll of parchment and labelled "Mortgages, Sixty thousand pounds!"

At length the ten days of his stay came to an end, and upon a certain morning the old Rosham coachman appeared at the door of Monk's Lodge to drive him home again.

"I don't know how to thank you, Levinger," he said, "for your kindness and hospitality to me here. I have not had such a good time for many a long day. It has been a rest to me, and I have come to the conclusion that rest is the best thing in the whole world. Now I must go back to face my anxieties."

"Meaning the eleventh of October?" said Mr. Levinger.

"Yes, meaning the eleventh of October and other things. I am sure I do not know what on earth I am to do about those farms. But I won't begin to bore you with business now. Good-bye, and again, many thanks."

"Good-bye, Graves, and don't fret. I dare say that something will turn up. My experience is that something generally does turn up—that is to say, when one is the right side of forty."

"Oh, Sir Henry!" said Emma, appearing at the door of the drawing-room, "will you take a note to your sister for me? It is just ready."

"Certainly," he answered, following her to the writing-table.

"It is about my going to town with her next month," she went on. "I have been speaking to my father, and he says that I may if I like. It is a question of trousseau—not that I know anything about such matters, but I am glad of the excuse for a change. Are you going with her?"

"I don't know. An old messmate of mine always gives a dinner at the Rag on the twentieth, to celebrate an adventure in which we were concerned together. I had a letter from him the other day asking me to come. I haven't answered it yet, but if you like I will accept. I believe you go up on the eighteenth, don't you?"

Emma coloured faintly. "Of course it would be pleasant if you came," she answered. "We might go to some picture galleries, and to the British Museum to look at those Egyptian things."

"All right," said Henry; "we've got to get there first. And now good-bye. I can assure you that I shall never forget your goodness to me."

"The goodness is on your side, Sir Henry: it is very kind of you to have come to see us."

"And it is very nice of you to say so, Miss Levinger. Again good-bye, or rather au revoir."

CHAPTER XXIII

A NEW DEPARTURE

Joan reached town in safety. Willie Hood called for her box as he had promised, and conveyed it to the station before anybody at the inn was up, whither she followed after breakfast. It gave Joan a new and strange sensation to sit opposite her aunt, who took the opportunity of a tete-a-tete to scold and grumble at her from one end of the meal to the other, and to reflect that they were about to separate, for aught she knew, never to meet again. She could not pretend any affection for Mrs. Gillingwater, and yet the thought moved her, for after all she belonged to the familiar round of daily life from which Joan was about to cut herself adrift. Still more did it move her, yes, even to silent tears, when for the last time she looked upon the ancient room that had been hers, and in which she had nursed Henry back to health. Here every chair and picture was an old friend, and, what is more, connected with his presence, the presence which to-day she finally refused.

In turning her back upon that room she forsook all hope of seeing him again, and not till she had closed the door behind her did she learn how bitter was this renunciation.

Finding her luggage at the station, she saw it labelled, and took her seat in the train. Just as it was about to start Willie Hood sauntered up.

"Oh! there you are, Joan Haste," he said. "I thought that you would be following your box, so I've just dropped round to say good-bye to you. Good-bye, Joan: I hope that you will have a pleasant time up in London. Let me know your address, and I shouldn't wonder if I looked you up there one day, for somehow I don't feel as though there were room for another smart young man in Bradmouth, and the old place won't seem the same without you. Perhaps, if you ain't going to marry him after all," and Willie jerked his red head in the direction of Rosham, "if you'll have the patience to wait a year or two, we might set up together yonder in the grocery line."

"You impudent young monkey!" said Joan, laughing in spite of herself; and then the train steamed off, leaving Master Willie on the platform, kissing his hand in the direction of her carriage.

On arriving at Liverpool Street, Joan took a cab and directed the man to Kent Street, Paddington, whither she came after a drive that seemed interminable.

Kent Street, Paddington, was a shabby little place in the neighbourhood of the Edgware Road. The street itself ended in a cul-de-sac, a recommendation to the lover of quiet, as of course no traffic could pass through it; but, probably on this account, it was the happy hunting ground of hundreds of dirty children, whose shrill voices echoed through it from dawn to dark, as they played and fought and screamed. The houses were tall, and covered with a dingy stucco, that here and there had peeled away in flakes, exposing patches of yellow brick; the doors were much in need of paint, some of the area railings were broken, and the window curtains for the most part presented the appearance of having been dried in a coal cellar. Indeed, the general squalor and the stuffy odours of the place filled Joan's heart with dismay, for she had never before visited the poorer quarters of a large town.

"Are you sure that this is Kent Street, Paddington?" she asked feebly of the driver.

"If you don't believe me, miss, look for yourself," he answered gruffly, pointing to the corner of a house upon which the name was painted. "No. 13, you said, didn't you? Well, here it is, and here's your box," he added, bumping her luggage down upon the steps; "and my fare is three-and-six, please."

Joan paid the three-and-sixpence, and the sulky cabman drove off, yelling at the children in front of get out of the way of his horse, and lashing with his whip at those who clung behind.

Left to herself, Joan pulled the bell and waited. Nobody came, so she pulled it again, and yet a third time; after which she discovered that it was broken, and there being no knocker, was reduced to rapping on the door with the handle of her umbrella. Presently it was opened with great violence, and a sour-faced slattern with a red nose asked shrilly—

"Who the dickens are you, that you come a-banging of the door to bits? This ain't the Al'ambra, my fine miss. Don't you make no mistake."

"My name is Haste," said Joan humbly, "and I have come here to lodge."

"Then you'd better haste out of this, for you won't lodge here." And the vixen prepared to slam the door.

"Does not Mrs. Thomas live here?" asked Joan desperately.

"No, she don't. Mrs. Thomas was sold up three days ago, and you'll find her in the Marylebone Workhouse, I believe. I am the caretaker. Now take that box off those steps, and cut it sharp, or I'll send for the policeman." And before Joan could say another word the door was shut in her face.

She turned round in despair. Where was she to go, and what could she do in this horrible place? By now a crowd had collected about her, composed largely of dirty children and dreadful blear-eyed men in very wide-skirted tattered coats, who made audible remarks about her personal appearance.

"Now then," screamed the vixen from the area, "will you take thim things off the steps?"

Thus adjured, Joan made a desperate effort to lift the box, but she was weak with agitation and could not stir it.

"Carry yer things for yer, miss?" said one creature in a raucous whisper. "Don't you mind him, miss," put in another; "he's a blooming area sneak, he is. You give 'em me." "Hullo, Molly, does your mother know you're out?" asked a painted-faced slut, who evidently had taken more to drink than was good for her; and so forth.

For a few moments Joan bore it. Then she sank down upon the box and began to weep—a sight that touched the better feelings of some of the men, for one of them offered to punch the "blooming 'ead" of anybody who annoyed her.

It was at this juncture that Joan, chancing to look up, saw a little pale-faced, straw-coloured woman, who was neatly dressed in black, pushing her way through the crowd towards her.

"What is the matter, my dear?" said the little woman, in a small and gentle voice.

"I have come from the country here to lodge," answered Joan, choking back her tears; "and there's nobody in the house except that dreadful person, and I don't know where to go."

The little woman shook her head doubtfully; and at that moment once more the fiend in the area yelled aloud, "If you don't get off thim steps I'll come and put you off. I'm caretaker here, and I'll show you."

"Oh! what can I do?" said Joan, wringing her hands.

The sight of her distress seemed to overcome the scruples of the little woman; at any rate she made one of the loafers lift the box and bring it across the street.

"Now, my dear, take your bag and your umbrella, and follow me."

Joan obeyed with joy: just then she would have followed her worst enemy anywhere, also her new friend's face inspired her with confidence. On the other side of the street the little woman opened the door of a house—it was No. 8—with a latchkey, and Joan noticed that on it was a brass plate inscribed "Mrs. Bird, Dressmaker."

"Go in," she said. "No, I will settle with the man; he will cheat you."

She went in, and found herself in a tiny passage of spotless cleanliness; and, her luggage having been set down beside her, the door was closed, and the crowd which had accompanied them across the street melted away.

"Oh! thank you," said Joan. "What do I owe you?"

"Threepence, my dear; it is a penny too much, but I would not stop to argue with the man."

Joan fumbled in her pocket and found the threepence.

"Thank you, my dear. I am glad to see that you pay your debts so readily. It is a good sign, but, alas! appearances are often deceptive"; and her hostess led the way into a small parlour, beautifully neat and well kept. "Sit down," said the little woman, lifting a dress that she was in process of making from a chair which she offered to Joan, "and take a cup of tea. I was just going to have some myself. Bobby, will you be quiet?" This last remark was addressed to a canary, which was singing at the top of its voice in a cage that hung in the window. "I am afraid that you find him rather shrill," she went on, nodding towards the canary, "but I have so much to do with silence that I don't mind the noise."

"Not at all: I like birds," said Joan.

"I am glad of that, my dear, for my name is Bird. Quite a coincidence, isn't it—not but what coincidences are deceptive things. And now, here is your tea."

Joan took the tea and drank it thankfully, while Mrs. Bird watched her.

"My dear, you are very handsome," she said at length, "if you will forgive me for making a personal remark—dreadfully handsome. I am sure that, being so handsome, you cannot be happy, since God does not give us everything; and I only hope that you are good. You look good, or I should not have come to help you just now; but it is impossible to put any trust in appearances."

"I am afraid that I am neither very happy nor very good," answered Joan, "but I am most grateful to you. I have come up from the country to look for work, and I want to find a decent lodging. Perhaps you can help me, for I have never been to London before, and do not know where to go. My name is Joan Haste."

"Perhaps I can, and perhaps I can't," said Mrs. Bird. "It depends. Yours is a very strange story, and I am not sure that I believe it. It is not usual for beautiful young women like you to wander to London in this kind of way—that is, if they are respectable. How am I to know that you are respectable? That you look respectable does not prove you to be so. Do your friends know that you have come here, or have you perhaps run away from home?"

"I hope that I am respectable," answered Joan meekly; "and some of my friends know about my coming."

"Then they should have made better arrangements for you. That house to which you were going was not respectable; it is a mercy that it was shut up."

"Not respectable!" said Joan. "Surely Mr. Levinger could never have been so wicked," she added to herself.

"No: it used to be a while ago—then there were none but very decent people there; but recently the woman, Mrs. Thomas, took to drink, and that was why she was sold up."

"Indeed," said Joan; "I suppose that my friend did not know. I fancy it is some years since he was acquainted with the house."

"Your friend! What sort of friend?" said Mrs. Bird suspiciously.

"Well, he is a kind of guardian of mine."

"Then he ought to have known better than to have sent you to a house without making further inquiries. This world is a changeable place, but nothing changes in it more quickly than lodging-houses, at any rate in Kent Street."

"So it seems," answered Joan sadly; "but now, what am I to do?"

"I don't know, Miss Haste—I think you said Haste was your name; although," she added nervously, sweeping off her lap some crumbs of the bread and butter that she had been eating, "if I was quite sure that you are respectable I might be able to make a suggestion."

"What suggestion, Mrs. Bird?"

"Well, I have two rooms to let here. My last lodger, a most estimable man, and a very clever one too—he was an accountant, my dear—died in them a fortnight ago, and was carried out last Friday; but then, you see, it is not everybody that would suit me as a tenant, and there are many people whom I might not suit. There are three questions to be considered; the question of character, the question of rent, and the question of surroundings. Now, as to the question of character—"

"I have a certificate," broke in Joan mildly, as she produced a document that she had procured from Mr. Biggen, the clergyman at Bradmouth. Mrs. Bird put on a pair of spectacles and perused it carefully.

"Satisfactory," she said, "very satisfactory, presuming it to be genuine; though, mind you, I have known even clergymen to be deceived. Now, would you like to see my references?"

"No, thank you, not at all," said Joan. "I am quite sure that you are respectable."

"How can you be sure of anything of the sort? Well, we will pass over that and come to the rent. My notion of rent for the double furnished room on the first floor, including breakfast, coals, and all extras, is eight shillings and sixpence a week. The late accountant used to pay ten-and-six, but for a woman I take off two shillings; not but what I think, from the look of you, that you would eat more breakfast than the late accountant did."

"That seems very reasonable," said Joan. "I should be very glad to pay that."

"Yes, my dear, you might be very glad to pay it, but you will excuse me for saying that the desire does not prove the ability. How am I to know that you would pay?"

"I have plenty of money," answered Joan wearily; "I can give you a month's rent in advance, if you like."

"Plenty of money!" said the little woman, holding up her hands in amazement, "and that very striking appearance! And yet you wander about the world in this fashion! Really, my dear, I do not know what to make of you."

"For the matter of that, Mrs. Bird, I do not quite know what to make of myself. But shall we get on with the business?—because, you see, if we do not come to an agreement, I must search elsewhere. What was it you said about surroundings?"

"That reminds me," answered Mrs. Bird; "before I go a step further I must consult my two babies. Now, do you move your chair a little, and sit so. Thank you, that will do." And she trotted off through some folding doors, one of which she left carefully ajar.

Joan could not in the least understand what this odd little person was driving at, nor who her two babies might be, so she sat still and waited. Presently, from the other side of the door, there came a sound as though several people were clapping their hands and snapping their fingers. A pause followed, and the door was pushed a little farther open, apparently that those on the farther side might look into the room where she was sitting. Then there was more clapping and snapping, and presently Mrs. Bird re-entered with a smile upon her kind little face.

"They like you, my dear," she said, nodding her head—"both of them. Indeed, Sal says that she would much prefer you as a lodger to the late accountant."

"They? Who?" asked Joan.

"Well, my dear, when I spoke of surroundings you may have guessed that mine were peculiar; and so they are—very peculiar, though harmless. The people in the next room are my husband and my daughter; he is paralytic, and they are both of them deaf and dumb."

"Oh, how sad!" said Joan.

"Yes, it is sad; but it might have been much sadder, for I assure you they are not at all unhappy. Now, if I had not married Jim it would have been otherwise, for then he must have gone to the workhouse, or at the best into a home, and of course there would have been no Sal to love us both. But come in, and you shall be introduced to them." And Mrs. Bird lit a candle and led the way into the small dark room.

Here Joan saw a curious sight. Seated in an armchair, his withered legs supported on a footstool, was an enormous man of about forty, with flaxen hair and beard, mild blue eyes, and a face like an infant's, that wore a perpetual smile. Sometimes the smile was more and sometimes it was less, but it was always there. Standing by his side was a sweet and delicate-faced little girl of about twelve; her eyes also were blue and her hair flaxen, but her face was alight with so much fire and intelligence that Joan found it hard to believe that she could be deaf and dumb. Mrs. Bird pointed to her, and struck her hands together this way and that so swiftly that Joan could scarcely follow their movements, whereon the two of them nodded vigorously in answer, and Sal, advancing, held out her hand in greeting. Joan shook it, and was led by her to where Mr. Bird was sitting, with his arm also outstretched.

"There, my dear—now you are introduced," said Mrs. Bird. "This is my family. I have supported them for many many years, thanks be to God; and I hope that I have managed that, if I should die before them, there will be no need for them to go to the workhouse; so you see I have much to be grateful for. Though they are deaf and dumb, you must not think them stupid, for they can do lots of things—read and write and carve. Oh, we are a very happy family, I can assure you; though at times I want somebody to talk to, and that is one of the reasons why I like to have a lodger—not that the late accountant was much use in that respect, for he was a very gloomy man, though right-thinking. And now that you have seen the surroundings, do you think that you would wish to stay here for a week on trial?"

"I should like nothing better," answered Joan.

"Very well, then. Will you come upstairs and see your rooms and wash your hands for supper? I will call the girl, Maria, to help you carry up the box."

Presently Maria arrived. She was a strong, awkward-looking damsel of fifteen, "a workinghouse girl," Mrs. Bird explained, but, like everything else in that house, scrupulously clean in appearance. With her assistance the box was dragged upon the narrow stairs, and Joan found herself in the apartments of the late accountant. They were neat little rooms, separated from each other by double doors, and furnished with a horsehair sofa, a round deal table with a stained top, and some old chairs with curly backs and rep-covered seats.

"They look a little untidy," said Mrs. Bird, eyeing these chairs; "but the fact is that the late accountant was a careless man, and often upset his coffee over them. However, I will run you up some chintz covers in no time, and for the sofa too if you like. And now do you think that the rooms will do? You see here is a good cupboard and a chest of drawers."

"Very nicely, thank you," answered Joan. "I never expected a sitting-room all to myself."

"I am glad that you are pleased. And now I will leave you. Supper will be ready in half an hour—fried eggs and bacon and bread and butter. But if you like anything else I dare say that I can get it for you."

Joan hastened to assure her that eggs and bacon were her favourite food; and, having satisfied herself that there was water in the jug and a clean towel, Mrs. Bird departed, leaving her to unpack. Half an hour later Joan went down and partook of the eggs and bacon. It was an odd meal, with a deaf-and-dumb child pouring out the tea, a deaf-and-dumb giant smiling at her perpetually across the table, and her little hostess attending to them all, and keeping up a double fire of conversation, one with her lips for Joan's benefit, and one with her head and hands for that of her two "babies."

After supper the things were cleared away; and having first inquired whether Joan objected to the smell of smoke, Mrs. Bird filled a large china pipe for her husband, and brought him some queer-shaped tools, with which he began to carve the head of a walking-stick.

"I told you that he was very clever," she said; "do you know, he sometimes makes as much as four shillings a week. He gives me the money, and thinks that I spend it, but I don't; not a farthing. I put it all into the Savings Bank for him and Sally. There is nearly forty pounds there on that account alone. There, do you know what he is saying?"

Joan shook her head.

"He says that he is going to carve a likeness of you. He thinks that you have a beautiful head for a walking-stick. Oh! don't be afraid; he will do it capitally. Look, here is the late accountant. I keep it in memory of him," and Mrs. Bird produced a holly stick, on the knob of which appeared a dismal, but most lifelike, countenance.

"He wasn't very handsome," said Joan.

"No, he wasn't handsome—only right-thinking; and that is why Jim would like to carve you, because you see you are handsome, though whether or no you are right-thinking remains to be proved."

Joan smiled; there was something very quaint about the little lady.

"I hope that Mr. Bird does not want me to sit to him to-night," she said, "for, do you know, I am dreadfully tired, and I think that I will go to bed."

"No, no; he will only make a beginning to-night, perhaps of two or three sticks, and afterwards he will study you. You will be much better for some sleep after your journey—though you have not yet told me where you came from," and she shook her straw-coloured head doubtfully.

Joan made no answer, not feeling inclined to submit herself to cross-examination at the moment; but, going round the table, she shook hands with Mr. Bird and with Sally, who had been watching her all the evening and now put up her face to be kissed in a way that quite won Joan's heart.

"That shows that Sally likes you," said Mrs. Bird, in a gratified voice; "and if Sally likes you I shall too, for she is never wrong about people. And now good night, my dear. We breakfast at half-past seven; but first I read some prayers if you would like to attend them: I read, and my two 'babies' follow in a book. Be sure you put your light out."

Joan stumbled upstairs, and, too tired even for thought, was soon in bed. Beneath her she could hear a clapping and cracking of fingers, which told her that she was being vigorously discussed by the Bird family after their own strange fashion; and to this queer lullaby she went to sleep.

CHAPTER XXIV

MESSRS. BLACK AND PARKER

Joan slept well that night, and woke to find the sunlight streaming in at her window. Coming down to the sitting-room at a quarter past seven, she saw that, early as it was, it had been swept and garnished and the breakfast laid.

"Good morning, my dear!" said Mrs. Bird: "I am glad to see that you are an early riser. I suppose it is a habit which you bring with you from the country. It was not so with the late accountant, who would never breakfast till nine if he could help it, and on Sundays not till ten; but I think that an affection of the liver from which he suffered made him sleepy. And now I am going to have prayers. Maria, come to prayers."

Maria shuffled in, obedient, and diving into the back room reappeared wheeling her master before her, who, as he came, smiled sweetly and waved his hand in greeting to Joan. Mrs. Bird handed two Bibles to her husband and her daughter, pointing out the passage which was to be read with her finger, then she gave them each a manual of prayer. These preparations finished, she began to read the chapter of the Bible aloud; and it was curious and touching to see the attention with which her deaf-and-dumb audience followed the words they could not hear, glancing from time to time at the motions of her lips to make sure that they were keeping pace with her. When the reading was finished, she shut the Bible and knelt down—an example that Mr. Bird could not follow, for his limbs were paralysed. Sally, however, placed herself near Joan, making it clear to her by signs that she was to indicate by pointing each sentence as it passed her mother's lips.

Prayers being over—and surely family worship was never carried on under greater difficulties—breakfast followed, and then the business of the day began. Mr. Bird carved while Mrs. Bird and her daughter sewed at gowns that they were making. For a time Joan looked on helplessly; then, wearying of idleness, asked if she could not do something.

"Can you sew, my dear?" said Mrs. Bird.

"Pretty well," she answered; "but not like you."

"That is scarcely wonderful, considering that I have done nothing else for more than twenty years; but here are some seams to be run up, if you have nothing better to do."

Joan took the seams and began to run them; indeed, she "ran" until her back ached with stooping.

"You are getting tired, my dear," said Mrs. Bird, "as I expected you would, not being accustomed to the work," and she peered at her kindly through her spectacles. "Now you had better rest awhile and talk. What part of England do you come from?"

"From the Eastern counties," answered Joan.

"Dear me! that is strange—quite a coincidence, I declare. I come from the East coast myself. I was born at Yarmouth, though it is many and many a year since I have seen a herring boat. You see, my story is a very simple one. I was an orphan girl, for my dear father was drowned in an October gale when fishing at sea, and I came to London with a family as nursemaid. They did not treat me kindly—even now I cannot say that they did, although I wish to be charitable—for they discharged me because I was not strong enough to do the work, and if I had not been taken in out of pity by a widow woman, a dressmaker and my predecessor in this very house, I do not know what would have become of me. My husband was her only child, and it was part of my duty, and indeed of my pleasure, to look after him in his affliction so far as I was able. Then when his mother died I married him, for I could not make up my mind to leave him alone, and this of course I must have done unless I became his wife. So you see, my dear, I took him on and the business with him, and we have been very happy ever since—so happy that sometimes I wonder why God is so good to me, who am full of faults. One sorrow we have had, it is true, though now even that seems to have become a joy: it was after Sally was born. She was a beautiful baby, and when for the first time I grew sure that she would be deaf and dumb also, I cried till I thought my heart would break, and wished that she might die. Now I see how wicked this was, and every night I thank Heaven that I was not taken at my word, for then my heart would have broken indeed." And the dear little woman's eyes filled with tears as, putting her arm round the child's waist, she kissed her tenderly.

There was something so beautiful in the scene that Joan almost cried in sympathy, and even Jim, who seemed to understand everything, for one moment ceased to smile, and having wiped away a tear from his round blue eye, stretched out his great arms and swept both the mother and the daughter into a confused embrace.

"You say that you are full of faults," said Joan, turning her head until the three of them had recovered their composure, "but I think you are an angel."

"If to tend and care for those whom one loves is to be an angel, I think that we shall most of us get to heaven," she answered, shaking her head; then added, "Oh! you wretched Jim, you have broken my spectacles—the new ones."

Jim, watching his wife's lip and the damaged glasses, looked so comically distressed that Joan burst out laughing, while Sally, seeing what was the matter, ran to the back room to fetch another pair.

"And now, my dear," Mrs. Bird said presently, "you say that you have come to London to get work, though why you should want work if you have plenty of money I do not quite understand. What kind of employment do you wish to take? For my part I cannot think, for, to be frank with you, my dear, you seem too much of a lady for most things."

"I thought," said Joan diffidently, "that I might perhaps get a situation as one of those girls in shops whom they use to hang cloaks on for the approval of customers. You see, I am—tall, and I am not clever enough to teach, so I know nothing else for which I should be fit."

Mrs. Bird shook her head. "I dare say that you might come by such employment, my dear, but I tell you at once that I do not approve of it. I know something of the wickedness of London, and I think that this sort of occupation puts too many temptations in the way of a young lady like you, who are so beautiful, and do not seem to have any home ties to keep your thoughts from them. We are most of us weak, remember; and flattery, and promises, and grand presents, all of which would be offered to you, are very nice things."

"I am not afraid of such temptations, Mrs. Bird," Joan answered, with a sad confidence that at once attracted the quick little woman's attention.

"Now, when a person tells me that she is not afraid of a thing," she said, glancing at her, "I conclude that she is either totally without experience and foolhardy, or that, having won the experience and passed through the fire, she no longer fears a danger which she has overcome, or—" and she stopped.

This vein of speculative reflection did not seem to recommend itself to Joan; at any rate she changed the subject.

"You have twice called me a lady, Mrs. Bird," she said, "but I must tell you that I am nothing of the sort. Who my father was I don't even know, though I believe him to have been a gentleman, and my mother was the daughter of a yeoman farmer."

"Married?" asked Mrs. Bird interrogatively.

Joan shook her head.

"Ah! I understand," said Mrs. Bird.

"That is partly why I left home," explained Joan.

"Meaning Bradmouth? Don't look surprised, my dear. I saw the name on the clergyman's testimonial, and also on your box."

"Yes, Bradmouth. I lived there with an aunt, and everybody looked down upon me because of my position."

"That was very wicked of them. But did they begin to look down upon you all at once, or had you, perhaps, some other reason for coming away? I suppose your aunt knew that you were coming?"

"No, she did not know. We do not get on together, and I thought it best not to tell her. Also, she wanted me to marry somebody whom I dislike."

"Because there is somebody else whom you do like, I suppose, my dear. Well, it is no affair of mine. But if you will not think me impertinent, where then do you get your money from?"

"A gentleman—"

"A gentleman!" exclaimed Mrs. Bird, dropping her work in horror.

"Oh! no, not that," said Joan, blushing; "he is a kind of guardian, a friend of my father's, I believe. At any rate he has paid for me all these years, and says that he will allow me five pounds a month; though I would rather earn my own living if possible."

"A friend of your father's? What a strange story! I suppose that he is not your father, my dear?"

"My father!" said Joan, opening her eyes wide in amazement—"Mr. Levinger my father! Of course not. Why, if he were, would he have treated me like a stranger all my life?"

"It is possible," said Mrs. Bird drily; "I have heard of such things."

"Oh no, he is not bad enough for that; in fact, he is very good and kind. He knew that I was coming away, and gave me five-and-twenty pounds to start on, and he told me himself that he was left my trustee by my father, who is dead, but whose name he was bound not to reveal."

"Indeed," answered Mrs. Bird, pursing up her lips. "And now I must go and see about the dinner. As it happens, I do work for some of the big shops; and I will inquire if there is any situation vacant that might suit you. Look: Jim wants you to turn your head a little, so that he can see your nose. Is he not making a beautiful likeness?" And, nodding affectionately to her husband, she left the room.

Once outside the door, Mrs. Bird stood still and reflected. "There is a mystery about that girl," she thought, "and she has not told me all her story: she has left out the love affair—I could see it in her face. Now, if I were wise, I should send her about her business without more words; but, somehow, I cannot find the heart to do it. I suppose it is because she is so beautiful, and seems so sad and friendless; and after all it is one's duty to help those who are placed thus—yes, even if they have not been quite respectable, though of course I have no right to suppose that she has not. No, I cannot turn her away. To do so might be to bring her to ruin, and that would be a dreadful thing to have upon one's mind. But I do not think much of that guardian of hers, Mr. Levinger she called him, who can send such a lovely girl to take her chance in London without providing her with a proper home. It looks almost as if he wished to be rid of her: altogether it is a very strange story. I must say that it interests me; but then curiosity always was one of my sins, and I have not conquered it yet." And again shaking her head, this time at the thought of her own depravity, Mrs. Bird made her way to the kitchen.

After dinner was over she announced to Joan that they were all going out for a walk in the Park, and asked her if she would like to accompany them. Joan, of course, was delighted, for already she began to feel a want of the fresh air to which she was accustomed; but as she accepted she looked inquiringly at Mr. Bird.

"Ah, my dear," said his wife, "you are wondering how he can come out walking when his legs are crippled. Well, presently you shall see. Now go and put on your hat."

By the time that Joan was ready she found that a long wheel-chair, which she had noticed standing in the passage, had been run into the sitting-room, and into this chair Mr. Bird shifted himself with marvellous agility by the help of his muscular arms, nodding and smiling at Joan the while.

"How on earth will they get it down the steps?" she wondered. Soon the mystery was solved, for, the front door having been opened, Sally appeared with three grooved boards which reached from the lintel to the pavement. The three wheels of the chair having been set in the grooves, Mr. Bird grasped the iron railings on either side of the steps, and, smiling triumphantly, launched himself with much dignity into the street.

"There, my dear!" said Mrs. Bird, while Sally replaced the boards in the passage and shut the door, "necessity is the mother of invention. Quite clever, isn't it? But we have other contrivances that are even cleverer."

Then they started, Mr. Bird guiding himself, while Sally and Mrs. Bird who was arrayed in a prim little bonnet and mantle, pushed behind. Joan offered to assist, but was not allowed this honour because of her inexperience of the streets, at any rate until they reached the Park. So she walked by the side of the chair, wondering at the shops and the noise and bustle of the Edgware Road.

Presently they came to the corner opposite the Marble Arch, where, as usual, the wide roadway was blocked with traffic. "How will they ever get across there?" thought Joan; "it frightens me to look at it."

But it did not frighten Mrs. Bird and her family, who, without a moment's hesitation, plunged into the thick of it, calling to Joan to keep close to them. It was really wonderful to see the skill with which the transit was accomplished; cabs, omnibuses and carriages bore down upon them from all directions, but the Bird family were not dismayed. Here and there the chair headed, now passing under the nose of a horse and now grazing the wheel of a cab, till at length it arrived safely at the farther pavement. Joan was not so fortunate, however; about half-way across she lost her head, and, having been nearly knocked down by the pole of an omnibus, stood bewildered till a policeman seized her by the arm and dragged her into safety.

"You see, my dear," said Mrs. Bird, "although you are so strong, you are not quite competent to wheel Jim at present. First you must learn to look after yourself."

Then they went for their walk in the Park, which Joan enjoyed, for it was all new to her, especially when she was allowed to push the precious chair; and returned to Kent Street in time for tea.

The rest of the afternoon and evening passed like those of the previous day, and the morrow was as the yesterday had been. Indeed, there was little variety in the routine of the Bird menage—so little that Joan soon began to wonder how they distinguished one month or one year from another. Few customers came to the house, for most of the dress-making was put out to Mrs. Bird by the managers of large shops, who had confidence in her, and were not afraid to trust her with costly materials, which she made up, generally into skirts, and took back in the evenings.

So it came about that all day long Mrs. Bird and Sally sewed, while Jim carved endless walking-sticks, and Joan sat by giving such help as she could, now listening to her hostess's good-natured chatter and now to the shrill song of the canary. At first, after all that she had gone through, this mode of life was a rest to her. It was delightful to be obliged neither to think nor to work unless she so wished; it was delightful to know that she was beyond the reach of Samuel Rock, and could not be harried by the coarse tongue of Mrs. Gillingwater or by the gossip of her neighbours. The atmosphere of goodness in which she lived was very soothing also: it was a new thing for Joan to pass her days where there was no hate, no passion, no jealousy, and no violence—where, on the contrary, charity and loving-kindness reigned supreme. Soon she grew very fond of little Mrs. Bird, as, indeed, anybody must have done who had the good fortune to know her; and began to share her adoration of the two "babies," the great patient creature who faced his infirmities with a perpetual smile, and the sweet child from whom love seemed to radiate.

But after a while, as her body and mind shook off their weariness, these things began to pall; she longed for work, for anything that would enable her to escape from her own thoughts—and as yet no work was forthcoming. At times, tiring of Jim's smile as he hewed out libellous likenesses of herself upon his walking-sticks, and of the trilling of the canary, she would seek refuge in her own sitting-room, where she read and re-read the books that Henry had given her; and at times, longing for air, she would escape from the stuffy little house to the Park, to walk up and down there till she grew weary—an amusement which she found had its drawbacks. At last, when she had been a fortnight in Kent Street, she asked Mrs. Bird if there was any prospect of getting employment.

"My dear," was the answer, "I have inquired everywhere, and as yet without success. To-night I am taking this skirt back to Messrs. Black and Parker, in Oxford Street, and I will ask their manager, who is quite a friend of mine, if he has an opening. Failing this I think you had better advertise, for I see that you are getting tired of doing nothing, and I do not wonder at it—though you should be most thankful that you can afford to live without work, seeing that many people in your position would now be reduced to starvation."

That night, Mrs. Bird returned from Messrs. Black and Parker's with a radiant countenance.

"My dear," she said, "there is a coincidence, quite a wonderful coincidence. The young woman at Messrs. Black and Parker's whose business it was to fit on the cloaks in the mantle department has suddenly been called away to nurse a sick uncle in Cornwall from whom she has expectations, and they are looking out for some one to take her place, for, as it chances, there is no one suitable for the post in their employ. I told the manager about you, and he said that I was to bring you there to-morrow morning. If they engaged you your pay would be eighteen shillings a week to begin with; which is not much, but better than nothing."

Accordingly, on the following morning, having arrayed herself in her best dress, and a pretty little bonnet that she had made with the help of Sally, Joan set out for Messrs. Black and Parker's in the company of Mrs. Bird.

Messrs. Black and Parker's establishment was an enormous one, having many departments.

"You see it is a first-class shop, my dear," said Mrs. Bird, glancing with veneration at the huge windows filled with chefs-d'oeuvres of the milliner's and other arts. "Now follow me, and don't be nervous." And she led the way through various divisions till she reached a large box built of mahogany and glass labelled "Manager's Office. No admittance except on business."

At this moment the door of the box opened, and from it issued an oiled and curled specimen of manhood, with very white hands and hair so wavy that it conveyed a suggestion of crimping tongs.

His eye fell upon Joan, and he bowed obsequiously.

"Can I do anything for you, madam?" he said. "We are so full this morning that I fear you are not being attended to."

"She is not a customer, Mr. Waters," said Mrs. Bird, emerging from behind Joan's tall shape: "she is the young person about whom I spoke to you, who wants a situation as show-woman."

"Oh! is she?" said Mr. Waters, with a complete change of manner; "then why didn't you say so at first? Well, she's a pretty girl anyway. Step in here, miss, and take off your jacket, please, so that I can see what your figure is like."

Joan did as she was told, although she felt a hate of this individual swelling in her heart. Mr. Waters surveyed her critically for half a minute or more, shutting first one eye and then the other, as though to bring her better into focus.

"Any experience?" he said laconically—"I mean of business."

"No, sir, none," Joan answered.

"Ah! I see: a lady, I suppose."

"I am not a lady, sir," replied Joan.

"Ain't you?—then you imitate the article very well."

"Just what I feared," murmured Mrs. Bird, shaking her head.

"However," he went on, "we can overlook that fault; but I have another doubt about you. You're too good-looking. Our customers like to see their things tried on a fine figure, of course, but they don't like to see them tried on a girl who makes them look common dowds beside her. Why, a three-guinea mantle would seem a better thing on your back than a forty-pound cloak on most of them. You'd show off the goods, I dare say, but I doubt that you would frighten away custom."

"I thought that tall people were always wanted," hesitated Joan.

"Tall people!" said Mr. Waters, with an admiring snigger; "just you look at yourself in this pier glass, and I think that you will see something else there beside height. Now, I'll give you a bit of advice: you drop this show and go on to the stage. You'll draw there; yes, even if you can't sing or act a bit, there are hundreds who would pay to come and look at you. By George! I'm not sure that I wouldn't myself."

"I do not wish to go on the stage," answered Joan stiffly; and Mrs. Bird behind her murmured, "No! never!" in sympathetic tones. "If you think that I shall not suit," she added, "I will not take up your time any longer."

"I didn't say that, miss. Here!"—and he put his head out of the door and called to a shop-woman—"just give me that velvet mantle, will you? Now, miss," he said: "you fancy that Mrs. Bird's a customer, and let me see you try to sell her this cloak."

Joan's first impulse was to refuse, but presently a sense of the fun of the situation prevailed, and she rose to it, mincing, smiling, and praising up the garment, which she hung upon her own shoulders, bending her graceful shape this way and that to show it in various lights and attitudes, till at length Mrs. Bird exclaimed, "Well, I never!—you're a born actress, my dear. You might have been bred to the business. I should have bought that cloak long ago, I should, though, saving your presence, Mr. Waters, I don't think it is worth the price asked."

"You'll do," said the manager, rubbing his hands, "if only you can forget that you are a lady, and have nous enough to flatter when you see that it is welcome, and that's always where ladies and their clothes are concerned. What's your name?"

"Haste: Joan Haste."

"Very well, Miss Haste. Let's see: to-day is Saturday, so you may as well begin on Monday. Hours nine to seven, dinner and tea provided, also black silk dress, that you put on when you come and take off when you leave. I should think that the last young lady's would fit you pretty well with a little alteration, unless you like to buy one yourself at cost price."

"Thank you, I think that I will buy one for myself."

"Indeed! Well, so much the better for us. It is usual to ask for references as to character, and security, or a sum on deposit; but I understand that Mrs. Bird guarantees all that, so we will say no more about it. The wages will be eighteen shillings a week for the first six months, and after that a pound if we are satisfied with you. Do you agree to these terms?"

"Yes."

"Very well, then. Good morning."

"There's a smart girl," reflected Mr. Waters to himself, "and a real beauty too. But she's a fool for all that; she ought to go on the boards—she'd have a future there. However, it's her affair, not mine."

"Well, my dear," said Mrs. Bird to Joan, "you got through that capitally. At first I thought that he would never engage you, but he seemed to take quite a liking to you before the end. What do you think of him?"

"I think him odious," said Joan.

"Odious, my dear! What a strong term! Free and easy, if you like, but not odious. He is much better than most of them, I can tell you."

"Then the rest must be very bad indeed," said Joan, and continued on her way in silence.

CHAPTER XXV

"I FORBID YOU."

On the following Monday morning Joan began her career as a shop-girl, to describe which in detail would be too long, however instructive it might prove. Her actual work, especially at this, the dead season of the year, was not so hard as she had expected, nor was she long in mastering her duties; but, accustomed as she had been to a country life and the fresh air, she soon found confinement for so many hours a day in the close atmosphere of the shop exceedingly irksome. From Kent Street to Messrs. Black and Parker's was but a quarter of an hour's walk; and, as Joan discovered by experiment, without exposing herself to many annoyances it was impossible for her to wander about the streets after dark in search of exercise. As a last resource she was driven to rising at the peep of day and taking her walks abroad in the Park so soon as the gates were open—a daily constitutional which, if wholesome, was not exhilarating, and one that could only be practised in fine weather and while the days were long. This craving for air, however, was among the least of her troubles, for soon it became clear to her that she had no vocation for shop life; indeed, she learned to loathe it and its surroundings. At first the humours of the business amused her a little, but very shortly she discovered that even about these there was a terrible sameness, for one cannot be perpetually entertained by the folly of old ladies trying to make themselves look young, or by the vanity of the young ones neglected by nature and attempting to supply their deficiencies with costly garments.

What galled her chiefly, however, were the attentions with which she was honoured by the young men of the establishment. Worst of all, the oiled and curled Mr. Waters singled her out as the object of his especial admiration, till at length she lost her temper, and answered him in such a fashion as to check his advances once and for all. He left her muttering "You shall pay for that"; and he kept his word, for thenceforth her life was made a misery to her, and it seemed that she could do nothing right. As it chanced, he could not actually discharge her, for Joan had attracted the favourable notice of one of the owners of the business, who, when Mr. Waters made some trumped-up complaint against her, dismissed it with a hint that he better be more careful as to his facts in future.

For the rest, she had no amusements and no friends, and during all the time she spent in London she never visited a theatre or other place of entertainment. Her only recreation was to read when she could get the books, or, failing this, to sit with little Mrs. Bird in the Kent Street parlour and perfect herself in the art of conversation with the deaf and dumb.

As may be imagined, such an existence did not tend to cause Joan to forget her past, or the man who was to her heart what the sun is to the world. She could renounce him, she could go away vowing that she would never see him more; but to live without him, and especially to live such a life as hers, ah! that was another matter.

Moreover, as time went on, a new terror took her, that, vague in the beginning, grew week by week more definite and more dreadful. At first she could scarcely believe it, for somehow such a thing had never entered into her calculations; but soon she was forced to acknowledge it as a fact, an appalling, unalterable fact, which, as yet secret to herself, must shortly become patent to the whole world. The night that the truth came home to her without the possibility of further doubt was perhaps the most terrible which she ever spent. For some hours she thought that she must go mad: she wept, she prayed, she called upon the name of her lover, who, although he was the author of her woe, in some mysterious fashion had grown doubly dear to her, till at last sleep or insensibility brought her relief. But sleep passes with the darkness, and she awoke to find this new spectre standing by her bedside and to know that there it must always stand till the end came. All that day she went about her work dazed by her secret agony of mind, but in the evening her senses seemed to come back to her, bringing with them new and acuter suffering.

Where was she to go and what was she to do, she who had no friend in the wide world, or at least none in whom she could confide? Soon they would turn her out upon the streets; even the Bird family would shrink from her as though she had a leprosy. Would it not be better to end it at once, and herself with it? Abandoning her usual custom, Joan did not return home, but wandered about London heedless of the stares and insults of the passers-by, till at length she came to Westminster Bridge. She had not meant to come there—indeed, she did not know the way—but the river had drawn her to its brink, as it has drawn so many an unfortunate before her. There beneath those dim and swirling waters she could escape her shame and find peace, or at least take it to a region beyond all familiar things, whereof the miseries and unrest would not be those of the earth, even if they surpassed them. Twice she crossed the bridge; once she tore herself away, walking for a while along the Embankment; then she returned to it again, brought back by the irresistible attraction of the darkling river.

Now she thought that she would do it, and now her hand was on the parapet. She was quite alone for the moment, there were none to stop her—alone with her fear and fate. Yes, she would do it: but oh! what of Henry? Had she a right to make him a murderer? Had she the right to be the murderess of his child? What would he say when he heard, and what would he think? After all, why should she kill herself? Was it so wicked to become a mother? According to religion and custom, yes—that is, such a mother as she would be—but how about nature? As for the sin, she could not help it. It was done, and she must suffer for it. She had broken the law of God, and doubtless God would exact retribution from her; indeed, already He was exacting it. At least she might plead that she loved this man, and there were many married women who could bear their children without shame, and could not say as much. Yet they were virtuous and she was an outcast—that was the rule. Well, what did it matter to her? They could not put her in prison, and she had no name to lose. Why should she kill herself? Why should she not bear her baby and love it for its father's sake and its own? Now she came to think of it, there was nothing that she would like better. Doubtless there would be difficulties and troubles, but she was answerable to no one. However much she might be ashamed of herself, there were none to be ashamed of her, and therefore it was a mere question of pounds, shillings, and pence. She could get these from Mr. Levinger, or, failing him, from Henry. He would not leave her to starve, or his child either—she knew him too well for that. What a fool she had been! Had she not come to her senses, by now she would be floating on that river or lying in the mud at the bottom of it. Well, she had done with that, and so she might as well go home. The future and the wrath of Heaven she must face, that was all; she had sown, and she must reap—as we always do.

Accordingly she hailed a passing hansom and told the driver to take her to the Marble Arch, for she was too weary to walk; moreover she did not know the road.

It was ten o'clock when she reached Kent Street. "My dear," said Mrs. Bird, "how flushed you look! Where have you been? We were all getting quite anxious about you."

"I have been walking," answered Joan: "I could not stand the heat of that shop any longer, and I felt as though I must get some exercise or faint."

"I do not think that young women ought to walk about the streets by themselves at night," said Mrs. Bird, reprovingly. "If you were so very anxious for exercise I dare say that I could have managed to accompany you. Have you had supper?"

"No, and I don't want any. I think that I will go to bed. I am tired."

"You will certainly not go to bed, Joan, until you have had something to eat. I don't know what has come to you—I don't indeed."

So Joan was forced to sit down and go through the farce of swallowing some food, while Sally ministered to her, and Jim, perceiving that something was wrong, smiled sympathetically across the table. How she got through the meal she never quite knew, for her mind was somewhat of a blank; though she could not help wondering vaguely what these good people would say, could they become aware that within the last hour she had been leaning on the parapet of Westminster Bridge purposing to cast herself into the Thames.

Next morning Joan went to her work as usual. All day long she stood in the shop attending to her duties, but it seemed to her as though she had changed her identity, as though she were not Joan Haste, but a different woman, whom as yet she could not understand. Once before she had suffered this fancied change of self: on that night when she lay in the churchyard clasping Henry's shattered body to her breast; and now again it was with her. That was the hour when she had passed from the regions of her careless girlhood into love's field of thorns and flowers—the hour of dim and happy dream. This, the second and completer change, came upon her in the hour of awakening; and though the thorns still pierced her soul, behold, the red bloom she had gathered was become a bitter fruit, a very apple of Sodom, a fruit of the tree of sinful knowledge that she must taste of in the wilderness which she had won. Love had been with her in the field, and still he was with her in the desert; but oh! how different his aspect! Then he was bright and winged and beautiful, with lips of honey, and a voice of promise murmuring many a new and happy word; now he appeared terrible and stern, and spoke of sin, of sorrow, and of shame. Then also her lover had been at her side, now she was utterly alone, alone with the accusing angel of her conscience, and in this solitude she must suffer, with no voice to cheer her and no hand to help.

From the hour of their parting she had longed for him, and desired the comfort of his presence. How much more, then, did she long for him now! Soon indeed this craving swallowed up every other need of her nature, and became a physical anguish that, like some deadly sickness, ended in the conquest of her mind and body. Joan fought against it bravely, for she knew what submission meant. It meant that she would involve Henry in her own ruin. She remembered well what he had said about marrying her, and the tale which she had heard as to his refusing to become engaged to Miss Levinger on the ground that he considered himself to be already bound to her. If she told him of her sore distress, would he not act upon these declarations? Would he not insist upon making her his wife, and could she find the strength to refuse his sacrifice? Beyond the barrier that she herself had built between them were peace and love and honour for her. But what was there for him? If once those bars were down—and she could break them with a touch—she would be saved indeed, but Henry must be lost. She was acquainted with the position of his affairs, and aware that the question was not one of a masalliance only. If he married her, he would be ruined socially and financially in such a fashion that he could never lift up his head again. Of course even in present circumstances it was not necessary that he should marry her, especially as she would never ask it of him; but if once they met, if once they corresponded even, as she knew well, the whole trouble would begin afresh, and at least there would be an end of his prospects with Miss Levinger. No, no; whatever happened, however great her sufferings, her first duty was silence.

Another week went by, leaving her resolution unchanged; but now her health began to fail beneath the constant strain of her anxieties, and a physical languor that rendered her unfit for long hours of work in a heated shop. Now she lacked the energy to tramp about in the Park before her early breakfast; indeed, the advance of autumn, with its rain and fogs, made such exercise impossible. Her first despair, the despair that suggested suicide, had gone by, but then so had the half-defiant mood which followed it. Whatever may have been her faults, Joan was a decent-minded woman, and one who felt her position bitterly. Never for one moment of the day or night could she be free from remorse and care, and the weight of apprehension that seemed to crush all courage out of her. Even if from time to time she could succeed in putting aside her mental troubles, their place was taken by anxieties for the future. Soon she must leave the home that sheltered her, and then where was she to go?

One afternoon, about half-past three o'clock, Joan was standing in the mantle department of Messrs. Black and Parker's establishment awaiting customers. The morning had been a heavy one, for town was filling rapidly, and she felt very tired. There was, it is true, no fixed rule to prevent Messrs. Black and Parker's employees from from seating themselves when not actually at work; but since a pique had begun between herself and Mr. Waters, in practice Joan found few opportunities of so doing. On two occasions when she ventured to rest thus for a minute, the manager had rated her harshly for indolence, and she did not care to expose herself to another such experience. Now she was standing, the very picture of weariness and melancholy, leaning upon a chair, when of a sudden she looked up and saw before her—Ellen Graves and Emma Levinger. They were speaking.

"Very well, dear," said Ellen, "you go and buy the gloves while I try on the mantles. I will meet you presently in the doorway."

"Yes," said Emma, and went.

Joan's first impulse was to fly; but flight was impossible, for with Ellen, rubbing his white hands and bowing at intervals, was Mr. Waters.

"I think you asked for velvet mantles, madam, did you not? Now, miss, the velvet mantles—quick, please—those new shapes from Paris."

Almost automatically, Joan obeyed, reaching down cloak after cloak to be submitted to Miss Graves's critical examination. Three or four of them she put by as unsuitable, but at last one was produced that seemed to take her fancy.

"I should like the young person to try on this one, please," she said.

"Certainly, madam. Now, miss: no, not that, the other. Where are your wits this afternoon?"

Joan put on the garment in silence, turning herself round to display its perfections, with the vain hope that Ellen's preoccupation and the gathering gloom in the shop would prevent her from being recognised.

"It's very dark here," Ellen said presently.

"Yes, madam; but I have ordered them to turn on the electric light. Will you be seated for a moment, madam?"

Ellen took a chair, and began chatting with the manager about the advantages of the employment of electricity in preference to gas in shops, while Joan, with the cloak still on her shoulders, stood before them in the shadow.

Just then she heard a footstep, the footstep of a lame man who was advancing towards them from the stairs, and the sound set her wondering if Henry had recovered from his lameness. Next moment she was clinging to the back of a chair to save herself from falling headlong to the floor, for the man was speaking.

"Are you here, Ellen?" he said: "it is so infernally dark in this place. Oh! there you are. I met Miss Levinger below, and she told me that I should find you upstairs trying on bodices or something."

"One does not generally try on bodices in public, Henry. What is the matter?"

"Nothing more than usual, only I have made up my mind to go back to Rosham by the five o'clock train, and thought that I would come to see whether you had any message for my mother."

"Oh! I understood that you were not going till Wednesday, when you could have escorted us home. No, I have no particular message, beyond my love. You may tell her that I am getting on very well with my trousseau, and that Edward has given me the loveliest bangle."

"I have to go," answered Henry: "those confounded farms, as usual," and he sighed.

"Oh! farms," said Ellen—"I am sick of farms. I wish that the art of agriculture had never been invented. Thank goodness"—as the electric light sprang out with a sudden glare—"we can see at last. If you have a minute, stop and give me your opinion of this cloak. Taste is one of your redeeming virtues, you know."

"Well, it is about all the time I have," he said, glancing at his watch. "Where's the article?"

"There, before you, on that young woman."

"Oh!" said Henry, "I see. Charming, I think; but a little long, isn't it? Now I'm off."

At this moment for the first time Ellen saw Joan's face. She recognised her instantly—there was no possibility of mistake in that brilliant and merciless light. And what a despairing face it was! so much so, indeed, that it touched even Ellen's imagination and moved her to pity. The great brown eyes were opened wide, the lips were set apart and pale, the head was bent forward, and from beneath the rich folds of the velvet cloak the hands were a little lifted, as though in entreaty.

In an instant Ellen grasped the facts: Joan Haste had seen Henry, and was about to speak to him. Trying as was the situation, Ellen proved herself its mistress, as she had need to do, for an instinct warned her that if once these two recognised each other incalculable trouble must result. With a sudden movement she threw herself between them.

"Very well, dear," she said: "good-bye. You had better be going, or you will miss the train."

"All right," answered Henry, "there is no such desperate hurry; let me have another look at the cloak."

"You will have plenty of opportunities of doing that," Ellen said carelessly; "I have settled to buy it. Why, here comes Emma; I suppose that she is tired of waiting."

Henry turned and began to walk down the stairs. Joan saw that he was going, and made an involuntary movement as though to follow him, but Ellen was too quick for her. Stepping swiftly to one side, she spoke, or rather whispered into her ear:

"Go back: I forbid you!"

Joan stopped bewildered, and in another moment Henry had spoken some civil words to Emma and was gone.

"Will you be so good as to send the cloak with the other things?" said Ellen to Mr. Waters. "Come, Emma, we must be going, or we shall be late for the 'at home,'" and, followed by the bowing manager, she left.

"Oh, my God!" murmured Joan, putting her hands to her face—"oh, my God! my God!"

CHAPTER XXVI

A LOVE LETTER

Joan never knew how she got through the rest of that afternoon. She did not faint, but she was so utterly overcome and bewildered that she could do nothing right. Three times Mr. Waters spoke to her, with ever-increasing harshness, and on the third occasion she answered him saying—

"I am very sorry, but it is not my fault. I feel ill: let me go home."

"Yes, you'd better go, miss," he said, "and so far as I am concerned you can stop there. I shall report your conduct to the proprietors, so you need not trouble to return unless you hear from me again."

Joan went without a word; and so ended her life as a show-woman, for never again did she set eyes upon the establishment of Messrs. Black and Parker, or upon their estimable manager, Mr. Waters.

The raw damp of the October evening revived her somewhat, but before she reached Kent Street she knew that she had not exaggerated when she said that she was ill—very ill, in body as well as in mind. The long anxiety and mental torture, culminating in the scene of that afternoon, together with confinement in the close atmosphere of the shop and other exciting causes, had broken down her health at last. Sharp pains shot through her head and limbs; she felt fever burning in her blood, and at times she trembled so violently that she could scarcely keep her feet. Sally opened the door to her with an affectionate smile, for the dumb girl had learned to worship her; but Joan went straight to her room without noticing her, and threw herself upon the bed. Presently Mrs. Bird, learning from the girl that something was wrong, came upstairs bringing a cup of tea.

"What is the matter with you, my dear?" she asked.

"I don't know," answered Joan; "I feel very bad in my head and all over me."

"Influenza, I expect," said Mrs. Bird; "there is so much of it about now. Let me help you off with your cloak and things, then drink this tea and try to go to sleep. If you are not better to-morrow morning, we shall have to send for the doctor."

Joan obeyed listlessly, swallowing the tea with an effort.

"Are you sure that you have nothing on your mind, my dear?" asked Mrs. Bird. "I have been watching you for a long while, and I find a great change in you. You never did seem happy from the hour that you came here, but of late you have been downright miserable."

Joan laughed: the sound of that laugh gave Mrs. Bird "the creeps," as she afterwards expressed it.

"Anything on my mind? Yes, I have everything on my mind, enough to drive me mad twice over. You've been very kind to me, Mrs. Bird, and I shall never forget your goodness; but I am going to leave you to-morrow—they have dismissed me from the shop already—so before I go I may as well tell you what I am. To begin with, I am a liar; and I'm more than that, I am— Listen!" and she bent her head forward and whispered into the little woman's ear. "Now," she added, "I don't know if you will let me stop the night in the house after that. If not, say so, and I'll be off at once. I dare say that they would take me in at a hospital, or a home, or if not there is always the Thames. I nearly threw myself into it the other day, and this time I should not change my mind." And again she laughed.

"My poor child! my poor, poor child!" said Mrs. Bird, wiping her eyes, "please don't talk like that. Who am I, that I should judge you?—though it is true that I do like young women to be respectable; and so they would be if it wasn't for the men, the villains! I'd just like to tear the eyes out of this wicked one, I would, who first of all leads you into trouble and then deserts you."

"Don't speak of him like that," said Joan: "he didn't lead me—if anything, I led him; and he didn't desert me, I ran away from him. I think that he would have married me if I had asked him, but I will have nothing to do with him."

"Why, the girl must be mad!" said Mrs. Bird blankly. "Is he a gentleman?"

"Yes, if ever there was one; and I'm not mad, only can't you understand that one may love a man so much that one would die rather than bring him into difficulties? There, it's a long story, but he would be ruined were he to marry me. There's another girl whom he ought to marry—a lady."

"He would be ruined, indeed! And what will you be, pray?"

"I don't know, and I don't care: dead, I hope, before long. Oh!" and she wrung her hands piteously, "I saw him in the shop this afternoon; he was quite close to me. Yes, he looked at a cloak that I was showing, and never knew me who wore it. That's what has broken me down: so long as I did not see him I could bear it, but now my heart feels as though it would burst. To think that he should have been so close to me and not have known me, oh! it is cruel, cruel!"

"Dear, dear!" said Mrs. Bird, "really I feel quite upset, I am not accustomed to this sort of thing. If you will excuse me I will go and look for my salts. And now you get into bed like a good girl, and stop there."

"Am I not to go away, then?" asked Joan.

"Certainly not—at any rate not for the present. You are much too ill to go anywhere. And now there is just one thing that I should like to know, and you may as well tell it me as you have told me so much. What is this gentleman's name?"

"I'll not tell you," answered Joan sullenly: "if I told you, you would be troubling him; besides, I have no right to give away his secrets, whatever I do with my own."

"Perhaps it is no such great secret after all, my dear. Say now, isn't his name Henry Graves, and doesn't he live at a place called Rosham?"

"Who told you that?" asked Joan, springing up and standing over her. Then she remembered herself, and sat down again on the bed. "No, that's not the name," she said; "I never heard that name."

"Nobody told me," answered Mrs. Bird quietly, ignoring Joan's denial. "I saw the name in those poetry books that you are so fond of, and which you lent me to read; and I saw one or two notes that you had made in them also, that's all. I've had to watch deaf-and-dumb people for many years, my dear, and there's nothing like it for sharpening the wits and teaching one how to put two and two together. Also you could never hear the name of Henry without staring round and blushing, though perhaps you didn't know it yourself. Bless you, I guessed it all a month ago, though I didn't think that it was so bad as this."

"Oh! it's mean of you to have spied on me like that, Mrs. Bird," said Joan, giving in; "but it's my fault, like everything else."

"Don't you fret about your faults, but just go to bed, there's a good girl. I will come back in half an hour, and if I don't find you fast asleep I shall be very angry." And she put her arms about her and kissed her on the forehead, as a mother might kiss her child.

"You are too kind to me, a great deal too kind," said Joan, with a sob. "Nobody ever was kind to me before, except him, and that's why I feel it."

When Mrs. Bird had gone, Joan undressed herself and put on a wrapper, but she did not get into bed. For a while she wandered aimlessly backwards and forwards through the doors between the two rooms, apparently without much knowledge of what she was doing. Some note-paper was lying on the table in the sitting-room, where the gas was burning, and it caught her eye.

"Why shouldn't I write?" she said aloud; "not to him, no, but just to put down what I feel; it will be a comfort to play at writing to him, and I can tear it up afterwards."

The fancy seemed to please her excited brain; at any rate she sat down and began to write rapidly, never pausing for a thought or words. She wrote:—

"My Darling,—

"Of course I have no business to call you that, but then you see this is not a real letter, and you will never get it, for I shall post it presently in the fire: I am only playing at writing to you. Henry, my darling, my lover, my husband—you can see now that I am playing, or I shouldn't call you that, should I?—I am very ill, I think that I am going to die, and I hope that I shall die quickly, quickly, and melt away into nothingness, to be blown about the world with the wind, or perhaps to bloom in a flower on my own grave, a flower for you to pick, my own. Henry, I saw you this afternoon; I wore that cloak your sister was choosing, and I think that I should have spoken to you, only she forbade me, and looked so fierce that she frightened me. Wasn't it strange—it makes me laugh now, though I could have cried then—to think of my standing there before you with that mantle on my shoulders, and of your looking at it, and taking no more notice of me than if I were a dressmaker's shape? Perhaps that is what you took me for; and oh! I wish I was, for then I couldn't feel. But I haven't told you my secret yet, and perhaps you would like to know it. I am going to have a child, Henry—a child with big blue eyes, like yours. I was ashamed about it at first, and it frightened me. I used to dream at nights that everybody I knew was hunting me through the streets, pointing and gibbering at me, with my aunt, Mrs. Gillingwater, at the head of them.

Now I'm not ashamed any more. I don't care: why should I? Nobody will bother because a nameless girl has a nameless baby—nobody except me; and I shall love it, and love it, and love it almost as much as I love you, my dear. But I forgot: I am going to die—kiss me when I am dead, Henry—pale lips for you to kiss, my own!—so there will be no child after all, and that is a pity, for you won't be able to see it. If it is born at all it will be born in heaven, or wherever poor girls who have gone wrong are sent to. I wonder what is the meaning of it, Henry; I wonder, not why I should love you, for I was bred to that, that was my birth-luck, but why I should suffer so because I love you? Is it my fault, or somebody else's?—I don't mean yours, dear—or is it simply a punishment because I am wicked?—because, if so, it seems curious. You see, if I had taken you at your word and married you, then I shouldn't have been wicked—that is, in the eyes of others—and I shouldn't have suffered. I should have been as good as all married women are, and oh! a great deal happier than most of them. But because I couldn't think of marrying you, knowing that it would be your ruin, I am wicked and I suffer; at least I can guess no other reason. Well, Henry, I don't mind suffering so long as you are happy, and I hope that you will always be happy. But I am selfish too: When I am dead, I hope that you will think of me at times—yes, and of the baby that wasn't born—and if I can, I shall try to wander into your sleep now and again, and you will see me there white robed, and with my hair spread out—for you used to praise my hair—holding the dream-baby in my arms. And at last you will die also and come to find me; not that you will need to seek, for though I am a sinner God will be good and pitiful to me because I have endured so much, and I shall be waiting at your bedside to draw your passing spirit to my breast. Oh! I have been lonely, so dreadfully lonely; I have felt as though I stood by myself in a world where nobody understood me and everybody scorned and hated me. But I know now that this was only because I could not see you. If only I could see you I should die happy. Oh! my darling, my darling, if only I could see you, and you were kind to me for one short hour, I would—"

Here Joan's letter came to an abrupt termination, for the simple reason that the agony in her head grew so sharp that she fainted for a moment, then, recovering herself, staggered to her bed, forgetting all about the disjointed and half-crazy epistle which it had been her fancy to write.

A few minutes later Mrs. Bird entered the room accompanied by a doctor—not a "red lamp" doctor, but a very clever and rising man from the hospital, who made a rapid examination of the patient.

"Um!" he said, after taking her temperature, "looks very like the beginnings of what you would call 'brain fever,' though it may be only bad influenza; but I can't tell you much about it at present. What do you know of the history of the case, Mrs. Bird?"

She told him, and even repeated the confession that Joan had made to her.

"When did she say all this?" he asked.

"About an hour and a half ago, sir."

"Then you must not pay too much attention to it. She is in a state of cerebral excitement with high fever, and was very likely wandering at the time. I have known people invent all sorts of strange stories under such conditions. However, it is clear that she is seriously ill, though a woman with such a splendid physique ought to pull through all right. Indeed, I do not feel anxious about her. What a beautiful girl she is, by the way! You'll sit up with her to-night, I suppose? I'll be round by eight o'clock to-morrow morning, and I will send you something in half an hour that I hope will keep her quiet till then."

Mrs. Bird did not go to bed that night, the most of which she spent by Joan's side, leaving her now and again to rest herself awhile upon the sofa in the sitting-room. As she was in the act of lying down upon this sofa for the first time, her eye fell upon the written sheets of Joan's unfinished letter. She took them up and glanced at them, but seeing from its opening words that the letter was of a strictly confidential character, she put it down and tried to go to sleep. The attempt, however, was not successful, for whenever Mrs. Bird closed her eyes she saw those passionate words, and a great desire seized her to learn to whom they were addressed, and whether or no the document threw any light upon the story that Joan had told her. Now, if Mrs. Bird had a weak point it was curiosity; and after many struggles of conscience, the end of it was, that in this instance temptation got the better of her. From time to time glancing guiltily over her shoulder, as though she feared to see the indignant writer rise from the bed where she lay in semi-torpor, she perused the sheets from beginning to end.

"Well, I never did!" she said, as she finished them—"no, not in all my born days. To think of the poor girl being able to write like that: not but what it is mad enough, in all conscience, though there's a kind of sense in the madness, and plenty of feeling too. I declare I could cry over it myself for sixpence, yes, that I could with all this silly talk about a babe unborn. She seems to have thought that she is going to die, but I hope that isn't true; it would be dreadful to have her die here, like the late accountant, let alone that we are all so fond of her. Well, I know her aunt's name now, for it's in the letter; and if things go bad I shall just take the liberty to write and tell her. Yes, and I'm by no means sure that I won't write to this Mr. Graves too, just to harrow him up a bit and let him know what he has done. If he's got the feelings of a man, he'll marry her straight away after this—that is, if she's left alive to marry him. Anyhow I'll make bold to keep this for a while, until I know which way things are going." And she placed the sheets in an envelope, which she hid in the bosom of her dress.

Next morning the doctor came, as he had promised, and announced that Joan was worse, though he still declined to express any positive opinion as to the nature of her illness. Within another twenty-four hours, however, his doubts had vanished, and he declared it to be a severe case of "brain fever."

"I wish I had moved her to the hospital at once," he said; "but it is too late for that now, so you will have to do the best you can with her here. A nurse must be got: she would soon wear you out; and what is more, I dare say she will take some holding before we have done with her."

"A nurse!" said Mrs. Bird, throwing up her hands, "how am I to afford all that expense?"

"I don't know; but can't she afford it? Has she no friends?"

"She has friends, sir, of a sort, but she seems to have run away from them, though I think that I have the address of her aunt. She's got money too, I believe; and there's some one who gives her an allowance."

"Very likely, poor girl," answered the doctor drily. "Well, I think that under the circumstances you had better examine her purse and see what she has to go on with, and then you must write to this aunt and let her know how things are. I dare say that you will not get any answer, but it's worth a penny stamp on the chance. And now I'll be witness while you count the money."

Joan's purse was easily found; indeed, it lay upon the table before them, for, notwithstanding Mr. Levinger's admonitions, she was careless, like most of her sex, as to where she put her cash. On examination it was found to contain over fifteen pounds.

"Well, there's plenty to go on with," said the doctor; "and when that's gone, if the relations won't do anything, I must get a sister to come in and nurse her. But I shouldn't feel justified in recommending her case to them while she has so much money in her possession."

Within three hours the nurse arrived—a capable and kindly woman of middle age who thoroughly understood her business. As may be imagined, Mrs. Bird was glad enough to see her; indeed, between the nursing of Joan, who by now was in a high fever and delirious, upstairs, and attending to her paralytic husband below, her strength was well-nigh spent, nor could she do a stitch of the work upon which her family depended for their livelihood. That afternoon she composed a letter to Mrs. Gillingwater. It ran as follows:—

"Madam,—

"You may think it strange that I should write to you, seeing that you never heard of me, and that I do not know if there is such a person as yourself, though well enough acquainted with the name of Gillingwater down Yarmouth way in my youth; but I believe, whether I am right or wrong—and if I am wrong this letter will come back to me through the Post Office—that you are the aunt of a girl called Joan Haste, and that you live at Bradmouth, which place I have found on the map. I write, then, to tell you that Joan Haste has been lodging with me for some months, keeping herself quiet and respectable, and working in a situation in Messrs. Black & Parker's shop in Oxford Street, which doubtless is known to you if ever you come to London. Two nights ago she came back from her work ill, and now she lies in a high fever and quite off her head (so you see she can't tell me if you are her aunt or not). Whether she lives or dies is in the hands of God, and under Him of the doctor; but he, the doctor I mean, thinks that I ought to let her relations, if she has any, know of her state, both because it is right that they should, and so that they may help her if they will. I have grown very fond of her myself, and will do all I can for her; but I am a poor woman with an invalid husband and child to look after, and must work to support the three of us, so that won't be much. Joan has about fifteen pounds in her purse, which will of course pay for doctor, food and nursing for a few weeks; but her illness, if things go well with her, is likely to be a long one, and if they don't, then there will be her funeral expenses to meet, for I suppose that you would wish to have her buried decent in a private grave. Joan told me that there is some one who is a kind of guardian to her and supplies her with money, so if you can do nothing yourself, perhaps you will send him this letter, as I can't write to him not knowing his address. Madam, I do hope that even if you have quarrelled with Joan, or if she hasn't behaved right to you, that you will not desert her now in her trouble, seeing that if you do and she dies, you may come to be sorry for it in after years. Trusting to hear from you,

"Believe me, Madam,
"Obediently yours,
"Jane Bird, Dressmaker.

"P.S.—I enclose my card, and you will find my name in the London Directory."

When she had finished this letter, and addressed it thus,

"Mrs. Gillingwater,
"Bradmouth,

"Please deliver at once,"

Mrs. Bird posted it with her own hands in the pillar-box at the corner of Kent Street.

Then she returned to the house and sat down to reflect as to whether or not she should write another letter—namely, to the Mr. Henry Graves of Rosham, who, according to Joan's story, was the author of her trouble, enclosing in it the epistle which the girl had composed at the commencement of her delirium. Finally she decided not to do so at present, out of no consideration for the feelings of this wicked and perfidious man, but because she could not see that it would serve any useful purpose. If Joan's relations did not come forward, then it would be time enough to appeal to him for the money to nurse or to bury her. Or even if they did come forward, then she might still appeal to him—that is, if Joan recovered—to save her from the results of his evil doings and her folly by making her his wife. Until these issues were decided one way or another, it seemed to Mrs. Bird, who did not lack shrewdness and a certain knowledge of the world, that it would be wisest to keep silent, more especially in view of the fact that, as the doctor had pointed out, the whole tale might be the imagining of a mind diseased.

And here it may be convenient to say that some weeks went by before it was known for certain whether Joan would die or live. Once or twice she was in considerable if not in imminent danger; moreover, after periods of distinct improvement, she twice suffered from relapses. But in the end her own splendid constitution and youth, aided by the care and skill with which she was nursed, pulled her through triumphantly. When her return to life and health was assured, Mrs. Bird again considered the question of the advisability of communicating with Henry in the interests of her patient.

CHAPTER XXVII

LUCK AT LAST

On the morning after the posting of Mrs. Bird's letter, Mrs. Gillingwater was sitting at breakfast in the parlour of the Crown and Mitre, in no happy frame of mind. Things had gone very ill with her since Joan disappeared, some months previously. To begin with, the ample allowance that Mr. Levinger had been in the habit of paying for his ward's support no longer found its way into her pocket, and the sums received from that quarter were now inconsiderable, amounting indeed to a remission of rent only. Then, try as she would, she could not extract another farthing from Samuel Rock, who, in fact, had shown the very nastiest temper when she ventured to ask him for a trifle, having gone so far as to allege that she had been playing a double game with him as to Joan, and was concealing from him the secret of that young lady's whereabouts.

"Look here, mum," he had said in conclusion, "if you want money you must give value, do you understand? At present you have had lots of money out of me, but I have had precious little value out of you. On the day that you tell me Joan's true address, there will be five-and-twenty sovereigns to go into your pocket. Look, I keep them ready,"—and going to a drawer he unlocked it and showed her the gold, at which Mrs. Gillingwater glared avariciously. "Yes, and on the day that I marry her there'll be fifty more to follow. Don't you be afraid but what I can afford it and will keep my word. But till I get that address you sha'n't have a sixpence—no, not if it was to save you from the poorhouse."

"I tell you, Mr. Rock, that I have no more notion where she has flitted to than a babe unborn. If any one knows, it's old Levinger or Sir Henry."

"And if they know, they keep their mouths shut," said Samuel. "Well, ma'am, you have got my answer, so now I will wish you good morning. When you can let me have that address I shall be glad to see you, but till then perhaps you'll keep clear, as it don't look well for a married woman to be always hanging about my house."

"Any one with a grain of sense in his head might be pretty certain that she wasn't hanging after an oily-tongued half-bred saint like you," retorted Mrs. Gillingwater furiously. "I don't wonder that Joan never could abide you, that I don't, with your sneaking, shuffling ways, and your eye cocked round the corner. She hates the sight of you, and that's why she's run away. She hates you as much as she loves Sir Henry, and small blame to her: ay, you may turn green with jealousy if you like, but it's true for all that. She'd rather run a mile barefoot to kiss his little finger than she would be carried in a coach-and-four to marry you. So there, you put that in your pipe and smoke it, Mr. Rock!" And she retired, slamming the office and kitchen doors behind her.

When her just wrath against Samuel had subsided, Mrs. Gillingwater considered the position, and since she must get money by hook or by crook, she determined to renew her attack upon Henry, this time by letter. Accordingly she wrote a long and rambling epistle, wherein among other things she accused him of the abduction of her niece, mildly suggesting even that he had murdered her in order to hide his misdeeds. The letter ended with a threat that she would publish his true "karacter" from one end of the county to the other unless the sum of ten pounds was immediately forthcoming. In a few days the answer came; but on opening it Mrs. Gillingwater discovered, to her disgust and dismay, that it was from a firm of lawyers, who informed her in the most pointed language that if any further attempt was made to blackmail their client she would be prosecuted with the utmost rigour of the law.

All this was bad enough, yet it was but a beginning of troubles. Since Joan's departure Mr. Gillingwater had been drunk at least twice as often as usual—as he declared in his sober moments, and with some truth, in order to console himself for the loss of Joan, who was the one human creature to whom he was attached. One of these drinking bouts culminated in his making a furious attack, in the bar of the Crown and Mitre, upon a customer who was also drunk. For this assault he was fined at the petty sessions; and on the matter coming before the bench on licensing day, his license to keep a public-house, that already had been twice endorsed by the police, was taken away from him—which meant, of course, that the Crown and Mitre was closed as a place of refreshment for man and beast so long as the landlord, Mr. Levinger, chose to allow him to occupy it.

No wonder, then, that on this morning of the receipt of Mrs. Bird's letter Mrs. Gillingwater was depressed in mind as she sat drinking her tea and trying to master an invitation from no less a person than "Victoria, by the grace of God, etc.," to attend a county court and show cause why she should not pay a certain sum of four pounds three and ninepence halfpenny, with costs, for various necessaries of life bought by and duly delivered to her, the said defendant.

Hearing a knock at the door, Mrs. Gillingwater threw down the summons with an expression that was more forcible than polite—having reference, indeed, to the temporal and spiritual welfare of her august sovereign and of all those who administer justice under her. Then, having looked carefully through the window to make sure that her visitor was not another bailiff or policeman, she opened the door and took her letter.

"I don't know the writing," she muttered, turning it round and round suspiciously. "It may be another of those dratted summonses, or something of that sort; I've half a mind to throw it into the fire and swear that I never got it, only then that fool of a postman would give me the lie, for I took it from him myself."

In the end she opened the letter and spelt through its contents with difficulty and ever growing astonishment.

"Well," she said, as she put it down, "here's some luck at last, anyway. If that silly girl doesn't go and die it will be hard if I don't turn an honest penny out of her, now that I know where she's got to. Samuel would pay up to learn, but it's best to let him lie awhile, for I can work more out of him when she gets well again—if she does. I'm off up to the old man's, for that's the safest game: he'll scarcely bow me out with this in my hand; and if I don't give him a nip or two before I am done with him, the mean old scamp, then my fingers grow on my feet, that's all!" For be it known that on two recent occasions when Mrs. Gillingwater called, Mr. Levinger had declared himself not to be at home, and this when she could plainly see him standing by the study window.

Reaching Monk's Lodge in due course, Mrs. Gillingwater, who was not afflicted with Joan's humility, went to the front door and rang the bell boldly. Its sound disturbed Mr. Levinger from his reading, and he stepped to the window to perceive her standing on the doorstep, red and hot from her walk, and looking, as he thought, unusually large, coarse and violent.

"There is that dreadful woman again," he said to himself. "I can't bear the sight of her. I wonder now if, had she lived, poor Mary would have looked like her by this time. Perhaps," and he sighed; then, opening the door, told the servant to say that he was not at home.

She obeyed, and presently there arose sounds of altercation. "It ain't no use, you impudent barefaced thing, for you to stand there a-lying your soul away, when I saw him with my own eyes," shrilled the rough voice of Mrs. Gillingwater.

"Not at home: them's my orders," answered the girl with warmth, as she attempted to shut the door.

"No, you don't, hussy!" retorted the visitor, thrusting her foot between it and the jamb. "I've got some orders for you too. You go to your master and tell him that I must see him, about Joan Haste, and if he won't let me in I'll holler what I've got say outside the house."

Alarmed by the violence of her antagonist, the girl retreated, and, returning presently, showed Mrs. Gillingwater into the study without a word. Here she found Mr. Levinger standing by the fire, his face white with anger.

"Be seated, Mrs. Gillingwater," he said in a quiet voice, "and tell me what you mean by coming to make a disturbance here."

"I mean that I want to see you, sir," she answered sullenly, "and that I won't be driven away from your door like a dog. Once for all I tell you, sir, that you'd better be careful how you treat me, for if you turn dirty on me, I'll turn dirty on you. It's only the dead that don't speak, sir, and I'm very much alive, I am." Then she paused and added threateningly, "You can't treat me as I've heard say you did another, Mr. Levinger."

"Have you quite done?" he asked. "Very well, then; be so good as to listen to me: you can tell nothing about me, for the best of all possible reasons, that you know nothing. On the other hand, Mrs. Gillingwater, I can, if necessary, tell something about you—perhaps you may remember to what I refer, if not I can refresh your memory—ah! I see that there is no need. A moment's reflection will show you that you are entirely in my power. If you dare to make any attack upon my character, or even to repeat such a disturbance as you have just caused, I will ruin you and drive you to the workhouse, where, except for me, you would have been long ago. In earnest of what I say, your husband will receive to-morrow a summons for the rent that he owes me, and a notice to quit my house. I trust that I have made myself clear."

Mrs. Gillingwater knew Mr. Levinger well enough to be aware that he would keep his word if she drove him to it; and, growing frightened at the results of her own violence, she began to whimper.

"You never would be so cruel as to deal with a poor woman like that, sir," she said. "If I've spoken rash and foolish it's because I'm as full of troubles as a thistle-head with down; yes, I'm driven mad, that's what I am. What with having lost the license, and that brute of a husband of mine always drunk, and Joan, my poor Joan, who was like a daughter to me, a-dying—"

"What did you say?" said Mr. Levinger. "Stop that snivelling, woman, and tell me."

"Now you see, sir, that you would have done foolish to send me away," Mrs. Gillingwater jerked out between her simulated sobs, "with the news that I had to tell you. Not as I can understand why it should trouble you, seeing that of course the poor dear ain't nothing to you; though if it had been Sir Henry Graves that I'd gone to, it wouldn't have been surprising."

"Will you tell me what you are talking about?" broke in Mr. Levinger, striking his stick upon the floor. "Come, out with it: I'm not to be trifled with."

Mrs. Gillingwater glanced at him out of the corner of her eyes, wondering if it would be safe to keep up the game any longer. Coming to an adverse conclusion, she produced Mrs. Bird's letter, saying, "This is what told me about it, sir."

He took, or rather snatched the letter from her hand, and read it through with eagerness. Apparently its contents moved him deeply, for he muttered, "Poor girl! to think of her being so ill! Pray Heaven she may not die." Then he sat down at the table, and taking a telegram form, he filled it in as follows:—

"To Mrs. Bird, 8 Kent Street, London, W.

"Your letter to Mrs. Gillingwater received. Spare no expense. Am writing by to-day's post.

"James Levinger, Monk's Lodge, Bradmouth."

"Would you mind ringing the bell, Mrs. Gillingwater?" said Mr. Levinger, as he re-read the telegram and, placing it in an envelope, directed it to the postmaster at Bradmouth. "No, stay: I will see to the matter myself." And he left the room.

Presently he returned. "I do not know that I need keep you, Mrs. Gillingwater," he said, "or that I have anything more to say. I shall do my best to look after your niece, and I will let you know how she goes on."

"Thank you, sir; and about the rent and the notice?"

"At present, Mrs. Gillingwater, I shall dispense with both of them. I do not wish to deal hardly with you unless you force me to it. I suppose that you are in a bad way, as usual?"

"Well, yes, sir, I am. In fact, I don't quite know what I can do unless I get a little help."

"Ten pounds?" suggested Mr. Levinger.

"That will tide me over for a bit, sir."

"Very well, then, here you are," and he produced the money. "But mind, I give you this for the sake of old associations, little as you deserve it; and if there is any more trouble you will get nothing further from me. One more thing: I expect you to hold your tongue about poor Joan's illness and her address—especially to Sir Henry Graves and Mr. Rock. Do you understand me?"

"Perfectly, sir."

"Then remember what I say, and good morning; if you want to communicate with me again, you had better write."

Mrs. Gillingwater departed humbly enough, dropping an awkward curtsey at the door.

"Like the month of March, she came in like a lion and has gone out like a lamb," reflected Mr. Levinger as the door closed behind her. "She is a dangerous woman, but luckily I have her in hand. A horrible woman I call her. It makes me shudder to think of the fate of anybody who fell into the power of such a person. And now about this poor girl. If she were to die many complications would be avoided; but the thing is to keep her alive, for in the other event I should feel as though her blood were on my hands. Much as I hate it, I think that I will go to town and see after her. Emma is to start for home to-morrow, and I can easily make an excuse that I have come to fetch her. Let me see: there is a train at three o'clock that would get me to town at six. I could dine at the hotel, go to see about Joan afterwards, and telegraph to Emma that I would fetch her in time for the eleven o'clock train to-morrow morning. That will fit in very well."

Two hours later Mr. Levinger was on his road to London.

Mrs. Gillingwater returned to Bradmouth, if not exactly jubilant, at least in considerably better spirits than she had left it. She had wrung ten pounds out of Mr. Levinger, which in itself was something of a triumph; also she had hopes of other pickings, for now she knew Joan's address, which it seemed was a very marketable commodity. At present she had funds in hand, and therefore there was no need to approach Samuel Rock—which indeed she feared to do in the face of Mr. Levinger's prohibition; still it comforted her not a little to think that those five-and-twenty sovereigns also were potentially her own.

CHAPTER XXVIII

THE PRICE OF INNOCENT BLOOD

A month went by, and at the end of it every farthing of Mr. Levinger's ten pounds was spent, for the most part in satisfying creditors who either had sued, or were threatening to sue, for debts owing to them. Finding herself once more without resources, Mrs. Gillingwater concluded that it was time to deal with Samuel Rock, taking the chance of her breach of confidence being found out and visited upon her by Mr. Levinger. Accordingly, towards dusk one evening—for she did not wish her errand to be observed by the curious—Mrs. Gillingwater started upon her mission to Moor Farm.

Moor Farm is situated among the wind-torn firs that line the ridge of ground which separates the sea heath between Bradmouth and Ramborough from the meadows that stretch inland behind it. Perhaps in the whole county there is no more solitary or desolate building, with its outlook on to the heath and the chain of melancholy meres where Samuel had waylaid Joan, beyond which lies the sea. The view to the west is more cheerful, indeed, for here are the meadows where runs the Brad; but, as though its first architect had determined that its windows should look on nothing pleasant, the house is cut off from this prospect by the straggling farm buildings and the fir plantation behind them.

The homestead, which stands quite alone, for all the labourers employed about the place live a mile or more away in the valley, is large, commodious, and massively built of grey stone robbed from the ruins of Ramborough. When the Lacons, Joan's ancestors on the mother's side, who once had owned the place, went bankrupt, their land was bought by Samuel Rock's grandfather, an eccentric man, but one who was very successful in his business as a contractor for the supply of hay to His Majesty's troops. After he had been the possessor of Moor Farm for little more than a year, this James Rock went suddenly mad; and although his insanity was of a dangerous character, for reasons that were never known his wife would not consent to his removal to an asylum, but preferred to confine him in the house, some of the windows of which are still secured by iron bars. The end of the tale was tragic, for one night the maniac, having first stunned his keeper, succeeded in murdering his wife while she was visiting him. This event took place some seventy years before the date of the present story, but the lapse of two generations has not sufficed to dispel the evil associations connected with the spot, and that portion of the house where the murder was committed has remained uninhabited from that day to this.

Mrs. Gillingwater was not a person much troubled by imaginative fears, but the aspect of Moor House as she approached it on that November evening affected her nerves, rudimentary as they were. The day had been very stormy, and angry rays from the setting sun shone through gaps in the line of naked firs behind the house, and were reflected from the broken sky above on to the surface of the meres and of the sea beyond them. The air was full of the voices of wind and storm, the gale groaned and shrieked among the branches of the ancient trees; from the beach a mile away came the sound of the hiss of the surge and of the dull boom of breakers, while overhead a flock of curlews appeared and disappeared as they passed from sunbeam into shadow and from shadow into sunbeam, until they faded among the uncertain lights of the distance, whence the echo of their unhappy cries still floated to the listener's ear. The front of the house was sunk in gloom, but there was still light enough to enable Mrs. Gillingwater, standing by the gate of what in other times had been a little pleasure garden, but was now a wilderness overrun with sea grasses, to note its desolate aspect, and even the iron bars that secured the windows of the rooms where once the madman was confined. Nobody could be seen moving about the place, and she observed no lamp in the sitting-room.

"I hope those brutes of dogs are tied up, for I expect he's out," Mrs. Gillingwater said to herself; "he's fond of sneaking about alone in weather like this."

As the thought passed through her mind, she chanced to glance to her left, where some twenty paces from her, and beyond the intercepting bulk of the building, a red sunbeam pierced the shadows like a sword. There in the centre of this sunbeam stood Samuel Rock himself. He was wrapped in his long dark cloak that fell to the knees, but his hat lay on the ground beside him, and his upturned face was set towards the dying sun in such a fashion that the vivid light struck full upon it, showing every line of his clear-cut features, every hair of the long beard that hung from the square protruding chin, and even the motion of his thin lips, and of the white hands that he moved ceaselessly, as though he were washing them in the blood-red light.

There was something so curious about his aspect that Mrs. Gillingwater started.

"Now what's he a-doing there?" she wondered: "bless me if I know, unless he's saying prayers to his master the devil. I never did see a man go on like that before, drunk or sober;—he gives me the creeps, the beast. Look, there he goes sneaking along the wall of the house, for all the world like a great black snake wriggling to its hole. Well, he's in now, so here's after him, for his money is as good as anybody else's, and I must have it."

In another half-minute she was knocking at the door, which was opened by Samuel.

"Who's that?" he said. "I don't want no visitors at this time of day."

"It's me, Mr. Rock—Mrs. Gillingwater."

"Then I want you least of all, you foul-mouthed, lying woman. Get you gone, or I'll loose the dogs on you."

"You'd better not," she answered, "for I've something to tell you that you'd like to hear."

"Something that I'd like to hear," he answered, hesitating: "is it about her?"

"Yes, it's about her—all about her."

"Come in," he said.

She entered, and he shut and locked the door behind her.

"What are you a-doing that for?" asked Mrs. Gillingwater suspiciously.

"Nothing," he answered, "but doors are best locked. You can't tell who will come through them, nor when, if they're left open."

"That's just another of his nasty ways," muttered Mrs. Gillingwater, as she followed him down the passage into the sitting-room, which was quite dark except for some embers of a wood fire that glowed upon the hearth.

"Stop a minute, and I will light the lamp," said her host.

Soon it burnt brightly, and while Samuel was making up the fire Mrs. Gillingwater had leisure to observe the room, in which as it chanced she had never been before, at any rate since she was a child. On the occasions of their previous interviews Samuel had always received her in the office or the kitchen.

It was long and low, running the depth of the house, so that the windows faced east and west. The fireplace was wide, and over it hung a double-barrelled muzzle-loading gun, which Mrs. Gillingwater noticed was charged, for the light shone upon the copper caps. There were two doors—one near the fireplace, leading to the offices and kitchen, and one by which she had entered. The floor was of oak, half covered with strips of matting, and the ceiling also was upheld by great beams of oak, that, like most of the materials in this house, had been bought or stolen from the Abbey at the time when it was finally deserted, a hundred and fifty years before. This was put beyond a doubt, indeed, by the curious way in which it had been the fancy of the builder to support these huge beams—namely, by means of gargoyles that once had carried off the water from the roofs of the Abbey. It would be difficult to imagine anything more grotesque, or indeed uncanny, than the effect of these weather-worn and grinning heads of beasts and demons glaring down upon the occupants of the chamber open-mouthed, as though they were about to spring upon and to devour them. Indeed, according to a tale in Bradmouth, a child of ten, finding herself left alone with them for the first time, was so terrified by their grizzly appearance that she fell into a fit. For the rest, the walls of the room were hung with a dingy paper, and adorned with engravings of a Scriptural character, diversified by prints taken from Fox's "Book of Martyrs." The furniture was good, solid and made of oak, like everything else in the place, with the sole exception of an easy chair, in which it was Samuel's custom to smoke at night.

"I suppose now, Mr. Rock," said Mrs. Gillingwater, pointing to the grinning gargoyles, "that you don't find it lonesome up here at nights, with those stone parties for company."

"Not a bit of it, Mrs. Gillingwater; why, I've known them all ever since I was a child, as doubtless others have before me, and they are downright good friends to me, they are. I have names for every one of them, and talk to them sometimes too—now this and now that, as the fancy takes me."

"Just what I should have expected of you, Mr. Rock," answered Mrs. Gillingwater significantly; "not but what I dare say it is good training."

"Meaning?" said Samuel.

"Meaning, Mr. Rock, that as it is getting late, and it's a long and windy walk home, we'd better stop talking of stone figures and come to business—that is, if you have a mind for it."

"By all means, Mrs. Gillingwater. But what is the business?"

"Well, it's this: last time we met, when we parted in anger, though through no fault of mine, you said that you wanted Joan's address: and now I've got it."

"You've got it? Then tell it me. Come, be quick!" and he leaned towards her across the polished oak table.

"No, no, Mr. Rock: do you think that I am as green as an alder shoot, that you should ask such a thing of me? I must have the money before you get the address. Do you understand?"

"I understand, Mrs. Gillingwater; but be reasonable. How can you expect me to pay you five-and-twenty pounds for what may be gammon after all?"

"Five-and-twenty pounds, Mr. Rock! No such thing, indeed: it is fifty pounds I want, every farthing of it, or you get nothing out of me."

"Fifty pounds!" answered Samuel; "then I don't think that we need talk no longer, Mrs. Gillingwater, seeing that I ain't going to give you fifty pounds, no, not for the address of all the angels in heaven."

"I dare say not, Mr. Rock: they'd be precious little use to you when you'd got them, either now or at any future time, to judge from what I know of you"—and she glanced significantly at the sculptured demons beneath the ceiling—"but you see Joan's whereabouts is another matter, more especially since she isn't an angel yet, though she's been nigh enough to it, poor dear."

"What do you mean by that, ma'am? Is she ill, then?"

"When I've got the fifty pounds in my pocket, Mr. Rock, I'll be glad enough to tell you all about it, but till then my mouth is sealed. Indeed, it's a great risk that I run letting you know at all, for if the old man yonder finds it out, I think that he'll be the ruin of me. And now, will you pay, or won't you?"

"I won't give you the fifty pounds," he answered, setting his teeth; "I'll give you thirty, and that's the last farthing which you'll screw out of me—and a lot of money too, seeing that there's no reason why I should pay you anything at all."

"That's just where you're wrong, Mr. Rock," she answered: "not that I'm denying that thirty pounds is a lot of money; but then, you see, I've got that to sell that you want to buy, and badly. Also, as I told you, I take risks in selling it."

"What risks?"

"The risks of being turned out of house and home, and being sold up, that's all. Old Levinger don't want no one to know Joan's address; I can't tell you why, but he don't, and if he finds out that I have let on, it will be a bad business for me. Now look here: I fancy that there is another person as wouldn't mind giving a trifle for this address, and if you're so mean that you won't cash up, I shall take a walk out yonder to-morrow morning," and she nodded in the direction of Rosham.

Samuel groaned, for he knew that she was alluding to his rival. "I doubt that he knows it already, curse him," he said, striking his hand upon the table. "Thirty-five—there, that's the last."

"You're getting along, Mr. Rock, but it won't do yet," sneered Mrs. Gillingwater. "See here now, I've got something in my hand that I'll show you just for friendship's sake," and producing Mrs. Bird's letter, she read portions of it aloud, pausing from time to time to watch the effect upon her hearer. It was curious, for as he listened his face reflected the extremes of love, hope, terror and despair.

"O God!" he said, wringing his hands, "to think that she may be dead and gone from me for ever!"

"If she were dead, Mr. Rock, it wouldn't be much use my giving you her address, would it? since, however fond you may be of her, I reckon that you would scarcely care to follow her there. No, I'll tell you this much, she is living and getting well again, and I fancy that you're after a live woman, not a dead one. This was written a month ago and more."

"Thank heaven!" he muttered. "I couldn't have borne to lose her like that; I think it would have driven me mad. While she's alive there's hope, but what hope is there in the grave?" Samuel spoke thus somewhat absently, after the fashion of a man who communes with himself, but all the while Mrs. Gillingwater felt that he was searching her with his eyes. Then of a sudden he leant forward, and swiftly as a striking snake he shot out his long arm across the table, and snatched the letter from her grasp.

"You think yourself mighty clever, Mr. Rock," she said, with a harsh laugh; "but you won't get the address for nothing in that way. If you take the trouble to look you'll see that I've tore it off. Ah! you've met your match for once; it is likely that I was going to trust what's worth fifty pounds in reach of your fingers, isn't it?"

He looked at the letter and saw that she spoke truth.

"I didn't take it for that," he said, gnawing his hand with shame and vexation; "I took it to see if there was a letter at all, or if you were making up lies." And he threw it back to her.

"No doubt you did, Mr. Rock," she answered, jeering at him. "Well, and now you're satisfied, I hope; so how about them fifty sovereigns?"

"Forty," he said.

"Fifty. Never a one less."

Samuel sprang up from his seat, and, coming round the table, stood over her.

"Look here," he said in a savage whisper, "you're pushing this game too far: if you're a wise woman you'll take the forty and go, or—"

"Or what?"

"Or I'll twist what I want to know out of that black heart of yours, and not a farthing shall you get for it. Perhaps you've forgotten that the door is locked and we are alone in the house. Yes, you might scream till you brought the roof down, but nobody would hear you; and scream you shall if I take hold of you."

Mrs. Gillingwater glanced at his face, and read something so evil in it, and in the lurid eyes, that she grew frightened.

"Very well," she said, as unconcernedly as possible, "I won't stand out for a tenner between friends: down with the cash, and you shall have it."

"Ah! ma'am, you're afraid of me now—I can feel it—and I've half a mind to beat you down; but I won't, I'll stand by my word. Now you write that address upon this piece of paper and I'll get the coin." And rising he left the room by the door near the fireplace, which he took the precaution of locking behind him.

"The murdering viper!" reflected Mrs. Gillingwater; "I pinched his tail a little too much that time, and I sha'n't be sorry to find myself outside again, though there's precious little chance of that until he chooses, as he's locked me in. Well, I must brazen it out now." And somewhere from the regions of her ample bosom she produced the fragment that she had torn off Mrs. Bird's letter, on which was written the address and a date.

Presently Samuel returned holding a small bag of money in his hand, from which he counted out forty sovereigns.

"There's the cash, ma'am," he said; "but before you touch it be so good as to hand me that bit of writing: no, you needn't be afraid, I'll give you the money as I take the paper."

"I'm not afraid, Mr. Rock; when once I've struck a bargain I stick to it like an honest woman, and so, I know, will you. Never you doubt that the address is the right one; you can see that it is torn off the letter I read to you. Joan is there, and through the worst of her illness, so the party she's lodging with wrote to me; and if you see her I hope you'll give her my love." As she spoke she pushed the scrap of paper to him with her left hand, while with her right she drew the shining heap of gold towards herself.

"Honest!" he said: "I may be honest in my way, Mrs. Gillingwater; but you are about as honest as other traitors who sell innocent blood for pieces of money."

"What do you mean by that, Mr. Rock?" she replied, looking up from her task of securing the forty sovereigns in her pocket-handkerchief. "I've sold no innocent blood; I'd scorn to do such a thing! You don't mean to do any harm to Joan, do you?"

"No, ma'am, I mean her no harm, unless it's a harm to want to make her my wife; but it would have been all one to you if I meant to murder her and you knew it, so your sin is just as great, and verily the betrayers of innocent blood shall have their reward," and he pointed at her with his long fingers. "I've got what I want," he went on, "though I've had to pay a lot of money for it; but I tell you that it won't do you any good; you might as well throw it into the mere and yourself after it, as expect to get any profit out of that forty pounds, the price of innocent blood—the price of innocent blood." Then once more Samuel pointed at her and grinned maliciously, till to her fancy his face looked like that of the stone demon above him.

By now Mrs. Gillingwater was so frightened that for a moment or two she hesitated as to whether it would not be wiser to return the money and free herself from the burden of a dreadful thought. In the end her avarice prevailed, as might have been expected, and without another word she rose and walked towards the front door, which Samuel unlocked and opened for her.

"Good-bye," he said, as she went down the passage. "You've done me a good turn, ma'am, and now I'm sure that I'll marry Joan; but for all that a day shall come when you will wish that your hand had been cut off before you touched those forty sovereigns: you remember my words when you lie a-dying, Mrs. Gillingwater, with all your deeds behind you and all the doom before."

Then the woman fled through the storm and the night, more terrified than ever she had been in her life's day, nor did the gold that she clasped to her heart avail to comfort her. For Rock had spoken truth; it was the price of innocent blood, and she knew it.

CHAPTER XXIX

THROUGH THE VALLEY OF THE SHADOW

Upon his arrival in town, Mr. Levinger drove to a private hotel in Jermyn Street, where he was in the habit of staying on the rare occasions when he visited London. He dressed and dined; then, having posted a letter to Emma stating that he would call for her and Miss Graves on the following morning in time to catch the eleven o'clock train, and escort them home, he ordered a hansom and told the cabman to take him to 8, Kent Street.

"It's many a year since I have been in this place," he thought to himself with a sigh, as the cab turned out of the Edgware Road, "and it doesn't seem much changed. I wonder how she came to go to another house. Well, I shall know the worst, or the best of it, presently." And again he sighed as the horse stopped with a jerk in front of No. 8.

Telling the man to wait, he rang the bell. The door was opened by Mrs. Bird herself, who, seeing an elderly gentleman in a fur coat, dropped a polite curtsey.

"Is this Mrs. Bird's house, pray?" he asked in his gentle voice.

"Yes, sir; I am Mrs. Bird."

"Indeed: then perhaps you received a telegram from me this morning—Mr. Levinger?"

"Yes, sir, it came safely, and I ordered some things on the strength of it. Will you be so good as to step in, sir? I have heard poor Joan speak of you, though I never could make out what you were to her from her father down."

"In a certain sense, madam, I am her guardian. Will you allow me to help you with that door? And now, how is she?"

"About as bad as she can be, sir; and if you are her guardian, I only wish that you had looked after her a little before, for I think that being so lonesome has preyed upon her mind, poor dear. And now perhaps you'll step upstairs into her sitting-room, making as little noise as possible. The doctor and the nurse are with her, and you may wish to see them; it's not a catching fever, so you can come up safely."

He bowed, and followed Mrs. Bird to the little room, where she offered him a chair. Through the thin double doors that separated them from the bedchamber he could hear the sound of whispering, and now and again of a voice, still strong and full, that spoke at random. "Don't cut my hair," said the voice: "why do you cut my hair? He used to praise it; he'd never know me without my hair."

"That's her raving, poor love. She'll go on in this kind of way for hours."

Mr. Levinger turned a shade paler. He was a sensitive man, and these voices of the sick room pained him; moreover, he may have found a meaning in them.

"Perhaps you will give me a few details, Mrs. Bird," he said, drawing his chair close to the window. "You might tell me first how Joan Haste came to be your lodger."

So Mrs. Bird began, and told him all the story, from the day when she had seen Joan sitting upon her box on the opposite doorstep till the present hour—that is, she told it to him with certain omissions. Mr. Levinger listened attentively.

"I was very wrong," he said, when she had finished, "to allow her to come to London in this fashion. I reproach myself much about it, but the girl was headstrong and—there were reasons. It is most fortunate that she should have found so kind a friend as you seem to have been to her."

"Yes, sir," answered Mrs. Bird severely, "I must say that I think you were wrong. London is not a place to throw a young woman like Joan into to sink or to swim, even though she may have given you some trouble; and if anything happens to her I think that you will always have it on your conscience." And she put her head on one side and looked at him through her spectacles.

Mr. Levinger winced visibly, and did not seem to know what to answer. At that moment the doctor came out of the sick room, leaving the door open; and, looking through it, Mr. Levinger saw a picture that he could never forget. Joan was lying upon an iron bedstead, and on a chair beside it, shimmering in the light, lay the tumbled masses of her shorn hair. Her face was flushed, and her large eyes shone with an unnatural brightness. One hand hung downwards almost to the floor, and with the other she felt feebly at her head, saying in a piteous voice, "Where is my hair? What have you done with my hair? He will never know me like this, or if he does he will think me ugly. Oh! please give me back my hair." Then the nurse closed the door, and Mr. Levinger was glad of it.

"This is the gentleman, Doctor," said Mrs. Bird, "who is interested in—"

The doctor bowed stiffly; then, seeing what manner of man Mr. Levinger was, relaxed, and said, "I beg your pardon. I suppose that your interest in my patient is of a parental character?"

"Not exactly, sir, but I consider myself in loco parentis. Can you give me any information, or perhaps I should say—any hope?"

"Hope? Oh yes—lots of it," answered the doctor, who was an able middle-aged man of the brusque and kindly order, one who understood his business, but took pleasure in disparaging both himself and it. "I always hope until I see a patient in his coffin. Not that things are as bad as that in this case. I trust that she will pull through—I fancy that she will pull through; but all the same, as I understand that expense is no longer an object, I am going to get in a second opinion to-morrow. You see I am barely forty myself, and my experience is consequently limited," and he smiled satirically. "I have my views, but I dare say that they stand in need of correction; at any rate, without further advice I don't mean to take the responsibility of the rather heroic treatment which I propose to adopt. The case is a somewhat peculiar one. I can't understand why the girl should be in this way at all, except on the hypothesis that she is suffering from some severe mental shock; and I purpose, therefore, to try and doctor her mind as well as her body. But it is useless to bore laymen with these matters. I can only say, sir, that I am deeply interested in the case, and will do my utmost to pull her through. I would rather that she had been at the hospital; but, on the whole, she is not badly off here, especially as I have succeeded in getting the best nurse for her that I know anywhere. Good night."

"Good night, Doctor, and whatever the issue, pray accept my thanks in advance, and remember that you need not spare money."

"Don't be afraid, sir—I sha'n't. I'll spend a thousand pounds over her, if necessary; and save your thanks at present—three weeks hence it may be another matter, or there may be only the bill to pay. Well, I must be off. Good night. Perhaps, Mrs. Bird, you will send out for the things the nurse wants," and he went.

"That seems a capable man," said Mr. Levinger; "I like the look of him. And now, madam, you will need some cash in hand. I have brought twenty pounds with me, which I suppose will be enough to go on with, without touching Joan's money," and he placed that sum upon the table.

"By the way, Mrs. Bird," he added, "perhaps you will be good enough to send me a note or a telegram every day informing me of your patient's progress—here is my address—also to keep an account of all sums expended, in which you can include an extra allowance of a pound a week to yourself, to compensate you for the trouble and anxiety to which this illness must put you."

"Thank you, sir," she answered, curtseying—"I call that very liberal; though, to tell you the truth, I am so fond of Joan that I would not take a farthing if I could afford it. But, what between two deaf-and-dumb people to look after and her on my mind, it is no use pretending that I can get through as much dressmaking work as I ought; and so, as you seem well able to pay, I will put my pride in my pocket, and the money along with it. Also I will keep you informed daily, as you ask."

"Two deaf-and-dumb people?"

"Yes, sir,"—and she told him about her husband and Sally.

"Really," he said, when she had finished, surveying the frail little woman with admiration, "you seem to have more than your share of this world's burden, and I respect you, madam, for the way in which you bear it."

"Not a bit, sir," she answered cheerily; "while it pleases God to give me my health, I wouldn't change places with the Queen of England and all her glory."

"I admire you still more, Mrs. Bird," he answered, as he bowed himself out politely; "I wish that everybody could face their trials so cheerfully." But within himself he said, "Poor Joan! no wonder she was wretched, shut up in this dreadful little house with deaf-and-dumb folk for companions. Well, I have done all I can for her now, but I wish that I had begun earlier. Oh! if I could have the last twenty-five years over again, things would be very different to-day."

Mrs. Bird was delighted with Mr. Levinger. Never before, as she explained presently with much gesticulation to Jim, had she met so charming, so handsome, so thoughtful, and so liberal an elderly gentleman.

"But," gesticulated Jim back, "if he is all this, why didn't he look after Joan better before?"—a question that his wife felt herself unable to answer, beyond saying that Joan and all connected with her were "most mysterious, my dear, and quite beyond me."

Indeed, now that she came to think of it, she saw that whereas she had given Mr. Levinger every information in her power, he had imported none to her. To this moment she did not know what was the exact relationship in which he stood towards Joan. Though there were many dissimilarities between them, it had struck her, observing him, that his eyes and voice were not unlike Joan's. Could he be her father? And, if so, how did it come about that he had allowed her to wander to London and to live there unprotected? Like the rest, it was a mystery, and one that after much cogitation Mrs. Bird was forced to give up as insoluble, though on the whole she came to the conclusion that her visitor was not a blood relation of Joan.

Mr. Levinger duly carried out his programme, and on the morrow escorted his daughter and Ellen back to Bradmouth. He did not, however, think fit to tell them the true cause of his visit to London, which he accounted for by saying that he had come up to bargain with a dealer in curiosities about some ancient British ornaments that were on the market. Nor, oddly enough, did Ellen chance to mention that she had seen Joan selling mantles at Messrs. Black and Parker's; the fact being that, as regards this young woman, there reigned a conspiracy of silence. Neither at Rosham nor at Monk's Lodge was her name ever mentioned, and yet she was seldom out of the minds of the members of either of those households. Ellen, when the preparations for her approaching marriage allowed her time for thought, never ceased to congratulate herself upon her presence of mind in preventing the recognition of Joan by Henry. It was clear to her that her obstinate brother had begun to settle down and to see matters in a truer light, especially as regarded Emma; but it was also clear that had he once found the missing Joan there would have been new troubles. Well, he had not found her, so that danger was gone by. And Ellen rejoiced accordingly.

Mrs. Bird kept her promise, writing and telegraphing regularly to Mr. Levinger to inform him of Joan's progress. Indeed, for some time the messenger from the Bradmouth post-office arrived almost daily with a yellow envelope at Monk's Lodge. One of these telegrams Emma opened by chance, as her father happened to be out and the boy said that it required an answer. It ran: "Patient had serious relapse last night. Doctor proposes to call in—" [here followed the name of a very eminent authority on such ceases]—"do you sanction expense? Reply, Bird." Emma was naturally quite unable to reply, and so soon as he came in she handed the telegram to Mr. Levinger, explaining why she had opened it. He read it, then said, with as much severity as he ever showed towards his daughter:—

"I wish, my dear Emma, that in future you would be so kind as to leave my letters and telegrams alone. As you have opened it, however, and your curiosity is doubtless excited, I may as well tell you that this is a business cypher, and has to do with nothing more romantic than the Stock Exchange."

"I am very sorry, father," she answered coldly—for, trusting as she was by nature, she did not believe him—"I will be more careful in the future."

Then she left the room, feeling that another enigma had been added to the growing stock of family mysteries.

Slowly the days went by, till at length it became clear to those who tended her that Joan would recover from her illness.

The last and greatest crisis had come and gone, the fever had left her, and she no longer wandered in her mind, but lay upon the bed a shadow of her former self, so weak that she could scarcely speak above a whisper. All day long she lay thus, staring at the dingy ceiling above her with her brown eyes, which, always large, now looked positively unnatural in her wasted face—a very pathetic sight to see. At times the eyes would fill with tears, and at times she would sigh a little, but she never smiled, except in acknowledgment of some service of the sick room. Once she asked Mrs. Bird if any one had discovered that she was ill, or come to see her, and on receiving a reply in the affirmative, asked eagerly—

"Who? What was his name?"

"Mr. Levinger," the little woman answered.

"It is very kind of him," Joan murmured, and turned her head upon the pillow, where presently Mrs. Bird saw such a mark as might have been left by the falling of a heavy raindrop.

Then it was that Mrs. Bird's doubts and difficulties began afresh. From what she had heard while attending on Joan in her delirium, she was now convinced that the poor girl's story was true, and that the letter which she had written was addressed not to any imaginary person, but to a living man who had worked her bitter wrong. This view indeed was confirmed by the doctor, who added, curiously enough, that had it not been for her condition he did not believe that she would have lived. In these circumstances the question that tormented Mrs. Bird was whether or no she would do right to post that letter. At one time she thought of laying the matter before Mr. Levinger, but upon consideration she refrained from so doing. He was the girl's guardian, and doubtless he knew nothing of her disgrace. Why, then, should she expose it, unless such a step became absolutely necessary? Ultimately he would have to be told, but there seemed no need to tell him until an appeal to the man's honour and pity had failed. After much thought Mrs. Bird adopted a third course, and took the doctor into her confidence. He was a man of rough manners, plain speech, and good heart, and her story did not in the least surprise him.

"There's nothing wonderful about this, Mrs. Bird," he said. "I have seen the same thing with variations dozens of times in my twenty years of experience. It's no use your starting off to call this man a scoundrel and a brute. It's fashionable, I know, but it does not follow that it is accurate: you see it is just possible that the girl may have been to blame herself, poor dear. However, she is in a mess, and the thing is to get her out of it, at the expense of the man if necessary, for we are interested in her and not in him. That letter of hers is a beautiful production in a queer kind of way, and ought to have an effect on the individual, if he is not already married, or a bad lot—both of which things are probable. I tell you what, I will make a few inquiries to-morrow. What did you say his name was? Henry Graves? Thanks; good-bye. No, no opiate to-night, I think."

On the following day the doctor returned, and having visited Joan and reported favourably of her progress, he descended to the front parlour, where Mrs. Bird was waiting for him.

"She's getting on well," he said—"a good deal better than I expected, indeed. Well, I have looked up Sir Henry Graves, for he's a baronet. As it chanced, I came across a man at the hospital last night who used to stay with his father down at Rosham. The old man, Sir Reginald, died a few months ago; and Henry, the second son—for his elder brother broke his neck in a steeplechase—succeeded him. He is, or was, a captain in the Navy, rather a distinguished man in a small way; and not long ago he met with an accident, broke his leg or something of that sort, and was laid up at an inn in a place called Bradmouth. It seems that he is a good sort of fellow, though rather taciturn. That's all I could find out about him."

"Joan comes from Bradmouth, and she lived in an inn there," answered Mrs. Bird.

"Oh! did she? Well, then there you have the whole thing; nothing could be more natural and proper, or rather improper."

"Perhaps so, sir," said Mrs. Bird reprovingly; "though, begging your pardon, I cannot see that this is a matter to joke about. What I want to know now is—shall I send the gentleman that letter?"

The doctor rubbed his nose reflectively and answered, "If you do he will probably put it at the back of the fire; but so far as I can judge, being of course totally unacquainted with the details, it can't hurt anybody much, and it may have a good effect. She has forgotten that she ever wrote it, and you may be sure that unless he acts on it he won't show it about the neighbourhood. Yes, on the whole I think that you may as well send it, though I dare say that it will put him in a tight place."

"That is where I should like to see him," she answered, pursing up her lips.

"I dare say. You're down on the man, are you not, Mrs. Bird? And so am I, speaking in a blessed ignorance of the facts. By all means let him be put into a tight place, or ruined, for anything I care. He may be comparatively innocent, but my sympathies are with the lady, whom I chance to know, and who is very good looking. Mind you let me know what happens—that is, if anything does happen."

That afternoon Mrs. Bird wrote her letter, or rather she wrote several letters, for never before did the composition of an epistle give her so much thought and trouble. In the end it ran as follows:—

"Sir,—

"I am venturing to take what I dare say you will thing a great liberty, and a liberty it is, indeed, that only duty drives me to. For several months a girl called Joan Haste has been staying in my house as a lodger. Some weeks ago she was taken seriously ill with a brain fever, from which she has nearly died; but it pleased God to spare her life, and now, though she is weak as water, the doctor thinks that she will recover. On the night that she became ill she returned home not at all herself, and made a confession to me, about which I need say nothing. Afterwards she wrote what I enclose to you. You will see from the wording of it that she was off her head when she did it, and now I am sure that she remembers nothing of it. I found the letter and kept it; and partly from what fell from her lips while she was delirious, partly because of other circumstances, I became sure that you are the man to whom that letter is addressed. If I have made any mistake you must forgive me, and I beg that you will then return the enclosed and destroy my letter. If, sir, I have not made a mistake, then I hope that you will see fit to act like an honest man towards poor Joan, who, whatever her faults may be—and such as they are you are the cause of them—is as good-hearted as she is sweet and beautiful. It is not for me to judge you or reproach you: but if you can, I do pray you to act right by this poor girl, who otherwise must be ruined, and may perhaps drift into a life of sin and misery, the responsibility of which will be upon your hands.

"Sir, I have nothing more to say: the paper I enclose explains everything.

"I am, sir,
"Your humble servant,
"Jane Bird.

"P.S.—Sir, I may say that there is no need for you to hurry to answer this, since, even if you wished to do so, I do not think that it would be safe for you to see Joan, or even to write anything that would excite her, for ten days at least."

CHAPTER XXX

REAPING THE WHIRLWIND

The day that Mrs. Bird wrote her letter to Henry was the day of Ellen's marriage with Mr. Edward Milward. It was settled that the ceremony should be a quiet one, because of the recent death of the bride's father—an arrangement which suited Lady Graves and her daughter very well, seeing that it was necessary to cut down the expenses to the last farthing. Indeed, the possibility of a financial esclandre at Rosham before she was safely married and independent of such misfortunes, haunted Ellen like a nightmare. Edward, it is true, was now perfectly in hand, and showed no further symptoms of backsliding. Still, slips between the cup and the lip are many, and in the event of a public scandal anything might happen. However private the marriage, it proved, in fact, impossible to dispense with a certain amount of the hospitality usual upon these occasions: thus a dinner must be given to the tenants, and a reception held after the wedding to which all the neighbouring families were invited. In these preparations Henry took but a small part, though, as head of the family, it would be his duty to give away the bride and to receive the guests. This marriage, and everything connected with it, was hateful to him, but not the less on that account must he keep up appearances before the world. There had been no reconciliation between himself and his sister, though outwardly they were polite and even affectionate to each other; and he had scarcely exchanged a word in private with his future brother-in-law since the day when Edward read him a lecture upon morals and conduct.

Thus it came about that not even Ellen herself was more anxious that the marriage should be over and done with. As it chanced, the bride's good luck did not desert her, and everything went smoothly. At the last moment, indeed, Edward showed some disposition to jib at the settlements, which, considering that the lady brought him nothing, were disproportionate and unfair; but Ellen's lawyers, assisted by a judicious letter from herself, were equal to the emergency, and he grumbled and signed.

At length, to everybody's relief, the day came—one of those rare and beautiful November days when the falling leaves dropped silently as snowflakes through the crisp and sunlit air to the frosted grass beneath. Rosham church was full, and when the bride, looking very stately and handsome in her wedding robes, swept up the aisle on her brother's arm, followed by her two bridesmaids, Emma

Levinger and an aristocratic cousin of Mr. Milward's, a low hum of admiration ran round the crowded pews. Then Edward, exceedingly uncomfortable in the newest of coats and the shiniest of boots, took his place by her side; the service began, Henry, wearing anything but an amiable expression of countenance, gave his sister away, and presently Mr. and Mrs. Milward were receiving the congratulations of their relatives and friends.

The wedding took place at two o'clock, so that there were no speeches or breakfast, only a glorified tea with champagne, at which the rector of the parish, vice Sir Henry Graves, who declared himself quite incapable of public speaking, proposed the bride and bridegroom's health in a few well-chosen words and a Latin quotation. Edward responded, stuttering horribly, saying with much truth, but by inadvertence, "that this was the proudest moment of his wife's life," whereat Henry smiled grimly and everybody else tittered. Then the company wandered off to inspect the marriage offerings, which were "numerous and costly"; the newly married pair vanished, and reappeared in appropriate travelling costume, to be driven away amid showers of slippers and rice, and after a little feeble and flickering conversation the proceedings terminated.

Mr. Levinger and Emma were the last to go.

"You look tired, Graves," said the former, as his trap came round.

"Yes," he answered, "I never was more tired in my life. Thank Heaven that it is done with!"

"Well, it is a good business well over, and, even if you don't quite like the man, one that has many advantages."

"I dare say," Henry replied briefly. "Good-bye, Miss Levinger; many thanks for coming. If you will allow me to say so, I think that dress of yours is charming, with those shimmering ornaments—moonstones, are they not?"

"I am glad you like it, Sir Henry," she answered, looking pleased.

"By the way, Graves," broke in Mr. Levinger, "can you come over next Friday week and stop till Tuesday? You know that old donkey Bowles rears a few pheasants in the intervals of attending the public-house. There ought to be three or four hundred to shoot, and they fly high on those hillside covers—too high for me, anyway. If you can come, I'll get another gun or two—there's a parson near who has a couple of pupils, very decent shots—and we'll shoot on Saturday and Monday, and Tuesday too if you care for driven partridge, resting the Sabbath."

"I shall be delighted," answered Henry sincerely. "I don't think that I have any engagement; in fact, I am sure that I have none," and he looked at Emma and, for the first time that day, smiled genially.

Emma saw the look and smile, and wondered in her heart whether it were the prospect of shooting the three or four hundred pheasants that "flew high" with which Henry was delighted, or that of visiting Monk's Lodge—and herself. On the whole she thought it was the pheasants; still she smiled in answer, and said she was glad that he could come. Then they drove off, and Henry, having changed his wedding garments for a shooting coat, departed to the study, there to smoke the pipe of peace.

That night he dined tete-a-tete with his mother. It was not a cheerful meal, for the house was disorganised and vestiges of the marriage feast were all about them. There had been no time even to remove the extra leaves from the great oval dining-table, and as Henry and his mother's places were set at its opposite extremes, conversation was, or seemed to be, impossible.

"I think that this is a little dismal, dear," said Lady Graves, speaking across the white expanse of cloth, when the butler had served the dessert and gone.

"Yes," answered Henry; "it reminds me of South Africa, where the natives talk to each other across the kloofs. Suppose that we go into the study—we sha'n't want a speaking trumpet there."

His mother nodded in assent, and they adjourned, Henry taking a decanter of wine with him.

"I think that it went off very well," she said presently, when he had made up the fire.

"Oh, yes, I suppose so. You don't mind my smoking, do you, mother?"

"I know that you didn't like the marriage, Henry," she went on, "nor do I altogether, for Edward is not—well, quite the class of man that I should have selected. But different people have different tastes, and I think that he will suit Ellen admirably. You see, she will rule him, and she could never have got on with a man who tried to be her master; also he is rich, and wealth is necessary to her comfort. I shall be very much surprised if she does not make a great success of her marriage."

"Ellen would make a success of anything, mother—even of Edward Milward. I have a great admiration for Ellen, but somehow I do not envy my brother-in-law his bargain, though he has married a lady, which, strictly speaking, is more than he deserves. However, I dare say that he will find his place."

"I have no doubt that they will settle it to their mutual satisfaction, dear; and, to look at the matter from another point of view, it certainly is a relief to me to know that your sister is removed out of reach of our troubles here." And she sighed. "It has been a great struggle, Henry, to keep up appearances so far, and I was in constant fear lest something awful should happen before the marriage. One way and another, difficulties have been staved off; indeed, the fact that Ellen was going to become the wife of such a rich man—for he is very rich—has helped us a great deal. But now the money is done; I doubt if there is a hundred pounds to go on with, and what is to happen I am sure I do not know."

Henry puffed at his pipe, staring into the fire, and made no answer.

"I scarcely like to ask you, dear," Lady Graves went on presently, "but—have you in any way considered the matter of which we spoke together after your father's funeral?"

"Yes, mother, I have considered—I have considered it a great deal."

"And what conclusion have you come to, Henry?" she asked, making pretence to arrange her dress in order to conceal the anxiety with which she awaited his answer.

He rose, and, although it was only half smoked, knocked out the contents of his pipe upon the fire-guard. Then he turned round and spoke suddenly, almost fiercely indeed.

"The conclusion which I have come to, mother, is that, taking everything into consideration, I ought to try my luck yonder. I don't know that she will have me, indeed I think that she will be foolish if she does, but I'll ask her. The other has vanished Heaven knows where; I can't find her, and perhaps it is best that I shouldn't, for if I did my resolutions might melt. And now, if you don't mind, let us talk of something else. I will let you know the end of the adventure in due course."

"One question, Henry. Are you going to Monk's Lodge again?"

"Yes, on Friday week. I have accepted an invitation to stay there from Friday till Tuesday, or perhaps longer."

Lady Graves uttered a sigh of the most intense and heartfelt relief. Then she rose, and coming to where her son was sitting, she kissed him upon the forehead, murmuring, "God bless you, my dear boy!—you have made me a happier woman than I have been for many a long day. Good night."

He returned his mother's embrace, lit a bedroom candle for her, and watched her pass from the room and across the hall. As she went he noticed that her very gait seemed different, so great was the effect of his words upon her. Of late it had been uncertain, almost timid; but now she was walking as she used to walk in middle life, with grace and dignity, holding her head high.

"Poor mother!" he thought to himself as he resumed his seat, "she has had much to bear, and it is a comfort to be able to please her for once. Heaven knows that had I alone been concerned I would have done it long ago for her sake. Oh, Joan, Joan! I wonder where you are, and why your eyes haunt me so continually. Well, wherever you may be, it is all over between us now, Joan." And he put his hands before his face and groaned aloud.

On the following morning, while Henry was dressing, the butler brought him up his letters, in accordance with the custom of the house. One by one, as the exigencies of his toilet gave him opportunity, he opened them and glanced through their contents. Some were circulars, some were on business connected with the estate, two were invitations to shoot, and one was a bill for saddlery supplied to his brother three years before.

"That's the lot, I think," he said, and was crushing up the circulars preparatory to throwing them into the fireplace, when another rather bulky letter, in a common thin envelope and addressed in an unformed handwriting, fell from among them. He picked it up and examined it, a certain distrust of this innocent-looking epistle creeping into his mind. "I wonder what it is?" he thought to himself: "another of Reginald's bills, or a fresh application for money from one of his intimate friends? Any way I don't know the writing and I have half a mind to tear it up unread. Letters that look like that always contain something disagreeable."

He threw it down on the dressing-table while he arranged his necktie, and hunted for a stud which had rolled under a chest of drawers. Indeed, the excitement of this wild pursuit put the letter out of his mind till he went to brush his hair, when the inaccurate superscription of "Sir H. Grave" immediately caught his eye, and he opened it at once. The first words that he saw were "see fit to act like an honest man."

"As I thought," he said aloud, "here's another of Reginald's legacies with the bill inside." And uttering an exclamation he lifted the letter to throw it into the fireplace, when its enclosure slipped out of it.

Then Henry turned pale, for he knew the writing: it was Joan Haste's. In five more minutes he had read both the documents through, and was sitting on his bed staring vacantly before him like a man in a trance. He may have sat like this for ten minutes, then he rose, saying in a perfectly quiet voice, as though he were addressing the bodily presence of Mrs. Bird:—

"Of course, my dear madam, you are absolutely right; the only thing to do is to marry her at once, and I am infinitely obliged to you for bringing these facts to my notice; but I must say that if ever a man got into a worse or more unlucky scrape, I never heard of it." And he laughed.

Then he re-read Joan's wandering words very carefully, and while he did so his eyes filled with tears.

"My darling! What you must have suffered!" he said, pressing the letter against his heart. "I love you! I love you! I would never say it before, but I say it now once and for all, and I thank God that He has spared you and given me the right to marry you and the chance of making you happy. Well, the thing is settled now, and it only remains to carry it through. First of all my mother must be told, which will be a pleasant business—I am glad, by the way, that Ellen has gone before I got this, for I believe that I should have had words with her. To think of my looking at that cloak and never seeing the woman who wore it, although she saw me! I remember the incident perfectly well, and one would have imagined— But so much for thought transference and the rest of it. Well, I suppose that I may as well go down to breakfast. It is a very strange world and a very sad one too."

Henry went down to breakfast accordingly, but he had little appetite for that meal, at which Lady Graves did not appear; then he adjourned to the study to smoke and reflect. It seemed to him that it would be well to settle this matter beyond the possibility of backsliding before he saw his mother. Ringing the bell, he gave an order that the boy should saddle the pony and ride into Bradmouth in time to catch the midday post; then he wrote thus to Mrs. Bird:—

"Dear Madam,—

"I have to thank you for your letter and its enclosure, and I hope that my conduct under the circumstances which you detail will not be such as to disappoint the hopes that you express therein. I shall be very much obliged if you will kindly keep me informed of Joan's progress. I purpose to come and see her within a week or so; and meanwhile, if you think it safe, I beg that you will give her the enclosed letter. Perhaps you will let me know when she is well enough to see me. You seem to have been a kind friend to Joan, for which I thank you heartily.

"Believe me to remain
"Very faithfully yours,
"Henry Graves."

To Joan he wrote also as follows:—

"Dearest Joan,—

"Some months since you left Bradmouth, and from that day to this I have heard nothing of you. This morning, however, I learned your address, and how terribly ill you have been. I have received also a letter, or rather a portion of a letter, that you wrote to me on the day when the fever took you; and I can only say that nothing I ever read has touched me so deeply. I do not propose to write to you at any length now, since I can tell you more in half an hour than I could put on paper in a week. But I want to beg you to dismiss all anxieties from your mind, and to rest quiet and get well as quickly as possible. Very shortly, indeed as soon as it is safe for me to do so without disturbing you, I hope to pay you a visit with the purpose of asking you if you will honour me by becoming my wife. I love you, dearest Joan—how much I never knew until I read your letter: perhaps you will understand all that I have neither the time nor the ability to say at this moment. I will add only that whatever troubles and difficulties may arise, I place my future in your hands with the utmost happiness and confidence, and grieve most bitterly to think that you should have been exposed to doubt and anxiety on my account. Had you been a little more open with me this would never have happened; and there, and there alone, I consider that you have been to blame. I shall expect to hear from Mrs. Bird, or perhaps from yourself, on what day I may hope to see you. Till then, dearest Joan,

"Believe me
"Most affectionately yours,
"Henry Graves."

By the time that he had finished and directed the letters, enclosing that to Joan in the envelope addressed to Mrs. Bird, which he sealed, Thomson announced that the boy was ready.

"Very well: give him this to post at Bradmouth, and tell him to be careful not to lose it, and not to be late."

The butler went, and presently Henry caught sight of his messenger cantering down the drive.

"There!" he thought, "that's done; and so am I in a sense. Now for my mother. I must have it out before my courage fails me."

Then he went into the drawing-room, where he found Lady Graves engaged in doing up little boxes of wedding cake to be sent to various friends and connections.

She greeted him with a pleasant smile, made some little remark about the room being cold, and throwing back the long crape strings of her widow's cap, lifted her face for Henry to kiss.

"Why, my dear boy, what's the matter with you?" she said, starting as he bent over her. "You look so disturbed."

"I am disturbed, mother," he answered, seating himself, "and so I fear you will be when you have heard what I have to tell you."

Lady Graves glanced at him in alarm; she was well trained in bad tidings, but use cannot accustom the blood horse to the whip or the heart to sorrow.

"Go on," she said.

"Mother," he began in a hoarse voice, "last night I told you that I intended to propose to Miss Levinger; now I have come to tell you that such a thing is absolutely impossible."

"Why, Henry?"

"Because I am going to marry another woman, mother."

"Going to marry another woman?" she repeated, bewildered. "Whom? Is it that girl?"

"Yes, mother, it is she—Joan Haste. You remember a conversation that we had shortly after my father's death?"

She bowed her head in assent.

"Then you pointed out to me what you considered to be my duty, and begged me to take time to think. I did so, and came to the conclusion that on the whole your view was the right one, as I told you last night. This morning, however, I have received two letters, the first news of Joan Haste that has reached me since she left Bradmouth, which oblige me to change my mind. Here they are: perhaps you will read them."

Lady Graves took the letters and perused them carefully, reading them twice from end to end. Then she handed them back to her son.

"Do you understand now, mother?" he asked.

"Perfectly, Henry."

"And do you still think that I am wrong in determining to marry Joan Haste—whom I love?"

"No, Henry: I think that you are right if the girl desires it—since," she added with a touch of bitterness, "it seems to be conceded by the world that the duty which a man owes to his parents and his family cannot be allowed to weigh against the duty which he owes to the partner of his sin. Oh! Henry, Henry, had you but kept your hands clean to this temptation as I know that you have done in others, these sorrows would not have fallen upon us. But it is useless to reproach you, and perhaps you are as much sinned against as sinning. At least you have sown the wind and you must reap the whirlwind, and whoever is to blame, it has come about that the fortunes of our house are fallen irretrievably, and that you must give your honour and your name into the keeping of a frail girl who has neither." And with a tragic gesture of despair Lady Graves rose and left the room.

"Whether or not virtue brings its own reward I cannot say," reflected Henry, looking after her, "but that vice does so is pretty clear. It seems to me that I am a singularly unfortunate man, and so, I suppose, I shall remain."

CHAPTER XXXI

THE GATE OF PARADISE

For some days Lady Graves was completely prostrated by this new and terrible misfortune, which, following as it did hard upon the hope of happier things, seemed to her utterly overwhelming. She dared not even trust herself to see her son, but kept her room, sending a message to him to say that she was unwell and did not wish to be disturbed. For his part Henry avoided the house as much as possible. As it chanced, he had several invitations to shoot during this particular week, one of them coupled with an engagement to dine and sleep; and of all these he availed himself, though they brought him little enjoyment. On the third morning after he had posted his letter, there came a short answer from Mrs. Bird, stating that Joan would be well enough to see him on the following Thursday or Friday; but from Joan herself he received no reply. This note reached him on a Friday, just as he was starting to keep his aforesaid engagement to shoot and sleep. On Saturday he returned to Rosham to find that his mother had gone to town, leaving a note of explanation to be given to him. The note said:—

"Dear Henry,—

"I am going to London to stay for a few days with my old friend and your grandmother, Lady Norse. Circumstances that have recently arisen make it necessary that I should consult with the lawyers, to see if it is possible for me to recover any of the sums that from time to time have been expended upon this estate out of my private fortune. I am not avaricious, but if I can obtain some slight provision for my remaining years, of course I must do so; and I desire that my claim should be made out legally, so as to entitle me to rank as a creditor in the bankruptcy proceedings which are now, I suppose, inevitable.

"Your affectionate mother,
"E. Graves."

Henry put the letter into his pocket with a sigh. Like everything else, it was sad and humiliating; but he was not sorry to find that his mother had gone, for he had no more wish to meet her just now than she had to meet him. Then he began to wonder if he ought to take any steps to advise Mr. Levinger of his intentions, so that the mortgagee might proceed to recover such portion of the capital advanced as the assets would realise. On the whole he determined to let the matter be for a while. He was sick to death of arguments, reproaches, and affairs; it would be time enough to face these and other disagreeables when he had seen Joan and was about to marry her, or had already done so. There was no pressing need for hurry. By Mr. Levinger's help arrangements had been made under which the vacant farms were being carried on for the present, and he had a little money in hand. He remembered, indeed, that he was engaged to stay at Monk's Lodge on the following Friday. Well, he could telegraph from London making his apologies and saying that he was detained in town by business, which would save the necessity of writing an explanatory letter. One step he did take, however: he wrote to an old messmate of his who held an under-secretaryship in the Government, explaining the condition of the estate to which he had succeeded, and asking him to interest himself to obtain him a consulship, no matter how remote, or any other suitable employment. Also he put himself in communication with the Admiralty, to arrange for the commutation of his pension, which of course was not liable for his father's debts, so that he might have some cash in hand wherewith to start in married life. Then he composed himself to wait quietly at Rosham till the following Friday, when he purposed to go to town.

Lady Graves's note to Henry was true in substance, but it was not the whole truth. She was still an able and an energetic woman, and her mind had not been idle during those days when she kept her room, refusing to see her son. On the contrary, she considered the position in all its bearings, recalling every word of her interviews with Henry, and of Joan's letter to him, no sentence of which had escaped her memory. After much thinking she came to a conclusion—namely, that while it would be absolutely useless to make any further attempt to turn Henry from his purpose, it was by no means certain that the girl herself could not be appealed to with success. She recollected that, according to Henry's story, Joan had all along declined to entertain the idea of marrying him, and that even in the mad rhapsody which

Mrs. Bird had forwarded, she stated that she could never suffer such a thing, because it would mean his ruin. Of course, as she was well aware, should these two once meet it was probable, it was almost certain, that Joan Haste would be persuaded to retract her self-denying ordinance, and to allow herself to be made Henry's wife and a respectable member of society. The woman who was so circumstanced and did otherwise would be more than human, seeing that her own honour and the honour of her child were at stake, and that consent meant social advancement to her, and the lifelong gratification of a love which, however guilty it might have been in its beginning, was evidently sincere. But if she could be appealed to before they met, it might be different. At any rate it seemed to Lady Graves that the experiment was worth trying.

Should she be justified in making such an appeal? This girl had been wronged, and she had rights: could she then be asked to forgo those rights? Lady Graves answered the question in the affirmative. She was not a hard and worldly woman, like her daughter, nor was she careful of her own advantage in this matter, but her dead husband's wishes were sacred to her and she had her son's best interests at heart. Moreover, she was of opinion, with Ellen, that a man has no right to undo his family, and bring the struggle of generations to an inglorious end, in order that he may gratify a personal passion or even fulfil a personal duty. It was better that this girl should be wronged, if indeed she was wronged, and that Henry should suffer some remorse and shame, than that a day should come when others would learn that the family had been ousted out of its place and heritage because he had chosen to pay a debt of honour at their expense.

The reasoning may have been faulty, and perhaps Lady Graves was not the person to give judgment upon a case in which she was so deeply interested; but, such as it was, it carried conviction to her mind, and she determined to act upon it. There was but one way to do this—to see the girl face to face, for she would trust nothing to letters. She had learned through Thomson the butler that Henry was not going to town for some days, and she must be beforehand with him. She had Joan's address—that is, she had seen it at the head of Mrs. Bird's letter, and she would take the chance of her being well enough to receive her. It was a forlorn hope, and one that Lady Graves had no liking for; still, for the sake of all that had been and of all that might be, she made up her mind to lead it.

Henry's letter reached Kent Street in due course, and when she read it Mrs. Bird was a proud and happy woman. She also had led a forlorn hope, and never in her wildest moments had she dreamed that the enemy would capitulate thus readily. She could scarcely believe her eyes: the wicked baronet, the penny-novel villain of her imaginings, had proved himself to be an amenable creature, and as well-principled as any common man; indeed, she gathered, although he did not say so in so many words, that actually he meant to marry the victim of his vices. Mrs. Bird was dumfoundered; she read and re-read Henry's note, then she examined the enclosure addressed to Joan, holding it to the light and trying to peep beneath the edges of the envelope, to see if perchance she could not win some further word of comfort. So great was her curiosity, indeed, that she looked with longing at the kettle boiling on the hearth, wondering if she would not be justified in reducing the gum upon the envelope to a condition that would enable her to peruse the writing within before she handed it seemingly inviolate to Joan. But at this point conscience came to her rescue and triumphed over her curiosity, devouring as it was.

When first she read Henry's letter she had determined that in the interests of Joan's health the enclosure must not be given to her for some days, but by degrees she modified this decision. Joan was out of danger now, and the doctor said that she might read anything; surely, therefore, it would be safe for her to peruse this particular sheet of paper. Accordingly, when the nurse came down to say that her patient was awake after her morning sleep, and that if Mrs. Bird would sit with her, she proposed to take a walk in the Park till dinner-time, the little woman hurried upstairs with the precious document in her pocket. Joan, who was sitting on the sofa, received her with a smile, and held up her face to be kissed.

"How are you this morning, my dear?" she asked, putting her head on one side and surveying her critically.

"I feel stronger than I have for weeks," answered Joan; "indeed, I believe that I am quite well again now, thanks to you and all your kindness."

"Do you think that you are strong enough to read a letter, dear?—because I have one for you."

"A letter?" said Joan anxiously: "who has taken the trouble to write to me? Mr. Levinger?"

Mrs. Bird shook her head and looked mysterious.

"Oh! don't torment me," cried Joan; "give it me—give it me at once."

Then Mrs. Bird put her hand into her pocket and produced Henry's enclosure.

Joan saw the writing, and her poor white hands trembled so that she could not unfasten the envelope. "Open it for me," she whispered. "Oh! I cannot see: read it to me. Quick, quick!"

"Don't be in a hurry, my dear; it won't fly away," said Mrs. Bird as she took the letter. Then she put on her spectacles, cleared her throat, and began.

"'Dearest Joan—' Really, my love, do you not think that you had better read this for yourself? It seems so—very—confidential."

"Oh! I can't; I must hear it at once. Go on, pray."

Thus encouraged, Mrs. Bird went on, nothing loath, till she reached the last word of the letter.

"Well," she said, laying it upon her knees, "now, that is what I call behaving like a gentleman. At any rate, my dear, you have been lucky in falling into the hands of such a man, for some would not have treated you so well—having begun wicked they would have gone on wickeder. Why, good gracious! what's the matter with the girl? She's fainted, I do believe." And she ran to get water, reproaching herself the while for her folly in letting Joan have the letter while she was still so weak. By the time that she returned with the water, the necessity for it had gone by. Joan had recovered, and was seated staring into vacancy, with a rapt smile upon her face that, so thought Mrs. Bird, made her look like an angel.

"You silly girl!" she said: "you gave me quite a turn."

"Give me that letter," answered Joan.

Mrs. Bird picked it up from the floor, where it had fallen, and handed it to her. Joan took it and pressed it to her breast as though it were a thing alive—much, indeed, as a mother may be seen to press her new-born infant when the fear and agony are done with and love and joy remain. For a while she sat thus in silence, holding the letter to her heart, then she spoke:—

"I do not suppose that I shall ever marry him, but I don't care now: whatever comes I have had my hour, and after this and the rest I can never quite lose him—no, not through all eternity."

"Don't talk nonsense, Joan," said Mrs. Bird, who did not understand what she meant. "Not marry him, indeed!—why shouldn't you?"

"Because something is sure to prevent it. Besides, it would be wrong of me to do so. Letting other things alone, he must marry a rich woman, not a penniless girl like me."

"Oh! stuff and nonsense with your 'rich woman': the man who'll go for money when he can get love isn't worth a row of pins, say I; and this one isn't of that sort, or he would never have written such a letter."

"He can get both love and money," answered Joan; "and it isn't for himself that he wants the money—it is to save his family. He had an elder brother who brought them to ruin, and now he's got to set them up again by taking the girl who holds the mortgages, and who is in love with him, as his wife—at least, I believe that's the story, though he never told it me himself."

"A pretty kettle of fish, I am sure. Now look here, Joan, don't you talk silly, but listen to me, who am older than you are and have seen more. It isn't for me to blame you, but, whatever was the truth of it, you've done what isn't right, and you know it. Well, it has pleased God to be kind to you and to show you a way out of a mess that most girls never get clear of. Yes, you can become an honest woman again, and have the man you love as a husband, which is more than you deserve perhaps. What I have to say is this: don't you be a fool and cut your own throat. These money matters are all very well, but you have got nothing to do with them. You get married, Joan, and leave the rest to luck; it will come right in the end. If there's one thing that's more of a vanity than any other in this wide world, it is scheming and plotting about fortunes and estates and suchlike, and in nine cases out of ten, the woman who goes sacrificing herself to put cash into her lover's pocket—or her own either for that matter—does him no good in the long run, but just breaks her heart for nothing, and his too very likely. There, that's my advice to you, Joan; and I tell you that if I thought that you would go on as you have begun and make this man a bad wife, I shouldn't be the one to give it. But I don't think that, dear. No; I believe that you would be as good as gold to him, and that he'd never regret marrying you, even though he is a baronet and you are—what you are."

"Oh! indeed I would," said Joan.

"Don't say 'indeed I would,' dear; say 'indeed I shall,' and mind you stick to it. And now I hear the nurse coming back, and it is time for me to go and see about your dinner. Don't you fuss and make yourself ill again, or she won't be able to go away to-morrow, you know. I shall just write to this gentleman and say that he can come and see you about next Friday; so mind, you've got to be well by then. Good-bye."

Weak as she was still from illness, when her first wild joy had passed a great bewilderment took possession of Joan.

As her body had been brought back to the fulness of life from the very pit of death, so the magic of Henry's letter changed the blackness of her despair to a dawn of hope, by contrast so bright that it dazzled her mind. She had no recollection of writing the letter to which Henry alluded; indeed, had she been herself she would never have written it, and even now she did not know what she had told him or what she had left untold. What she was pleased to consider his goodness and generosity in offering to make her his wife touched her most deeply, and she blessed him for them, but neither the secret pleading of her love nor Mrs. Bird's arguments convinced her that it would be right to take advantage of them. The gate of what seemed to be an earthly paradise was of a sudden thrown open to her feet: behind her lay solitude, sorrow, sin and agonising shame, before her were peace, comfort, security, and that good report which every civilised woman must desire; but ought she to enter by that gate? A warning instinct answered "No," and yet she had not strength to shut it. Why should she, indeed? If she might judge the future from the past, Fate would do her that disservice; such happiness could not be for one so wicked. Yet—till the blow fell—she might please her fancy by standing upon the threshold of her heaven, and peopling the beyond with unreal glories which her imagination furnished without stay or stint. She was still too weak to struggle against the glamour of these visions, for that they could become realities Joan did not believe—rather did she submit herself to them, and satisfy her soul with a false but penetrating delight, such as men grasp in dreams. Of only one thing was she sure—that Henry loved her—and in that knowledge, so deep was her folly, she found reward for all she had undergone, or that could by any possibility be left for her to undergo; for had he not loved her, as she believed, he would never have offered to marry her. He loved her, and she would see him; and then things must take their chance, meanwhile she would rest and be content.

CHAPTER XXXII

THE CLOSING OF THE GATE

While Lady Graves was standing at the Bradmouth station on that Saturday in November, waiting for the London train, she saw a man whose face she knew and who saluted her with much humility. He was dressed in a semi-clerical fashion, in clothes made of smooth black cloth, and he wore a broad wide-awake, the only spot of colour about him being a neck-scarf of brilliant red, whereof the strange incongruity caught and offended her eye. For a long time she puzzled herself with endeavours to recollect who this individual might be. He did not look like a farmer; and it was obvious that he could not belong to the neighbouring clergy, since no parson in his senses would wear such a tie. Finally Lady Graves concluded that he must be a dissenting minister, and dismissed the matter from her mind. At Liverpool Street, however, she saw him again, although he tried to avoid her, or so she thought; and then it flashed across her that this person was Mr. Samuel Rock of Moor Farm, and she wondered vaguely what his business in London could be.

Had Lady Graves possessed the gift of clairvoyance she would have wondered still more, for Mr. Rock's business was curiously connected with her own, seeing that he also had journeyed to town, for the first time in his life, in order to obtain an interview with Joan Haste, whose address he had purchased at so great a price on the previous day. As yet he had no very clear idea of what he should say or do when he found himself in Joan's presence. He knew only that he was driven to seek that presence by a desire which he was absolutely unable to control. He loved Joan, not as other men love, but with all the strength and virulence of his distempered nature; and this love, or passion, or incipient insanity, drew him to her with as irresistible a force as a magnet draws the fragment of steel that is brought within its influence. Had he known her to be at the uttermost ends of the earth, it would have drawn him thither;

and though he was timid and fearful of the vengeance of Heaven, there was no danger that he would not have braved, and no crime which he would not have committed, that he might win her to himself.

Till he learned to love Joan Samuel Rock had been as free from all human affections as it is possible for a man to be; there was no one creature for whom he cared, and, though he was naturally passionate, his interest and his strict religious training had kept him from giving way to the excesses that in secret he brooded over and desired. During his early manhood all his energies had been devoted to money-making, and in the joy of amassing wealth and of overreaching his fellows in every kind of legitimate business he found consolation for the absence of all that in the case of most men makes life worth living. Then on one evil day he met Joan, grown from a child into a most lovely woman; and that which he had hidden in his heart arose suddenly and asserted itself, so that from this hour he became a slave bound to the chariot-wheels of a passion over which he had lost command. The rebuffs that he had received at her hands served only to make the object of his affections dearer and more desirable in his eyes, while the gnawing ache of jealousy and the daily torment of long-continued disappointment drove him by slow degrees to the very edge of madness. She hated him, he knew, as he knew that she loved his rival; but if only he could see her, things might yet go well with him, or if they did not, at least he would have seen her.

But of all this Lady Graves was ignorant, and, had she known it, anxious though she was to win her end, it is probable that she would have shrunk from an enterprise which, if successful, must expose Joan Haste to the persecution of such a man as Samuel Rock, and might end in delivering her into his hands.

On the following afternoon—it was Sunday—Lady Graves informed her hostess that she was going to visit a friend, and, declining the offer of the carriage, walked to the corner of the square, where she chartered a four-wheeled cab, directing the driver to take her to Kent Street. As they crawled up the Edgware Road she let down the window of the cab and idly watched the stream of passers-by. Presently she started, for among the hundreds of faces she caught sight of that of Mr. Samuel Rock. It was pale, and she noticed that as he went the man was muttering to himself and glancing at the corner of a street, as though he were seeking some turn with which he was not familiar.

"I wonder what that person is doing here," she thought to herself; "positively he seems to haunt me." Then the cab went on, and presently drew up in front of No. 8, Kent Street.

"What a squalid-looking place!" Lady Graves reflected, while she paid the man and rang the bell.

As it chanced, Mrs. Bird was out and the door was answered by the little serving-girl, who, in reply to the question of whether Miss Haste was in, said "Yes" without hesitation and led the way upstairs.

"Some one to see you," she said, opening the door in front of Lady Graves and almost simultaneously shutting it behind her.

Joan, who was seated on the horsehair sofa reading, or pretending to read a book, rose instinctively at the words, and started at her veiled and stately-looking visitor.

"Surely," she said, "you are Lady Graves?"

"Yes, Miss Haste, I am Lady Graves, and I have taken the liberty of coming to see you. I am told that you have been ill."

Joan bowed her head and sank back upon the sofa, pointing towards a chair. At the moment she could not trust herself to speak, for she felt that the blow which she dreaded was about to fall, and that Henry's mother came as a messenger of ill.

Lady Graves sat down, and for a while there was silence.

"I trust that you are better," she said at length.

"Thank you, yes, your ladyship; I am almost well again now."

"I am glad of that, Miss Haste, for I do not wish to upset you or retard your recovery, and I have come to speak to you, if I have your permission, upon a very delicate and important matter."

Again Joan bowed, and Lady Graves went on.

"Miss Haste, certain things have come to my knowledge of which I need only allude to one—namely, that my son Henry is anxious to make you his wife, as indeed, if what I have learned is true, you have a right to expect," and she paused.

"Please go on," murmured Joan.

"I am here," she continued hesitatingly, "to submit some questions to your consideration; but pray understand that my son knows nothing of this visit, and that I have not come to reproach you in any way. We are all human and liable to fall into temptation, though our temptations vary with age, disposition, and other circumstances: it is quite possible, for instance, that in speaking to you thus I am at this moment yielding to a temptation which I ought to resist. Perhaps I am right in supposing that it is your intention to accept my son's offer of marriage?"

"I have not made up my mind, Lady Graves."

"Well," she answered, with a faint smile, "you will doubtless make it up when you see him, if you do see him. I think that I may take it for granted that, unless what I have to say to you should change your views, you will very shortly be married to Sir Henry Graves."

"I suppose you do not wish that," said Joan: "indeed, how can you wish it, seeing what I am, and his reason for asking me to marry him?"

"No, I do not wish it, though not altogether for these reasons. You are a very beautiful woman and a sweet one, and I have no doubt but that you could soon learn to fill any position which he might be able to give you, with credit to yourself and to him. As for the rest, he is as much to blame as you are, and therefore owes you reparation, so I will say no more upon that point. My reasons are simple and to a certain extent selfish, but I think that they will appeal to you. I believe that you love Henry. Well, if you marry him you will bring this man whom you love to the most irretrievable ruin. I do not know if you have heard of it, but the place where he lives, and where his ancestors have lived for three centuries before him, is deeply encumbered. Should he marry a girl without means it must be sold, leaving us all, not only beggars, but bankrupt. I will not insult you by supposing that the fact that you would find yourself in the painful position of the penniless wife of a person of nominal rank can influence you one way or another, but I do hope that the thought of the position in which he will find himself may influence you. He would be driven from his home, his name would be tarnished, and he would be left burdened with a wife and family, and without a profession, to seek such a living as chance might offer to him."

"I know all this," said Joan quietly; "but have you quite considered my side of the question, Lady Graves? You seem to have heard the facts: have you thought, then, in what state I shall be left if I refuse the offer that Sir Henry has so generously made to me?"

"Doubtless," answered Lady Graves confusedly—"forgive me for speaking of it—adequate provision, the best possible, would be made—"

She stopped, for Joan held up her hand in warning, and said: "If you are going to offer me money compensation, I may as well tell you at once, it is the one thing that I shall not be able to forgive you. Also, where is the provision to come from? Do you wish to endow me with Miss Levinger's money? I have not sunk to that, Lady Graves."

"I ask your pardon," she answered; "it is so terribly hard to deal with such a subject without giving offence. Believe me, I have considered your side of the question, and my heart bleeds for you, for I am asking more of you than any one has a right to ask of a woman placed in your position. Indeed, I come to you as a suppliant, not for justice, but for pity; to implore you, in the name of the love which you bear my son, to save him from himself—yes, even at the cost of your own ruin."

"You put things plainly, Lady Graves; but how if he loves me? In that event will it be any real kindness to save him from himself? Naturally I do not wish to sacrifice my life for nothing."

"It will be a kindness, Miss Haste, if not to him, at any rate to his family. To the chance that a man in after years might learn to dislike, or even to hate the woman who has been forced upon him as a wife under such painful circumstances, I will only allude; for, although it is a common experience enough, it is possible, indeed I think that it is probable, that such a thing would never arise in your case. If he loves you, in my opinion he should sacrifice that love upon the altar of his duty; he has sinned, and it is right that he should suffer for his sin, as you have already suffered. Although I am his mother, Miss Haste, for Henry I have little sympathy in this matter; my sympathy is for you and you alone."

"You spoke of his family, Lady Graves: a man is not his family. Surely his duty is towards himself, and not towards the past and the future."

"I cannot agree with you. The duty of a man placed as Henry is, is chiefly owing to the house which for some few years he represents—in which, indeed, he has but a brief life interest—and to the name that has descended to him. The step which he contemplates would bring both to destruction; also it would bring me, his mother, who have given my all to bolster up the fortunes of his family, to utter penury in my old age. But of that I do not complain; I am well schooled in trouble, and it makes little difference to me in what fashion I drag out my remaining years. I plead, Miss Haste, not for myself and not for my son Henry, but for his forefathers and his descendants, and the home that for three centuries has been theirs. Do you know how his father, my beloved husband, died? He died broken-hearted, because in his last moments he learned that his only surviving son purposed to sacrifice all these on your account. Therefore although he is dead I plead for him also. Putting Henry out of the account, this is the plain issue, Miss Haste: are you to be deserted, or is Rosham to be sold and are the members of the family into which I have married to be turned out upon the world bankrupt and dishonoured?"

"Putting myself aside, Lady Graves, is your son to suffer for difficulties that he did not create? Did he spent the money which if not repaid will make him a bankrupt? Indeed, will he be made a bankrupt at all? Was he not earning his living in a profession which his family forced him to abandon, in order that he might take these troubles upon his own shoulders, and put an end to them by bartering himself in marriage to a rich lady for whom he has no affection?"

"These things are true; but still I say that he must suffer, and for the reasons that I have given."

"You say that, Lady Graves, but what you mean is that he will not suffer. I will put your thoughts into words: you think that your son has been betrayed by me into a troublesome position, from which most men would escape simply enough—namely, by deserting the woman. As it chances, he is so foolish that, when he has heard of her trouble, he refuses to do this—from a mistaken sense of honour. So you come to appeal to that fallen and unfortunate woman, although it must be an insult to you to be obliged even to speak to her, and because you are kind-hearted, you say that your son must suffer. How must he suffer according to your view? His punishment will be, firstly, that at the cost of some passing pain he escapes from a disgraceful marriage with a nameless girl—a half-lady—born of nobody knows whom and bred up in a public-house, with such results that on the first opportunity she follows her mother's example; and secondly, that he must marry a sweet and beautiful lady who will bring him love as well as fortune, and having shaken himself clear from trouble of every sort, live happy and honoured in the position that he has inherited. And if, as you wish, I inflict all this upon him by refusing to marry him, what will be my reward? A life of shame and remorse for myself and my unborn child, till at length I die of a broken heart, or perhaps—" and she stopped.

"Oh! how can I ask it of you?" broke in Lady Graves.

"I do not know—that is a matter for your own conscience; but you have asked it, understanding all that it means to me. Well, Lady Graves, I will do as you wish, I will not accept your son's offer. He never made me a promise of marriage, and I never asked or expected any. Whatever I have done I did for love of him, and it was my fault, not his—or as much my fault as his—and I must pay the price. I love him so well that I sacrifice my child and myself, that I put him out of my life—yes, and give him to the arms of my rival!"—and Joan made a movement with her hands as though to push away some unseen presence.

"You are a very noble woman," said Lady Graves—"so noble that my mind misgives me; and notwithstanding all that I have said, I am inclined to ask you to forget that promise and let things take their chance. Whatever may have been your faults, no man could do wrong to marry such a wife."

"No, no—I have promised, and there's an end; and may God have mercy on me, for He alone knows how I shall perform what now I undertake! Forgive me, your ladyship, but I am very tired."

Then her visitor rose.

"My dear girl," she said, "my dear, dear girl, in asking all this of you I have done only what I believed to be my duty; and should you, on reflection, come to any different conclusion from what which you have just expressed, I can only say that I for one shall not blame you, and that, whatever the event, you will always have me for your friend." And, moved to it by a sudden impulse, she bent down and kissed Joan upon the forehead.

"Thank you," said Joan, smiling faintly, "you are too good to me. Do not distress yourself; I dare say that I should have come to the same mind if I had not seen you, and I deserve it all."

Then Lady Graves went. "It was very painful," she reflected, as she left the house. "That girl has a heart of gold, and I feel as though I had done something wicked, though Heaven knows that I am acting for the best. Why, there is that man Rock again, staring at the house! What can he be looking for? Somehow I don't like him; his face and manner remind me of a cat watching a caged bird."

Joan watched the door close behind Lady Graves, then, pressing her hands to her head, she began to laugh hysterically. "It is like a scene out of a book," she said aloud. "Well, the dream has come to an end sooner than I thought even. I knew it would, so what does it matter? And now what am I to do?" She thought a while, then went to the table and began to write. She wrote thus:—

"Dear Sir Henry,—

"I have received your letter, but could not answer it before because I was so ill. I am very much honoured by what you say in it, but it is not to be thought of that a gentleman in your position should marry a poor girl like me; and, if you did, I dare say that we should both of us be very unhappy, seeing that, as they say in Bradmouth, pigeons can't nest with crows. It seems, from what you tell me, that I have written you some stuff while I was ill. I remember nothing about it, but if so, you must pay no attention to it, since people often talk and write nonsense when they are off their heads. You will be glad to know that I hope to get well again soon, but I am still too sick to see anybody at present, so it will be no use your coming to London to call upon me. I do not mind my life here at all, and hope to find another situation as soon as I can get about. Thanking you again,

"Believe me
"Your affectionate
"Joan.

"P.S.—You must not take any notice of what Mrs. Bird writes, as she is very romantic. I cannot help thinking how sorry you would be if I were to take you at your word. Just fancy Sir Henry Graves married to a shop-girl!"

Joan gave much thought and care to the composition of this precious epistle, with the result that it was in its way a masterpiece of art—indeed, just the kind of letter that a person of her position and bringing up might be expected to write to a former flame of whom, for reasons of her own, she wished to see no more.

"There," she said, as she finished re-reading her fair copy, "if that does not disgust him with me, I don't know what will. Bah! It makes me sick myself. Oh! my darling, it is bitter hard that I should have to write to you like this. I know that I shall not be able to keep up for long: some day I shall see you and tell you the truth, but not till you are married, dear." And she rested her head, that now was clustered over with little curls, upon the edge of the table, and wept bitterly, till she heard the girl coming up with her tea, when she dried her eyes and sent her letter to the post.

Thus, then, did Joan begin to keep her promise.

On the afternoon of the day following the interview between Lady Graves and Joan, it occurred to Henry, who chanced to be in Bradmouth, that he might as well call at the post-office to get any letters which had been despatched from London on the Sunday. There was but one, and, recognising the handwriting on the envelope, he read it eagerly as he sat upon his horse.

Twice did he read it, then he put it in his pocket and rode homewards wondering, for as yet he could scarcely believe that it had been written by Joan Haste. There was nothing in the letter itself that he could find fault with, yet the tone of it disgusted him. It was vulgar and flippant. Could the same hand have written these words and those other words, incoherent and yet so touching, that had stirred his nature to its depths? and if so, which of them reflected the true mind of the writer? The first letter was mad, but beautiful; the second sane, but to his sense shocking. If it was genuine, he must conclude that the person who penned it, desired to have done with him: but was it genuine? He could not account for the letter, and yet he could not believe in it; for if Joan wrote it of her own free will, then indeed he had misinterpreted her character and thrown his pearls, such as they were, before the feet of swine. She had been ill, she might have fallen under other influences; he would not accept his dismissal without further proof, at any rate until he had seen her and was in a position to judge for himself. And yet he must send an answer of some sort. In the end he wrote thus:—

"Dear Joan,—

"I have received your note, and I tell you frankly that I cannot understand it. You say that you do not wish to marry me, which, unless I have altogether misunderstood the situation (as may be the case), seems incomprehensible to me. I still purpose to come to town on Friday, when I hope that you will be well enough to see me and to talk this matter over.

"Affectionately yours,
"Henry Graves."

Joan received this note in due course of post.

"Just what I expected," she thought: "how good he is! Most people would have had nothing more to do with me after that horrid, common letter. How am I to meet him if he comes? I cannot—simply I cannot. I should tell him all the truth, and where would my promise be then! If I see him I shall marry him—that is, if he wishes it. I must not see him, I must go away; but where can I go? Oh! Heaven help me, for I cannot help myself."

The journey to London had not changed Mr. Samuel Rock's habits, which it will be remembered were of a furtive nature. When Lady Graves saw him on the Sunday, he was employed in verifying the information as to Joan's address that he had obtained from Mrs. Gillingwater. Any other man would have settled the matter by inquiring at No. 8 as to whether or not she lived there, but he preferred to prowl up and down in the neighbourhood of the house till chance assured him of the fact.

As it happened, Fortune favoured him from the outset, for if Lady Graves saw him, he also saw her as she left the house, and was not slow to draw conclusions from her visit, though what its exact object might be he could not imagine. One thing was clear, however: Mrs. Gillingwater had not lied, since to suppose that by the merest coincidence Lady Graves was calling at this particular house for some purpose unconnected with Joan Haste, was an idea too improbable to be entertained. Still his suspicious mind was not altogether satisfied: for aught he knew Joan had left the place, or possibly she might be dead. In his desire to solve his doubts on these points before he committed himself to any overt act, Samuel returned on the Monday morning to Kent Street from the hotel where he had taken a room, and set himself to watch the windows of No. 8; but without results, for the fog was so thick that he could see nothing distinctly. In the afternoon, when the fog lifted, he was more successful, for, just as the November evening was closing in, the gas was lit in the front room on the first floor, and for a minute he caught a glimpse of Joan herself drawing down a blind. The sight of her filled him with a strange rapture, and he hesitated a while as to whether he should seek an interview with her at once, or wait until the morrow. In the end he decided upon the latter course, both because his courage failed him at the moment, and because he wished to think over his plan of action.

On the Tuesday morning he returned about ten o'clock, and with many inward tremblings rang the bell of No. 8. The door was answered by Mrs. Bird, whom he saluted with the utmost politeness, standing on the step with his hat off.

"Pray, ma'am, is Miss Haste within?" he asked.

"Yes, sir, being so ill, she has not been out for many weeks."

"So I have heard, ma'am; and I think that you are the lady who has nursed her so kindly."

"I have done my best, sir: but what might be your errand?"

"I wish to see her, ma'am."

Mrs. Bird looked at him doubtfully, and shook her head, "I don't think that she can see any one at present—unless, indeed, you are the gentleman from Bradmouth whom she expects."

An inspiration flashed into Samuel's mind. "I am the gentleman from Bradmouth," he answered.

Again Mrs. Bird scanned him curiously. To her knowledge she had never set eyes upon a baronet, but somehow Samuel did not fulfil her idea of a person of that class. He seemed too humble, and she felt that there was something wrong about the red tie and the broad black hat. "Perhaps he is disguising himself," she thought; "baronets and earls often do that in books"; then added aloud, "Are you Sir Henry Graves?"

By now Samuel understood that to hesitate was to lose all chance of seeing Joan. His aim was to obtain access to the house; once there, it would be difficult to force him to leave until he had spoken to her. After all he could only be found out, and if he waited for another opportunity, it was obvious that his rival, who was expected at any moment, would be beforehand with him. Therefore he lied boldly, answering,—

"That is my name, ma'am. Sir Henry Graves of Rosham."

Mrs. Bird asked him into the passage and shut the door.

"I didn't think you would be here till Friday, sir," she said, "but I dare say that you are a little impatient, and that your mother told you that Joan is well enough to see you now"; for Mrs. Bird had heard of Lady Graves's visit, though Joan had not spoken to her of its object.

"Yes, ma'am, you are right: I am impatient—very impatient."

"That is at it should be, sir, seeing all the lost time you have to make up for. Well, the past is the past, and you are acting like a gentleman now, which can never be a sorrow to you, come what may."

"Quite so, ma'am: but where is Joan?"

"She is in that room at the top of the stairs, sir. Perhaps you would like to go to her now. I know that she is up and dressed, for I have just left her. I do not think that I will come with you, seeing that you might feel it awkward, both of you, if a third party was present at such a meeting. You can tell me how you got on when you come down."

"Thank you, ma'am," said Samuel again. And then he crept up the stairs, his heart filled with fear, hope, and raging jealousy of the man he was personating. Arriving at the door, he knocked upon it with a trembling hand. Joan, who was reading Henry's note for the tenth time, heard the knock, and having hastily hidden the paper in her pocket, said "Come in," thinking that it was her friend the doctor, for she had caught the sound of a man's voice in the passage. In another moment the door had opened and shut again, and she was on her feet staring at her visitor with angry, frightened eyes.

"How did you come here, Mr. Rock?" she said in a choked voice: "how dare you come here?"

"I dare to come here, Joan," he answered, with some show of dignity, "because I love you. Oh! I beg of you, do not drive me away until you have heard me; and indeed, it would be useless, for I shall only wait in the street till I can speak to you."

"You know that I do not wish to hear you," she answered; "and it is cowardly of you to hunt me down when I am weak and ill, as though I were a wild beast."

"I understand, Joan, that you are not too ill to see Sir Henry Graves; surely, then, you can listen to me for a few minutes; and as for my being cowardly, I do not care if I am—though why a man should be called a coward because he comes to ask the woman he loves to marry him, I can't say."

"To marry you!" exclaimed Joan, turning pale and sinking back into her chair; "I thought that we had settled all that long ago, Mr. Rock, out by the Bradmouth meres."

"We spoke of it, Joan, but we did not settle it. We both grew angry, and said and did things which had best be forgotten. You swore that you would never marry me, and I swore that you should live to beg me to marry you, for you drove me mad with your cruel words. We were wrong, both of us; so let's wipe all that out, for I believe I shall marry you, Joan, and I know that you will never plead with me to do it, nor would I wish it so. Oh! hear me, hear me. You don't know that I have been filled with all the tortures of hell; I have thought of you by day and dreamed of you by night, till I began to believe my brain would burst and that I must go mad, as I shall do if I lose you altogether. At last I heard that you had been ill and got your address, and now once more I come to pray you to take pity on me and to promise to be my wife. If only you will do that, I swear to you I will be the best husband that ever a woman had: yes, I will make myself your slave, and you shall want for nothing which I can give you. I do not ask your love, I do not even ask that you should treat me kindly. Deal with me as you will, be bitter and scornful and trample me in the dirt, and I will be content if only you will let me live where I can see you day by day. This isn't a new thing with me, Joan—it has gone on for years; and now it has come to this, that either I must get the promise of you or go mad. Then do not drive me away, but have mercy as you hope for mercy. Pity me and consent." And with an inarticulate sound that was half a sob and half a groan, he flung himself upon his knees and, clasping his hands, looked up at her with a rapt face like that of a man lost in earnest prayer.

Joan listened, and as she listened a new and terrible idea crept into her mind. Here, if she chose to take it—if she could bring herself to take it—was an easy path out of her difficulty: here was that which would effectually cure Henry of any desire to ruin himself by marrying her, and would put her beyond the reach of temptation. The thought made her faint and sick, but still she entertained it, so desperate was the case between her love and what she conceived to be her duty. If it could be done—with certain safeguards and reservations—why should it not be done? This man was in a humour to consent to anything; it was but a question of the sacrifice of her miserable self, whereby, so they said and so she believed, she would save her lover. In a minute she had made up her mind: at least she would sound the man and put the matter to proof.

"Do not kneel to me," she said, breaking the silence; "you do not know what sort of woman it is to whom you are grovelling. Get up, and now listen. I love another man; and if I love another man, what do you think that my feelings are to you?"

"I think that you hate me, but I do not mind that—in time you would come to care for me."

"I doubt it, Mr. Rock; I cannot change my heart so easily. Do you know what terms I stand on with this man?"

"If you mean Sir Henry Graves, I have heard plenty of all that, and I am ready to forgive you."

"You are very generous, Mr. Rock, but perhaps I had better explain a little. I think it probable that, unless I change my mind, within a week I shall be married to Sir Henry Graves."

"Oh! my God!" he groaned; "I never thought that he would marry you."

"Well, as it happens he will—that is, if I consent. And now do you know why?"

He shook his head.

"Then I will tell you, so that you may understand exactly about the woman whom you wish to make your wife. Do not think that I am putting myself in your power, for in the first place, if you use my words against me I shall deny them, and in the second I shall be married to Sir Henry and able to defy you. This is the reason, Mr. Rock:" and she bent forward and told him all in a few words, speaking in a low, clear voice.

Samuel's face turned livid as he heard.

"The villain!" he muttered. "Oh! I should like to kill him. The villain—the villain!"

"Don't talk in that kind of way, Mr. Rock, or, if you wish to do so, leave me. Why should you call him a villain, seeing that he loves me as I love him, and is ready to marry me to-morrow? Are you prepared to do as much—now? Stop before you answer: you have not heard all the terms upon which, even if you should still wish it, I might possibly consent to become your wife, or my reason for even considering the matter. First as to the reason; it would be that I might protect Sir Henry Graves from the results of his own good feeling, for it cannot be to his advantage to burden his life with me, and unless I take some such step, or die, I shall probably marry him. Now as to the condition upon which I might consent to marry anybody else—you, for instance, Mr. Rock: it is that I should be left alone to live here or wherever I might select for a year from the present date, unless of my own free will I chose to shorten the time. Do you think that you, or any other man, Mr. Rock, could consent to take a woman upon such terms?"

"What would happen at the end of the year?" he asked.

"At the end of the year," she answered deliberately, "if I still lived, I should be prepared to become the faithful wife of that man, provided, of course, that he did not attempt to violate the agreement in any particular. If he chose to do so, I should consider the bargain at an end, and he would never see me again."

"You want to drive a hard trade, Joan."

"Yes, Mr. Rock—a very hard trade. But then, you see, the circumstances are peculiar."

"It's too much: I can't see my way to it, Joan!" he exclaimed passionately.

"I am very glad to hear that, Mr. Rock," she answered, with evident relief; "and I think that you are quite right. Good-bye."

Samuel picked up his hat, and rose as though to go.

"Shall you marry him?" he said hoarsely.

"I do not see that I am bound to answer that question, but it is probable—for my own sake I hope so."

He took a step towards the door, then turned suddenly and dashed his hat down upon the carpet.

"I can't let you go—to him," he said, with an oath: "I'll take you upon your own terms, if you'll give me no better ones."

"Yes, Mr. Rock: but how am I to know that you will keep those terms?"

"I'll swear it; but if I swear, when will you marry me?"

"Whenever you like, Mr. Rock. There's a Bible on the table: if you are in earnest, take it and swear, for then I know you will be afraid to break your oath."

Samuel picked up the book, and swore thus at her dictation:—

"I swear that for a year from the date of my marrying you, Joan Haste, I will not attempt to see you, but will leave you to go your own way without interfering with you by word or deed, upon the condition that you have nothing to do with Sir Henry Graves" (this sentence was Samuel's own), "and that at the end of the year you come to me, to be my faithful wife." And, kissing the book, he threw it down upon the table, adding, "And may God blast me if I break this oath! Do you believe me now, Joan?"

"On second thoughts I am not sure that I do," she answered, with a contemptuous smile, "for I think that the man who can take that vow would also break it. But if you do break it, remember what I tell you, that you will see no more of me. After all, this is a free country, Mr. Rock, and even though I become your wife in name, you cannot force me to live with you. There is one more thing: I will not be married to you in a church—I will be married before a registrar, if at all."

"I suppose that you must have your own way about that too, Joan; though it seems an unholy thing not to ask Heaven's blessing on us."

"There is likely to be little enough blessing about the business," she answered; then added, touched by compunction: "You had best leave it alone, Mr. Rock; it is wicked and wrong from beginning to end, and you know that I don't love you, nor ever shall, and the reasons why I consent to take you. Be wise and have done with me, and find some other woman who has no such history who will care for you and make you a good wife."

"No, Joan; you have promised to do that much when the time comes, and I believe you. No other woman could make up to me for the loss of you, not if she were an angel."

"So be it, then," she answered: "but do not blame me if you are unhappy afterwards, for I have warned you, and however much I may try to do my duty, it can't make up to a man for the want of love. And now, when is it to be?"

"You said whenever I liked, Joan, and I say the sooner we are married the sooner the year of waiting will be over. If it can be done, to-morrow or the next day, as I think—for you have been living a long while in this parish—I will go and make arrangements and come to tell you."

"Don't do that, Mr. Rock, as I can't talk any more to-day. Send me a telegram. And now good-bye: I want to rest."

He waited for her to offer him her hand, but she did not do so. Then he turned and went, walking so softly that until she heard the front door close Mrs. Bird was unaware that he had left the room above. Throwing down her work she ran upstairs, for her curiosity would not allow her to delay. Joan was seated on the sofa staring out of the window, with wide-opened eyes and a face so set that it might have been cut in stone.

"Well, my dear," said the little woman, "so you have seen Sir Henry, and I hope that you have arranged everything satisfactorily?"

Joan heard and smiled; even then it struck her as ludicrous that Mrs. Bird could possibly mistake Samuel Rock for Sir Henry Graves. But she did not attempt to undeceive her, since to do so would have involved long explanations, on which at the moment she had neither the wish nor the strength to enter; moreover, she was sure that Mrs. Bird would disapprove of this strange contract and oppose it with all her force. Even then, however, she could not help reflecting how oddly things had fallen out. It was as though some superior power were smoothing away every difficulty, and, to fulfil secret motives of its own, was pushing her into this hideous and shameful union. For instance, though she had never considered it, had not Mrs. Bird fatuously taken it for granted that her visitor must be Sir Henry and no other man, it was probable that she would have found means to prevent him from seeing her, or, failing that, she would have put a stop upon the project by communicating with Henry. For a moment Joan was tempted to tell her the truth and let her do what she would, in the hope that she might save her from herself. But she resisted the desire, and answered simply,—

"Yes; I shall probably be married to-morrow or the next day."

"To-morrow!" ejaculated Mrs. Bird, holding up her hands. "Why, you haven't even got a dress ready."

"I can do without that," she replied, "especially as the ceremony is to be before a registrar."

"Before a registrar, Joan! Why, if I did such a thing I should never feel half married; besides, it's wicked."

"Perhaps," said Joan, smiling again; "but it is the only fashion in which it can be arranged, and it will serve our turn. By the way, shall you mind if I come back to live here afterwards?"

"What, with your husband? There would not be room for two of you; besides, a baronet could never put up with a place like this."

"No, without him. We are going to keep separate for a year."

"Good heavens!" exclaimed Mrs. Bird, "what an extraordinary arrangement!"

"There are difficulties, Mrs. Bird, and it is the only one that we could come to. I suppose that I can stay on?"

"Oh! yes, if you like; but really I do not understand."

"I can't explain just at present, dear," said Joan gently. "I am too tired; you will know all about it soon."

"Well," thought Mrs. Bird, as she left the room, "somehow I don't like that baronet so much as I did. It is all so odd and secret. I hope that he doesn't mean to deceive Joan with a false marriage and then to desert her. I have heard of people of rank doing such things. But if he tries it on he will have to reckon with me."

That afternoon Joan received the following telegram: "All arranged. Will call for you at two the day after to-morrow. Samuel."

CHAPTER XXXIV

THE OPENING OF THE GATE

It was a quarter to two on the Thursday and Joan, dressed in the black silk gown that she used to wear when on duty at Messrs. Black & Parker's, awaited the arrival of her intended husband in the little sitting-room, where presently Mrs. Bird joined her, attired in a lilac dress and a bonnet with white flowers and long tulle strings.

"What, my dear, are you going to be married in black? Pray don't: it is so unlucky."

"It is the best dress that I have," answered Joan.

"There is the pretty grey one."

"No," she replied hastily, "I will not wear that. Besides, the black one is more suitable."

"Joan, Joan," cried Mrs. Bird, "is everything right? You don't look as you ought to—not a bit happy."

"Quite right, thank you," she answered, with an unmoved countenance. "I have been shut up for so long that the idea of going out upsets me a little, that is all."

Then Mrs. Bird collapsed and sat silent, but Joan, moving to the window, looked down the street. The sight was not an inspiring one, for it was a wet and miserable afternoon even for London in November, and the rain trickled ceaselessly down the dirty window-panes. Presently through the mist Joan saw a four-wheeled cab advancing towards the house.

"Come," she said, "here it is." And she put on a heavy cloak over her other wrappings.

At the door she paused for a moment, as though her resolution failed her; then passed downstairs with a steady step. Mr. Rock was already in the passage inquiring for her from Maria.

"Here I am," she said; "let us go at once. I am afraid of catching cold if I stand about."

Apparently Samuel was too much taken aback to make any answer, and in another minute they were all three in the cab driving towards the nearest registry.

"I managed it all right, Joan," he said, bending forward and raising his voice to make himself heard above the rattling of the crazy cab. "I was only just in time, though, for I had to give forty-eight hours' clear notice at the registry, and to make all sorts of affidavits about your age, and as to your having been resident in the parish for more than fifteen days."

Joan received this information in silence, and nothing more was said until they arrived at the office.

From that moment till the end of the ceremony, so far as her immediate surroundings were concerned, Joan's mind was very much of a blank. She remembered, indeed, standing before a pleasant-looking gentleman with gold spectacles and a bald head, who asked her certain questions which she answered. She remembered also that Samuel put a ring upon her finger, for she noticed how his long white hands shook as he did so, and their hateful touch for a few instants stirred her from her lethargy. Then there arose in her mind a vision of herself standing on a golden summer afternoon by the ruins of an ancient church, and of one who spoke to her, and whom she must never see again. The vision passed, and she signed something. While her pen was yet upon the paper, she heard Mrs. Bird exclaim, in a shrill, excited voice—

"I forbid it. There's fraud here, as I believed all along. I thought that he used the wrong name, and now he's gone and signed it."

"What do you mean, madam?" asked the registrar. "Pray explain yourself."

"I mean that he is deceiving this poor girl into a false marriage. His name is Sir Henry Graves, Bart., and he has signed himself there Samuel Rock."

"The good lady is under a mistake," explained Samuel, clasping his hands and writhing uncomfortably: "my name is Rock, and I am a farmer, not a baronet."

"Well, I must say, sir," answered the registrar, "that you look as little like the one as the other. But this is a serious matter, so perhaps your wife will clear it up. She ought to know who and what you are, if anybody does."

"He is Mr. Samuel Rock, of the Moor Farm, Bradmouth," Joan answered, in an impassive voice. "My friend here is mistaken. Sir Henry Graves is quite a different person."

Mrs. Bird heard, and sank into a chair speechless, nor did she utter another syllable until she found herself at home again. Then the business went on, and presently the necessary certificates, of which Samuel was careful to obtain certified copies, were filled in and signed, and the party left the office.

"There's something odd about that affair," said the registrar to his assistant as he entered the amount of the fee received in a ledger, "and I shouldn't wonder if Mr. and Mrs. Samuel Rock make their appearance in the Courts before they are much older. However, all the papers are in order, so they can't blame me. What a pretty woman she is!—but she looked very sad and ill."

In the waiting-room of the office Joan held out her hand to Samuel, and said, "Good-bye."

"Mayn't I see you home?" he asked piteously.

She shook her head and answered, "On this day year, if I am alive, you may see as much of me as you like, but till then we are strangers," and she moved towards the door.

He stretched out his arms as though to embrace her; but, followed by the bewildered Mrs. Bird, she swept past him, and soon they were driving back to Kent Street, leaving Samuel standing bare-headed upon the pavement in the rain, and gazing after her.

In the passage of No. 8 Sally was waiting to present Joan with a bouquet of white flowers, that she had found no opportunity to give her as she went out. Joan took the flowers and, bending down, kissed the dumb child; and that kiss was the only touch of nature in all the nefarious and unnatural business of her marriage. Mrs. Bird followed her upstairs, and so soon as the door was closed, said,—

"For pity's sake, Joan, tell me what all this means. Am I mad, or are you?"

"I am, Mrs. Bird," she answered. "If you want to know, I have married this man, who has been in love with me a long while, but whom I hate, in order to prevent Sir Henry Graves from making me his wife."

"But why, Joan? but why?" Mrs. Bird gasped.

"Because if I had married Sir Henry I should have ruined him, and also because I promised Lady Graves that I would not do so. Had I once seen him I should have broken my promise, so I have taken this means to put myself out of temptation, having first told Mr. Rock the whole truth, and bargained that I should not go to live with him for another year."

"Oh! this is terrible, terrible!" said Mrs. Bird, wringing her hands; "and what a reptile the man must be to marry you on such terms, and knowing that you loathe the sight of him!"

"Do not abuse him, Mrs. Bird, for on the whole I think that he is as much wronged as anybody; at least he is my husband, whom I have taken with my eyes open, as he has taken me."

"He may be your husband, but he is a liar for all that; for he told me that he was Sir Henry Graves, and that is why I let him come up to see you, although I thought, from the look of him, that he couldn't be a baronet. Well, Joan, you have done it now, and as you've sown so you will have to reap. The wages of sin is death, that's the truth of it. You've gone wrong, and, like many another, you have got to suffer. I don't believe in your arguments that have made you marry this crawling creature. They are a kind of lie, and, like all lies, they will bring misery. You have a good heart, but you've never disciplined it, and a heart without discipline is the most false of guides. It isn't for me to reproach you, Joan, who am, I dare say, ten times worse than you are, but I can't hold with your methods. However, you are married to this man now, so if you're wise you'll try to make the best of him and forget the other."

"Yes," she answered, "I shall if I am wise, or if I can find wisdom."

Then Mrs. Bird began to cry and went away. When she had gone, Joan sat down and wrote this letter to catch the post:—

"Dear Sir,

"I have received your kind letter, and write to tell you that it is of no use your coming to London to see me to-morrow, as I was married this afternoon to Mr. Samuel Rock; and so good-bye! With all good wishes,

"Believe me, dear sir,
"Ever yours,
"Joan."

Joan was married on a Thursday; and upon the following morning Henry, who had slept but ill, rose early and went out before breakfast. As it chanced, the weather was mild, and the Rosham fields and woods looked soft and beautiful in the hazy November light. Henry walked to and fro about them, stopping here to admire the view, and there to speak a few kindly words to some labourer going to his daily toil, or to watch the pheasants drawing back to covert after filling their crops upon the stubble. Thus he lingered till long past the hour for breakfast, for he was sad at heart and loath to quit the lands that, as he thought, he would see no more, since he had determined not to revisit Rosham when once he had made Joan his wife.

He felt that he was doing right in marrying her, but it was idle to deny that she was costing him dear. For three centuries his forefathers had owned these wide, familiar lands; there was no house upon them that they had not built; with the exception of a few ancient pollards there was scarcely a tree that they had not planted; and now he must send them to the hammer because he had been unlucky enough to fall in love with the wrong woman. Well, such was his fortune, and he must make the best of it. Still he may be pardoned if it wrung his heart to think that, in all human probability, he would never again see those fields and friendly faces, and that in his person the race of Graves were looking their last upon the soil that for hundreds of years had fed them while alive and covered them when dead.

In a healthy man, however, even sentiment is not proof against hunger, so it came about that at last Henry limped home to breakfast with a heavy heart, and, having ordered the dog that trotted at his heels back to its kennel, he entered the house by the side door and went to the dining-room. On this plate were several letters. He opened the first, which he noticed had an official frank in the left-hand corner. It was from his friend the under-secretary, informing him that, as it chanced, there was a billet open in Africa, and that he had obtained a promise from a colleague, in whose hands lay the patronage of the appointment, that if he proved suitable in some particulars, he, Henry, should have the offer of it. The letter added that, although the post was worth only six hundred a year, it was in a good climate, and would certainly lead to better things; and that the writer would be glad if he would come to town to see about the matter as soon as might be convenient to him, since, when it became known that the place was vacant, there were sure to be crowds of people after it who had claims upon the Government.

"Here's a bit of good news at last, anyway," thought Henry, as he put down the letter: "whatever happens to us, Joan and I won't starve, and I dare say that we can be jolly enough out there. By Jove! if it wasn't for my mother and the thought that some of my father's debts must remain unpaid, I should almost be happy," and for a moment or two he gave himself over to a reverie in which the thought of Joan and of her tender love and beauty played the largest part (for he tried to forget the jarring tone of that second letter)—Joan, whom, after so long an absence, he should see again that day.

Then, remembering that the rest of his correspondence was unread, he took up an envelope and opened it without looking at the address. In five seconds it was on the floor beside him, and he was murmuring, with pale lips, "'Married this afternoon to Samuel Rock.' Impossible! it must be a hoax!" Stooping down, he found the letter and examined it carefully. Either it was in Joan's writing, or the forgery was perfect. Then he thought of the former letter, of which the tenor had disgusted him; and it occurred to him that it was an epistle which a woman contemplating some such treachery might very well have written. had he, then, been deceived all along in this girl's character? It would seem so. And yet—and yet! She had sworn that she loved him, and that she hated the man Rock. What could have been her object in doing this thing? Only one that he could see—money. Rock was a rich man, and he—was a penniless baronet.

If this letter were genuine, it became clear that she thought him good enough for a lover but not for a husband; that she had amused herself with him, and now threw him over in favour of the solid advantage of a prosperous marriage with a man in her own class of life. Well, he had heard of women playing such tricks, and the hypothesis explained the attitude which Joan had all along adopted upon the question of becoming his wife. He remembered that from the first she disclaimed any wish to marry him. Oh! if this were so, what a blind fool he had been, and how unnecessarily had he tormented himself with doubts and searchings for the true path of duty! But as yet he could not believe that it was true. There must be some mistake. At least he would go to London and ascertain the facts before he passed judgment on the faith of such evidence. Why had he not gone before, in defiance of the doctor and Mrs. Bird?

Half an hour later he was driving to the station. As he drew near to Bradmouth he perceived a man walking along the road, in whom he recognised Samuel Rock.

"There's an end of that lie," he thought to himself, with a sigh of relief; "for if she married him yesterday afternoon he would be in London with her, since he could scarcely have returned here to spend his honeymoon."

At any rate he would settle the question. Giving the reins to the coachman, he jumped down from the cart, and, bidding him drive on a few yards, waited by the roadside. Presently Samuel caught sight of him, and stopped as though he meant to turn back. If so, he changed his mind almost instantly and walked forward at a quick pace.

"Good day, Mr. Rock," said Henry: "I wish to have a word with you. I have heard some strange news this morning, which you may be able to explain."

"What news?" asked Samuel, looking at him insolently.

"That you were married to Joan Haste yesterday."

"Well, what about that, Sir Henry Graves?"

"Nothing in particular, Mr. Rock, except that I do not believe it."

"Don't you?" answered Samuel with a sneer. "Then perhaps you will throw your eye over this." And he produced from his pocket a copy of the marriage certificate.

Henry read it, and turned very white; then he handed it back without a word.

"It is all in order, I think?" said Samuel, still sneering.

"Apparently," Henry answered. "May I ask if—Mrs. Rock—is with you?"

"No she isn't. Do you think that I am fool enough to bring her here at present, for you to be sneaking about after her? I know what your game was, 'cause she told me all about it. You were going up to town to-day to get hold of her, weren't you. Well, you're an hour behind the fair this time. Joan may have been a bit flighty, but she's a sensible woman at bottom, and she knew better than to trust herself to a scamp without a sixpence, like you, when she might have an honest man and a good home. I told you I meant to marry her, and you see I have kept my word. And now look you here, Sir Henry Graves: just you keep clear of her in future, for if I catch you so much as speaking to her, it will be the worse both for yourself and Joan—not that she cares a rotten herring about you, although she did fool you so prettily."

"You need not fear that I shall attempt to disturb your domestic happiness, Mr. Rock. And now for Heaven's sake get out of my way before I forget myself."

Samuel obeyed, still grinning and sneering with hate and jealousy; and Henry walked on to where the dog-cart was waiting for him. Taking the reins, he turned the horse's head and drove back to Rosham.

"Thomson," he said to the butler, who came to open the door, "I have changed my mind about going to town to-day; you can unpack my things. Stop a minute, though: I remember I am due at Monk's Lodge, so you needn't meddle with the big portmanteau. When does my mother come back?"

"To-morrow, her ladyship wrote me this morning, Sir Henry."

"Oh! very well. Then I sha'n't see her till Tuesday; but it doesn't matter. Send down to the keeper and tell him that I want to speak to him, will you? I think that I will change my clothes and shoot some rabbits after lunch. Stop, order the dog-cart to be ready to drive me to Monk's Lodge in time to dress for dinner."

To analyse Henry's feelings during the remainder of that day would be difficult, if not impossible; but those of shame and bitter anger were uppermost in his mind—shame that he had laid himself open to such words as Rock used to him, and anger that his vanity and blind faith in a woman's soft speeches and feigned love should have led him into so ignominious a position. Mingled with these emotions were his natural pangs of jealousy and disappointed affection, though pride would not suffer him to give way to them. Again and again he reviewed every detail of the strange, and to his sense, appalling story; and at times, overpowering as was the evidence, his mind refused to accept its obvious moral—namely, that he had been tricked and made a tool of—yes, used as a foil to bring this man to the point of marriage. How was it possible to reconcile Joan's conduct in the past and that wild letter of hers with her subsequent letters and action? Thus only: that as regards the first she had been playing on his feelings and inexperience of the arts of women; and that, as in sleep men who are no poets can sometimes compose verse which is full of beauty, so in her delirium Joan had been able to set on paper words and thoughts that were foreign to her nature and above its level. Or perhaps that letter was a forgery written by Mrs. Bird, who was "so romantic." The circumstances under which it reached him were peculiar, and Joan herself expressly repudiated all knowledge of it. Notwithstanding his doubts, perplexities and suffering, as might have been expected, the matter in the end resolved itself into two very simple issues: first, that, whatever may have been her exact reasons, Joan Haste had broken with him once and for all by marrying another man; and second, that, as a corollary to her act, many dangers and difficulties which had beset him had disappeared, and he was free, if he wished it, to marry another woman.

Henry was no fool, and when the first bitterness was past, and he could consider the matter, if not without passion as yet, at least more calmly, he saw, the girl being what she had proved herself to be, that all things were working together for his good and the advantage of his family. Supposing, for instance, that he had found her out after marriage instead of before it, and supposing that the story which she told him in her first letter had been true, instead of what it clearly was—a lie? Surely in these and in many other ways his escape had been what an impartial person might call fortunate. At the least, of her own act she had put an end to an imbroglio that had many painful aspects, and there remained no stain upon his honour, for which he was most truly thankful.

And now, having learnt his lesson in the hard school of experience, he would write to his friend the under-secretary, saying he could not be in town till Wednesday. Meanwhile he would pay his visit to Monk's Lodge.

CHAPTER XXXV

DISENCHANTMENT

It was Sunday evening at Monk's Lodge, and Henry and Mr. Levinger were sitting over their wine after dinner. For a while they talked upon indifferent subjects, and more particularly about the shooting on the previous day and the arrangements for the morrow's sport. Then there was a silence, which Mr. Levinger broke.

"I have heard a curious bit of news," he said, "about Joan Haste. It seems that she is married."

Henry drank half a glass of port wine, and answered, "Yes, I know. She has married your tenant Samuel Rock, the dissenter, a very strange person. I cannot understand it."

"Can't you? I think I can. It is a good match for her, though I don't altogether approve of it, and know nothing of the details. However, I wasn't consulted, and there it is. I hope that they may be happy."

"So do I," said Henry grimly. "And now, Mr. Levinger, I want to have a word with you about the estate affairs. What is to be done? It is time that you took some steps to protect yourself."

"It seems to me, Graves," he answered deliberately, "that my course of action must very much depend upon your own. You know what I mean."

"Yes, Mr. Levinger; but are you still anxious that I should propose to your daughter? Forgive me if I speak plainly."

"That has always been my wish, and I see no particular reason to change it."

"But do you think that it is her wish, Mr. Levinger? I fancy that her manner has been a little cold to me of late, perhaps with justice; and," he added, rather nervously, "naturally I do not wish to lay myself open to a rebuff. I find that I am very ignorant of the ways of women, as of various other things."

"Many of us have made that discovery, Graves; and of course it is impossible for me to guarantee your success, though I think that you will be successful."

"There is another matter, Mr. Levinger: Emma has considerable possessions; am I then justified, in my impoverished condition, in asking her to take me? Would it not be thought, would she not think, that I did so from obvious motives?"

"On that point you may make your mind quite easy, Graves; for I, who am the girl's father, tell you that I consider you will be giving her quite as much as she gives you. I have never hidden from you that I am in a sense a man under a cloud. My follies came to an end many years ago, it is true, and I have never fallen into the clutches of the law, still they were bad enough to force me to change my name and to begin life afresh. Should you marry my daughter, and should you wish it, you will of course have the right to learn my true name, though on that point I shall make an appeal to your generosity and ask you not to press your right. I have done with the past, of which even the thought is hateful to me, and I do not wish to reopen old sores; so perhaps you may be content with the assurance that I am of a good and ancient family, and that before I got into trouble I served in the army with some distinction: for instance, I received the wound that crippled me at the battle of the Alma."

"I shall never press you to tell that which you desire to keep to yourself, Mr. Levinger."

"It is like you to say so, Graves," he answered, with evident relief; "but the mere fact that I make such a request will show you what I mean when I say that Emma has as much or more to gain from this marriage than you have, since it is clear that some rumours of her father's disgrace must follow her through life; moreover she is humbly born upon her mother's side. I do trust and pray, my dear fellow, that it will come off. Alas! I am not long for this world, my heart is troubling me more and more, and the doctors have warned me that I may die at any moment; therefore it is my most earnest desire to see the daughter whom I love better than anything on earth, happily settled before I go."

"Well, Mr. Levinger," Henry answered, "I will ask her to-morrow if I find an opportunity, but the issue does not rest with me. I only wish that I were more worthy of her."

"I am glad to hear it. God bless you, and God speed you, my dear Graves! I hope when I am gone that, whatever you may learn about my unfortunate past, you will still try to think kindly of me, and to remember that I was a man, cursed by nature with passions of unusual strength, which neither my education nor the circumstances of my early life helped me to control."

"It is not for me to judge you or any other man; I leave that to those who are without sin," said Henry, and the conversation came to an end.

That night Henry was awakened by hearing people moving backwards and forwards in the passages. For a moment he thought of burglars, and wondered if he should get up; but the sounds soon ceased, so he turned over and went to sleep again. As he learned in the morning, the cause of the disturbance was that Mr. Levinger had been seized with one of his heart attacks, which for a few minutes threatened to be serious, if not fatal. Under the influence of restoratives, that were always kept at hand, the danger passed as quickly as it had arisen, although Emma remained by her father's bedside to watch him for a while.

"That was a near thing, Emma," he said presently: "for about thirty seconds I almost thought—" and he stopped.

"Well, it is over now, father dear," she answered.

"Yes, but for how long? One day I shall be taken in this fashion and come back no more."

"Pray don't talk like that, father."

"Why not, seeing that it is what I must accustom my mind to? Oh! Emma, if I could but see you safely married I should not trouble so much, but the uncertainty as to your future worries me more than anything else. However, you must settle these things for yourself; I have no right to dictate to you about them. Good night, my love, and thank you for your kindness. No, there is no need for you to stop up. If I should want anything I will touch the bell."

"I wonder why he is so bent upon my getting married," thought Emma, as she went back to her bed, "especially as, even did anything happen to him, I should be left well off—at least, I suppose so. Well, it is no use my troubling myself about it till the time comes, if ever it does come."

After his attack of the previous night, Mr. Levinger was unable to come out shooting as he had hoped to do. He said, however, that if he felt well enough he would drive in the afternoon to a spot known as the Hanging Wood, which was to be the last and best beat of the day; and it was arranged that Emma should accompany him and walk home, a distance of some two miles.

The day was fine, and the shooting very fair; but, fond as he was of the sport, Henry did not greatly enjoy himself—which, in view of what lay behind and before him, is scarcely to be wondered at.

After luncheon the guns and beaters were employed in driving two narrow covers, each of them about half a mile long, towards a wood planted upon the top of a rise of ground. On they went steadily, firing at cock pheasants only, till, the end of the plantations being unstopped, the greater number of the birds were driven into this Hanging Wood, which ended in a point situated about a hundred and twenty yards from the borders of the two converging plantations. Between these plantations and the wood lay a little valley of pasture land, through which ran a stream; and it was the dip of this valley, together with the position of the cover on the opposite slope, that gave to the Hanging Wood its reputation of being the most sporting spot for pheasant shooting in that neighbourhood. The slaughter of hand-reared pheasants is frequently denounced, for the most part by people who know little about it, as a tame and cruel amusement; and it cannot be denied that this is sometimes so, especially where the object of the keeper, or of his master, is not to show sport, but to return a heavy total of slain at the end of the day. In the case of a cover such as has been described, matters are very different, however; for then the pheasants, flying towards their homes, from which they have been disturbed, come over the guns with great speed and at a height of from eight-and-twenty to forty yards, and the shooting must be good that will bring to bag more than one in four of them.

By the banks of the stream between the covers Henry and his companions found Mr. Levinger and Emma waiting for them, the pony trap in which they had come having been driven off to a little distance, so as not to interfere with the beat.

"Here I am," said Mr. Levinger: "I don't feel up to much, but I was determined to see the Hanging Wood shot again, even if it should be for the last time. Now then, Bowles, get your beaters round as quick as you can, and be careful that they keep wide of the cover, and don't make a noise. I will place the guns. You've no time to lose: the light is beginning to fade."

Bowles and his small army moved off to the right, while Mr. Levinger pointed out to each sportsman the spot to which he should go upon the banks of the stream; assigning to Henry the centre stand, both because he was accompanied by a loader with a second gun, and on account of his reputation of being the best shot present.

"The wind is rising fast and blowing straight down the cover," said Mr. Levinger, when he had completed his arrangements; "those wild-bred birds will take some stopping, unless I am much mistaken. I tell you what, Graves: I bet you half a crown that you don't kill a pheasant for every four cartridges you fire, taking them as they come, without shirking the hard ones."

"All right," answered Henry, "I can run to that"; and they both laughed, while Emma, who was standing by, dressed in a pretty grey tweed costume, looked pleased to see her father show so much interest in anything.

Ten minutes passed, and a shrill whistle, blown far away at the end of the cover, announced that the beaters were about to start. Henry cocked his gun and waited, till presently a brace of pheasants were seen coming towards him with the wind in their tails, and at a tremendous height, one bird being some fifty yards in front of the other.

"Over you, Graves," said Mr. Levinger.

Henry waited till the first bird was at the proper angle, and fired both barrels, aiming at least three yards ahead of him; but without producing the slightest effect upon the old cock, which sailed away serenely. Snatching his second gun with an exclamation, he repeated the performance at the hen that followed, and with a similar lack of result.

"There go four cartridges, anyway," said Mr. Levinger.

"It isn't fair to count them," answered Henry, laughing; "those birds were clean out of shot."

"Yes, out of your shot, Graves. You were yards behind them. You mustn't be content with aiming ahead here, especially in this wind; if you don't swing as well, you'll scarcely kill a bird. Look out: here comes another. There! you've missed him again. Swing, man, swing!"

By this time Henry was fairly nettled, for, chancing to look round, he saw Emma was laughing at his discomfiture. The next time a bird came over him he took his host's advice and "swung" with a vengeance, and down it fell far behind him, dead as a stone.

"That's better, Graves; you caught him in the head."

Now the fun became fast and furious, and Emma, watching Henry's face as he fired away with as much earnestness and energy as though the fate of the British Empire depended upon each shot, thought that he was quite handsome. Handsome he was not, nor ever would be; but it is true that, like most

Englishmen, he looked his best in his rough shooting clothes and when intent upon his sport. Five minutes more, and the firing, which had been continuous all along the line, began to slacken, and then died away altogether, Henry distinguishing himself by killing the last two birds that flew over with a brilliant right and left. Still, when the slain came to be counted it was found that he had lost his bet by one cartridge.

"Don't be depressed," said Levinger, as he pocketed the half-crown; "the other fellows have done much worse. I don't believe that young Jones has touched a feather. The fact is that a great many of the birds you fired at were quite impossible. I never remember seeing them fly so high and fast before. But then this wood has not been shot in half a gale of wind for many years. And now I must say good-bye to these gentleman and be off, or I shall get a chill. You'll see my daughter home, won't you?"

As it chanced, Emma had gone to fetch a pheasant which she said had fallen in the edge of the plantation behind them. When she returned with the bird, it was impossible for her to accompany her father, even if she wished to do so, for he had already driven away.

Henry congratulated her upon the skill with which she had marked down the cock, at the same time announcing his intention of reclaiming the half-crown from her father. Then, having given his guns to the loader, they started for the high road, accompanied by the two pupils of the neighbouring clergyman. A few hundred yards farther on these young gentlemen went upon their way rejoicing, bearing with them a leash of pheasants and a hare.

"You must show me the road home, Miss Levinger," said Henry, by way of making conversation, for they were now alone.

"The shortest path is along the cliff, if you think that we can get over the fence," she answered.

The hedge did not prove unclimbable, and presently they were walking along the edge of the cliff. Below them foamed an angry sea, for the tide was high, driven shoreward by the weight of the easterly gale, while to the west the sky was red with the last rays of a wintry sunset.

For a while they walked in silence, which Emma broke, saying, "The sea is very beautiful to-night, is it not?"

"It is always beautiful to me," he answered.

"I see that you have not got over leaving the Navy yet, Sir Henry."

"Well, Miss Levinger, to tell you the truth I haven't had a very pleasant time ever since I came ashore. One way and another there have been nothing but sorrow and worries and disagreeables, till often and often I have wished myself off the coast of Newfoundland, with ice about and a cotton-wool fog, or anywhere else that is dangerous and unpleasant."

"I know that you have had plenty of trouble, Sir Henry," she said in her gentle voice, "and your father's death must have been a great blow to you. But perhaps your fog will lift, as I suppose that it does sometimes—even on the coast of Newfoundland."

"I hope so; it is time that it did," he answered absently, and then for a minute was silent. He felt that, if he meant to propose, now was his chance, but for the life of him he could not think how to begin. It was an agonising moment, and, though the evening had turned bitterly cold, he became aware that the perspiration was running down his forehead.

"Miss Levinger," he said suddenly, "I have something to ask you."

"To ask me, Sir Henry? What about?"

"About—about yourself. I wish to ask you if you will honour me by promising to become my wife?"

Emma heard, and, stopping suddenly in her walk, looked round as though to find a refuge, but seeing none went on again.

"Miss Levinger," Henry continued, "I am not skilled at this sort of thing, and I hope that you will make allowances for my awkwardness. Do you think that you could care enough for me to marry me? I know very well that I have little to recommend me, and there are circumstances connected with my financial position which make it almost presumptuous that I should ask you."

"I think, Sir Henry," she answered, speaking for the first time, "that we may leave money matters out of the question. I have heard something of the state of affairs at Rosham, and I know that you are not responsible for it, though you are expected by others to remedy it."

"It is very generous of you to speak like that, Miss Levinger; and it helps me out of a great difficulty, for I could not see how I was to explain all this business to you."

"I think that it is only just, Sir Henry, not generous. Provided that there is enough on one side or the other, money is not the principal question to be considered."

"No, Miss Levinger, I agree with you, though I have known others who thought differently. The main thing is whether you can care enough about me."

"That is one thing, Sir Henry," she answered in a low voice; "also there are others."

"I suppose that you mean whether or no I am worthy of you, Miss Levinger. Well, even though it should destroy my chances with you, I will tell you frankly that, in my judgment, I am not. Listen, Miss Levinger: till within a few months ago I had never cared about any woman; then I saw you for the second time, and thought you the sweetest lady that I had ever met, for I understood how good and true you are, and in my heart I hoped that a day would come when I might venture to ask you what I am asking you now. Afterwards trouble arose through my own weakness and folly—trouble between myself and another woman. I am sure that you will not press me for details, because, in order to give them, I must betray another person's secret. To be brief, I should probably have married this woman, but she threw me over and chose another man."

"What!" said Emma, startled out of her self-control, "is Joan Haste married?"

"I see that you know more about me than I thought. She is married—to Mr. Samuel Rock."

"I cannot understand it at all; it is almost incredible."

"Nor can I, but the fact remains. She wrote to tell me of it herself, and, what is more, her husband showed me the marriage certificate. And now I have made a clean breast of it, for I will not sail under false colours, and you must judge me. If you choose to take me, I promise you that no woman shall ever have a better husband than I will be to you, for your happiness and welfare shall be the first objects of my life. The question is, after what I have told you, can you care for me?"

Emma stopped, for all this while they had been walking slowly, and looked him full in the eyes, a last red ray of the dying light falling on her sweet face.

"Sir Henry," she said, "you have been frank with me, and I honour you for it, none the less because I happen to know something of the story. And now I will be equally frank with you, though to do so is humbling to me. When I stayed in the same house with you more than two years ago, you took little notice of me, but I grew fond of you, and I have never changed my mind. Still I do not think that, as things are, I should marry you on this account alone, seeing that a woman looks for love in her marriage; and, Sir Henry, in all that you have said to me you have spoken no word of love."

"How could I, knowing what I had to tell you?" he broke in.

"I cannot say, but it is so; and therefore, speaking for myself alone, I should be inclined to answer you that we had best go our separate ways in life, though I am sure that, as you promise, you would be a good and kind husband to me. But there are other people to be considered; there is my father, who is most anxious that I should make a satisfactory marriage—such as I know this would be for me, for I am nobody and scarcely recognised in society here—and who has the greatest respect and affection for you, as he had for your father before you. Then there is your family: if I refuse you it would mean that you would all be ruined, and though it may hurt your pride to hear me say so, I shrink from such a thought—"

"Oh! pray do not let that weigh with you," he interrupted. "You know well that, although much of what you say is unhappily true, I am not seeking you that you may mend my broken fortunes, but because you are what you are, and I desire above all things to make you my wife."

"I am sorry, Sir Henry, but, though I believe every word you say, I must let it weigh with me, for I wish to be a blessing to those about me, and not a curse. Well, for all these reasons, and chiefly perhaps, to be honest, because I am fond of you though you do not care very much for me, I will be your wife, Sir Henry, as you are good enough to wish it," and she gave him her hand.

He took it and kissed it, and they walked on in silence till they were near to the house. Then Henry spoke, and his voice betrayed more emotion than he cared to show.

"How can I thank you, Emma!" he said; "and what am I to say to you? It is useless to make protestations which you would not believe, though perhaps they might have more truth in them than you imagine. But I am sure of this, that if we live, a time will come soon when you will not doubt me if I tell you that I love you." And, drawing her to him, he kissed her upon the forehead.

"I hope so, Henry," she said, disengaging herself from his arms, and they went together into the house.

Within ten weeks of this date Henry and Emma were spending a long honeymoon among the ruined temples of the Nile.

CHAPTER XXXVI

THE DESIRE OF DEATH—AND THE FEAR OF HIM

Joan remained at Kent Street, and the weary days crept on. When the first excitement of her self-sacrifice had faded from her mind, she lapsed into a condition of melancholy that was pitiable to see. Every week brought her rambling and impassioned epistles from her husband, most of which she threw into the fire half-read. At length there came one that she perused eagerly enough, for it announced the approaching marriage of Sir Henry Graves and Miss Levinger—tidings which were confirmed in a few brief words by a note from Mr. Levinger himself, enclosing her monthly allowance; for from Samuel as yet she would take nothing. Then in January another letter reached her, together with a copy of the local paper, describing the ceremony, the presents, the dress and appearance "of the lovely bride and the gallant bridegroom, Captain Sir Henry Graves, Bart., R.N."

"At least I have not done all this for nothing," said Joan, as she threw down the paper; and then for the rest of that day she lay upon her bed moaning with the pain of her bitter jealousy and immeasurable despair.

She felt now that, had she known what she must suffer, she would never have found the strength to act as she had done, and time upon time did she regret that she had allowed her impulses to carry her away. Rock had been careful to inform her of his interview with Henry, putting his own gloss upon what passed between them; and the knowledge that her lover must hate and despise her was the sharpest arrow of the many which were fixed in her poor heart. All the rest she could bear, but than this Death himself had been more kind. How pitiable was her state!—scorned by Henry, of whose child she must be the mother, but who was now the loving husband of another woman, and given over to a man she hated, and who would shortly claim his bond. Alas! no regrets, however poignant, could serve to undo the past, any more than the fear of it could avert the future; for Mrs. Bird was right—as she had sown so she must reap.

One by one the weary days crept on till at length the long London winter gave way to spring, and the time of her trial grew near. In health she remained fairly well, since sorrow works slowly upon so vigorous a constitution; but the end of each week found her sadder and more broken in spirit than its beginning. She had no friends, and went out but little—indeed, her only relaxations were found in reading, with a vague idea of improving her mind, because Henry had once told her to do so, or conversing in the deaf-and-dumb language with Jim and Sally. Still her life was not an idle one, for as time went by the shadow of a great catastrophe fell upon the Kent Street household. Mrs. Bird's eyesight began to fail her, and the hospital doctors whom she consulted, were of opinion that the weakness must increase.

"Oh! my dear," she said to Joan, "what is to happen to us all if I go blind? I have a little money put away—about a hundred and fifty pounds, or two hundred in all, perhaps; but it will soon melt, and then I suppose that they will take us to the workhouse; and you know, my dear, they separate husband and wife in those places." And, quite broken down by such a prospect, the poor little woman began to weep.

"At any rate, there is no need for you to trouble yourself about it at present," answered Joan gently, "since Sally helps, and I can do the fine work that you cannot manage."

"It is very kind of you, Joan. Ah! little did I know, when I took you in out of the street that day, what a blessing you would prove to me, and how I should learn to love you. Also, it is wicked of me to repine, for God has always looked after us heretofore, and I do not believe that He Who feeds the ravens will suffer us to starve, or to be separated. So I will try to be brave and trust in Him."

"Ah!" answered Joan, "I wish that I could have your faith; but I suppose it is only given to good people. Now, where is the work? Let me begin at once. No, don't thank me any more; it will be a comfort; besides, I would stitch my fingers off for you."

Thenceforth Mrs. Bird's orders were fulfilled as regularly as ever they had been, and as Joan anticipated, the constant employment gave her some relief. But while she sat and sewed for hour after hour, a new desire entered into her mind—that most terrible of all desires, the desire of Death! Of Death she became enamoured, and her daily prayer to Heaven was that she might die, she and her child together, since her imagination could picture no future in another world more dreadful than that which awaited her in this.

Only once during these months did she hear anything of Henry; and then it was through the columns of a penny paper, where, under the heading of "Society Jottings," she read that "Sir Henry Graves, Bart., R.N., and his beautiful young bride were staying at Shepheard's Hotel in Cairo, where the gallant Captain was very popular and Lady Graves was much admired." The paragraph added that they were going to travel in the Holy Land, and expected to return to their seat at Rosham towards the end of May.

It was shortly after she read this that Joan, who from constantly thinking about death, had convinced herself that she would die, went through the formality of making a will on a sixpenny form which she bought for that purpose.

To Sir Henry Graves she left the books that he had given her, and a long letter, which she was at much trouble to compose, and placed carefully in the same envelope with the will. All the rest of her property, of any sort whatsoever, whereof she might die possessed—it amounted to about thirty pounds and some clothes—she devised to Mrs. Bird for the use of her unborn child, should it live, and, failing that, to Mrs. Bird absolutely.

At last the inevitable hour of her trouble came upon her, and left her pale and weak, but holding a little daughter in her arms. From the first the child was sickly, for the long illness of the mother had affected its constitution; and within three weeks from the day of its birth it was laid to rest in a London cemetery, leaving Joan to drink the cup of a new and a deeper agony than any that it had been her lot to taste.

Yet, when her first days of grief and prostration had gone by, almost could she find it in her heart to rejoice that the child had been taken from her and placed beyond the possibilities of such a life as she had led; for, otherwise, how would things have gone with it when she, its mother, passed into the power of Samuel Rock? Surely he would have hated and maltreated it, and, if fate had left it without the protection of her love in the hands of such a guardian, its existence might have been made a misery. Still, after the death of that infant those about her never saw a smile upon Joan's face, however closely they might watch for it. Perhaps she was more beautiful now than she had ever been, for the chestnut hair that clustered in short curls upon her shapely head, and her great sorrowful eyes shining in the pallor of her sweet face, refined and made strange her loveliness; moreover, if the grace of girlhood had left her, it was replaced by another and a truer dignity—the dignity of a woman who has loved and suffered and lost.

One morning, it was on the ninth of June, Joan received a letter from her husband, who now wrote to her every two or three days. Before she opened it she knew well from past experience what would be the tenor of its contents: an appeal to her, more or less impassioned, to shorten the year of separation for which she had stipulated, and come to live with him as his wife. She was not mistaken, for the letter ended thus:—

"Oh! Joan, have pity on me and come to me, for if you don't I think that I shall go crazed. I have kept my promise to you faithful so far, so if you are made of flesh and blood, show mercy before you drive me to something desperate. It's all over now; the child's dead, you tell me, and the man's married, so let's turn a new leaf and begin afresh. After all, Joan, you are my wife before God and man, and it is to me that your duty lies, not to anybody else. Even if you haven't any fondness for me, I ask you in the name of that duty to listen to me, and I tell you that if I don't I believe that I shall go mad with the longing to see your face, and the sin if it will be upon you. I've done up the house comfortable for you, Joan; no money has been spared, and if you want anything more you shall have it. Then don't go on hiding yourself away from me, but come and take the home that waits you."

"I suppose he is right, and that it is my duty," said Joan to herself with a sigh, as she laid down the letter. "Love and hope and happiness have gone from me, nothing is left except duty, so I had better hold fast to it. I will write and say that I will go soon—within a few days; though what the Birds will do without me I do not know, unless he will let me give them some of my allowance."

Having come to this determination, Joan wrote her letter and posted it, fearing lest, should she delay, her virtuous resolution might fail her. As she returned from the pillar box, a messenger, who was standing on the steps of No. 8, handed her a telegram addressed to herself. Wondering what it might be, she opened it, to read this message:—

"Come down here at once. I am ill and must see you before it is too late. The carriage will meet the five o'clock train at Monk's Vale station. Wire reply.

"Levinger,
"Monk's Lodge."

"I wonder what he can want to see me for," thought Joan; then, asking the boy to wait in the passage, she went in to consult Mrs. Bird.

"You had best go, my dear," she said; "I have always thought that there was some mystery about this Mr. Levinger, and now I expect that it is coming out. If you take a cab at once, you will just have time to catch the twelve o'clock train at Liverpool Street."

Joan nodded, and writing one word upon the prepaid answer—"Coming,"—gave it to the boy and ran upstairs to pack a few things in a bag. In ten minutes a hansom was at the door and she was ready to start. First she bade good-bye to the two invalids, who were much disturbed at this hurried departure; and then to Mrs. Bird, who followed her into the passage kissing her again and again.

"Do you know, Joan," she said, beginning to cry, "I feel as if you were going away for good and I should never see you any more."

"Nonsense, dear," she answered briefly, for a queer contraction in her throat made a lengthened speech impossible, "I hope to be back in a day or two if all is well."

"Yes, Joan—if all is well, and there's hope for everybody. Well, good-bye, and God bless you wherever you go—God bless you here and hereafter, for ever and ever!"

Then Joan drove away, and as she went it came into her mind that it would be best if she returned no more. She had promised to join her husband in a few days. Why should she not do so at once, and thus avoid the pain of a formal parting with the Birds, her true and indeed her only friends?

By half-past four that afternoon the train pulled up at Bradmouth, where she must change into the light railway with tramcar carriages that runs for fifteen or twenty miles along the coast, Monk's Vale being the second station from the junction.

The branch train did not start for ten minutes, and Joan employed the interval in walking up and down the platform, looking at the church tower, the roofs of the fishing village, the boats upon the beach, and the familiar view of land and sea. Everything seemed quite unchanged; she alone was changed, and felt as though a century of time had passed over her head since that morning when she ran away to London.

"Hullo, Joan Rock!" said a half-remembered voice at her elbow. "I'm in luck, it seems: I saw you off, and here I am to welcome you back. But you shouldn't have married him, Joan; you should have waited for me as I told you. I'm in business for myself now—four saddle donkeys and a goat chaise, and doing grand. I shall die a rich man, you bet."

Joan turned round to see a youth with impudent blue eyes and a hair of flaming red, in whom she recognised Willie Hood, much elongated, but otherwise the same.

"Oh! Willie, is that you?" she said, stretching out her hand, for she was pleased to see a friendly face; "how are you, and how do you know that I am married?"

"Know? Why, if you sent the crier round with a bell to call it, folks would hear, wouldn't they? And that's just about what Mr. Samuel Rock has done, talking of 'my wife, Joan Haste as was,' here, there, and everywhere; and telling how as you were stopping in foreign parts awhile for the benefit of your health—which seems a strange tale to me, and I know a thing or two, I do. Not that it has done you much good, anyway, to judge from the air of you, for you look like the ghost of what you used to be. I'll tell you what, Joan: for the sake of old times you shall have a ride every morning on my best donkey, all for love, if Sammy won't be jealous. That'll bring the colour back into your cheeks, you bet."

"How are my uncle and aunt?" asked Joan, hastening to change the conversation.

"How are they? Will you promise to bear up if I tell you? Well, then, Mrs. G. is lodging for three months at the public expense in Ipswich jail, which the beaks gave her for assault 'with intent to do grievous bodily harm'—them was the words, for I went to hear the case—'upon the person of her lawful husband, John Gillingwater'—and my! she did hammer him too—with a rolling pin! His face was like a squashed pumpkin, with no eyes left for a sinner to swear by. The guardians have taken pity on him too, and are nursing him well again, all for nothing, in the Union. I saw him hoeing taters there the other day, and he asked me if I couldn't smuggle him a bottle of gin—yes, and nearly cried when I told him that it wasn't to be done unless I had the cash in hand and a commission."

At this moment Willie's flow of information was interrupted by the guard, who told Joan that she must get into the train if she did not wish to be left.

"Ta-ta, Mrs. Rock," cried Willie after her: "see you again soon; and remember that the donkey is always ready. Now," he added to himself, "I wonder why the dickens she is going that way instead of home to her loving Sammy? He's a nasty mean beast, he is, and it's a rum go her having married him at all, but it ain't no affair of mine. All the same, I mean to let my dickies run down by the meres to-night, for I'm sure he can't grudge an armful of rough grass to an old friend of his wife's as has been the first to welcome her home. By the way, why ain't the holy Samuel here to welcome her home himself?" and Master Willie scratched his red head and departed speculating, with the full intention of pasturing his donkeys that night upon lands in the possession or hire of the said Samuel.

At Monk's Vale station Joan found a dog-cart waiting for her. When she had taken her seat she asked the groom if Mr. Levinger was ill. He replied that he didn't rightly know, but that his master had kept the house almost ever since Miss Emma—he meant Lady Graves—had married, and that last night, feeling queer, he had sent for a doctor.

Then Joan asked if Lady Graves was at Monk's Lodge, and was informed that she and her husband were not expected home at Rosham from abroad till this night or the next morning.

By this time they had reached the house, which was not more than half a mile distant from the station. The servant who opened the door took Joan to a bedroom and said that tea was waiting for her. When she was ready she went downstairs to the dining-room, where presently she received a message that Mr. Levinger would be glad to see her, and was shown to his room on the first floor. She found him seated in an armchair by a fire, although the weather was warm for June; and noticed at once that he was much changed since she had last seen him, his face being pale and thin and his form shrunken. His eyes, however, retained their brightness and intelligence, and his manner its vivacity. As she entered the room he attempted to rise to receive her, only to sink back into his chair with a groan, where for a while he remained speechless.

"It is very good of you to come to see me, Joan," he said presently. "Pray be seated."

"I am sorry to hear that you have not been well, sir," she answered.

"No, Joan, I have not; there never was a man further from health or much nearer to death than I am at this moment, and that is why I have sent for you, since what I have to say cannot be put off any longer. But you do not look very well yourself, Joan."

"I feel quite strong, thank you, sir. You know I had a bad illness, for you very kindly came to see me, and it has taken me a while to recover."

"I hear that you are married, Joan, although you are not living with your husband, Samuel Rock. It would, perhaps, have been well if you had consulted me before taking such a step, but you have a right to manage your own affairs. I trust that you are happy; though, if so, I do not understand why you keep away." And he looked at her anxiously.

"I am as happy as I ever shall be, sir, and I go to live with Mr. Rock to-morrow: till now I have been detained in town by business."

"You know that my daughter is married to Sir Henry Graves," he went on after a pause, again searching her face with his eyes. "They return home to-night or to-morrow; and not too soon if they wish to see me alive, though they know nothing of that, for I have told them little of my state of health."

"Yes, sir," she answered imperturbably, though her hands shook as she spoke. "But I suppose that you did not send for me to tell me that, sir."

"No, Joan, no. Is the door shut? I sent for you—O my God, that I should have to say it!—to throw myself upon your mercy, since I dare not die and face the Judgment-seat till I have told you all the truth. Listen to me"—and his voice fell to a piercing whisper—"Joan, you are my daughter!"

CHAPTER XXXVII

THE TRUTH, THE WHOLE TRUTH

"Your daughter!" she said, rising in her astonishment—"you must be mad! If I were your daughter, could you have lied to me as you did, and treated me as you have done?"

"I pray you to listen before you judge, and at present spare your reproaches, for believe me, Joan, I am not fit to bear them. Remember that I need have told you nothing of this; the secret might have been buried in my grave—"

"As it would have been, sir, had you not feared to die with such falsehood on your soul."

He made an imploring gesture with his hand, and she ceased.

"Joan," he went on, "I will tell you the whole truth. You are not only my child, you are also legitimate."

"And Miss Levinger—Lady Graves, I mean—is she legitimate too?"

"No, Joan."

She heard, and bit her lip till the blood ran, but even so she could not keep silence.

"Oh!" she cried, "I wonder if you will ever understand what you have done in hiding this from me. Do you know that you have ruined my life?"

"I pray that you may be mistaken, Joan. Heaven is my witness that I have tried to act for the best. Listen: many years ago, when I was still a youngish man, it was my fate to meet and to fall in love with your mother, Jane Lacon. Like you, she was beautiful, but unlike you she was hot-tempered, violently jealous, and, when she was angered, rough of speech. Such as she was, however, she obtained a complete empire over my mind, for I was headstrong and passionate; indeed, so entirely did I fall into her power that in the end I consented to marry her. This, however, I did not dare to do here, for in those days I was poor and struggling, and it would have ruined me. Separately, and without a word being said to any one, we went to London, and there were secretly married in an obscure parish in the East End. In proof of my words here is a copy of the certificate,"—and, taking a paper from a despatch-box that stood on the table beside him, he handed it to Joan, then went on:—

"As you may guess, a marriage thus entered into between two people so dissimilar in tastes, habits and education did not prove successful. For a month or so we were happy, then quarrels began. I established her in lodgings in London, and, while ostensibly carrying on my business as a land agent here, visited her from time to time. With this, however, she was not satisfied, for she desired to be acknowledged openly as my wife and to return with me to Bradmouth. I refused to comply—indeed, I dared not do so—whereupon she reviled me with ever-increasing bitterness. Moreover she became furiously jealous, and extravagant beyond the limit of my means. At length matters reached a climax, for a chance sight that she caught of me driving in a carriage with another woman, provoked so dreadful an outburst that in my rage and despair I told her a falsehood. I told her, Joan, that she was not really my wife, and had no claim upon me, seeing that I had married her under a false name. This in itself was true, for my own name is not Levinger; but it is not true that the marriage was thereby invalidated, since neither she nor those among whom I had lived for several years knew me by any other. When your mother heard this she replied only that such conduct was just what she should have expected from me; and that night I returned to Bradmouth, having first given her a considerable sum of money, for I did not think that I should see her again for some time. Two days afterwards I received a letter from her—here it is," and he read it:—

"'George,

"'Though I may be what you call me, a common woman and a jealous scold, at least I have too much pride to go on living with a scoundrel who has deceived me by a sham marriage. If I were as bad as you think, I might have the law of you, but I won't do that, especially as I dare say that we shall be best apart. Now I am going straight away where you will never find me, so you need not trouble to look, even if you care to. I haven't told you yet that I expect to have a child. If it comes to anything, I will let you know about it; if not, you may be sure that it is dead, or that I am. Good-bye, George: for a week or two we were happy, and though you hate me, I still love you in my own way; but I will never live with you again, so don't trouble your head any more about me.

"'Yours,
"'Jane —?

"'P.S.—Not knowing what my name is, I can't sign it.'

"When I received this letter I went to London and tried to trace your mother, but could hear nothing of her. Some eight or nine months passed by, and one day a letter came addressed to me, written by a woman in New York—I have it here if you wish to see it—enclosing what purports to be a properly attested American certificate of the death of Jane Lacon, of Bradmouth in England. The letter says that Jane Lacon, who passed herself off as a widow, and was employed as a housekeeper in a hotel in New York, died in childbirth with her infant in the house of the writer, who, by her request, forwarded the certificate of death, together with her marriage ring and her love.

"I grieved for your mother, Joan; but I made no further inquiries, as I should have done, for I did not doubt the story, and in those days it was not easy to follow up such a matter on the other side of the Atlantic.

"A year went by and I married again, my second wife being Emma Johnson, the daughter of old Johnson, who owed a fleet of fishing boats and a great deal of other property, and lived at the Red House in Bradmouth. Some months after our marriage he died, and we came to live at Monk's Lodge, which we inherited from him with the rest of his fortune. A while passed, and Emma was born; and it was when her mother was still confined to her room that one evening, as I was walking in front of the house after dinner, I saw a woman coming towards me carrying a fifteen-months' child in her arms. There was something in this woman's figure and gait that was familiar to me, and I stood still to watch her pass. She did not pass, however; she came straight up to me and said:—

"'How are you, George? You ought to know me again, though you won't know your baby.'

"It was your mother, and, Joan, you were that baby.

"'I thought that you were dead, Jane,' I said, so soon as I could speak.

"'That's just what I meant you to think, George,' she answered, 'for at that time I had a very good chance of marrying out there in New York, and didn't want you poking about after me, even though you weren't my lawful husband. Also I couldn't bear to part with the baby; though it's yours sure enough, and I've been careful to bring its birth papers with me to show you that it is not a fraud; and here they are, made out in your name and mine, or at least in the name that you pretended to marry me under.' And she gave me this certificate, which, Joan, I now pass on to you.

"'The fact of the matter is,' she went on, 'that when it came to the point I found that I couldn't marry the other man after all, for in my heart I hated the sight of him and was always thinking of you. So I threw him up and tried to get over it, for I was doing uncommonly well out there, running a lodging-house of my own. But it wasn't any use: I just thought of you all day and dreamed of you all night, and the end of it was that I sold up the concern and started home. And now if you will marry me respectable so much the better, and if you won't—well, I must put up with it, and sha'n't show you any more temper, for I've tried to get along without you and I can't, that's the fact. You seem to be pretty flourishing, anyway; somebody in the train told me that you had come into a lot of money and bought Monk's Lodge, so I walked here straight, I was in such a hurry to see you. Why, what's the matter with you, George? You look like a ghost. Come, give me a kiss and take me into the house. I'll clear out by-and-by if you wish it.'

"These, Joan, were your mother's exact words, as she stood there in the moonlight near the roadway, holding you in her arms. I have not forgotten a syllable of them.

"When she finished I was forced to speak. 'I can't take you in there,' I said, 'because I am married and it is my wife's house.' She turned ghastly white, and had I not caught her I think that she would have fallen.

"'O my God!' she said, 'I never thought of this. Well, George, you won't cast me off for all that, will you? I was your wife before she was, and this is your daughter.'

"Then, Joan, though it nearly choked me, I lied to her again, for what else was I to do? 'You never were my wife,' I said, 'and I've got another daughter now. Also all this is your own fault, for had I known that you were alive, I would not have married. You have yourself to thank, Jane, and no one else. Why did you send me that false certificate?'

"'I suppose so,' she answered heavily. 'Well, I'd best be off; but you needn't have been so ready to believe things. Will you look after the child if anything happens to me, George? She's a pretty babe, and I've taught her to say Daddy to nothing.'

"I told your mother not to talk in that strain, and asked her where she was going to spend the night, saying that I would see her again on the morrow. She answered, at her sister's, Mrs. Gillingwater, and held you up for me to kiss. Then she walked away, and that was the last time that I saw her alive.

"It seems that she went to the Crown and Mitre, and made herself known to your aunt, telling her that she had been abroad to America, where she had come to trouble, but that she had money, in proof of which she gave her notes for fifty pounds to put into a safe place. Also she said that I was the agent for people who knew about her in the States, and was paid to look after her child. Then she ate some supper, and saying that she would like to take a walk and look at the old place, as she might have to go up to London on the morrow, she went out. Next morning she was found dead beneath the cliff, though how she came there, there was nothing to show.

"That, Joan, is the story of your mother's life and death."

"You mean the story of my mother's life and murder," she answered. "Had you not told her that lie she would never have committed suicide."

"You are hard upon me, Joan. She was more to blame than I was. Moreover, I do not believe that she killed herself. It was not like her to have done so. At the place where she fell over the cliff there stood a paling, of which the top rail, that was quite rotten, was found to have been broken. I think that my poor wife, being very unhappy, walked along the cliff and leaned upon this rail wondering what she should do, when suddenly it broke and she was killed, for I am sure that she had no idea of making away with herself.

"After her death Mrs. Gillingwater came to me and repeated the tale which her sister had told her, as to my having been appointed agent to some person unknown in America. Here was a way out of my trouble, and I took it, saying that what she had heard was true. This was the greatest of my sins; but the temptation was too strong for me, for had the truth come out I should have been utterly destroyed, my wife would have been no wife, her child would have been a bastard, I should have been liable to a prosecution for bigamy, and, worse of all, my daughter's heritage might possibly have passed from her to you."

"To me?" said Joan.

"Yes, to you; for under my father-in-law's will all his property is strictly settled first upon his daughter, my late wife, with a life interest to myself, and then upon my lawful issue. You are my only lawful issue, Joan; and it would seem, therefore, that you are legally entitled to your half-sister's possessions, though of course, did you take them, it would be an act of robbery, seeing that the man who bequeathed them certainly desired to endow his own descendants and no one else, the difficulty arising from the fact of my marriage with his daughter being an illegal one. I have taken the opinions of four leading lawyers upon the case, giving false names to the parties concerned. Of these, two have advised that you would be entitled to the property, since the law is always strained against illegitimate issue, and two that equity would intervene and declare that her grandfather's inheritance must come to Emma, as he doubtless intended, although there was an accidental irregularity in the marriage of the mother.

"I have told you all this, Joan, as I am telling you everything, because I wish to keep nothing back; but I trust that your generosity and sense of right will never allow you to raise the question, for this money belongs to Emma and to her alone. For you I have done my best out of my savings, and in some few days or weeks you will inherit about four thousand pounds, which will give you a competence independent of your husband."

"You need not be afraid, sir," answered Joan contemptuously; "I would rather cut my fingers off than touch a farthing of the money to which I have no right at all. I don't even know that I will accept your legacy."

"I hope that you will do so, Joan, for it will put you in a position of complete independence, will provide for your children, and will enable you to live apart from your husband, should you by any chance fail to get on with him. And now I have told you the whole truth, and it only remains for me to most humbly beg your forgiveness. I have done my best for you, Joan, according to my lights; for, as I could not acknowledge you, I thought it would be well that you should be brought up in your mother's class—though here I did not make sufficient allowance for the secret influences of race, seeing that, notwithstanding your education, you are in heart and appearance a lady. I might, indeed, have taken you to live with me, as I often longed to do; but I feared lest such an act should expose me to suspicion, suspicion should lead to inquiry, and inquiry to my ruin and to that of my daughter Emma. Doubtless it would have been better, as well as more honest, if I had faced the matter out; but at the time I could not find the courage, and the opportunity went by. My early life had not been altogether creditable, and I could not bear the thought of once more becoming the object of scandal and of disgrace, or of imperilling the fortune and position to which after so many struggles I had at length attained. That, Joan, is my true story; and now again I say that I hope to hear you forgive me before I die, and promise that you will not, unless it is absolutely necessary, reveal these facts to your half-sister, Lady Graves, for if you do I verily believe that it will break her heart. The dread lest she should learn this history has haunted me for years, and caused me to strain every nerve to secure her marriage with a man of position and honourable name, so that, even should it be discovered that she had none, she might find refuge in her disgrace. Thank Heaven that I, who have failed in so many things, have at least succeeded in this, so that, come what may when I am dead, she is provided for and safe."

"I suppose, sir, that Sir Henry Graves knows all this?"

"Knows it! Of course not. Had he known it I doubt if he would have married her."

"Possibly not. He might even have married somebody else," Joan answered. "It seems, then, that you palmed off Miss Emma upon him under a false description."

"I did," he said, with a groan. "It was wrong, like the rest; but one evil leads to another."

"Yes, sir, one evil leads to another, as I shall show you presently. You ask me to forgive you, and you talk about the breaking of Lady Graves's heart. Perhaps you do not know that mine is already broken through you, or to what a fate you have given me over. I will tell you. Your daughter's husband, Sir Henry Graves, and I loved each other, and I have borne his child. He wished to marry me, though, believing myself to be what you have taught me to believe, I was against it from the first. When he learned my state he insisted upon marrying me, like the honourable man that he is, and told his mother of his intention. She came to me in London and pleaded with me, almost on her knees, that I should ward off this disgrace from her family, and preserve her son from taking a step which would ruin him. I was moved by her entreaties, and I felt the truth of what she said; but I knew well that, should he come to marry me, as within a few days he was to do, for our child's and our love's sake, if not for my own, I could never find the strength to deny him.

"What was I to do? I was too ill to run away, and he would have hunted me out. Therefore it came to this, that I must choose between suicide—which was both wicked and impossible, for I could not murder another as well as myself—and the still more dreadful step that at length I took. You know the man Samuel Rock, my husband, and perhaps you know also that for a long while he has persecuted me with his passion, although again and again I have told him that he was hateful to me. While I was ill he obtained my address in London—I believe that he bought it from my aunt, Mrs. Gillingwater, the woman in whose charge you were satisfied to leave me—and two days after I had seen Lady Graves, he came to visit me, gaining admission by passing himself off as Sir Henry to my landlady, Mrs. Bird.

"You can guess the rest. To put myself out of temptation, and to save the man I loved from being disgraced and contaminated by me, I married the man I hated—a man so base that, even when I had told him all, and bargained that I should live apart from him for many months, he was yet content to take me. I did more than this even: I wrote in such a fashion to Sir Henry as I knew must shock and revolt him; and then I married, leaving him to believe that I had thrown him over because the husband whom I had chosen was richer than himself. Perhaps you cannot guess why I should thus have dishonoured both of us, and subjected myself to the horrible shame of making myself vile in Sir Henry's eyes. This was the reason: had I not done so, had he once suspected the true motives of my sacrifice, the plot would have failed. I should have sold myself for nothing, for then he would never have married Emma Levinger. And now, that my cup may be full, my child is dead, and to-morrow I must give myself over to my husband according to the terms of my bond. This, sir, is the fruit of all your falsehoods; and I say, Ask God to forgive you, but not the poor girl—your own daughter—whom you have robbed of honour and happiness, and handed over to misery and shame."

Thus Joan spoke to him, in a quiet, almost mechanical voice indeed, but standing on her feet above the dying man, and with eyes and gestures that betrayed her absorbing indignation. When she had finished, her father, who was crouched in the chair before her, let fall his hands, wherewith he had hidden his face, and she saw that he was gasping for breath and that his lips were blue.

"'The way of transgressors is hard,' as we both have learned," he muttered, with a deathly smile, "and I deserve it all. I am sorry for you, Joan, but I cannot help you. If it consoles you, you may remember that, whereas your sorrows and shame are but temporal, mine, as I fear—will be eternal. And now, since you refuse to forgive me, farewell; for I can talk no more, and must make ready, as best I can, to take my evil doings hence before another, and, I trust, a more merciful Judge."

Joan turned to leave the room, but ere she reached the door the rage died out of her heart and pity entered it.

"I forgive you, father," she said, "for it is Heaven's will that these things should have happened, and by my own sin I have brought the worst of them upon me. I forgive you, as I hope to be forgiven. But oh! I pray that my time here may be short."

"God bless you for those words, Joan!" he murmured.

Then she was gone.

CHAPTER XXXVIII

A GHOST OF THE PAST

Lady Graves sat at breakfast in the dining-room at Rosham, where she had arrived from London on the previous evening, to welcome home her son and her daughter-in-law. Just as she was rising from the table the butler brought her a telegram.

"Your master and mistress will be here by half-past eleven, Thomson," she said. "This message is from Harwich, and they seem to have had a very bad crossing."

"Indeed, my lady!" answered the old man, whose face, like the house of Graves, shone with a renewed prosperity; "then I had better give orders about the carriage meeting them. It's a pity we hadn't a little more notice, for there's many in the village as would have liked to give Sir Henry and her ladyship a bit of a welcome."

"Yes, Thomson; but perhaps they can manage something of that sort in a day or two. Everything is ready, I suppose? I have not had time to go round yet."

"Well, I can't say that, my lady. I think that some of them there workmen won't have done till their dying day; and the smell of paint upstairs is awful. But perhaps your ladyship would like to have a look?"

"Yes, I should, Thomson, if you will give the orders about the carriage and to have some breakfast ready."

Thomson bowed and went, and, reappearing presently, led Lady Graves from room to room, pointing out the repairs that had been done to each. Emma's money had fallen upon the nakedness of Rosham like spring rains upon a desert land, with results that were eminently satisfactory to Lady Graves, who for many years had been doomed to mourn over threadbare carpets and shabby walls. At last they had inspected everything, down to the new glass in the windows of the servants' bedrooms.

"I think, Thomson," said Lady Graves, with a sigh of relief, "that, taking everything into consideration, we have a great deal to be thankful for."

"That's just what I says upon my knees every night, my lady. When I remember that if it hadn't been for the new mistress and her money (bless her sweet face!) all of us might have been sold up and in the workhouse by now, or near it, I feel downright sick."

"Well, you can cheer up now, Thomson, for, although for his position your master will not be a rich man, the bad times are done with."

"Yes, my lady, they are done with; and please God they won't come no more in my day. If your ladyship is going to walk outside I'll call March, as I know he's very anxious to show you the new vinery."

"Thank you, Thomson, but I think I will sit quiet and enjoy myself till Sir Henry comes, and then we can all go and see the gardens together. Mr. and Mrs. Milward are coming over this afternoon, are they not?"

"Yes, I believe so, my lady; that is, Miss Ellen—I mean Mrs. Milward—drove round with her husband yesterday to look at the new furniture in the drawing-room, and said that they should invite themselves to dinner to-night to welcome the bride. He's grown wonderful pleasant of late, Mr. Milward has, and speaks quite civil to the likes of us since Sir Henry's marriage; though March, he do say it's because he wants our votes—for I suppose you've heard, my lady, that he's putting up for Parliament in this division—but then March never was no believer in the human heart."

"Yes, I have heard, and I am told that Miss Ellen will pull him through. However, we need not think of that yet. By the way, Thomson, tell March to cut a bowlful of sweet peas and have them put in your mistress's room. I remember that when she was here as a girl, nearly three years ago, she said that they were her favourite flower."

When Thomson had gone Lady Graves sat herself down near the open door of the hall, whence she could see the glowing masses of the rose-beds and the light shifting on the foliage of the oaks in the park beyond, to read the morning psalms in accordance with her daily custom. Soon, however, the book dropped from her hand and she fell to musing on the past, and how strangely, after all its troubles, the family that she loved, and with which her life was interwoven, had been guided back into the calm waters of prosperity. Less than a year ago there had been nothing before them but ruin and extinction—and now! It was not for herself that she rejoiced; her hopes and loves and fears were for the most part buried in the churchyard yonder, whither ere long she must follow them; but rather for her dead husband's sake, and for the sake of the home of his forefathers, that now would be saved to their descendants.

Truly, with old Thomson, she felt moved to render thanks upon her knees when she remembered that, but for the happy thought of her visit to Joan Haste, things might have been otherwise indeed. She had since heard that this poor girl had married a farmer, that same man whom she had seen in the train when she went to London; for Henry had told her as much and spoken very bitterly of her conduct. The story seemed a little curious, and she could not altogether understand it, but she supposed that her son was right, and that on consideration the young woman, being a person of sense, had chosen to make a wise marriage with a man of means and worth, rather than a romantic one with a poor gentleman. Whatever was the exact explanation, without doubt the issue was most fortunate for all of them, and Joan Haste deserved their gratitude. Thinking thus, Lady Graves fell into a pleasant little doze, from which she was awakened by the sound of wheels. She rose and went to the front door to find Henry, looking very well and bronzed, helping his wife out of the carriage.

"Why, mother, is that you?" he said, with a pleasant laugh. "This is first-rate: I didn't expect from your letter that you would be down before to-morrow," and he kissed her. "Look, here is my invalid; I have been twenty years and more at sea, but till last night I did not imagine that a human being could be so sick. I don't know how she survived it."

"Do stop talking about my being sick, Henry, and get out of the way, that I may say how you do to your mother."

"Well, Emma," said Lady Graves, "I must say that, notwithstanding your bad crossing, you look very well—and happy."

"Thank you, Lady Graves," she answered, colouring slightly; "I am both well and happy."

"Welcome home, dear!" said Henry; and putting his arm round his wife, he gave her a kiss, which she returned. "By the way," he added, "I wonder if there is any news of your father."

"Thomson says he has heard that he is not very grand," answered Lady Graves. "But I think there is a postcard for you in his writing; here it is."

Henry read the card, which was written in a somewhat shaky hand. It said:—

"Welcome to both of you. Perhaps Henry can come and give me a look to-morrow; or, if that is not convenient, will you both drive over on the following morning?

"Yours affectionately,
"G. L."

"He seems pretty well," said Henry. "But I'll drive to Bradmouth and take the two o'clock train to Monk's Vale, coming back to-night."

"Ellen and her husband are going to be here to dinner," said Lady Graves.

"Oh, indeed! Well, perhaps you and Emma will look after them. I dare say that I shall be home before they go. No, don't bother about meeting me. Probably I shall return by the last train and walk from Bradmouth. I must go, as you remember I wrote to your father from abroad saying that I would come and see him to-day, and he will have the letter this morning."

After her interview with Mr. Levinger, for the first time in her life Joan slept beneath her father's roof—or rather she lay down to sleep, since, notwithstanding her weariness, the scene through which she had passed, together with the aching of her heart for all that she had lost, and its rebellion against the fate which was in store for her on the morrow, made it impossible that she should rest. Once towards morning she did doze off indeed, and dreamed.

She dreamt that she stood alone upon a point of rock, out of all sight or hope of shore, while round her raged a sea of troubles. From every side they poured in upon her to overwhelm her, and beneath the black sky above howled a dreary wind, which was full of voices crying to each other of her sins and sorrows across the abysm of space. Wave after wave that sea rolled on, and its waters were thick with human faces, or rather with one face twisted and distorted into many shapes, as though reflected from a thousand faulty mirrors—now long, now broad, and now short; now so immense that it filled the ocean and overflowed the edge of the horizon, and now tiny as a pin's point, yet visible and dreadful.

Gibbering, laughing, groaning, and shouting aloud, still the face was one face—that of Samuel Rock, her husband. Nearer it surged and nearer, till at length it flowed across her feet, halving itself against them; then the one half shouted with laughter and the other screamed in agony, and joining themselves together, they rose on the waters of that sea, which of a sudden had grown red, and, smiting her upon the breast, drove her down and down and down into the depths of an infinite peace, whence the voice of a child was calling her.

Then she awoke, and rejoiced to see the light of day streaming into the room; for she was frightened at her nightmare, though the sense of peace with which it closed left her strangely comforted. Death must be like that, she thought.

At breakfast Joan inquired of the servant how Mr. Levinger was; and, being of a communicative disposition, the girl told her that he had gone to bed late last night, after sitting up to burn and arrange papers, and said that he should stop there until the doctor had been. She added that a letter had arrived from Sir Henry announcing his intention of coming to see her master after lunch. Joan informed the woman that she should wait at Monk's Lodge to hear Dr. Childs's report, but that Mr. Levinger need not be troubled about her, since, having only a handbag with her, she could find her own way back to Bradmouth, either on foot or by train. Then she went to her room and sat down to think.

Henry was coming here, and she was glad of it; for, dreadful as such an interview would be, already she had made up her mind that she must see him alone and for the last time. Everything else she could bear, but she could no longer bear that he should think her vile and faithless. To-day she must go to her husband, but first Henry should learn why she went. He was safely married now, and no harm could come of it, she argued. Also, if she did not take this opportunity, how could she know when she might find another? An instinct warned her that her career in Bradmouth as the wife of Mr. Rock would be a short one; and at least she was sure that, when once she was in his power, he would be careful that she should have no chance of speaking with the man whom he knew to have been her lover. Yes, it might be unheroic and inconsistent, but she could keep silence no longer; see him she must and would, were it only to tell him that his child had lived, and was dead.

Moreover, there was another matter. She must warn him to guard against the secret which she had learned on the previous night being brought directly or indirectly to the knowledge of his wife. Towards Emma her feelings, if they could be defined at all, were kindly; and Joan guessed that, should Henry's wife discover how she had been palmed off upon an unsuspecting husband, it would shatter her happiness. For her own part, Joan had quickly made up her mind to let all this sad history of falsehood and dishonour sink back into the darkness of the past. It mattered to her little now whether she was legitimate or not, and it was useless to attempt to clear the reputation of a forgotten woman, who had been dead for twenty years, at the expense of blasting that of her own father. Also, she knew that if Samuel got hold of this story, he would never rest from his endeavours to wring from its rightful owner the fortune that might pass to herself by a quibble of the law. No, she had the proofs of her identity; she would destroy them, and if any others were to be found among her father's papers after his death Henry must do likewise.

When Dr. Childs had gone, about one o'clock, Joan saw the servant, who told her the doctor said that Mr. Levinger remained in much the same condition, and that he yet might live for another month or two. On the other hand, he might die at any moment, and, although he did not anticipate such immediate danger, he had ordered him to stay in bed, and had advised him to send for a clergyman if he wished to see one; also to write to his daughter, Lady Graves, asking her to come on the morrow and to stay with him for the present. Joan thanked the maid, and leaving a message for Mr. Levinger to the effect that she would come to see him again if he wished it, she started on her way, carrying her bag in her hand.

There were only two roads by which Henry could approach Monk's Lodge: the cliff road; and that which ran, through woodlands for the most part, to the Vale station, half a mile away. Joan knew that about three hundred yards from the Lodge at the end of the shrubberies, there was a summer-house commanding a view of the cliff and sea, and standing within twenty paces of the station road. Here she placed herself, so as to be able to intercept Henry by whichever route he should come; for she wished their meeting to be secret, and, for obvious reasons, she did not dare to await him in the immediate neighbourhood of the house.

She came to the summer-house, a rustic building surrounded at a little distance by trees, and much overgrown with masses of ivy and other creeping plants. Here Joan sat herself down, and picking up a mouldering novel left there long ago by Emma, she held it in her hand as though she were reading, while over the top of it she watched the two roads anxiously.

Nearly an hour passed, and as yet no one had gone by whom even at that distance she could possibly mistake for Henry; when suddenly her heart bounded within her, for a hundred yards or more away, and just at the turn of the station road, a view of which she commanded through a gap in the trees, she caught sight of the figure of a man who walked with a limp. Hastening from the summer-house, she pushed her way through the undergrowth and the hedge beyond, taking her stand at a bend in the path. Here she waited, listening to the sound of approaching footsteps and of a man's voice, Henry's voice, humming a tune that at the time was popular in the streets of London. A few seconds passed, which to her seemed like an age, and he was round the corner advancing towards her, swinging his stick as he came. So intent was he upon his thoughts, or on the tune that he was humming, that he never saw her until they were face to face. Then, catching sight of a lady in a grey dress, he stepped to one side, lifting his hand to his hat—looked up at her, and stopped dead.

"Henry," she said in a low voice.

"What! are you here, Joan," he asked, "and in that dress? For a moment you frightened me like a ghost—a ghost of the past."

"I am a ghost of the past," she answered. "Yes, that is all I am—a ghost. Come in here, Henry; I wish to speak to you."

He followed her without a word, and presently they were standing together in the summer-house.

Henry opened his lips as though to speak; but apparently thought better of it, for he said nothing, and it was Joan who broke that painful silence.

"I have waited for you here," she began confusedly, "because I have things that I must tell you in private."

"Yes, Mrs. Rock," he answered; "but do you not think, under all the circumstances, that it would be better if you told them to me in public? You know this kind of meeting might be misunderstood."

"Do not speak to me like that, I beg," she said, clasping her hands and looking at him imploringly; then added, "and do not call me by that name: I cannot bear it from you, at any rate as yet."

"I understand that it is your name, and I have no title to use any other."

"Yes, it is my name," she answered passionately; "but do you know why?"

"I know nothing except what your letters and your husband have told me, and really I do not think that I have any right to inquire further."

"No, but I have a right to tell you. You think that I threw you over, do you not, and married Mr. Rock for my own reasons?"

"I must confess that I do; you would scarcely have married him for anybody else's reasons."

"So you believe. Now listen to me: I married Samuel Rock in order that you might marry Emma Levinger. I meant to marry you, Henry, but your mother came to me and implored me not to do so, so I took this means of putting myself out of the reach of temptation."

"My mother came to you, and you did that! Why, you must be mad!"

"Perhaps; but so it is, and the plot has answered very well, especially as our child is dead."

"Our child!" he said, turning deathly pale: "was there any child?"

"Yes, Henry; and she was very like you. Her name was Joan. I thought that you would wish her to be called Joan. I buried her about a month ago."

For a moment he hid his face in his hands, then said, "Perhaps, Joan, you will explain, for I am bewildered."

So she told him all.

"Fate and our own folly have dealt very hardly with us, Joan," he said in a quiet voice when she had finished; "and now I do not see what there is to be done. We are both of us married, and there is nothing between us except our past and our dead child. By Heaven! you are a noble woman, but also you are a foolish one. Why could you not consult me instead of listening to my mother, or to any one else who chose to plead with you in my interests—and their own?"

"If I had consulted you, Henry, by now I should have been your wife."

"Well, and was that so terrible a prospect to you? As you know, I asked nothing better; and it chanced that I was able to obtain a promise of employment abroad which would have supported both of us in comfort. Or—answer me truly, Joan—did you, on the whole, as he told me, think that you would do better to marry Mr. Rock?"

"If Mr. Rock said that," she answered, looking at him steadily, "he said what he knew to be false, since before I married him I told him all the facts and bargained that I should live apart from him for a while.

Oh! Henry, how can you doubt me? I tell you that I hate this man whom I have married for your sake, that the sight of him is dreadful to me, and that I had sooner live in prison than with him. And yet to-day I go to him."

"I do not doubt you, Joan," he answered, in a voice that betrayed the extremity of his distress; "but the thing is so appalling that it paralyses me, and I know neither what to do nor to say. Do you want help to get away from him?"

She shook her head sadly, and answered, "I can escape from him in one way only, Henry—by death, for my bargain was that when the time of grace was ended I would come to be his faithful wife. After all he is my husband, and my duty is towards him."

"I suppose so—curse him for a cringing hound. Oh, Joan! The thought of it drives me mad, and I am helpless. I cannot in honour even say the words that lie upon my tongue."

"I know," she answered; "say nothing, only tell me that you believe me."

"Of course I believe you; but my belief will not save you from Samuel Rock, or me from my remorse."

"Perhaps not, dear," she answered quietly, "but since there is no escape we must accept the inevitable; doubtless things will settle themselves sooner or later. And now there is another matter of which I want to speak to you. You know your father-in-law is very ill, dying indeed, and yesterday he telegraphed for me to come to see him from London. What do you think that he had to tell me?"

Henry shook his head.

"This: that I am his legitimate daughter; for it seems that in marrying your wife's mother he committed bigamy, although he did not mean to do so."

"Oh! this is too much," said Henry. "Either you are mistaken, Joan, or we are all living in a web of lies and intrigues."

"I do not think that I am mistaken." Then briefly, but with perfect clearness, she repeated to him the story that Mr. Levinger had told her on the previous night, producing in proof of it the certificates of her mother's marriage and of her own birth.

"Why, then," he burst out when she had finished, "this old rogue has betrayed me as well as you! Now I understand why he was so anxious that I should marry his daughter. Did she know anything of this, Joan?"

"Not a word. Do not blame her, Henry, for she is innocent, and it is in order that she may never know, that I have repeated this story to you. Look, there go the proofs of it—the only ones." And taking the two certificates, she tore them into a hundred fragments and scattered them to the winds.

"What are you doing?" he said. "But it does not matter; they are only copies."

"It will be difficult for you to find the originals," she answered, with a sad smile, "for I was careful that you should see neither the name of the parish where my mother was married, nor the place of the registration of my birth."

"I will get those out of him," he said grimly, nodding his head towards the house.

"If you care for me at all, Henry, you will do nothing of the sort—for your wife's sake. I have been nameless so long that I can well afford to remain so; but should Lady Graves discover the secret of her birth and of her father's conduct, it would half kill her."

"That is true, Joan; and yet justice should be done to you. Oh! was ever a man placed so cruelly? What you have said about the money is just, for it is Emma's by right, but the name is yours."

"Yes, Henry; but remember that if you make a stir about the name, attempts will certainly be made to rob your wife of her fortune."

"By whom?"

"By my husband, to whose house I must now be going."

For a few moments there was silence, then Joan spoke again:—

"I forgot, Henry: I have something to give you that you may like to keep," and she took a tiny packet from her breast.

"What is it?" he said, shrinking back a little.

"Only—a lock of the—baby's hair." And she kissed it and gave it to him.

He placed the paper in his purse calmly enough. Then he broke down.

"Oh! my God," he said, with a groan, "forgive me, but this is more than I can bear."

Another second, and they were sobbing in each other's arms, seeing nothing of a man, with a face made devilish by hate and jealousy, who craned his head forward to watch them from the shelter of a thick bush some few yards away.

CHAPTER XXXIX

HUSBAND AND WIFE

When Joan parted from Henry she walked quickly to Monk's Vale station to catch the train. Arriving just in time, she bought a third-class ticket to Bradmouth, and got into an empty carriage. Already they were starting, when the door opened, and a man entered the compartment. At first she did not look at him, so intent was she upon her own thoughts, till some curious influence caused her to raise her eyes, and she saw that the man was her husband, Samuel Rock.

She gazed at him astonished, although it was not wonderful that she should chance to meet a person within a few miles of his own home; but she said nothing.

"How do you do, Joan?" Samuel began, and as he spoke, she noticed that his eyes were bloodshot and wild, and his face and hands twitched: "I thought I couldn't be mistook when I saw you on the platform."

"Have you been following me, then?" she asked.

"Well, in a way I have. You see it came about thus: this morning I find that young villain, Willie Hood, driving his donkeys off my foreshore pastures, and we had words, I threatening to pull him, and he giving me his sauce. Presently he says, 'You'd be better employed looking after your wife than grudging my dickies a bellyful of sea thistles; for, as we all know, you are a very affectionate husband, and would like to see her down here after she's been travelling so long for the benefit of her health.' Then, of course, I ask him what he may chance to mean; for though I have your letter in my pocket saying that you were coming home shortly, I didn't expect to have the pleasure of seeing you to-day, Joan; and he tells me that he met you last night bound for Monk's Vale. So you see to Monk's Vale I come, and there I find you, though what you may happen to be doing, naturally I can't say."

"I have been to see Mr. Levinger," she answered; "he is very ill, and telegraphed for me yesterday."

"Did he now! Of course that explains everything; though why he should want to see you it isn't for me to guess. And now where might you be going, Joan? Is it 'home, sweet home' for you?"

"I propose to go to Moor Farm, if you find it convenient."

"Oh, indeed! Well, then, that's all right, and you'll be heartily welcome. The place has been done up tidy for you, Joan, by the same man that has been working at Rosham to make ready for the bride. She's come home to-day too, and it ain't often in these parts that we have two brides home-coming together. It makes one wonder which of the husbands is the happier man. Well, here we are at Bradmouth, so if you'll come along to the Crown and Mitre I'll get my cart and we'll drive together. There are new folks there now. Your aunt's in jail, and your uncle is in the workhouse; and both well suited, say I, though p'raps you will think them a loss."

To all this talk, and much more like it, Joan made little or no answer. She was not in a condition to observe people or things closely, nevertheless it struck her that there was something very strange about Samuel's manner. It occurred to her even that he must have been drinking, so wild were his looks and so palpable his efforts to keep his words and gestures under some sort of control.

Presently they were seated in the cart and had started for Moor Farm. The horse was a young and powerful animal, but Samuel drove it quietly enough till they were clear of the village. Then he commenced to shout at it and to lash it with his whip, till the terrified beast broke into a gallop and they were tearing along the road at a racing pace.

"We can't get home too fast, can we, darling?" he yelled into her ear, "and the nag knows it. Come on, Sir Henry, come on! You know that a pretty woman likes to go the pace, don't you?" and again he bought down his heavy whip across the horse's flanks.

Joan clung to the rail of the cart, clenched her teeth and said nothing. Luckily the last half-mile of the road ran up a steep incline, and, notwithstanding Rock's blows and urgings, the horse, being grass-fed, became blown, and was forced to moderate its pace. Opposite the door of the house Rock pulled it up so suddenly that Joan was almost thrown on to her head; but, recovering her balance, she descended from the cart; which her husband gave into the charge of a labourer.

"Here's your missus come home at last, John," he said, with an idiotic chuckle. "Look at her: she's a sight for sore eyes, isn't she?"

"Glad to see her, I'm sure," answered the man. "But if you drive that there horse so you'll break his wind, that's all, or he'll break your neck, master."

"Ah! John, but you see your missus likes to go fast. We've been too slow up at Moor Farm, but all that's going to be changed now."

As he spoke two great dogs rushed round the corner of the house baying, and one of them, seeing that Joan was a stranger, leapt at her and tore the sleeve of her dress. She cried out in fear, and the man, John, running from the head of the horse, beat the dogs back.

"Ah! you would, Towser, would you?" said Rock. "You wait a moment, and I'll teach you that no one has a right to touch a lady except her husband," and he ran into the house.

"Don't go, pray," said Joan to the man; "I am frightened,"—and she shrank to his side for protection, for the dogs were still walking round her growling, their hair standing up upon their backs.

By way of answer John tapped his forehead significantly and whispered, "You look out for yourself, missus; he's going as his grandfather did. He's allus been queer, but I never did see him like this before."

Just then Rock reappeared from the house, carrying his double-barrelled gun in his hand.

"Towser, old boy! come here, Towser!" he said, addressing the dog in a horrible voice of pretended affection, that, however, did not deceive it, for it stood still, eyeing him suspiciously.

"Surely," Joan gasped, "you are not going—"

The words were scarcely out of her mouth when there was a report, and the unfortunate Towser rolled over on to his side dying, with a charge of No. 4 shot in his breast. The horse, frightened by the noise, started off, John hanging to the reins.

"There, Towser, good dog," said Rock, with a brutal laugh, "that's how I treat them that try to interfere with my wife. Now come in, darling, and see your pretty home."

Joan, who had hidden her eyes that she might not witness the dying struggles of the wretched dog, let fall her hand, and looked round wildly for help. Seeing none, she took a few steps forward with the idea of flying from this fiend.

"Where are you going, Joan?" he asked suspiciously. "Surely you are never thinking of running away, are you? Because I tell you, you won't do that; so don't you try it, my dear. If I'm to be a widower again, it shall be a real one next time." And he lifted the gun towards her and grinned.

Then, the man John having vanished with the cart, Joan saw that her only chance was to appear unconcerned, and watch for an opportunity to escape later.

"Run away!" she said: "what are you thinking of? I only wanted to see if the horse was safe," and she turned and walked through the deserted garden to the front door of the house, which she entered.

Rock followed her, locking the door behind her has he had done when Mrs. Gillingwater came to visit him, and with much ceremonious politeness ushered her into the sitting-room. This chamber had been re-decorated with a flaring paper, that only served to make it even more incongruous and unfit to be lived in by any sane person than before; and noting its gloom, which by contrast with the brilliant June sunshine without was almost startling, and the devilish faces of carven stone that grinned down upon her from the walls, Joan crossed its threshold with a shiver of fear.

"Here we are at last!" said Samuel. "Welcome to your home, Joan Rock!" And he made a movement as though to embrace her, which she avoided by walking straight past him to the farther side of the table.

"You'll be wanting something to eat, Joan," he went on. "There's plenty in the house if you don't mind cooking it. You see I haven't got any servants here at present," he added apologetically, "as you weren't expected so soon; and the old woman who comes in to do for me is away sick."

"Certainly I will cook the food," Joan answered.

"That's right, dear—I was afraid that you might be too grand but perhaps you would like to wash your hands first while I light the fire in the kitchen stove. Come here," and he led the way through the door near the fireplace to the foot of an oaken stair. "There," he said, "that's our room, on the right. It's no use trying any of the others, because they'll all locked up. I shall be just here in the kitchen, so you will see me when you come down."

Joan went upstairs to the room, which was large and well furnished, though, like that downstairs, badly lighted by one window only, and secured with iron bars, as though the place had been used as a prison at some former time. Clearly it was Samuel's own room, for his clothes and hat were hung upon some pegs near the door, and other of his possessions were arranged in cupboards and on the shelves.

Almost mechanically she washed her hands and tidied her hair with a brush from her handbag. Then she sat down and tried to think, to find only that her mind had become incapable, so numbed was it by all that she had undergone, and with the terrors mental and bodily of her present position. Nor indeed was much time allowed her for thought, since presently she heard the hateful voice of her husband calling to her that the fire was ready. At first she made no answer, whereon Samuel spoke again from the foot of the stairs, saying,—

"If you won't come down, dear, I must come up, as I can't bear to lose sight of you for so long at a time."

Then Joan descended to the kitchen, where the fire burnt brightly and a beef-steak was placed upon the table ready for cooking. She set to work to fry the meat and to boil the kettle and the potatoes; while Samuel, seated in a chair by the table, followed her every movement with his eyes.

"Now, this is what I call real pleasant and homely," he said, "and I've been looking forward to it for many a month as I sat by myself at night. Not that I want you to be a drudge, Joan—don't you think it. I've got lots of money, and you shall spend it: yes, you shall have your carriage and pair if you like."

"You are very kind," she murmured, "but I don't wish to live above my station. Perhaps you will lay the table and bring me the teapot, as I think that the steak is nearly done."

He rose to obey with alacrity, but before he left the room Joan saw with a fresh tremor that he was careful to lock the kitchen door and to put the key into his pocket. Evidently he suspected her of a desire to escape.

In a few more minutes the meal was ready, and they were seated tete-a-tete in the parlour.

When he had helped her Joan asked him if she should pour out the tea.

"No, never mind that wash," he said; "I've got something that I have been keeping against this day." And going to a cupboard he produced glasses and two bottles, one of champagne and the other of brandy. Opening the first, he filled two tumblers with the wine, giving her one of them.

"Now, dear, you shall drink a toast," he said. "Repeat it after me. 'Your health, dearest husband, and long may we live together.'"

Having no option but to fall into his humour, or run the risk of worse things, Joan murmured the words, although they almost choked her, and drank the wine—for which she was very thankful, for by now it was past seven o'clock, and she had touched nothing since the morning. Then she made shift to swallow some food, washing it down with sips of champagne. If she ate little, however, her husband ate less, though she noticed with alarm that he did not spare the bottle.

"It is not often that I drink wine, Joan," he said, "for I hold it sinful waste—not but what there'll always be wine for you if you want it. But this is a night to make merry on, seeing that a man isn't married every day," and he finished the last of the champagne. "Oh! Joan," he added, "it's like a dream to think that you've come to me at last. You don't know how I've longed for you all these months; and now you are mine, mine, my own beautiful Joan—for those whom God has joined together no man can put asunder, however much they may try. I kept my oath to you faithful, didn't I, Joan? and now it's your turn to keep yours to me. You remember what you swore—that you would be a true and good wife to me, and that you wouldn't see nothing of that villain who deceived you. I suppose that you haven't seen him during all these months, Joan?"

"If you mean Sir Henry Graves," she answered, "I met him to-day as I walked to Monk's Vale station."

"Did you now?" he said, with a curious writhing of the lips: "that's strange, isn't it, that you should happen to go to Monk's Lodge without saying nothing to your husband about it, and that there you should happen to meet him within a few hours of his getting back to England? I suppose you didn't speak to him, did you?"

"I spoke a few words."

"Ah! a few words. Well, that was wrong of you, Joan, for it's against your oath; but I dare say that they were to tell him just to keep clear in future?"

Joan nodded, for she dared not trust herself to speak.

"Well, then, that's all right, and he's done with. And now, Joan, as we've finished supper, you come here like a good wife, and put your arms round my neck and kiss me, and tell me that you love me, and that you hate that man, and are glad that the brat is dead."

Joan sat silent, making no answer. For a few moments he waited as though expecting her to move, then he rose and came towards her with outstretched arms.

Seeing his intention, she sprang from her chair and slipped to the other side of the table.

"Come," he said, "don't run from me, for our courting days are over, and it's silly in a wife. Are you going to say what I asked you, Joan?"

"No," she answered in a quiet voice, for her instincts overcame her fears; "I have promised to live with you, though you know why I married you, and I'll do it till it kills me, even if you are mad; but I'll not tell you a lie, for I never promised to love you, and I hate you now more than ever I did."

Samuel turned deadly white, then poured out a glass of neat brandy and drank it before he answered.

"That's straight, anyway, Joan. But it's queer that while you won't lie to me of one thing you ain't above doing it about another. P'raps you didn't know it, but I was there to-day when you had your 'few words' with your lover. He never saw me, but I followed him from Bradmouth step for step, though sometimes I had to hide behind trees and hedges to do it. You see I thought he would lead me to you; and so he did, for I saw you kissing and hugging—yes, you who belong to me—I saw you holding that man in your arms. Mad, do you say I am? Yes, I went mad then, though mayhap if you'd done that I asked you just now I might have got over it, for I felt my brain coming right; but now it is going again, going, going! And, Joan, since you hate me so bad, there is only one thing left to do, and that is—" And with a wild laugh he dashed towards the mantelpiece to reach down the gun which hung above it.

Then Joan's nerve broke down, and she fled. From the house itself there was no escape, for every door was locked; so, followed by the madman, she ran panting with terror upstairs to the room where she had washed her hands, and, shutting the door, shot the strong iron bolt—not too soon, for next instant her husband was dashing his weight against it. Very shortly he gave up the attempt, for he could make no impression upon oak and iron; and she heard him lock the door on the outside, raving the while. Then he tramped downstairs, and for a time there was silence. Presently she became aware of a scraping noise at the lattice; and, creeping along under shelter of the wall, she peeped round the corner of the window place. Already the light was low, but she could see the outlines of a white face glowering into the room through the iron bars without. Next instant there was a crash, and fragments of broken glass fell tinkling to the carpet. Then a voice spoke, saying, "Listen to me, Joan: I am here, on a ladder. I won't hurt you, I swear it; I was mad just now, but I am sane again. open the door, and let us make it up."

Joan crouched upon the floor and made no answer.

Now there came the sounds of a man wrenching at the bars, which apparently withstood all the strength that he could exert. For twenty minutes or more this went on, after which there was silence for a while, and gradually it grew dark in the room. At length through the broken pane she heard a laugh, and Samuel's voice saying:

"Listen to me, my pretty: you won't come out, and you won't let me in, but I'll be square with you for all that. You sha'n't have any lover to kiss to-morrow, because I'm going to make cold meat of him. It isn't you I want to kill; I ain't such a fool, for what's the use of you to me dead? I should only sit by your bones till I died myself. I've gone through too much to win you to want to be rid of you so soon. You'd be all right if it wasn't for the other man, and once he's gone you'll tell me that you love me fast enough; so now, Joan, I'm going to kill him. If he sticks to what I heard him tell his servant this morning, he should be walking back to Rosham in about an hour's time, by one of the paths that run past Ramborough Abbey wall. Well, I shall be waiting for him there, at the Cross-Roads, so that I can't miss him whichever way he comes, and this time we will settle our accounts. Good-bye, Joan: I hope you won't be lonely till I get home. I suppose that you'd like me to bring you a lock of his hair for a keepsake, wouldn't you? or will you have that back again which you gave him this day—the dead brat's, you know? You sit in there and say your prayers, dear, that it may please Heaven to make a good wife of you; for one thing's certain, you can't get out," and he began to descend the ladder.

Joan waited awhile and then peered through the window. She believed little of Samuel's story as to his design of murdering Henry, setting it down as an idle tale that he had invented to alarm her. Therefore she directed her thoughts to the possibility of escape.

While she was thus engaged she saw a sight which terrified her indeed: the figure of her husband vanishing into the shadows of the twilight, holding in his hand the double-barrelled gun with which he had shot the dog and threatened her. Could it, then, be true? He was walking straight for Ramborough, and swiftly—walking like a man who has some purpose to fulfil. She called to him wildly, but no answer came; though once he turned, looking towards the house, threw up his arm and laughed.

Then he disappeared over the brow of the slope.

CHAPTER XL

FULL MEASURE, PRESSED DOWN AND RUNNING OVER

Joan staggered back from the window, gasping in her terror. Her husband was mad with jealousy and hate and every other passion. She could see now that he had always been more or less mad, and that his frantic love for herself was but a form of insanity, which during the long months of their separation had deepened and widened until it obtained a complete mastery over his mind. Then by an evil fortune he had witnessed the piteous and passionate scene between Henry and herself, or some part of it, and at the sight the last barriers of his reason broke down, and he became nothing but an evil beast filled with the lust of revenge and secret murder. Now he had gone to shoot down his rival in cold blood; and this was the end of her scheming and self-sacrifice—that she had given herself to a lunatic and her lover to a bloody death!

So awful was the thought that for a while Joan felt as though her own brain must yield beneath it. Then of a sudden the desperate nature of the emergency came home to her, and her mind cleared. Henry was still unharmed, and perhaps he might be saved. Oh! if only she could escape from this prison, surely it would be possible for her to save him, in this way or in that. But how? If she could find any one about she might send to warn him and to obtain help; but this she knew was not likely, for nobody lived at Moor Farm except its master, and by now the labourers would have gone to their homes in the valley, a mile away. Well, once out of the house she might run to meet him herself? No, for then possibly she would be too late. Besides, there were at least three ways by which Henry could walk from Bradmouth—by the cliff road, by the fen path, or straight across the heath; and all these separate routes converged at a spot beneath the wall of the old Abbey, known as the Cross-Roads. That was why Samuel had chosen this place for his deed of blood: as he had told her, he knew that if he came at all his victim must pass within a few paces of a certain portion of the ruined churchyard fence.

What, then, could be done? Joan flung herself upon the bed and thought for a while, and as she lay thus a dreadful inspiration came into her mind.

If she could get free it would be easy for her to personate Henry. There upon the pegs hung a man's coat and a hat, not unlike those which he was wearing that day. They were much of a height, her hair was short, and she could copy the limp in his gait. Who then would know them apart, in the uncertain glimmer of the night? Surely not the maddened creature crouching behind some bush that he might satisfy his hate in blood. But so, if things went well, and if she did not chance to meet Henry in time to save him, as she hoped to do, she herself must die within an hour, or at the best run the risk of death! What of it? At least he would escape, for, whether or not her husband discovered his error, after all was over, she was sure that one murder would satiate his vengeance. Also would it not be better to die than to live the life that lay before her? Would it not even be sweet to die, if thereby she could preserve the man she loved more than herself a thousand times? She had made many a sacrifice for him; and this, the last, would be the lightest of them, for then he would learn how true she was to him, and always think of her with tenderness, and long to greet her beyond the nothingness of death. Besides, it might not come to this. Providence might interpose to rescue her and him. She might see him in time coming by the cliff road, or she might find her husband and turn him from his purpose.

Oh! her mind was mazed with terror for Henry, and torn by perplexities as to how she best might save his life. Well, there was no more leisure to search out a better plan; if she would act, it must be at once. Springing from the bed, she ran to the window, and throwing it wide, screamed for help. Her cries echoed through the silent air, but the only answer to them was the baying of the dog. There were matches on the mantelpiece—she had seen them; and, groping in the dark, she found the box and lit the candles. Then she tried the door; it was locked on the outside, and she could not stir it. Next she examined the window place, against which the ladder that Rock had set there was still standing. It was secured by three iron bars let into the brickwork at the top and screwed to the oaken sill at the bottom.

Scrutinising these bars closely, she saw that, although her husband had not been able to wrench them away, he had loosened the centre one, for in the course of many years the rust of the iron mixing with the tannin in the oak had widened the screw holes, so that the water, settling in them, had rotted that portion of the sill. Could she but force out this bar she would be able to squeeze her body through the gap and to set her feet upon the ladder.

There was a fireplace in the room, and, resting on the dogs in front of it, lay a heavy old-fashioned poker. Seizing it, she ran to the window and struck the bottom of the centre bar again and again with all her strength. The screws began to give. Now they were half-way out of the decaying woodwork, but she could force them no farther with blows. For a moment Joan seemed to be baffled, then she took refuge in a new expedient. Thrusting the poker outside of the bar to the right, and the end of it inside that which she was seeking to dislodge, she obtained a powerful leverage and pulled in jerks. At the third jerk her hand came suddenly in contact with the sharp angle of the brickwork, that rasped the skin from the back of it; the screws gave way, and the bar, slipping from the hole in which its top end was set, fell clattering down the ladder.

Now the road was open, and it remained only for her to dress herself to the part. Half crying with the pain of her hurt and bleeding hand, quickly Joan put on the hat and overcoat, remembering even then that they were the same which Rock had worn when he came to see her in London, and, going to the window, she struggled through the two remaining bars on to the ladder. Reaching the ground, she ran through the garden to the heathland, for she feared lest the surviving dog should espy and attack her. But no dog appeared: perhaps the corpse of its brother that still lay by the gate kept it away.

Now she was upon the heathland and heading straight for the ruins of Ramborough, which lay at a distance of about three-quarters of a mile from the house. The night was fine and the air soft, but floating clouds now and again obscured the face of the half-moon, that lay low in the sky, causing great shadows to strike suddenly across the moor. Her way ran past the meres, where the wind whispered drearily amongst the growing reeds and the nesting wildfowl called to each other across the water. There was a great loneliness about the place; no living creature was to be seen; and, at the moment, this feeling of solitude weighed more heavily upon her numbed heart than the sense of the death that she was courting. The world was still with her, and its moods and accidents affected her as they had always done; but the possibilities of that other unrisen world upon whose brink she stood, and the fear of it, moved her but little, and she scarcely thought of what or where she might or might not be within an hour. Those terrors were to come.

She was past the meres, and standing on a ridge of ground that lies between them and the cliff. Before her, when the moon shone out, she could see the glimmer of the ocean, the white ribbon of the road, and the ruins of Ramborough showing distinctly against the delicate beauty of the twilight summer sky. On she went, scanning the heath and the cliff with eager eyes, in the hope that she might discover the man she sought. It was in vain; the place was empty and desolate, a home of solitude.

At length she stood upon the border of the cliff road, and the Abbey was in line with her some two hundred yards to the right. Here she paused awhile, staring into the shadows and listening earnestly. But there was nothing to be seen except the varying outlines of the clouds, and nothing to be heard save the murmur of the sea, the stirring of the wind among the grasses, and now and again the cry of some gull seeking its food by night.

Now it was, as she stood thus, that a great fear of death took her, and it seemed as though all her past life went before her in pictures, full, every one of them, of exact and bewildering detail. For the most part these pictures were not pleasant, yet it chilled her to remember that the series might so soon be ended. At the least they were human and comprehensible, whereas what lay beyond might be inhuman and above her understanding. Also it came home to her that she was not fit to die: until her child was taken from her, she had never turned much to religion, and of late she had thought more of her own cruel misfortunes and of her lost lover than of her spiritual responsibilities, of the future welfare of her soul.

She was minded to fly; she had escaped from her prison, and no law could force her to live with a madman. Why should she not go back to Monk's Lodge, or to London, to seek a new existence for herself, leaving these troubles behind her? After all, she was young and beautiful, and it was sweet to live; and now that she was near to it the death which once she had so passionately desired seemed a grim, unfriendly thing.

But then there was Henry. He was lost to her, indeed, and the husband of another woman; yet, if she deserted him now, what would become of him? His career was before him—a long and happy career—and it was pitiable to think that within some few minutes he might be lying in the grass murdered for her sake by a wretched lunatic. And yet, if she offered herself up for him, what must be the end of it? It would be that after a period of shock and disturbance his life would fall back into its natural courses, and, surrounded by the love of wife and children, he would forget her, or, at the best, remember her at times with a vague, affectionate regret. No man could spend his days in mourning continually over a passionate and inconvenient woman, who had brought him much sorrow and anxiety, even though in the end she chanced to have given him the best proof possible of her affection, by laying down her life for his.

Well, so let it be. Afraid or not afraid, she would offer what she had, and the gift must be valued according to its worth in the eyes of him to whom it was given. Existence was a tangle which she had been quite unable to loose, and now, although her dread was deep, she was willing that Death should cut its knot; for here she had no hope, and, unless it pleased fate that it should be otherwise, to Death she would consign herself.

All these thoughts, and many others, passed through her mind in that brief minute, while, tossed between love and terror, Joan stood to search the landscape and recover her breath. Then, with one last glance over the moorland, she stepped on to the road and began to walk slowly towards the Abbey. Fifty yards away the three paths met, but the ground lay so that to reach the Cross-Roads, their junction, and to see even a little distance along the other two of them, she must pass the corner of the broken churchyard wall. Dared she do it, knowing that perchance there her death awaited her? Coward that she was, while she lingered Henry might be murdered! Even now, perhaps this very instant, he was passing to his doom by one of the routes which she could not see.

She paused a moment, looking up the main road in the hope that she might catch sight of Henry advancing down it. But she could perceive no one; an utter loneliness brooded on the place. Moreover, the moon at this moment was obscured by a passing cloud. For aught she knew, the deed was already done—only then she would have heard the shot—or perhaps Henry had driven to Rosham, or had gone by the beach, or the fit of homicidal mania had passed from her husband's mind. Should she go on, or wait there, or run away? No, she must reach the Cross-Roads: she would not run; she would play the hand out.

Of a sudden a strange excitement or exaltation of mind took possession of her; her nerves tingled, and the blood drummed in her ears. She felt like some desperate gambler staking his wealth and reputation on a throw, and tasted of the gambler's joy. For a moment, under the influence of this new mood, the uncertainty of her fate became delightful to her, and she smiled to think that few have played such a game as this, of which the issues were the salvation of her lover and the hazard of her mortal breath.

Now she began to act her part, walking forward with a limp like Henry's, till she was opposite to and some five yards away from the angle of the churchyard wall. Here a swift change came over her; the false excitement passed away, and again she grew mortally afraid. She could not do it! The Cross-Roads were now not twenty paces from her, and once there she might see him and save him. But never could she walk past that wall, knowing that behind it a murderer might be lurking, that every stone and bush and tuft of grass might hide him who would send her to a violent and cruel death. It was very well to make these heroic resolutions at a distance, but when the spot and moment of their execution were at hand—ah! then the thing was different! She prayed God that Henry had escaped, or might escape, but she could not take this way to preserve him. Her mind was willing, but the poor flesh recoiled from it. She would call aloud to her husband, and reveal herself to him if he were there. No, for then he would guess her mission, render her helpless in this way or that—what chance had she against a madman?—and afterwards do the deed. So it came to this: she must go back and wait, upon the chance of meeting Henry on the cliff road, for forward she dared not go.

Already she had turned to fly, when her ear caught a sound in the intense silence—such a sound as might have been made by some beast of prey dragging itself stealthily towards its victim. Instantly Joan became paralysed; the extremity of terror deprived her of all use of her limbs or voice, and so she stood with her back towards the wall. Now there was a new sound, as of something rising quickly through deep grass or brushwood, and then she heard the dull noise of the hammer of a gun falling upon an uncapped nipple. In a flash she interpreted its meaning: her husband had forgotten to reload that barrel with which he shot the dog!

There was still a chance of life for her, and in this hope Joan's vital powers returned. Uttering a great cry, she swung round upon her heel so swiftly that the hat fell from her head, and the moonlight passing from the curtain of a cloud, shone upon her ashy face. As she turned, her eyes fell upon another face, the face of a devil—of Samuel Rock. He was standing behind the wall, that reached to his breast, and the gun in his hand was levelled at her. A tongue of flame shot out, and, in the glare of it, it seemed to her that his countenance of hellish hate had changed its aspect to one of agony. Then Joan became aware of a dull shock at her breast, and down she sank senseless on the roadway.

Joan was right. Perceiving her from the Cross-Roads knoll, his place of outlook, whence, although himself invisible, he commanded a view of the three paths, Rock, deceived by her disguise and assumed lameness, into the belief that his wife was Henry advancing by the cliff road, had crept towards her under shelter of the wall to kill her as she stood. But in that last moment he learned his error—too late! Yes, before the deed was done he tasted the agony of knowing that he was wreaking murder upon the woman he desired, and not upon the man she loved. Too late! Already his finger had contracted on the trigger, and the swift springs were at their work. He tried to throw up the gun, but as the muzzle stirred, the charge left it to bury itself in the bosom of his wife.

Casting down the gun, he sprang over the wall and ran to her. She was lying on her back, dead as he thought, with opened eyes and arms thrown wide. Once he looked, then with yells of horror the madman bounded from her side and rushed away, he knew not whither.

When Henry parted with Joan in the Monk's Lodge summer-house that morning, anger and bitter resentment were uppermost in his mind, directed first against his father-in-law, and next against his family, more particularly his mother. He had been trapped and deluded, and now, alas! it was too late to right the wrong. Indeed, so far as his wife was concerned, he could not even speak of it. Joan spoke truly when she said that Emma must never hear of these iniquities, or learn that both the name she had borne and the husband whom she loved had been filched from another woman. Poor girl! at least she was innocent; it must be his duty to protect her from the consequences of the guilt of others, and even from a knowledge of it.

But Levinger, her father, was not innocent, and towards him he was under no such obligation. Therefore, sick or well, he would pour out his wrath upon him, and to his face would call him the knave and liar that he was.

But it was not fated that in this world Mr. Levinger should ever listen to the reproaches of his son-in-law. When Henry reached the house he was informed that the sick man had fallen into a restless sleep, from which he must not be disturbed. Till nine o'clock that sleep endured, while Henry waited with such patience as he could command; then suddenly there was a cry and a stir, and the news was brought to him that, without the slightest warning or premonition of immediate danger, Mr. Levinger had passed from sleep into death.

Sobered and calmed by the shock of such tidings, Henry gave those orders which were necessary, and then started for home, where he must break the fact of her father's death to Emma. He had arranged to return to Bradmouth by the last train; but it was already gone, so he drove thither in the dog-cart that went to advise Dr. Childs and others of what had happened, and thence set out to walk to Rosham half an hour or so later than he had intended. He might have hired a cart and driven, but being the bearer of this heavy news, naturally enough he had no wish to hurry; moreover he was glad of the space of quiet that a lonely walk by night afforded him, for he had much to think of and to grieve over. It was, he felt, a good thing that the old man should have died before he spoke with him; for though certainly he would have done it, there was little use in reproaching him with falsehoods and treachery the results of which could not now be remedied.

Poor Joan! Hers was indeed a hard lot—harder even than his own! It was a year this day, he remembered, since first he had met her yonder by the ruins of Ramborough Abbey. Who could know all that she had suffered during this eventful year, or measure what was left for her to suffer in the time to come? Alas! he could see no escape for her; she had entered on an unnatural marriage, but still it was a marriage, and she must abide by her bargain, from which nothing could free her except the death of her husband or of herself. And this she had done for his sake, to safeguard him: ah! there was the bitterest part of it.

While Henry walked on, chewing the cud of these unhappy reflections, suddenly from the direction of Ramborough Abbey, that was a quarter of a mile or more away, there floated to his ear the sound of a single cry—far off, indeed, but strangely piercing, followed almost instantly by the report of a gun loaded with black powder. He halted and listened, trying to persuade himself that the cry was that of some curlew which a poacher had shot out of season; only to abandon the theory so soon as he conceived it, for something in his heart told him that this scream was uttered by mortal lips—by the lips of a woman in despair or agony. A few seconds passed, and he heard other sounds, those of short, sharp yells uttered in quick succession, but of so inhuman a note that he was unable to decide if they proceeded from a man or from some wounded animal.

He started forward at a run to solve the mystery, and as he went on the yells grew louder and came nearer. Presently he halted, for there, from over the crest of a little rise in the road, and not fifteen paces away, appeared the figure of a man running with extraordinary swiftness. His hat had fallen from him, his long hair seemed to stand up upon his head, his eyes stared white in terror and were ablaze with the fire of madness, his face was contorted and ashy white, and from his open mouth issued hideous and unearthly sounds. So shocking was his aspect in the moonlight that Henry sprang to one side and bethought him of the tale of the Ramborough goblin. Now the man was level with him, and as he went by he turned his head to look at him, and Henry knew the face for that of Samuel Rock.

"Dead!" shrieked the madman, wringing his hands, "dead, dead!" and he was gone.

Henry gasped, for his heart grew cold with fear. Joan had left him to join her husband; and now, what had happened? That cry, the gunshot, and the sight that he had seen, all seemed to tell of suicide or murder. No, no, he would not believe it! On he went again, till presently he saw a lad running towards him who called to him to stop.

"Who are you?" he gasped, "and what is the matter here?"

"I'm Willie Hood, and that's just what I should like to know, Sir Henry," was the answer, "more especial as not five minutes since I thought that I saw you walking up to the Abbey yonder."

"You saw me walking there! Rubbish! I have just come from Bradmouth. Did you see that man, Rock, run by?"

"Yes, I see'd him fast enough. I should say by the looks of him that he has been doing murder and gone mad. Half an hour ago, before you came along, or begging your pardon, some one as limped like you, he had a gun in his hand, but that's gone now."

"Look here, young man," said Henry, as they went forward, "what are you doing here, that you come to see all these things?"

"Well, sir, to tell the truth, I was driving my donkeys to feed on Rock's land, and when I saw him coming along with a gun I hid in the bracken; for we had words about my taking his feed this very morning, and he swore then that if he caught me at it again he'd shoot me and the dickies too; so I lay pretty close till I saw the other man go by and heard the shriek and the shot."

"Come along, for Heaven's sake!" said Henry: "that devil must have killed some one."

Now they were near to the Abbey wall, and Willie, catching his companion by the arm, pointed to a dark shape which lay in the white dust of the roadway, and in a terrified whisper said, "Look there! what's that?"

Henry dashed forward and knelt down beside the shape, peering at its face. Then of a sudden he groaned aloud and said, "It is Joan Haste, and he has shot her!"

"Look at her breast!" whispered Willie, peeping over his shoulder. "I told her how it would be. It was I who found you both a year ago just here and looking like that, and now you see we have all come together again. I told her it was a bad beginning, and would come to a bad end."

"Be silent, and help me to lift her," said Henry in a hollow voice; "perhaps she still lives."

Then together they raised her, and at that moment Joan opened her eyes.

"Listen, you!" Henry said: "she is alive. Now run as you never ran before, to Dr. Childs at Bradmouth, to the police, and anybody else you can think of. Tell them what has happened, and bid them come here as fast as horses can bring them. Do you understand?"

"Yes, sir."

"Then go."

Willie sprang forward like an arrow, and presently the sound of his footsteps beating on the road grew faint and faded away.

"Oh! Joan, Joan, my darling," Henry whispered as he leant over her, pressing her cold hands. "Cannot you speak to me, Joan?"

At the sound of his voice the great empty eyes began to grow intelligent, and the pale lips to move, faintly at first, then more strongly.

"Is that you, Henry?" she said in a whisper: "I cannot see."

"Yes. How did you come thus?"

"He was going to murder you. I—I passed myself off for you—at least, I tried to—but grew afraid, and—was running away when he—shot me."

"Oh! my God, my God!" groaned Henry: "to think that such a thing should have been allowed to be!"

"It is best," she answered, with a faint smile; "and I do not suffer—much."

Then he knelt down beside her and held her in his arms, as once on a bygone day she had held him. The thought seemed to strike her, for she said:—

"A year ago, to-night; do you remember? Oh! Henry, if I have sinned, it has been paid back to me to the uttermost. Surely there can be nothing more to suffer. And I am happy because—I think that you will love me better dead than ever you did alive. 'The way of transgressors—the way of—'" and she ceased, exhausted.

"I shall love you now, and then, and always—that I swear before God," he answered. "Forgive me, Joan, that I should ever have doubted you for a moment. I was deceived, and did not understand you."

Again she smiled and said, "Then I have done well to die, for in death I find my victories—the only ones. But you must love the child also—our child—Henry, since we shall wait for you together in the place—of peace."

A while went by, and she spoke again, but not of herself or him:—

"I have left Mrs. Bird in London—some money. When Mr. Levinger is dead—there will be a good deal; see that—she gets it, for they were kind to me. And, Henry, try to shield my husband—for I have sinned against him—in hating him so much. Also tell your wife nothing—or you will make her wretched—as I have been."

"Yes," he answered, "and your father is dead; he died some hours ago."

After this Joan closed her eyes, and, bleeding inwardly from her pierced lungs, grew so cold and pulseless that Henry thought she must be gone. But it was not so, for when half an hour or more had passed she spoke, with a great effort, and in so low a whisper that he could scarcely hear her words, though his ear was at her mouth.

"Pray God to show me mercy, Henry—pray now and always. Oh, one hour of love—and life and soul to pay!" she gasped, word by word. Then the change came upon her face, and she added in a stronger voice, "Kiss me: I am dying!"

So he pressed his lips on hers; and presently, in the midst of the great silence, Joan Haste's last sobbing breath beat upon them in a sigh, and the agony was over.

Two hours later Henry arrived at Rosham, to find his mother and Mr. and Mrs. Milward waiting to receive him.

"My dear Henry, where have you been?" said Lady Graves, "It is twelve o'clock, and we were beginning to fear that something had gone wrong at Monk's Lodge."

"Or that you had met with another accident, dear," put in Ellen. "But I haven't given you a kiss yet, to welcome you home. Why, how pale you look! and what is the matter with your coat?"

"Where is Emma?" he asked, waving her back.

"She was so dreadfully tired, dear," said Lady Graves, "that I insisted upon her going to bed. But has anything happened, Henry?"

"Yes, a great deal. Mr. Levinger is dead: he died in his sleep this evening."

Lady Graves sank back shocked; and Ellen exclaimed, "How dreadfully sad! However, his health was very bad, poor man, so it is something of a release. Also, though you won't care to think of such things now, there will be advantage for Emma—"

"Be silent, Ellen. I have something more to tell you. Joan Haste, or rather Joan Rock, is dead also."

"Dead!" they both exclaimed.

"Yes, dead,—or, to be more accurate, murdered."

"Who murdered her?" asked Milward.

"Her husband. I was walking back from Bradmouth, and found her dying in the road. But there is no need to tell you the story now—you will hear plenty of it; and I have something else to say. Do you mind leaving the room for a moment, Mr. Milward? I wish to speak to my mother and sister."

"Edward is my husband, Henry, and a member of the family."

"No doubt, Ellen, but I do not desire that he should hear what I have to say. If you feel strongly about the matter I will go into the library with my mother."

"Oh! pray don't trouble about me," answered Edward; "I am accustomed to this sort of thing here, and I shall only be too glad to smoke a cigar in the hall, if Sir Henry does not object"; and he left the room, an example which Ellen did not follow.

"Now that we are quite alone, Henry, perhaps you will condescend to unbosom yourself," she said.

"Certainly, Ellen. I have told you that this unhappy woman has been murdered. She died in my arms"—and he glanced at his coat—"now I will tell you why and how. She was shot down by her husband, who mistook her for me, whom he meant to murder. She discovered his plan and personated me, dying in my stead. I do not wish to reproach either of you; the thing is too fearful for reproaches, and that account you can settle with your own consciences, as I must settle mine. But you worked so, both of you, that, loving me as she did, and feeling that she would have no strength to put me away otherwise, she gave herself in marriage to a man she hated, to the madman who to-night has slaughtered her in his blind jealousy, meaning to slaughter me. Do you know who this woman was, mother? She was Mr. Levinger's legitimate daughter: it is Emma who is illegitimate; but she died begging me to keep the secret from my wife, and if you are wise you will respect her wish, as I shall. I have nothing more to say. Things have gone amiss between us, whoever is to blame; and now—her life is lost, and—mine is ruined."

"Oh! this is terrible, terrible!" said Lady Graves. "God knows that, whatever I have done, I acted for what I believed to be the best."

"Yes, mother," said Ellen boldly, "and not only for what you believed to be the best, but for what is the best. This unfortunate girl is dead, it seems, not through any deed of ours, but by the decrees of Providence. Henry says that his life is ruined; but do not grieve, mother,—he is not himself, and he will think very differently in six months' time. Also he is responsible for this tragedy and no one else, since it springs from his own sin. 'Les desirs accomplis,'—you know the saying. Well, he has accomplished his desire; he sowed the seed, and he must reap the fruit and harvest it as best he may.

"And now, with your permission, Henry, I will order the carriage. I suppose that there will be policemen and reporters here presently, and you can understand that just at this moment, with the elections coming on, Edward and I do not wish to be mixed up in a most painful scandal."

H. Rider Haggard – A Short Biography

Sir Henry Rider Haggard, KBE was born on June 22nd, 1856 at Bradenham in Norfolk, England.

More familiarly known as H. Rider Haggard, he was the eighth of ten children born to Sir William Meybohm Rider Haggard, a barrister (born, incidentally, in St Petersburg, Russia), and Ella Doveton, an author, poet and daughter of a merchant in the East India Trading Company.

Haggard was initially schooled at Garsington Rectory in Oxfordshire where he studied under the tutelage of Reverend H. J. Graham. His elder brothers, who seemed to find more favour with their father, graduated from various private schools whilst Haggard was sent to Ipswich Grammar School, saving his father a considerable sum in fees.

He failed his army entrance exam, and was therefore sent to a private crammer in London in preparation for the entrance exam to the British Foreign Office, which he appears never to have sat. However, it was during his two years in London that Haggard came into contact with a circle of people interested in the study of psychical phenomena and for which he too now developed a life-long interest together with a series of enduring friendships.

In 1875, Haggard's father used his family's connections to send him to Southern Africa to take up an unpaid position as assistant to the secretary to Sir Henry Bulwer, Lieutenant-Governor of the Colony of Natal. In 1876 he was transferred to the staff of Sir Theophilus Shepstone, Special Commissioner for the Transvaal. It was in this role that Haggard was present in Pretoria in April 1877 for the official announcement of the British annexation of the Boer Republic of the Transvaal. The official who had been nominated to read out the Proclamation lost his voice and Haggard was his replacement. It was a moment in history.

Haggard was to remain in the country for six years, during which time he served as Master of the High Court of the Transvaal and an adjutant of the Pretoria Horse.

It was here that he fell in love with Mary Elizabeth "Lilly" Jackson. He hoped to marry her once he obtained more certainty in his career path.

In 1878 he became Registrar of the High Court in the Transvaal and now the time seemed opportune to write to his father to tell him of his hope to marry. The reply from his father was uncompromising. He forbade it until his son had made a proper career for himself.

The following year, 1879, Lily married Frank Archer, a well-to-do banker.

Haggard returned briefly to England to marry a friend of his sister's, Marianna Louisa Margitson, a 21 year old, in 1880, and the couple travelled to Africa together. Haggard's years in Africa had proved, at least on a writing level, rich and inspirational for him, and while still in Natal he wrote two articles for The Gentleman's Magazine describing his experiences.

Moving back to England in (and accounts here differ as to whether it was 1881 or 1882) the couple settled in Ditchingham, Norfolk, Louisa's ancestral home. Later they moved to Kessingland and established connections with the church in Bungay, Suffolk. The marriage produced four children. A son named Jack (who tragically died at age 10 of measles) and three daughters, Angela, Dorothy and Lilias. (Lilias grew to become an author and her father's biographer.)

In England Law was to be the fulcrum of his career. However, although he studied, writing was growing in its appeal to him. His first book, Cetywayo and His White Neighbours, was an account and study of Britain's policies in South Africa.

From this point his career as a writer began to take substantial hold and with it a dramatic shift to fiction. Two years later he published his first fiction, Dawn followed in 1885 by arguably his most popular novel, King Solomon's Mines—detailing the life of the adventurer Allan Quatermain. This was followed the following year, 1886, by She: A History of Adventure, which introduced the female character Ayesha. Both characters, Quatermain and Ayesha, developed a series of books about their adventures.

The study of Law now fell away entirely. He appeared also to have a keen sense of his commercial appreciation. Rather than sell the copyright of his first best-seller, King Solomon's Mines, for a £100 fee he, instead, accepted a 10% royalty. This book is also generally accepted as the first of the Lost World writing genre.

Haggard obviously thought there were many further adventures to tell and it would be hard to find a publisher who would disagree given the start he had made. Sequels soon followed. Allan Quatermain continued his epic and swash-buckling adventures in Africa whilst the sequel to She entitled Ayesha played out her adventures in Tibet. Interestingly Haggard would later extend his characters adventures around the world with Eric Brighteyes, being the basis for an epic Viking romance.

The Haggard family lived at 69 Gunterstone Road in Hammersmith, London, from mid-1885 to mid-1888. It was here that he wrote his most famous works. His time in Africa had given him the experience and atmosphere as well as several observations and friendships of the people who would so influence his fictional characters. Chief among them were the larger-than-life adventurers Frederick Selous and Frederick Russell Burnham. Both were men of Empire and huge ambition as they helped uncover the great mineral wealth of Africa, as well as the ruins of ancient lost civilisations of the continent, such as Great Zimbabwe.

Three of Haggard's books, The Wizard (1896), Black Heart and White Heart; a Zulu Idyll (1896), and Elissa; the Doom of Zimbabwe (1898), are dedicated to Burnham's daughter Nada, the first white child born in Bulawayo; she had been named after Haggard's 1892 book Nada the Lily.

As is typical of the writing of the time his novels contain many of the stereotypes associated with colonialism, yet they also sympathise, to a degree, with the native populations. Africans often play heroic roles in the novels, although the protagonists are more often than not European. The time around the turn of the century was, after all, the great sprint to Empire by many European countries intent on gaining possessions of land, people and resources.

Three of Haggard's novels were written in collaboration with his friend Andrew Lang who shared his interest in the spiritual realm and paranormal phenomena and who was also a greatly admired editor.

Haggard's stories are still widely read today. Ayesha, the female protagonist of She, has been cited as a prototype by psychoanalysts such as Sigmund Freud (in The Interpretation of Dreams) and Carl Jung. Her epithet is, of course, "She Who Must Be Obeyed" and has for decades been used tongue-in-cheek to describe the presumed balance of influence between the sexes.

As a legacy it is easy to establish Haggard, and his pioneering work, as the author of the Lost World branch of writing and its influence of such other writers as Edgar Rice Burroughs, Robert E. Howard and Talbot Mundy. The Allan Quatermain character influenced many 'serials' in Hollywood during the 30s & 40s and can readily be seen as a template for Indiana Jones, the American archaeologist and explorer and huge box office film character.

Years later, when Haggard was a successful novelist, he was contacted by his former love, Lilly Archer, née Jackson. Lily had been deserted by her husband, who had embezzled funds and fled bankrupt to Africa. Haggard installed her and her sons in a house and saw to the children's education. Lilly eventually followed her husband to Africa, where he infected her with syphilis before dying of it himself. Lilly returned to England in late 1907, where Haggard again supported her until her death on April 22nd, 1909.

Haggard also wrote about agricultural and social reform, in part inspired by his experiences in Africa, but also based on what he saw in Europe. By the end of his life, he was adamantly opposed to Bolshevism, a position that he shared with his life-long friend Rudyard Kipling. The two had found friendship upon Kipling's arrival at London in 1889 largely on the strength of their shared opinions.

Haggard was extremely interested in the social affairs of the Country and eager to play a more active part in attempting reform. In 1895 he stood unsuccessfully for Parliament as a Conservative candidate for the Eastern division of Norfolk losing by 198 votes.

Also in 1895 he served on a government commission to examine Salvation Army labour colonies. This, and his heavy involvement in agriculture reform, led to him being a member of several further commissions on land use and related affairs, work that involved several trips to the Colonies and Dominions. This work, in part, helped lead to the passage of the 1909 Development Bill.

In 1911 he served on the Royal Commission examining coastal erosion.

He was an absorbed and dedicated writer of letters to The Times, nearly one hundred were published by them and the bibliography attached below reveals much in the range of subjects he wished to bring attention to.

He was made a Knight Bachelor in 1912 and a Knight Commander of the Order of the British Empire in 1919. Haggard was a member of several clubs including the Athenaeum, Savile, and Authors' clubs.

The district of Rider in British Columbia, Canada, was named in his honour.

Henry Rider Haggard died on May 14th, 1925 at the age of 68. His ashes were buried at Ditchingham Church. His papers are held at the Norfolk Record Office.

The first chapter of his book People of the Mist (1894) is credited with inspiring the 1912 motto of the Royal Air Force (formerly the Royal Flying Corps), Per ardua ad astra. "Through adversity to the stars" (or alternately "Through struggle to the stars") it is also used by other Commonwealth air forces such as the RAAF, RCAF, RNZAF, and the SAAF.

H. Rider Haggard — A Concise Bibliography

Novels
Dawn (1884) Published in three volumes
The Witch's Head (1884) Published in three volumes
King Solomon's Mines (1885) Allan Quatermain series
She: A History of Adventure (1886) Ayesha series
Allan Quatermain (1887) Allan Quatermain series
Jess (1887)
A Tale of Three Lions (1887) Allan Quatermain series
Maiwa's Revenge, or the War of the Little Hand (1888) Allan Quatermain series
Colonel Quaritch, VC (1889) Published in three volumes
Cleopatra (1889)
Beatrice (1890)
The World's Desire (1890) Co-written with Andrew Lang
Eric Brighteyes (1891)
Nada the Lily (1892)
An Heroic Effort (1893)
Montezuma's Daughter (1893)
The People of the Mist (1894)
Heart of the World (1895)
Joan Haste (1895)
The Wizard (1896)
Doctor Therne (1898)
Swallow: A Tale of the Great Trek (1899)
Lysbeth (1901)
Pearl Maiden (1903)
Stella Fregelius: A Tale of Three Destinies (1903)
The Brethren (1904)
Ayesha: The Return of She (1905) Ayesha series
The Way of the Spirit (1906)
Benita (1906)
Fair Margaret (1907)
The Ghost Kings(1908)
The Yellow God (1908)
The Lady of Blossholme (1909)
Morning Star (1910)
Queen Sheba's Ring (1910)
Red Eve (1911)
The Mahatma and the Hare (1911)
Marie (1912) Allan Quatermain series
Child of Storm (1913) Allan Quatermain series
The Wanderer's Necklace (1914)
The Holy Flower (1915) Allan Quatermain series
The Ivory Child (1916) Allan Quatermain series
Finished (1917) Allan Quatermain series]
Love Eternal (1918)
Moon of Israel (1918)

When the World Shook (1919)
The Ancient Allan (1920) Allan Quatermain series
She and Allan (1921) Allan Quatermain series / Ayesha series
The Virgin of the Sun (1922)
Wisdom's Daughter (1923) Ayesha series
Heu-Heu (1924) Allan Quatermain series]
Queen of the Dawn (1925)
The Treasure of the Lake (1926) Allan Quatermain series
Allan and the Ice-Gods (1927) Allan Quatermain series
Mary of Marion Isle (1929)
Belshazzar (1930)

Short Story Collections
Allan's Wife and Other Tales (1889)
Black Heart and White Heart: A Zulu Idyll (1900)
Smith and the Pharaohs (1920)

Publications in Periodicals and Newspapers
A Zulu War-Dance (July 1877) The Gentleman's Magazine
A Visit to the Chief (September 1877) The Gentleman's Magazine
Hydrophobia (letter) (3 November 1885) The Times
The Land Question (letter) (28 April 1886) The Times
About Fiction (February 1887) The Contemporary Review
Mr Rider Haggard and His Critics (letter) (27 April 1887) The Times
Our Position in Cyprus (July 1887) The Contemporary Review
American Copyright (letter) (11 October 1887) The Times
On Going Back (November 1887) Longman's Magazine
Delagoa Bay (letter) (17 December 1887) The Times
South African Policy (letter) (27 December 1887) The Times
Suggested Prologue to a Dramatised Version of She (March 1888) Longman's Magazine
Mr. Meeson's Will (18 June 1888) The Illustrated London News
The Wreck of the Copeland (18 August 1888) The Illustrated London News
Cleopatra (3 December 1888) The Illustrated London News
Hydrophobia and Muzzling (letter) (25 October 1889) The Times
The Annals of Natal (23 November 1889) The Saturday Review
Mummy at St Mary/Woolnoth's (letter) (25 December 1889) The Times
Mummies (letter) (27 December 1889) The Times
The Fate of Swaziland (January 1890) The New Review
In Memoriam (17 May 1890) Thompson's Seasons
American Copyright (letter) (5 June 1890) The Times
Mr Herbert Ward and Mr Stanley (10 November 1890) The Times
Nada the Lily (2 January 1892) The Illustrated London News
A New Argument Against Creation (19 December 1892) The Times
My First Book. Dawn. By H. Rider Haggard (April 1893) The Idler
The Tale of Isandlwana and Rorke's Drift (4 October 1893) The True Story Book
Lobengula (letter) (19 October 1893) The Times

The New Sentiment (letter) (6 November 1893) The Times
Wanted—Imagination   (25 December 1893) The Times
The Fate of Captain Patterson's Party (28 December 1893) The Times
The Three Volume Novel (letter) (27 July 1894) The Times
The Adventures of John Gladwyn Jebb (letter) (30 October 1894) The Times
Agriculture in Norfolk (letter) (30 October 1894) The Times
The Nelson Bazaar (letter) (16 February 1895) The Times
Everything is Peaceful (letter) (20 March 1895) The Times
Lord Kimberley in Norfolk (letter) (17 April 1895) The Times
The East Norfolk Election (letter) (23 July 1895) The Times
The East Norfolk Election (letter) (29 July 1895) The Times
Wilson's Last Fight (7 October 1895) The True Story Book
The Crisis in the Transvaal (letter) (2 January 1896) The Times
The Transvaal Crisis (letter) (13 January 1896) The Times
Jameson's Surrender (letter) (14 March 1896) The Times
The Rinderpest in South Africa (letter) (5 November 1896) The Times
Mr Rider Haggard and Dr Neufeld (letter) (9 January 1899) The Times
Shrinkage of Population in Agricultural Districts (letter) (9 May 1899) The Times
The South African Crisis—An Appeal (letter) (1 July 1899) The Times
Commandant-General Joubert and Mr H Rider Haggard (letter) (8 September 1899) The Times
Anglo-African Writers' Club (17 October 1899) The Times
The War (letter) (25 October 1899) The Times
Farming in 1899 (letter) (22 December 1899) The Times
Farming in 1899 (letter) (1 January 1900) The Times
Settlement of Soldiers in South Africa (letter) (5 May 1900) The Times
1881 and 1900 (letter) (2 October 1900) The Times
Farming in 1900 (letter) (1 January 1901) The Times
Central and Associated Chambers of Agriculture (letter) (6 November 1901) The Times
Small Holdings (letter) (8 November 1901) The Times
Rural England (letter) (4 February 1903) The Times
Mr Rider Haggard on Rural Depopulation (3 May 1903) The Times
Agricultural Distress (letter) (11 June 1903) The Times
The Motor Problem (letter) (24 June 1903) The Times
Fiscal Policy and Agriculture (letter) (16 December 1903) The Times
Telepathy Between a Human Being and a Dog (letter) (21 July 1904) The Times
Telepathy Between a Human Being and a Dog (letter) (9 August 1904) The Times
Mr Rider Haggard on Small Holdings (12 September 1904) The Times
Case L.1139 Dream (October 1904) Journal of the Society for Psychical Research
Mr Rider Haggard on Agriculture (22 October 1904) The Times
Mr Rider Haggard on Rural Housing (27 October 1904) The Times
The Deserted Village (letter) (25 August 1905) The Times
Decrease of Population and the Land (letter) (6 January 1906) The Times
Prevention of Cruelty to Children (3 February 1906) The Times
The New Land and Tenure Bill (letter) (12 March 1906) The Times
Garden City Association (17 March 1906) The Times
Mr H. Rider Haggard on the Zulus (19 May 1906) The Illustrated London News
To Be Proof against British Bullets: A Zulu Incantation (19 May 1906) The Illustrated London News
Housing of the Working Classes (26 June 1906) The Times

Mr Rider Haggard on Small Holdings (4 July 1906) The Times
The Unemployed and Waste City Lands (letter) (19 July 1906) The Times
Mr Rider Haggard on the Transvaal Constitution (7 August 1906) The Times
Vanishing East Anglia (1 September 1906) The Saturday Review
The Land Grabbing at Plaistow (5 September 1906) The Times
The Land Tenure Bill (22 November 1906) The Times
Publishers and the Public (letter) (19 February 1907) The Times
The Careless Children (2 March 1907) The Saturday Review
The Government and the Land (letter) (29 April 1907) The Times
Chambers of Agriculture (2 May 1907) The Times
The Government and the Land (letter) (8 May 1907) The Times
Miss Jebb on Small Holdings (15 June 1907) Country Life
Rural Housing and Sanitation Association (27 June 1907) The Times
St Thomas Hospital Medical School (28 June 1907) The Times
The Land Question (4 July 1907) The Times
A Plea for the Sitting Tennant (letter) (12 August 1907) The Times
A Literary Coincidence (letter) (19 October 1907) The Spectator
Town Planning Conference (26 October 1907) The Times
Dr Barnardo's Homes (16 November 1907) The Times
The Proposed Agricultural Party (5 December 1907) The Times
Mr Rider Haggard and Small Holdings (10 January 1908) The Times
Mr Haggard and Children's Legislation (13 March 1908) The Times
The Drink Trade and Common Sense (letter) (2 April 1908) The Times
The Zulus: The Finest Savage Race in the World (June 1908) The Pall Mall Magazine
Sparrows (letter) (18 August 1908) The Times
Sparrows, Rats and Humanity (letter) (5 September 1908) The Times
The Letters of Queen Victoria (letter) (26 November 1908) The Times
The Romance of the World's Greatest Rivers (December 1908) Travel Magazine
Afforestation. Mr Rider Haggard's View (1 March 1909) The Times
The Late Sir Marshal Clarke (letter) (13 April 1909) The Times
Mr Rider Haggard on Agriculture (27 November 1909) The Times
Mr Rider Haggard on South Africa (11 March 1910) The Times
Why? (letter) (25 April 1910) The Times
Mr Rider Haggard on Irish Agriculture (23 May 1910) The Times
Why Not? (letter) (12 July 1910) The Times
Mr Rider Haggard on Agriculture (16 September 1910) The Times
Mr Rider Haggard on Vermin (8 November 1910) The Times
Danish High Schools (21 December 1910) The Times
Sugar Beet Growing in Norfolk (6 March 1911) The Times
Rural Denmark (letter) (22 March 1911) The Times
Rural Denmark (letter) (3 April 1911) The Times
The Copyright Bill (letter) (6 June 1911) The Times
Mr Rider Haggard on Poverty. The Burden of Civilization (15 July 1911) The Times
Mr Rider Haggard and the Public Records (28 July 1911) The Times
The Farmers' Burden (1 December 1911) The Times
Egyptian Date Farm. The Financial Aspect (11 October 1912) The Times
Umslopogaas and Makokel. Sir H. Rider Haggard on Zulu Types (letter) (16 August 1913) The Times
The Death of Mark Haggard (letter) (10 October 1914) The Times

On the Land. Old Problems and New Ways. The War—and After. (15 March 1915) The Times
Soldiers as Settlers. After-War Problem for the Empire (20 August 1915) The Times
Raids by Air. Zeppelins and Zeppelins (letter) (22 October 1915) The Times
Women's Work on the Land. A Palliative in Hard Times (letter) (29 November 1915) The Times
Women on the Land. Town Girls' Unfitness for Farm Work (letter) (9 December 1915) The Times
Soldiers as Settlers. Sir Rider Haggard's Oversea Mission (2 February 1916) The Times
Soldiers as Settlers (letter) (7 February 1916) The Times
Soldier Settlers. The Future of Rural England (letter) (10 February 1916) The Times
Farewell Luncheon to Sir Rider Haggard (March 1916) United Empire
Soldier Settlers for the Empire. Offer from Victoria (18 April 1916) The Times
Sir R Haggard's Tour. Land for Ex-Service Men (22 July 1916) The Times
Sir H. Rider Haggard's Mission. Land for Ex-Soldiers (1 August 1916) The Times
Land for Ex-Soldiers. Outline of Sir R. Haggard's Report   (12 August 1916) The Times
Empire Land Settlement Deputation to the Secretary of State for the Colonies and the President of the
Board of Agriculture (September 1916) United Empire
Empire Land Settlement by Sir Rider Haggard (December 1916) United Empire
A Journey through Zululand by Sir H Rider Haggard (December 1916) The Windsor Magazine
Mr Wilson's Note. British Publicity (28 December 1916) The Times
Home Produce (letter) (22 February 1917) The Times
The Milk Supply (letter) (11 April 1917) The Times
Corn Production Bill. A National Measure (letter) (13 June 1917) The Times
A Protest and a Plea. Farmers and Meat (letter) (9 October 1917) The Times
Pig-Breeding. A Subject for Municipal Enterprise (letter) (22 February 1918) The Times
The German Colonies. Interests of the Dominions (letter) (5 November 1918) The Times
Light—More Light! (letter) (19 November 1918) The Times
A Great American. Tributes to the Late Mr Roosevelt (letter) (8 January 1919) The Times
Shut the Door (letter) (10 March 1919) The Times
Population and Housing. Emigration v Birth Control (25 March 1919) The Times
The Ex-Kaiser (letter) (11 April 1919) The Times
Empire Birth-Rate. Sir Rider Haggard on Emigration (17 April 1919) The Times
Ex-Service Men Abroad. Warnings from California (letter) (10 May 1919) The Times
Edith Cavell (letter) (16 May 1919) The Times
The Ex-Kaiser. Uncertainties of Trial (letter) (8 July 1919) The Times
Race Suicide Peril. Western Civilization Threatened (11 October 1919) The Times
The British Cinema. Production of Reputable Films (letter) (5 November 1919) The Times
Horrors on the Film. Limits of Publicity (letter) (19 November 1919) The Times
The British Museum (letter) (24 January 1920) The Times
Air Exploration and Empire (letter) (7 February 1920) The Times
The Liberty League. A Campaign Against Bolshevism (letter) (3 March 1920) The Times
Bolshevist Peril. Counter-Propaganda (4 March 1920) The Times
The Empire's Vacant Lands. Settlers and the Food Supply (14 April 1920) The Times
Films and Happy Endings. The Tyranny of a Convention (letter)   (21 April 1921) The Times
Land and its Burdens. Evil of Grinding Taxation (letter) (8 August 1921) The Times
Boy Emigrants (letter) (31 March 1922) The Times
Migration and Morals. Declining Birther Rate (7 April 1922) The Times
Labour Party's Programme. Confiscation and Class Hatred (letter) (28 October 1922) The Times
Efficient Denmark. Keeping the People on the Land (7 December 1922) The Times
The Egyptian Find. Tombs of Eighteenth Dynasty Queens (letter) (19 December 1922) The Times

King Tutankhamen. Reburial in Great Pyramid (letter) (13 February 1923) The Times
The Norfolk Dispute. A Truce while There is Time (letter) (3 April 1923) The Times
Rural Post and Telephone. Minister's Reply to Deputation (19 April 1923) The Times
Liberalism and Land Reform (letter) (1 May 1923) The Times
Small Holdings. Influence of Heredity (letter) (4 July 1923) The Times
Agricultural Parcel Post (26 July 1923) The Times
Country Houses for Sale. Empty East Anglian Mansions (letter) (14 June 1924) The Times
Plight of Agriculture (24 July 1924) The Times
Loans From the British Museum (letter) (30 July 1924) The Times
Zinovieff Letter. Mr MacDonald and a Political Plot (letter) (29 October 1924) The Times
Two Centuries of Publishing. Tributes to Messrs. Longmans (6 November 1924) The Times
Imagination and War (26 November 1924) The Times

Non-Fiction

Cetywayo and His White Neighbours (1882)
A Farmer's Year (1899)
The Last Boer War (1899)
A Winter Pilgrimage (1901)
Rural England (1902)
A Gardener's Year (1905)
The Poor and the Land (1905)
Regeneration (1910)
Rural Denmark (1911)
The Days of My Life (1926)

Film Adaptations

King Solomon's Mines
This novel has been adapted at least six times. The first version, King Solomon's Mines, directed by Robert Stevenson, premiered in 1937. The best known version premiered in 1950: King Solomon's Mines, directed by Compton Bennett and Andrew Marton, was followed in 1959 by a sequel, Watusi. In 1979 a low-budget version directed by Alvin Rakoff, King Solomon's Treasure, combined both King Solomon's Mines and Allan Quatermain in one story. The 1985 film King Solomon's Mines was a tongue-in-cheek parody of the story, with a 1987 sequel in the same vein, Allan Quatermain and the Lost City of Gold. Around the same time an Australian animated TV film came out, King Solomon's Mines. In 2008 a direct-to-video adaptation, Allan Quatermain and the Temple of Skulls, was released.

She
She has been adapted for the cinema at least ten times, and was one of the earliest films to be made, in 1899 as La Colonne de feu (The Pillar of Fire), by Georges Méliès. A 1911 version starred Marguerite Snow, a British-produced version appeared in 1916, and in 1917 Valeska Suratt appeared in a production for Fox which is lost. In 1925 a silent film of She, starring Betty Blythe, was produced with the active participation of Rider Haggard, who wrote the intertitles. This film combines elements from all the books in the series.

A decade later another cinematic version of the novels was released, featuring Helen Gahagan, Randolph Scott and Nigel Bruce. Unlike the book and the other films, this 1935 version was set in the Arctic, rather than Africa, and depicts the ancient civilisation of the story in an Art Deco style, with music by Max Steiner.

The 1965 film She was produced by Hammer Film Productions; it starred Ursula Andress as Ayesha and John Richardson as her reincarnated love, with Peter Cushing and Bernard Cribbins as other members of the expedition.

In 2001 another adaption was released direct-to-video with Ian Duncan as Leo Vincey, Ophélie Winter as Ayesha and Marie Bäumer as Roxane.

Dawn
The film Dawn was released in 1917, starring Hubert Carter and Annie Esmond.

Jess
This book was filmed in 1912, featuring Marguerite Snow, Florence La Badie and James Cruze, in 1914 with Constance Crawley and Arthur Maude, and in 1917 as Heart and Soul, starring Theda Bara in the title role.

Beatrice
The book was adapted into a 1921 Italian silent drama film called The Stronger Passion, directed by Herbert Brenon and starring Marie Doro and Sandro Salvini.

Swallow
The novel was adapted into a 1922 South African film.

Stella Fregelius
The book was adapted into a 1921 British film, Stella.

Moon of Israel
This novel was the basis of a script by Ladislaus Vajda, for film-director Michael Curtiz in his 1924 Austrian epic known as Die Sklavenkönigin (Queen of the Slaves).

www.ingramcontent.com/pod-product-compliance
Lightning Source LLC
Chambersburg PA
CBHW070902180626
46817CB00003B/885